PRAISE FOR THIS BOOK

WINNER

The Sunday Times CNA Literary Awards, South Africa, 2021
Book of the Year

"A wrenching, deeply felt story about Stephen Malusi Mzamane, a young Anglican priest, trained in England but now marooned in a rundown mission in Fort Beaufort ... battling the prejudices of colonial society, and the church itself."

SHORTLISTED

The Walter Scott Prize for Historical Fiction, 2020

"It's a rare book that punishes the sins of the past with beauty, but Marguerite Poland knows the power of doing just that. Quietly, implacably, in writing that cuts to the heart of the matter, she draws us into the life of Stephen Mzamane, a young South African trained for Christian missionary work, eager to serve both God and his own people but hampered by conflicted loyalties and the entrenched prejudices of both society and the Anglican Church. Set in the late nineteenth century, the bells of Canterbury and the bells of Africa ring out a story of what was, what might have been, and what in some places, shamefully, still is. An important story, then, and a difficult one, but in the hands of Marguerite Poland, a story luminously told."

ENDORSEMENTS

John Mbangyeno, Africa Now
"An emotional rollercoaster—the astonishing love story of a man for a church, an ideal and a woman. Heart-wrenching."

Reverend Thabo Makgoba, Archbishop of Cape Town
"Marguerite Poland, as always, is able to use words to paint reality. She has written an incredibly moving and compassionate yet piercing historical account which both demands apologies for the sins of the past yet is also redemptive."

Dr Sindiwe Magona , writer
"I love the book and admire its courage, to say nothing of its skilfulness. The subject is painful. Reading the manuscript, I was driven to tears more times than I care to remember. I couldn't stop thinking: if this is what priests thought, why do we wonder Apartheid happened? It is horrifying but also humbling to see how, with the best intentions, we err and betray the very values we preach. Marguerite Poland is to be commended for writing such a revelatory account of societal attitudes. The book is fiction but is based on church history and bigotry parading as decency. This is a painful and humbling reminder that none of us is above erroneous judgment."

Mark Gevisser, novelist and critic
"Poland is a worthy descendant of Olive Schreiner in her heritage and passions."

A SIN OF OMISSION

MARGUERITE POLAND (born 3 April 1950 in Johannesburg) is an award-winning South African writer of books for adults and children. Brought up in the Eastern Cape, she studied Social Anthropology and Xhosa, took a master's in Zulu literature and folktales, and was awarded a doctorate for her study of the cattle of the Zulu people.

Two of her books—*The Mantis and the Moon* and *Woodash Stars*—won South Africa's Percy FitzPatrick Award. *The Train to Doringbult* was shortlisted for the CNA Awards; *Shades* has been a matriculation set text for over a decade; and *The Keeper* received the Nielsen Booksellers' Choice Award in 2015 as the title South African booksellers most enjoyed reading, selling and promoting the previous year.

With books translated into several languages, the author won South Africa's highest civic award in 2016 for her contribution to the field of indigenous languages, literature and anthropology.

MARGUERITE POLAND
A SIN OF OMISSION

ENVELOPE BOOKS

Originally published in South Africa in 2019
by Penguin Random House, South Africa
© 2019 Marguerite Poland

This revised UK/ROI edition published in Great Britain in 2022
by Envelope Books, London
© 2021 Marguerite Poland

A CIP catalogue record is available from the British Library

First edition 1 3 5 7 9 8 6 4 2
Printed by Severn, Gloucester, GL2 5EU
ISBN 9781838172039

Cover and interior designed by Stephen Games | Booklaunch

Envelope Books
12 Wellfield Avenue
London N10 2EA
www.envelopebooks.co.uk

IN MEMORIAM
Reverend Stephen Mtutuko Mnyakama
(1848–1885)

For my beloved family and for Bruce Howard, whose dedication and generosity provided the key to Stephen Mnyakama's life.

CHAP. 1:1

They have smashed the bells. All over Kaffraria the sound has ceased.

There is a great silence. More profound, more still than the dim before the dawn. A great conspiracy of emptiness except for the sound of the wind—vaulting, powerful.

Once, for Stephen Mzamane, every hour of every day had been marked by the ringing of the bell. In over twenty years, it had proclaimed the time for waking, washing, matins, breakfast, lessons, dinner, handwork, supper, prayers, bed. He had long forgotten how to allot his day by the rising or the setting of the sun, to sense the hour when the seed-eaters gather or the anvil bird marks the meridian at noon. He knew nothing of the swifts and swallows following the herds: this is dusk; this the time when we beg the last sweet drop of milk. All that had been exchanged, when he was nine, for the bell, its gong quartering the hours, hitching men to labour or to prayer.

YET ONE BELL had been spared: Albert Newnham's bell at St Paul's still hung on its scaffold of logs. Stephen had asked that it should be left alone—in tribute to all the bells that he and Newnham had answered together, especially the great cathedral bell in Canterbury which had summoned them as students every Sunday, marching two by two in their choir cassocks to the chime of God.

At his small mission in the hills—barely more than an outstation—Stephen had never had the funds to buy a bell and the Sunday offertories were so erratic it would have taken years to pay it off. Instead, he had hung a piece of scavenged iron piping in the old shrubby tree outside the parsonage door. He would strike it with a shorter piece of pipe to call the faithful to Sunday service and the children to school. The sound had neither melody nor weight. He was like a colonial farmer summoning hands to the fields.

Now he was glad he was without one.

Those holy bells he had rejoiced in on a Sunday in England belonged in another world, echoing from church to church, carolling out, underscored by the mighty tongue of the cathedral bell. Here, at Nodyoba, they were the doleful reminder of bondage to a thing called sin.

Hated by the heathens. Feared by the converted.

As he packed his suitcase and rubbed his extra pair of boots with a cloth, Stephen listened to the wind gathering outside, the lift and creak of the iron roof, the thrashing of the sturdy old tree before the house. He glanced at the cross on the wall above his bed, its varnished surface catching a spark of light from his lamp. It was made of English oak, a gift from the Warden of the Missionary College in Canterbury nine years before, in the winter of 1871, on the eve of the voyage home to the Cape.

How different his journey in the morning was to be—without the hope or exhilaration of that noisy embarkation from a great English port, his fellow students waving their hats as they stood on the quayside, his dear friend—his English 'brother'—Albert Newnham among them. The Warden had raised his hand in blessing as the rowing boat filled with passengers pulled away and swung out towards

2

where the ship was anchored. Stephen had shouted his farewell, standing legs astride, the wooden cross held aloft: he, at the start of his great adventure, his crusade of Faith.

A warrior of Christ.

He no longer felt like a warrior—nor armoured by his Faith. And in the three years of war that had just passed, he was neither soldier nor, it seemed, priest. He was just a frightened young man, forgotten by his fellow clergy and—if Mzamo's words were true—a traitor to his own Ngqika people.

At first light he would saddle up the borrowed horse and start out for the train station in the nearest town. From there, it was more than a hundred miles to Albert Newnham's mission, and the railway ran only a part of the way. He had no choice but to borrow money from the offertory fund for the journey. He would repay it from his stipend when it came. At Newnham's he would ask for another mount and travel east across the broken ridge of hills and down the pass into the drier stretches of Thembuland in search of the homestead of his mother's people.

She would be older, perhaps forgetful. Perhaps she would not recognise him or resent that he had come after being absent for so long, returning to her only as the bearer of bad news. It was eight years since he had seen her face, twenty-one since he was wrenched by his father from her care.

But he was compelled to go, compelled by the arrival of an official letter from the military prison authorities in the Cape, water-stained and dirty: it had lain unclaimed in Grahamstown, addressed as it had been to *Rev. S Mzamane, Kaffraria*.

Days old, weeks old, months old, retrieved by chance by the Director of Missions and sent on, additional directions written in his well-known hand on the front: *Trinity Mission, Nodyoba, via Fort Beaufort*.

He stowed it in the inner pocket of his coat, wrapped in a handkerchief. When he reached his uncle's home he would

3

open it and read it to his mother: *January 27th 1880*, translating every phrase, omitting none of its cold, clear words. The signing of the peace, the dousing of the fires, the surrender of all guns had not meant the end of war.

The smashing of the bells had been a greater, more insidious defiance.

THE REVEREND BASIL Rutherford had found him as a child in the Donsa bush. Searching for shade for his horse, he had dismounted, thrown the reins across a stump, relieved himself contemplatively, the beads of dust rolling in the sudden plash, and seen the boy.

If only he had taken another path, chosen another byway from the track ...

But he had not.

He had chosen, for that necessary moment, the privacy of the undergrowth. Had he kept his eyes on the valley falling away below or watched the sky for signs of rain, it would have been no omission, no conspiracy of God's in which he— unwillingly and with some irritation—became complicit.

The boy was grey-tinged, a husk-child, motionless in the shadow of a bush.

Basil Rutherford beckoned and then went forward to lift him onto the saddle of his horse. The child showed no fear, no disinclination: he was much too weak. Rutherford walked the horse the last five miles to his mission station. He laid the boy on the back porch of the church—some strange specimen of drought—and summoned his cook, the wife of the catechist, Mjodi.

She came, observed, said nothing but fetched a calabash of sour milk from the pantry and sat straight-legged on the ground, the boy between her knees, back to her chest, coaxing the whey into him over patient hours.

Basil Rutherford called his wife.

'I doubt I can fit another in the orphans' hut,' she said. 'This is not the last. How are we to keep feeding them all?'

They stood at a little distance and looked at the child mechanically opening his mouth, barely moving in the encircling arms of the cook.

'The people are starting to move west,' said Rutherford. 'I noticed at least five deserted homesteads near the pass. I suppose I should go back and make sure that no old people or children have been abandoned there but I dread what I might find.'

'It's the government's task to feed them.'

'The government!' snorted Rutherford. 'They think this famine is the finest way of forcing labour into digging roads.'

'There's barely a bag of flour left in the storeroom,' said his wife.

'Archdeacon Kitton wrote in his last letter that the Governor has forbidden his parish from running a feeding scheme in King William's Town. It breaks his heart to see the people starving in the street.'

'The Governor should be made to bury the corpses himself! I trust Kitton will ignore him.'

'And lose his parish grant?'

'What about his Christian duty?' she retorted. She bent to the child. 'He looks very bad,' she said. 'Perhaps you should baptise him at once. As a precaution.'

Rutherford gazed at him a moment, then he turned to his wife. 'We shall call him Stephen,' he said. 'It's very apt: he looks more like the relic of a martyr than a living child.'

Indeed he was, with his emaciated limbs, his sad, wary eyes, no longer vivid with life but already conceding death. Rutherford cocked his head, scrutinising him. 'Yes,' he said. 'Stephen is his name.'

BUT HIS NAME was not Stephen. It was Malusi Mzamane. He was nine years old. In foraging for food he had been left behind by his elder brother, Mzamo, suddenly separated by a thoughtless turn where the bush was thick. They were both children, starving and intent—the younger, in wandering off,

5

too weak to call or cry. When Mzamo reached home without him, he could not tell their mother where or how they had been separated.

Mzamo was too thin to beat. And, besides, their father did not have the strength to lift the stick. Their mother's tears were shed alone. Despite her own great hunger she went on, hour after hour, searching for her younger son. It was five days before their father ventured to the mission, brought by the catechist, Mjodi, who had gone about the district on *Mfundisi* Rutherford's horse asking if anyone had lost a child. He returned without the boy and all he said to his wife was,'He is found. He is fed. He will grow fat. He will forget us soon.'

He turned his back on the mother's cries.

Nor did she see her son for thirteen years. When he returned, so briefly, a sudden vision from across an unimagined and unimaginable sea with the gift of a prayer book that she could not read, he was a stranger to her. 'It is a prayer book, Mama,' he had said. And Mzamo—the eldest and their father's heir—had glanced at Stephen, then the book, and laughed.

This time, Stephen would not come before his mother with a prayer book. He would come with a letter.

Nor would Mzamo laugh. For he was dead.

THE BELLS. THE voice of *Thixo*, a reinvented God, ringing out across the pastures and the bush at morning and evening and five times on Sunday, when a white flag was hoisted on the hill above the mission to remind the people that they should not work—neither gather wood nor hoe their fields. Not even milk the cows. The clang of the mission bell would cut across the notes of singing in the heathen homesteads. Each Sunday morning as Stephen had helped *Mfundisi* Rutherford push the heavy flagpole upright on the hillock near the church and heard the sombre bell tolling for service he had seen old heathen women shaking their hoes defiantly at the sound.

6

The younger women sometimes hesitated, then retreated from the fields: better not tempt fate; better not defy the wisdom of the evangelist, Mjodi, always coming to their homes, talking of the Sabbath and of sin.

'God has given us six sheep,' he might say. 'But the seventh He has claimed as His own. What a sin'—hand raised in admonishment—'to kill the sheep belonging to God! What a sin to ignore the voice of God calling the faithful to service by the bell!'

STEPHEN KNEW WHY the rebels had left Albert Newnham's bell unharmed. It was due to his own urgent intercession with his brother Mzamo—and Mzamo's own obligation to Albert Newnham, even though Newnham was a man he had never met. That, and Stephen's promise to Mzamo: as solemn as if he'd made a covenant with God.

Stephen hung his travelling coat on the cupboard door, slipped his prayer book into the pocket, knelt by the side of his bed and said the Lord's Prayer as he had since he was nine years old except that when he was a child—coaxed by Mrs Rutherford for her own diversion—the words had been quaintly prefaced: 'God bless Stephen Mzamane and make Stephen Mzamane a good boy.'

Now he was not sure that God even knew that Stephen Mzamane existed.

IT HAD BEEN an unseasonably wet and windy December night in 1878 when Stephen's brother Mzamo had come to Stephen's parsonage door—unannounced—to warn him of the danger to the bells. It had been startling to see him carrying a stick and spears, a fusty old jacket keeping out the cold beneath the folds of an ochred cloak.

Stephen knew that jacket well. It had once belonged to Albert Newnham, worn with a nosegay in the buttonhole whenever he had gone to visit Miss Unity Wills. Now it was mud-streaked and shabby, the buttons lost, the sleeves too short for Mzamo's long arms. Gone, too, were Mzamo's tailored trousers, the stiff collar, the white waistcoat, gloves and cane, the rakish bowler hat he had worn when Stephen had seen him last.

And yet, there was something magisterial about him now. An innate authority and grace.

'Come in, brother,' Stephen had said in a low voice, standing quickly aside to let him pass, closing the door behind him and turning the key. 'Did anyone see you?'

Mzamo shook his head.

The greeting was brief and then Mzamo had walked to the furthest wall of the small room and gazed at the framed photograph of the Missionary College in Canterbury, his head on one side, saying nothing, just touching it with his stick. He could have lifted his weapon and smashed the glass. Stephen had half expected it.

'They chose you instead of me,' Mzamo said.

Stephen inclined his head.

Mzamo had glanced at him then. 'I've learned not to believe the lies of Englishmen.'

Stephen did not contradict him.

'You say nothing, Malusi—just like them. That, I think, is the same as a lie. The choice of a coward.'

'I heard that you had joined the rebels,' said Stephen. 'At first I did not believe it but now I see it's true.'

'We are not rebels. We are soldiers fighting for our land.'

Again, Stephen did not contradict him, his dark suit and clergyman's collar sombre in contrast to the ochre of his brother's robe.

'You should be fighting for your father's people,' said Mzamo. 'There are others from Grahamstown who have joined us. Gonya Sandile. The Duke. Julius Naka. They know where their duty lies. Why should you support the Church when it has not supported you? They promised you an English missionary to work with you and here you sit alone like a hen on a nest without eggs. Where is he, that

8

missionary? They say they will pay you as they pay the other clergymen—yet I know you earn half. They say they will ordain you priest when you can pass an examination in Greek and Latin. But here you are, still only a deacon, with no one to teach you. They send you to England where your comrades die from consumption like cattle with lung-sickness and yet they told us we would be healthy if we were chosen to go. All lies.'

Stephen had remained silent, the small flame of his hearth flickering and sending the shadow of Mzamo up against the whitewashed wall, subverting the neat arrangement of the pictures he had framed from the *Illustrated London News*, sagging now from the damp in the plaster. 'Brother,' he had said at last, 'you may no longer be a Christian and we may not serve the same God but I ask you not to doubt my Faith.'

'There is one God,' said Mzamo. '*Mveli-Nqangi*. He is not an Englishman.'

'Nor am I.'

'You are no longer a Ngqika.'

NO: HE HAD not been circumcised, he had not been *mkhwetha*, he had not learned the lore of manhood, the rituals of an heir. Nor did he know anything beyond the rudiments of Greek and Latin, the sole barrier to his ordination and the only hurdle to be overcome.

But where would he learn them on this barren hillside with his promised mentor, Albert Newnham, so far away and pre-occupied with minding a mission, with preaching and ploughing and raising a child?

A promise had been broken—the bargain between the Warden of the Missionary College in England and themselves: that Stephen would teach Albert Xhosa and Albert would coach Stephen in the Classics.

The perfect partnership. Comrades in their great crusade.

But Albert had always been less than diligent. 'Let's go

and play cricket,' he would say, rummaging for his bat and ball as Stephen appeared with his primers. 'There will be lots of time to teach you Latin at the mission. We will have nothing to entertain us in the evenings and nowhere to go.' And because Stephen was so skilled a bowler and loved the chance to throw off his jacket, flex his arms and stride out across the field, he had always acquiesced.

Mzamo had seated himself on the only chair in Stephen's parlour while Stephen prepared a pot of tea, glancing furtively through the window, afraid of watchers in the yard. Mzamo had held his fighting sticks across his knees—alert—and shifted his blanket on his shoulder. 'There is nothing I can do if our kinsmen smash your bell,' he said.

'I have no bell to smash.'

'A church without a bell?' Mzamo laughed.

That old derision, that vexing patronage. Stephen glanced away, said, almost apologetically, 'You are a mission-educated man, Mzamo. How can you allow it?'

'I am not a chief's son to be obeyed, like Duke or Gonya.'

'One thing I beg,' Stephen said, despising his age-old tone of supplication when speaking to his brother. 'Even if they burn my church and turn me out because I have no bell, ask them to spare Albert Newnham's mission.' He cast about, acutely conscious of a possible disloyalty. 'He's a good man. He will never be a threat to your cause.'

'As you well know,' said Mzamo, 'I have my own reasons for sparing Mr Newnham and his bell. Moreover, I have every intention of returning the money that I owe him. I will take it myself, despite the risk. As I am not an Englishman, I do not forget my obligations.' Mzamo looked directly at Stephen. 'Not to your friend, Albert Newnham. Nor to my son and his mother.'

'Or perhaps,' Stephen retorted, his voice rising at last, 'it has little to do with obligation. *Mhlawumbi sisazela.*'

An unquiet conscience.

'No, *Mntakwethu!* It is you who have an unquiet conscience

10

and know that you have failed our father's house. It is *you* who have forgotten your language. Even now, when you speak, you sound more like a white man.' Mzamo paused. 'Or an Mfengu. 'The intended insult stung. 'Yes—you are just like the other *Amahlungulu*, with their white collars and their black suits.'

White-necked ravens, collared priests, cawing from their pulpits.

Stephen turned away. Was his deacon's work to feed on carrion—the dregs and remnants of his people, devastated by war, torn by different loyalties, yoked by their dependence for work on farmers, tradesmen? Missionaries?

Mzamo gazed at him with shrewd appraisal, so familiar and yet so disconcerting. 'Our father,' Mzamo continued, 'always had you weighing on his heart. Up until the day he disappeared he had our mother crying, "Why did you give up my son to the missionary? It would have been better if he had died than to be lost to us, a vagabond, never herding his father's cattle." And our father said, "There are no cattle in the byre to herd."'

'Perhaps their loss was greater than the loss of his son,' Stephen had replied.

'Perhaps it was.'

PERHAPS IT WAS.

Stephen knew this. He knew the loss had been greater. It was a burden he had carried since he was a child of nine, abandoned at the mission after Basil Rutherford had sent out the catechist, Mjodi, to enquire if anyone had missed a boy.

Shrewdly, his father, Mzamane, had claimed him as his son, parleyed through Mjodi when Rutherford's Xhosa failed him, then retreated, giving him into the care of the priest and his acolyte.

Stephen had been too young to grasp the exigencies of need and opportunity, the logic of his abandonment. He had only watched in wretchedness as his father had walked away, a gaunt shadow-man, taking the wagon track that led past the door of the church. He had never heard his mother's keen lament, the fearful *ubulanzi*—the unassuaged and lonely longing—for her younger son. But it was something that he knew himself.

Ubulanzi. The word defied translation.

His father had simply said to the missionary, Rutherford, 'There is no food.'

'I am hard-pressed here,' Rutherford had replied. 'There are so many who are starving. I have thirteen children already.'

'We are being banished from our lands,' Mzamane had continued. 'We have been told to leave our homesteads and go beyond the Kei River. Where will our goats and sheep graze? Where will the cattle that are left find pasture? We leave behind the graves of our people and there will be corpses all along the road to that distant place. What will we eat? Where will we shelter?'

Rutherford frowned as Mjodi translated. 'If you had heeded the Magistrate's warnings, not sinned and killed your cattle ...' he retorted but Mzamane kept on speaking, a lament that did not need an answer.

'Will not those cattle turn their heads towards the Amathole, lowing? How can they graze the pasture of a stranger's herds? No. *Zibutisana!* They will lie down together to die.'

He shifted his gaze to the missionary's face. 'They have imprisoned our chiefs *esiqitini*—on Nxele's island. Maqoma, Siyolo, Xhoxho. They will die there and we will have no one to lead us. Now, any man who can lift a pick must leave his home and work on the Governor's roads.'

'Those chiefs were warmongers,' Rutherford had said irascibly enough for Mzamane to catch the tone before Mjodi had translated. 'They brought it on themselves. It is because of their foolish wickedness that you are starving.'

'*Ndingumphakati*. I am a councillor ...' said Mzamane.

'He is an important man,' said Mjodi. '*Unesithunzi*. '

12

Rutherford had waited for him to continue, one brow raised.

Mzamane had ignored the slight. 'A councillor is not a common man,' he had resumed. 'I have heard it said that the Governor is anxious to take away the sons of chiefs and make them Englishmen so they can teach their people to be servants of the English.'

'Indeed. But only the sons of chiefs.'

'No chief will ever give you the heir.'

'They have said they would.'

Mzamane had snorted, gazed off across the pasture. 'What man would be so foolish as to send his ancestral beast to another man's byre?'

He had scrutinised Rutherford a moment, then said, 'Since the cattle are killed and the crops are burned, there is no food. We were betrayed by those who failed to believe and now we are all starving. I have many wives and many children, but this child'—he indicated Stephen by the tilt of his head—'is the younger son of my Great Wife. I intend to bring you his elder brother—my heir. His name is Mzamo. He will be councillor after me. Make them *amagqobhoka*. Teach them to be Christians as the Governor has said. Perhaps they will learn to be missionaries like you. That will please the Governor very well.'

'THE INFERNAL IMPUDENCE!' Rutherford had fulminated to his wife. 'As if it were *he* who was doing the Governor a favour!'

But he knew the man to be right: councillors were as important to the purpose of Christianising the heathen as the chiefs. A grip on the frontier could only be sustained through wide political influence. Perhaps that influence could be gained more thoroughly through the councillors than through the whims or insecurities—or even the largesse —of an individual chief. He had heard all the arguments from his fellow clergy: wisdom from the Bishop and the Vestry, noted in the *Quarterly Review*:

13

—Of course, this cattle killing, wretched as it is, is really an unforeseen blessing!

The Chancellor of the Cathedral, ever eager to agree: *How else could we persuade the chiefs to hand over their sons to the missions?*

—And now, as churchmen, we will have all the influence that we could wish in bringing a new generation to God. This from the Archdeacon.

The plight of a decimated people could have a dozen different interpretations at Vestry meetings in the Cathedral in Grahamstown but not—Rutherford grumbled to his wife —for missionaries whose relentless lobby to both government and Church for money, medicines and supplies to aid their starving people went unheeded. How could they imagine the sights and scenes these isolated men had known?

Once, on a round of duty to his outstations, Rutherford—to his horror—had seen a starving dog nosing at a corpse at an abandoned homestead. He had turned away retching, soiling the front of his suit, gasping into his handkerchief. He had tethered his horse and searched in vain for an implement among the debris in the empty yard to dig a grave. And the dog, barely flinching at his curses or the hurled stones, had darted in again as soon as he, defeated, had mounted his horse.

WITHIN DAYS OF Stephen's rescue, Stephen's father Mzamane had appeared at the mission accompanied by Stephen's older brother. Seeing them approach, Stephen ran to them with a great cry. His father ignored him and pushed the boy forward as Rutherford came out onto the porch. 'Here is my son, Mzamo,' he said.

Mzamo was sullen, barely acknowledging the missionary. Incomparably thin, he glanced fleetingly at Stephen's trousers, boots and jacket and haughtily hitched his own frayed blanket up about his naked ribs.

Their father said, gesturing towards Mzamo, '*Unengqondo.*'

He is clever. '*Unesibindi.*' He is brave. 'You will teach him well.' He looked at Mzamo for a long moment, then beckoned Stephen to him and put his hand on his shoulder. 'Their mother is moving west with our people.' He raised his stick. 'I go to dig the roads.'

'And these children?'

'They are yours,' Mzamane had said. He stood, stick across his shoulders, arms bent up to grip it. He gazed silently at his sons. They gazed back at him until he turned away.

ALTHOUGH MZAMO WAS thirteen, Stephen knew he was afraid even though he had never cried and seemed indifferent. He had paid no attention to Stephen's shrill reproaches about leaving him in the bush on the day when *Mfundisi* Rutherford had found him. He retaliated, saying that it was Stephen who had wandered off—not he who had abandoned him. He made no answer to questions about their mother, except to say, 'Mothers weep.'

It was not only mothers.

At night, in the dormitory hut, Stephen cried in the darkness.

Despite Mzamo's presence and having no idea of where his mother was, he had tried to run away. *Mfundisi* Rutherford had sent Mjodi in pursuit before he'd reached the boundary of the mission lands and when he had caned him—guilty of ingratitude—he used the opportunity to lecture the other abandoned boys on the foolishness of the Ngqika people for laying waste to their herds of cattle.

—*If they are hungry it is their own fault.*

—*It is a punishment from God.*

—*It is a work of Satan.*

—*It is an unforeseen blessing:* he had read the Bishop's comments in the *Quarterly Review* three times.

It was not just Stephen's father, *Mfundisi* Rutherford said, who had given up his sons. Many chiefs and important men, humbled by their wickedness, were offering their children to the missions all through British Kaffraria. Not just to the English Church but to the Wesleyans and Scots and other Dissenters. 'But you are fortunate boys, indeed, that you have been given sanctuary by the English Church,' the *Mfundisi* had said, speaking very slowly so his words would have their weight and the interpreter, Mjodi, could emphasise each point. 'It is the Church of the Governor and it is possible that the most worthy among you may'—he lifted his great finger in emphasis—'may be sent to the new Native College in Grahamstown to be educated as teachers and catechists, perhaps even priests!' He had looked around at the upturned faces while the interpreter waited respectfully. 'It is your duty, therefore, to remain here until you are sent for—not run off like goats into the undergrowth!' He had cast an eye on Stephen. 'You are under the protection of our Father, God, in atonement for your own fathers' folly.'

Stephen had gazed back—uncomprehending—intent only on the missionary's large protruding ears, tufty as an owl's.

IF THE GOVERNOR had been brisk in turning tragedy to opportunity by proposing asylum for the children of high-ranking men with the chance of a Christian education, the Bishop, into whose care they had been delivered, had been ambivalent: he was perfectly aware of the Governor's more worldly motives in wishing to create native colleges in the name of the Church in both Cape Town and Grahamstown.

Saved for God by the Bishop; salvaged by the Governor in the interests of Empire.

At a meeting of the more prominent citizens of Grahamstown, the visiting Governor had said—in deference to the Bishop—'Education is the surest way to christianise the native.' He had turned to the wider audience, remarking, 'Choose the child with care and teach him. Keep him from the influence of home, especially from the heathen chiefs. Six to twelve years under rigorous supervision will transform the savage. It will ensure the peace and prosperity of this colony and supply willing servants of the state.'

'It sounds as if you mean to take them hostage,' the Bishop had said, a touch austerely.

'Ah,' the Cathedral's Precentor had murmured to the Chancellor, 'a step ahead of the Dissenters who would see no practical sense in isolating these youths from their families.'

'It is the purpose of the Church to bend the plant, to train the vine, to nourish and invigorate,' returned the Chancellor complacently.

That the Governor's speech had little to do with the Church had escaped them both.

Stephen would have had no idea of what a hostage was. He only knew that tears were useless. In time, the hills to the east where the track led up the pass no longer promised the vision of his mother hurrying down in search of him. Those he saw—men in their blankets trudging west—were not transformed by his eager gaze into her thin, angular frame. In the end, he ceased to look for her; in the end, the mother's voice became the voice of Mrs Rutherford.

'What a pious little fellow Stephen is,' she very often said to her husband. 'You should hear him say his prayers at night. "God bless Stephen whatever-it-is and make Stephen a good boy." Such a quaint character! Quite different from his brother. I fear we will have rebellions there unless we curb him carefully. He has come to us too old. It would be so much better if children were put into our care as infants. We could mould them from the start.'

'YOU MUST RAISE my son. You will be his guardian,' Mzamo had said on the night he came to Stephen's parsonage to warn him about the bells. 'As soon as it is safe to go to Port Elizabeth you must fetch him from his mother and bring him here.'

'He's little more than a baby!'

'You must teach him everything you know.' Mzamo was

urgent. 'And when he's old enough, send him to Grahams-town and then to England.'

'Why would his mother give him up?'

'Our mother gave us up when we were children. Why not her?'

Stephen began to object. 'It was our father, not our mother ...'

Mzamo cut him short, holding up his hand to silence him. 'There are two other matters, Malusi.' He pulled a leather pouch from the cord at his waist and extracted a paper, its folds brown with age. 'This is the letter from the Bishop about the grant of land which we were promised by the Governor when we were still at the Native College. Eight years on and nothing done. Eight years!' He opened it, pointed. 'Look at the date.' And thrust it into Stephen's hand.

Stephen held the sheet to the candle and scanned it. *December 1870.*

'Did you not get such a letter yourself?' asked Mzamo impatiently.

'I was in England then. No one wrote.'

Mzamo snorted. 'Of course they didn't! Only those who have begged and threatened have heard. All this time and we are still waiting for the land to be surveyed.'

'Why are you giving this to me?'

'Because that paper will be safer with you than with me. It may happen that one day you must claim the property for my son. 'Mzamo tied the pouch to his belt and let his blanket fall. 'And now'—he lowered his voice—'where is my gun?'

Stephen put the letter on the table, his back to his brother. 'It is not your gun, Mzamo. It is still our father's.' A relic, not a weapon.

'He is long dead,' said Mzamo. 'So it is mine.'

Stephen did not reply.

'Did you hand it in, Malusi?' Mzamo took a step forward and Stephen almost flinched—a child again, knowing the tone, expecting a cuff across his head.

18

'It's the law to hand it in.'

'What have you done with it?'

'If you're caught with a gun ...' Stephen spoke in English then, asserting himself and brushing past his brother.

'What have you done with it?' Mzamo grasped his shoulder.

Stephen hesitated, detached himself from his brother's grip. 'It's in the church,' he said. 'Under the altar.'

Mzamo almost laughed. 'Under the altar?' He clapped Stephen on the back. '*Kanti*—but you're a sly one. Wait till I tell our comrades about this.'

'You will say nothing!' Stephen said. 'Absolutely nothing! It is there,' he resumed in Xhosa, 'because it is our father's gun. Kept to honour him. If there was no danger to you on this journey I would have lied and told you I had handed it in but I cannot see you travel only armed with sticks. There are patrols all up and down the valley along the river. The people here are Mfengu. They would betray you if they saw you. There are some who might kill you even though you are my brother.' Stephen went briskly to the door. 'Wait here,' he said and let himself out into the yard.

He looked about. The wind thrashed in the old tree so that the iron bell-pipe hanging from its branches gonged every now and then. A candle flame still flickered in the window of the churchwarden's house beyond the garden. Stephen crossed the yard and slipped inside the church. His footfall on the dung floor was soundless.

Had it been sacrilege to lay his father's firearm under the wooden casing of the altar in the gap between its base and the floor? He had had no safer choice. It was the only place where none would dare to pry. It had lain there, safe from discovery ever since a mission circular had come to Ockert's shop from *Mfundisi* Rutherford in Grahamstown, a prelude to the Peace Preservation Act. The notice was headed in thick black print, declaring: *No native may carry arms.*

If you have a firearm please hand it in immediately to your District Magistrate. Please ensure that all those in possession of firearms at your mission (including outstations) do the same. Those who fail to comply risk imprisonment.

HE HAD WRITTEN to the *Mfundisi* and told him that fifteen guns had been handed over by him to the Magistrate. All had belonged to Mfengu and many had been used in combat in support of the government against the Ngqika in an earlier war.

He did not elaborate on the disbelief and anger—the betrayal—of these men at losing their weapons.

How could he blame them?

Angry and then conscience-stricken, he had lifted his father's gun from its hiding place at the back of the bookshelf to take to the Magistrate. Mzamo had trusted him to care for it, left instructions—but he had always thought of it as his father's gun, earned through heavy labour. He had examined it, smoothed the butt with his palm, felt its weight in his hands.

No, it was not Mzamo's. And even if Mzamo had appropriated it, it would always be their father's gun.

Proof of manhood, not a weapon of war.

Stephen had not taken the gun to the Magistrate. He had not done his civic duty.

—*He who robs his father is a son who brings shame and disgrace.*

Such was the Word of God. Greater than the Law.

He had hastily wrapped it in a cloth and concealed it in the only place he knew where others would not think—nor dare—to pry. He went at night when the mission workers thought he was at private prayer and, easing the boards from the base of the altar cabinet he had made to house his communion plate and Bible, he had hidden it between them and the earthen floor. He had kneeled in the darkness, his candle extinguished, head bowed, and recalled his father, so long ago, standing in the mission yard, gripping the travelling stick yoked across his shoulders on the day he had left Mzamo at the mission.

That terrible silence. That mute farewell. It was the last time he had seen him.

STEPHEN CREPT BACK to the house. He handed Mzamo the gun. A moment of exchange, fingers touching. He hesitated, then he said, 'My horse is in the shed.' More firmly, 'You must take it.'

He looked into his brother's face. 'Be careful when you let it out. The churchwarden lives close by.'

'I cannot take your horse,' said Mzamo, shaking his head.

'There's an old bridle at the back of the door,' urged Stephen, ignoring him. 'But don't take the saddle. *Mfundisi* Rutherford gave it to me. If you are caught they will trace you back here and I will be arrested for helping you. I do not wish to lie.'

'You have lied to them already.'

Stephen did not reply.

A dog barked in the distant valley, answered by another. 'You must go,' Stephen said. 'It will be sunrise soon.'

'When the fighting is over you may fetch the horse from our mother. As it is yours, she will guard it well.' Mzamo went to the door. 'And do not fear, I will repay my debt to your friend, Newnham.' He paused, turned. '*Baz' iindlebe!*' Attend me, brother.

Far off the dogs were barking once again, others joining as the challenge was taken up, homestead to homestead. 'You must go!'

'*Baz' iindlebe!*' Mzamo said more urgently. 'My son must inherit that land.'

'He is not the son of your wife. It will not be granted.'

'I will marry his mother.'

'You are already married to Nokhanyiso.'

21

'She is barren. And she has deserted me.'

'She is still your wife.'

'By someone else's laws.'

'They are the laws of the land. And of God's Christian Church.'

'Why do you think I have had to ask for money? Why do you think I humbled and abased myself before Canon Rutherford, asking for help? Why do you think I cannot buy a weapon to protect myself? Why do I, who once owned horses and a carriage, have to come on foot in the dead of night?' He paused, looked at Stephen squarely. 'It is because I have sold everything that was mine and sent every penny that I could to her. To sustain her. To sustain our son. To do what was honourable and right, even in your eyes and the eyes of the Church. And I will marry Elizabeth Madikane. By the same customary union as our father married our mother. She will be my Great Wife. It is my right to choose the mother of my heir.'

'She is a Christian. She is still someone else's wife. She will never agree.'

'How can you know?'

Stephen looked away. How indeed?

'In the meantime,' said Mzamo, 'you will fetch him and bring him here. You will teach him, Malusi, to be a man like you.'

'To speak like me?' Stephen's voice was unsteady. '*Ihlungulu?*'

'No.' Mzamo came forward and laid his hand on Stephen's shoulder, shaking it slightly—not in anger but in supplication. 'You are a man of stature. *Unesithunzi.* Yes, I know that now.' He gazed into Stephen's face, then dropped his hand and turned again towards the door. 'He must have an education, know English well. It's the only weapon left.'

'You can do that yourself, better than me.'

'I am a soldier,' Mzamo said. 'Soldiers die.'

CHAP. 2:23

The churchwarden at Nodyoba had lent Stephen a horse for his journey to the nearest railhead. It was a shanky bay—hardy, wayward, it preferred to triple. Old Dyoba's eagerness in helping his missionary was touching. At the time of Mzamo's secret visit, when Stephen's horse had so 'mysteriously disappeared', Dyoba had organised a party of boys to search the veld and hillsides. They had found the tracks across the high ground.

'It is the rebels,' Dyoba had said. 'I am surprised you did not hear them.'

'It was a night of high wind. It blows very loudly round this house.'

Dyoba had mused a moment. 'Perhaps you should get a dog, *Mfundisi*. To give a warning.'

'Perhaps.'

If Dyoba believed that the theft had been reported, Stephen omitted to contradict him and he avoided going into the town. He wanted no speculation by people there as to why he walked instead of trotting down the high street on his grey, raising his hat to passers-by: the war was reason enough to stay at the mission although visits to his nearest outstations could not be avoided. Having to go on foot meant he had had to spend the night at each of them. It had been many months before he was able to venture to the more distant settlements. When at last he did, in July 1879, it was from the headman at kwaJingqi that he had heard the news of Mzamo's capture.

The old man had said, 'I am grieved to hear about your brother.' Stephen had stared at him, uncomprehending. 'I do not understand you, *Mhlekazi*.'

'News does not lie in the road, *Mfundisi*,' the man had said gravely. *Iindaba azilali ndleleni.*

'What news?'

He glanced about and then hastily took Stephen into his house and closed the door. 'Your brother was captured many weeks ago like those other men from Grahamstown. All grand gentlemen indeed. *Zizinoni*. Very learned.' He paused. 'Christians like you.'

Stephen sat down on a chair, uninvited, steadying himself. 'I did not know.'

'*Yeh! intlekele!*' Indeed, it is a great misfortune!

'Where was he captured?'

'He was up near the Indwe, going, perhaps further into Thembuland. I cannot think why he was so far north.'

Stephen was silent.

The Indwe River and Albert Newnham's mission: I have my own reasons for sparing Mr Newnham's bell.

'Your brother had a gun.' The old man was defiant. 'Why may a man not carry his own gun? What treason is that? Why may he not ride his own horse?'

'Where is he now?'

'He was taken to the gaol in Grahamstown where the others they call rebels have been kept. Since then they have been sent to the Cape, some to the island, some to break stones in the harbour. Many have gone. Those that break stones can see across the water to the place—*esiqitini*—where our chief Jongumso-bomvu Maqoma has twice been exiled.'

The Breakwater of the harbour—and beyond, across a forbidding stretch of sea, the bleak small island where Maqoma, the finest of their generals, lay buried in an unmarked grave.

'*Kanti ke*, and yet,' the old man said, 'it is a lie that Jongumso-bomvu is dead. It is what the government wants us to believe, to break our spirit.'

Stephen did not contradict him. He knew the legend of Maqoma's immortality: Jingqi, Maqoma's great mottled riding-ox, had long been heard bellowing at night, lamenting its master. It was said that it had walked five hundred miles to the Cape and braved the surf and currents of the sea, swimming to the island to rescue the chief, and that sometime—unknown to any man—Maqoma would emerge from hiding, riding on the ox, and triumphantly lead his people out of bondage.

But Stephen knew that no man could escape from that island no matter how near the shore, no matter how close the city's lights might seem. It was a place where graves ranged side by side under a shrieking wind: convicts, lepers, lunatics —the discarded of the earth.

STEPHEN HAD LEFT the headman and kwaJingqi not knowing whom to call on, whom to confide in, how to confess that he had desecrated his church by concealing a gun in it—a gun that had led to his brother's arrest. There was no one from whom he could learn the truth of how it had happened without exposing his own role.

The gun. The horse.

Who would believe that both were stolen when each could be so clearly identified with him, the rebel's only brother?

And now—so many, many weary months after the confusion of that news, the anxious silence, the absence of any visits from a fellow missionary, the curfews, rumours and uncertainties—the truth of what had happened was explicit in the letter which he carried in the inner pocket of his coat as he rode east along the low escarpment towards the train station in the town.

It was a truth that he could share only with Albert Newnham—and not be judged.

As SOON AS the letter had arrived informing him of Mzamo's death the previous January, Stephen had written to Albert.

June 13th 1880

My dear Albert,
It is urgent that I see you, d.v., on Friday fortnight. I will ride to Stutterheim and leave the horse with an acquaintance and proceed by train to Queenstown. Could you meet me there on the 27th? If I could spend a day or two with you it would be a comfort to me in a time of great anxiety and sorrow. I will give you details when I see you. If I could impose on you further—I wonder if you could spare a horse which I would return within the week. If, by any chance, you are unable to meet me, I will make my own way to your mission.

He had given no details of the reason for his journey. It seemed unwise when his letter might fall into unfriendly hands and, though he was anxious to reach his mother, he was more anxious to be armed with Albert's counsel. He needed someone with whom he could pray. Someone to confide in. Someone to return to when his task was done.

The road from Stephen's mission at Nodyoba led along a hillside between clusters of huts. Many had been burned in the fighting the year before, left to disintegrate. The smell of smoke had long deserted them and the wind had sent the cinders of their thatch far and wide. Passing them, Stephen remembered the goats and the sheep, the flocks among the sweet thorns. But there had been few cattle. More than twenty years ago they had been slaughtered and the fields laid waste for the coming of a new Universe when herds

26

would arise, fat from the earth, the crops would sprout spontaneously and all white men would be driven into the sea. He had only a faint remembrance of those herds of cattle and the time of the great hunger when he was lost in the bush and *Mfundisi* Rutherford had found him and taken him to his mission. He could just recall—an earliest memory— the bellow of their dying, the vultures and the crows, the sky black with wingbeats, his fear of their beaks and venom eyes.

Now, picking his way down the hillside, taking a shortcut across the slope, he greeted women hoeing, he stopped to speak to a man in the path, an old wall-eyed heathen, his blanket draped across his shoulders.

'*Maneli*.' Reverend missionary.

'*Mnumzana*.'

The courtesy of titles, the tip of the old man's stick touched briefly to his forehead.

Usually, when he rode from homestead to homestead evangelising, Stephen sang hymns. He did not sing today. He wondered if he would ever raise his voice in song again or preach with conviction. He simply gazed across the arc of the horse's neck as the hills seemed to dip and stumble to its gait.

If belief was fragile and his hymns could give no comfort, he knew—he trusted absolutely—that Albert would be waiting for him. Albert with his long thin legs, his jaunty beard, his beaming little spectacles, his short-cropped sandy hair. At the Missionary College in Canterbury, even when he had chivvied Stephen, he had never been impatient, only rolled his eyes and laughed at Stephen's dawdling. 'Come on, old chap! You have no sense of time at all!'

And Stephen would shrug good-naturedly. What was the use of rushing?

'The teashop closes at five. The bell will go before we're done and we'll be late.' Ah yes, the bell!

But time was not the only constraint in visiting the

27

teashop. Stephen did not have the money and he could not always allow Albert to pay.

'Bother the Bishop!' Albert would say if Stephen shook his head at every invitation. 'After all, you're not earning fees to teach me your language and I'm hungry! So we'll have two Welsh cakes and bring a penny bun back with us. That's only fair. Come along.'

No, Albert would not let him down.

Even with his cheerful innocence about the world, he had a sense of duty and a touching loyalty on which Stephen had always depended. How many times Albert had saved him from awkward moments in the drawing rooms of Canterbury, or shown him unobtrusively the way to hold his knife, to greet a lady, to ignore a slight. If he could not share in the gravity of Stephen's burden now, Stephen could count on his kindliness and tact. Stephen knew he would help him in any way he could—with food, a bed, a horse.

And prayers.

When Albert prayed, he would always close his eyes quite tightly, raise his chin and chat confidingly with God—so different from the Warden of the Missionary College, Dr Bailey, or *Mfundisi* Basil Rutherford, intoning through their noses, alert to the sonorous sound of their own voices. So different from Stephen's own silent, apprehensive reverence. Albert did not have the gravity of a man in Holy Orders. He was more like a child kneeling at his bedside, looking up into his father's face before the candle was blown out and loving hands tucked him in between the sheets.

Once they had prayed, Stephen knew Albert would suggest a pot of tea and then divert him with memories of Canterbury—japes at the tutors; jokes in the dining hall; waylaying the Superintendent of Students or old Blunsom, the porter, with outrageous requests—and laugh at how the Warden had chided them both for irreverent behaviour.

They had been friends almost since the day that Stephen had walked through the door of the Missionary College,

28

standing, simply overwhelmed, his eyes scanning in bewilderment the towering arches and Gothic windows.

To begin with he was led about in a haze of staring confusion—unprepared, unrehearsed and silent—until he was taken to the workshop and given a lathe by the carpentry master, who began by speaking to him in a pidgin English and explaining the tool as if it were an artefact from another world and he an idiot.

But here Stephen was on familiar ground: Mr Simeon Gawe's coaching at the Native College had been expert and swift. 'Thank you, sir,' Stephen had said quietly to the master. 'On what would you like me to work?'

A little nettled, the carpenter had given him a length of wood. 'Round this off and let me see how you do.'

Expected to fail, Stephen had failed.

He had no vice to hold the wood and, under scrutiny, he had allowed the lathe to slip and clatter to the floor, damaging the handle. Everyone in the carpentry shop had stopped their work and looked up.

It would have been better to have been chastised, to have been cuffed as Mr Gawe would have done with a few well-aimed but not ill-natured curses, calling him '*Sidenge*', a useless fellow, rather than this polite and supercilious silence.

Except for Albert.

'Ah!' He hurried over—a young man with inordinately thin, long legs—ears flushed red as if the condescension had been directed at him instead of Stephen. 'Sorry, old chap,' he said under his breath as he picked the lathe up off the floor. He examined it. 'I know this lathe,' he said more loudly. 'It's got a tricky handle. I believe I split it long before today. Bad luck.'

'Newnham,' the carpentry teacher said, 'get back to your work.'

'Got a replacement?' said the young man airily, looking directly at the master.

'No.'

'I can share mine then,' he said and grinned ingenuously. He took Stephen by the arm, leading him away to his workbench. 'He always does that to new students,' he said, winking at Stephen. 'It's an old trick to put them in their place, especially if they're foreign.' He meant 'native'. He had often heard the master call them 'uncouth little animals'. But he was far too tactful to say it.

After that, Stephen—hanging back but eager—had looked for Albert Newnham, an anchor in his bewilderment. Albert had even been good enough—making a detour though pretending not to—to show him the more secluded lavatories behind the chapel. 'I find fellows bother one,' he laughed, 'when one doesn't want to be bothered!' And the reddening about his ears was more earnest than embarrassed. 'If you ever need a dose of castor oil, tell me rather than Mrs Blunsom, who will advertise your complaint all over College. She's used to me now and doesn't make remarks any more.'

It was Albert, too, who coached him for the College Vow —the solemn committal to vocation which every student made on enrolling. 'As it's a vow,' Albert had said more seriously than usual, 'and vows can't be broken, you must be absolutely sure you want to make it. If you're in doubt you must tell the Warden now.'

'I want to make it,' said Stephen.

'They say that only half the fellows end up keeping it.'

'I will keep it.'

Nor could Stephen doubt that the vow could be anything but binding after the Archbishop of Canterbury himself had given the sermon on Founders' Day, setting forth the urgent need of providing ministrations in the colonies and the consequences of a Failure of Faith.

'How lamentable the extent to which darkness, ignorance, heathenism and idolatry prevail among those who have been ignorant of the covenant of grace. But,' and he had paused and gazed around at the assembled students, 'if there are degrees of wretchedness, surely it is they who have once

30

tasted of the heavenly gift but who have forgotten the covenant of baptism and retained the name without the character of a Christian, it is they who are undoubtedly the most wretched of all.'

With the fear of such a wretchedness ringing in their ears, the vow was taken, student by student, before the Warden and the assembled clergy, before the benefactors of the College in their grandeur and their eminence, crowded into the College Chapel.

Stephen, awaiting his turn, had gazed along the pews in search of Albert, seated among the students who had been inducted the year before. Albert winked, nodded encouragingly, made a small gesture of support and Stephen had stood, slight and graven-faced under the weight of music, the smell of incense, of pomade and lavender and musty kneelers, enraptured by the vision of the clergy in their robes, the Bishop's mitre, the gleaming cross.

Struck by the magnificence of God.

At last he had stood before the Warden: 'Is it your deliberate intention to devote yourself, with all the powers of mind and body which God in His goodness has given you, to His service in the ministry in the Church of England in the distant dependencies of the British Empire or in the Foreign Mission Field?'

'It is my solemn intention,' Stephen replied—as Albert had coached him.

It was not long after, alert to aptitude and sympathies, that their tutor suggested that Albert should go to British Kaffraria instead of India. Stephen had agreed—delightedly —to teach Albert the rudiments of Xhosa. In exchange, Albert would coach him in Latin and Greek, a pre-requisite after ordination as a deacon to the elevation of the priesthood. 'Maybe, one day we'll both be bishops, Stephen!' Albert had exclaimed. They had laughed together at the absurdity of Stephen in a mitre or Albert as a prelate.

Until that time Stephen's mother tongue had almost been

lost to him. After the age of twelve, when he had been sent to the Native College in Grahamstown, speaking it had been forbidden during school hours. As students came from many different regions, English was an easier choice than Xhosa, Sotho, Zulu or Tswana, even in the dormitories at night. Here, at the Missionary College in Canterbury, any African language was completely unknown.

Stephen had not spoken a word of Xhosa since leaving the Cape—not until he was asked to teach Albert conversation. In tutoring, the words and their alliteration returned to him like a refrain and the first few tentative phrases that grew between them made an intimacy, a shared purpose that held promise for their work together in Kaffraria.

The Warden, too, had assured his students that if an African—or Indian or Melanesian or Chinese or any foreign student—taught a designated English classmate his native tongue, they could well be posted together. Experience had taught him that such mutual support would help the English clergyman understand his foreign flock and would obviate—for the 'native'—the risk of what he called 'backsliding into heathen ways': a bolster against the 'barbarous influences' that could be exerted on a young missionary returning alone to his own people. With an English missionary at his side, the Warden had declared, each would hold steady to his purpose. That the Englishman, and not the native, might have wavered in resolve was not conceded.

Yet the Warden knew all too well the chief cause of 'backsliding'. He had a sheaf of reports from colonial bishops in India, China, Kaffraria, the Cape: the isolated missionary without a wife, lured to immorality or worse. Or, more likely, the demanding, selfish English spouse wrecking the vocation of a worthy man!

The Church was littered with such cases.

AT NODYOBA, STEPHEN had no wife, either to support him or exert a baleful influence on his vocation. The mission community was surrounded by heathen homesteads. The young men had gone away to work at the diamond fields or in distant towns, the girls—traditional and illiterate—tilled the fields. Most of the converts at his mission were displaced: the elderly, the widowed, the destitute, the feeble, the very young. There were few with even a rudimentary education.

In England he had been too young, too preoccupied, too astonished by his situation to think of anything else. He had neither thought of women in his enthusiasm for his calling nor doubted the incalculable distance between him and the pale girls that he encountered in Canterbury. Then, one day, he had been walking down the high street on his way back to College from his lessons at the hospital. He was brought up short.

Stopped. Gazed.

There, in the window of Mr Baldwin's Photographic Studio, there among the small and modest rows of prints of comely matrons, bewhiskered gentlemen, solemn children; there, among the crinolines, the lace tippets, the furled parasols—a black face.

It was a woman.

So unexpected, so utterly arresting.

Underneath the picture was a caption: 'Kaffir Woman'.

He had stood, the small gusts of autumn wind sliding round the corner and catching the brim of his hat, the cold fingering his neck within the stiff, starched collar. All the other portraits were marked with a name, a rank, a place. But she—she was Kaffir Woman. A generic for all women from southern Africa: a species, a type.

As was he: Kaffir Man.

To be wondered over.

The woman in the portrait was turned to the left, her face untouched by consciousness of the lens, detached from this sombre city with its towers and turrets, its cold damp wind, its ivied walls.

Stephen put his hand on the knob of the door of the shop

and pushed gently. A bell tinkled as he entered. The man behind the counter looked at him keenly—a collector's fervour—as if already lining up a shot. 'Can I help you?'

At a loss to know what to say, to admit the irrational impulse of barging in, Stephen stammered, 'What is the cost of taking my picture?' He did not know why he had said it when he had scant money in his pocket. Was it some vague wish to be placed beside her in the window? A complementary specimen?

The portrait was far more than he could afford and he owed Albert tea—a dozen teas—but he counted out his coins, promising to pay the balance on collection, and pulled his collar straight. The photographer hesitated, clearly weighing up the chance of an interesting picture against Stephen's commitment to pay. 'Right,' he said. 'Come this way.'

Stephen was ushered into a studio. He was shown a mirror and adjusted his necktie. What luck that he had borrowed one of Albert's hats for the visit to town, his own shabby as a workman's. He rubbed the dome with his handkerchief, smoothing the nap, and patted his hair. It was styled as Mzamo's had always been, with a parting down the centre. He had waited, watching, as the man prepared the glass, painted on collodion and then, adjusting his instruments, indicated that Stephen should take up a position with one hand on the back of an ornamental chair placed before a draped curtain. Stephen had stood—quite agonisingly frozen—in a posture of feigned repose, one leg flexed across his ankle, cane and hat on the seat of the chair.

He stood very upright, his hand at his hip.

He set his gaze beyond the man behind the camera, staring into infinity as she had done, a counterpoint to her angled stance.

Set side by side, their glances would cross.

Kaffir Man.

34

When the picture had been taken he said, 'Who is the lady in the portrait in the window?'

'There are many portraits of ladies in the window.'

'The black woman.'

'Ah! She was a member of a choir that came to London some time ago. I went up to take their likenesses. They performed energetic heathen dances. Most exotic!'

'She is not dressed like a heathen.'

'No. They were engaged to show their savagery but I believe they were members of a Nonconformist church choir. They even sang before the Queen. A great fuss was made of them and—the lady herself told me—they were entertained most royally in a number of grand houses. She even sported a string of pearls a member of the nobility had given her. I took her picture when she was not performing.'

Stephen smiled. Should he have come dressed in skins and feathers?

He left the shop and stooped to look again at the print of that serene and haunting face.

It was a week later that he had returned to collect his photograph. As he entered the shop he noticed that the display in the window had changed. She was no longer there.

The photographer brought out the portrait of Stephen and handed it to him with some pride. It was a fine likeness. There he stood, keen and upright in his overcoat and shining boots.

'Thank you,' Stephen said. 'My mother will be pleased with this.' He scanned it again and slipped it into an envelope. Then he said, rather awkwardly, not looking at the man, 'What has happened to the picture of the native lady whose portrait was in your window?'

'I have changed my display and most of the prints have been claimed. I do not expect that lady to come for hers. She has returned to the Cape. It was a trifle for my own interest.'

'Is there a copy?'

The man appraised Stephen with the hint of a leer.

'Five shillings for the original.'

Twice what he'd paid for his own picture. 'I will come tomorrow.'

'Mind where you get the money.'

Stung, Stephen had left the shop.

CHAP. 3:37

I t was the first time that Stephen had asked—directly—to borrow money. He knew it was the surest way to strike at the heart of friendship but he had no choice. And Albert, rather too heartily, had said, 'Of course, old chap!' He'd cocked his head, anticipating an explanation. How could Stephen tell him it was to pay for the photograph of an unknown woman?

'Broke an instrument at a lesson in the hospital,' Stephen had said unconvincingly, knowing he could not even go to confession and admit to such a lie without the priest notching up a '?' against his name—proof, yet again, that Warden Bailey had been misled in admitting 'foreigners' to the College.

'Oh Lord,' said Albert scrummaging in his drawer under his shirts, 'I don't have an awful lot ...' Nor—a guilty omission—did he tell Stephen that, at last, he had been invited by Miss Wills, the Precentor's daughter, to have tea with her family that Sunday afternoon and that he had intended to buy her a small gift. 'How much do you need?' he'd said, hiding his vexation.

'Five shillings.'

Albert had coloured, hesitated, dived into the drawer again.

'I'm sure I can manage that.'

It was a lie, too.

When Stephen had gone with the money in his pocket, hastening downtown before his errand could be discovered, Albert had had to ask a senior student if he could beg a couple of florins from him, mortified by his own request and so earnest in his promises to repay within a week that the young man had said, with a knowing grin, 'I won't charge interest, Newnham. If it's all in pursuit of Miss Wills I won't begrudge you!'

With which, ears flaming, Albert had escaped.

Nor, when Stephen returned hastily to College in time for prep, could he show the picture to anyone. Especially Albert.

He hid it inside a book face to face with his own photograph, a slip of tissue paper between them, and wrestled with some way to pay his debt—knowing he could not. And no matter how he longed to ask Albert what he thought of that face—too distinctive to be posing, too detached to be self-aware—it must remain a secret, a deception.

Albert's preoccupations at that time were no secret. After he had repaid his debt to his fellow student—an urgent letter to his mother had sufficed—he took to loitering about at Dr Wills's gate at recreation time.

Clearly, Albert Newnham was in love.

He daydreamed in tutorials, mooned about, even in chapel, spent far longer in confession than before and did not suggest tea to Stephen for a fortnight. If Stephen was relieved to accept no favours—some remission from debt— he was alarmed at Albert's sudden inattention to their plan to go together to Kaffraria. Besides, courtship was a harrowing business, with exchanged letters, visits which were cut short by maiden aunts or happily prolonged through their absence, glances in church, detours round the Cathedral Close, dawdling after service near the Sunday school where Miss Unity was mistress. Stephen was impatient to meet the paragon who had claimed his friend's attention.

When she was introduced to him, she clasped his hand so long his palm began to sweat: such neat small teeth, her upper lip a little damp in her anxiety to please.

'How do you do, Mr Mana?'

'Miss Wills.'

At tea he watched her. She was decisive in everything she did, a merry girl with vivacious little hands, darting and busy. She reminded him of a musical box: open the lid and the notes would trip out, without pause or seeming continuity until they stopped—suddenly—eager to be wound again.

Like Albert, she laughed at everything, cocking her head with its short dark ringlets of springy curls. She chattered in a way he found incomprehensible in a woman, alighting on every subject, fluttering away again. She was too eager to please. She hadn't half the dignity he thought necessary in a missionary's wife. She had none of the authority of a Mrs Rutherford or the tough self-discipline of Mrs Turvey, the wife of the Principal of the Native College in Grahamstown, who could arrange a meal for a hundred without complaint, stay up all night sewing the students' clothes and still appear at matins before breakfast.

At *Mfundisi* Rutherford's mission and even in Grahamstown, the Xhosa girls were quiet, detached, eyes respectfully cast down. But they were capable and strong. They could hoe the fields, clean the church, carry water and wood—even those destined to be teachers or teachers' wives. They had a keen self-reliance and a power to slight as subtle as it might be silent. There was nothing inherently submissive as there was in the unmarried ladies he had met in Canterbury.

He often looked at the picture of the woman, hidden in his prayer book. That was the face of a missionary's wife!

Luminous, sufficient.

No, compared with her, Unity Wills was not a woman. She was a girl. She would always be a girl. She was not a soldier of Christ. She was a Sunday worshipper in her best bonnet.

'My busy little woman!' Albert called her, chuckling up his shoulders, twinkling behind his spectacles, pink about the neck.

Stephen had smiled. How foolish Englishmen could be!

FOOLISHNESS COULD BE indulged but not insanity!

'I have asked Unity—Miss Wills—to marry me,' Albert had announced.

'Marry you?' Stephen was aghast. 'What about our mission?'

'She will make a very fine missionary's wife,' retorted Albert. 'After all, her father was once a Fellow of our College.' He was flustered, casting around. 'She knows all about missionaries! She will teach the mission children.'

'There may not be any mission children to teach, Albert!' exclaimed Stephen. 'We may have to start from scratch, build ourselves a hut in the bush, cook on a fire and face hostile tribesmen who have never heard of Christ. We might even have to fight for our lives!'

'It's too late now!' Albert had been more abject than angry. Then he bristled a little and said, 'I didn't think I had to ask your permission to get married!'

'You don't.' Stephen had turned away. 'But you have no idea what you are going to.'

Nor, Stephen knew, had he.

He had been held a virtual hostage since he was nine years old, an ecclesiastical experiment, a pastiche of an Englishman. Only the remnants of his real provenance remained: his black face.

STEPHEN RODE ALL day. He stopped only once at a stream to water the horse and sat awhile on flat rocks under a tree. He was hungry but, on searching his saddlebag, he discovered that he had left his food behind in his hurry. No one was about. New homesteads, replacing those that had been burned by the rebels, clustered forlornly on the open hillsides. The Ngqika had cleared out the Mfengu in their passage through the Amathole the year before. The fields had been raided, trampled by men, not by browsing cattle. But the people had begun to drift back to rebuild their homes. Here and there a newly planted field had begun to sprout. As Stephen sat in the shade and his horse cropped the grass at the edge of the stream, he watched the first smoke of afternoon cooking fires drift up from thatched roofs, and a dog, disturbed by his presence, barked from a yard.

He considered approaching a nearby homestead and asking for food but decided against it. Despite being a clergyman, he could not forget, in this neighbourhood, that he was a stranger and a Ngqika, not an Mfengu—nor that his father had been councillor to a Ngqika chief.

He rode on and at dusk he came to the outskirts of the town. He passed through the quiet side streets to the huts and shacks where the Xhosa lived. There was a man, Eleazar Mbanda, who had worked at the Native College in Grahamstown as an assistant to the carpenter until he had removed to this village and set up on his own. Remembering Eleazar, he had sent a message with a carter a few days before his arrival in the hope that Eleazar would care for his horse while he travelled on to Queenstown by train.

Eleazar Mbanda was waiting on his porch, evidently on the lookout. 'Mfundisi!' A pleasant, cheerful greeting, acknowledging Stephen's new and greater status, with the pride of an avuncular schoolmaster, a generous hand outstretched to take the bridle and bring the horse into the yard.

Stephen unsaddled and hobbled the horse and entered the house, hat in hand. He sat at the table while Eleazar's wife made tea and cut slices of bread which she spread with jam. It was a better house than his, securely built. The shelves were lined with paper, the dishes and plates carefully arranged. An easy chair stood by the fireplace.

A Christian household with a wife and a picture of the Bishop on the wall.

They said grace before tea and read a passage from the Bible. Four small grandchildren clustered round, neat, clean and silent.

'Where are you going, *Mfundisi*?' asked Eleazar.

'To see my mother,' said Stephen, venturing no further. How could he tell these pious people—both Mfengu—the reason for his journey? Instead, to their delight and astonishment, he told them about England and about his own attempts at carpentry at the Missionary College. 'In fact,' he said, 'I was something of a wonder because I came with skills they did not expect, especially the master, who thought I must be a savage. I told him I was taught at the Native College in Grahamstown by very good carpenters who are my own people. At first he did not seem to believe me but after a while he chose me above others to help with commissions.'

The old man nodded his head, musing. 'Ah yes!' He sipped his tea. 'Mr Gawe was a good teacher.'

'And so were you!' said Stephen, recalling the carpenter's shop, the rough chisels, the single lathe. 'Just as good with half the tools!'

They talked on about the price of timber, the scarcity of work and how best to make a chapel window, while the reason for Stephen's journey remained concealed in his pocket.

The next day, leaving his borrowed horse in Eleazar's care, Stephen took the train to Queenstown. The unfolding scene—the aloes and the kiepersols, the euphorbia and the scrubby seams along the riverbeds—bore no resemblance to the familiar countryside of England which he had come to associate with train journeys. He tried to doze but the

42

benches were hard and the coach loud with the voices of passengers. This was not the way the English travelled, avoiding the eyes of their fellows, barricaded by their newspapers or even by prayer books.

'Always be prepared for accidents!' Albert had once whispered wryly in Stephen's ear as they had boarded a train together, nodding towards an elderly lady holding her Bible up to her face. 'Insurance against catastrophe! Nor can you imagine what a comfort it is to have a clergyman in the carriage!'

'We are not clergymen yet!'

'Ah, but we have the air!' said Albert, putting on his most pious face so that Stephen had to take out his handkerchief and blow his nose to stop his laughter.

Now, the people spoke loudly, excitedly, as if the uproar might check anxiety while they swayed and rocked together on the benches, shoulders touching, parcels between their feet, knee to knee. Stephen took his prayer book from his pocket—not as an antidote to disaster but so that he could open the page where he kept the precious photograph of the woman, the face transmuted now from vision to reality, each detail memorised and known, even the small blemish beside her ear.

How often he had gazed at it.

And how could he ever have a wife like her when he was not yet a man? Neither circumcised nor initiated into manhood as Mzamo was.

STEPHEN HAD ARRIVED in Canterbury in September 1869. It was nine months before he received a letter from Mzamo. He had long given up hearing from him—or anyone—except *Mfundisi* Turvey, the Principal of the Native College, acknowledging his frequent letters and relaying news of all his friends. Mzamo's letter had taken five months to reach him.

43

January 1870

My dear brother,

You will not have heard from me before but I wish to tell you that I have undertaken the rites of initiation, *ubukwetha*. Without them I cannot have authority as a Ngqika nor as my father's son. Do not fear: I am Christian still but this restriction on circumcision by the English is a mark of disrespect and a trick to oppress black Christians—for if our own people see the uninitiated as children, why shouldn't they continue to treat us as such as well?

After leaving the College and a tiresome time at Mfundisi Rutherford's mission I decided to seek our home and once there, obeyed my father's wish to proceed to the circumcision school. Afterwards, I did not return to the mission but went directly to Grahamstown and spoke to the Bishop about work. He was very high with me for 'disappearing' but, I suspect, he did not question too closely what I had been doing because he knows he cannot afford to throw away the expense of my education. Nor can he grieve for what he does not know so any word about circumcision was avoided! I do not think he will have mentioned it to Mfundisi Turvey either although I suspect that the wise old fellow knows better.

So, brother, I am now interpreter to the Magistrate. He is the gentleman who used to come to the College when we performed the scenes from Shakespeare. He speaks no Kaffir and is hard of hearing and asked for a man who could be trusted to understand and use his very words.

He had mentioned nothing further of their mother but wrote that their father had gone off again on yet another sojourn digging the government's roads. He had made no inquiries about England to which Stephen might reply. He had supplied an address in Grahamstown, care of their old school friend, Vuyo Tontsi. He added at the end of the letter:

44

I am shortly to be married to Tontsi's sister, Nokhanyiso. She is a member of the choir at St Philip's where I am choirmaster. The nuptials will take place in the new church which you have not seen. It will be an important gathering as her father is a chief.

The only other information had been of the cricket club he and Tontsi had started in the community: *We will soon be able to challenge the fellows at the Native College to a match.* Stephen had had to wait for his return to Grahamstown to appreciate Mzamo's prominence in the community or the lustre he'd acquired beyond the status of a man whose brother was in England.

As the train drew into the station, Stephen gathered up his things, gazing expectantly from the window, waiting for the last of the thorn trees to slip by and the platform to come into view. Albert would be waiting for him, his trap and horse in the yard.

—*Don't worry, old chap, I'll always be there to welcome you, wherever you might be.*

The remark had been made with touching eagerness long ago when Stephen was packing in the dormitory at the College in Canterbury on the eve of his return to the Cape. The great cathedral tower in its age and permanence had brooded beyond the window, an arc of pigeons flaring out across a pale evening sky.

'But we'll be together,' Stephen had said. 'They promised to post us in pairs.'

'Of course,' Albert had replied without conviction, bending to inspect his boots and rub his sleeve across the top of them.

Stephen had gazed at him in consternation. 'The Warden wouldn't break his promise!' Albert had not replied and Stephen had hurried on. 'Toyise and Wilson went together last year. Don't you remember? With that fellow who looks like a stork? We all have to work together or the whole venture will fail.'

'Politics,' said Albert.

'We are churchmen. '

'Same thing,' said Albert and laughed, as if it were a joke.

STEPHEN STEPPED DOWN from the train with his bag and looked about him. The other passengers were taking their luggage and walking out into the road beyond. There were some wagons drawn up, there was a horse or two tethered to a hitching post. There was no Albert Newnham pacing the platform, jaunty with welcome.

Long, long ago Mzamo had said, 'Never think that white men are your fathers or your brothers, no matter what they say. They will promise you one thing and they will do another. What about all those boys who thought they were Sir George Grey's sons because they took his name? When he went as Governor to New Zealand he did not even bother to answer their letters.'

'My father was still my father though he never wrote me a letter,' Stephen had retorted.

'Only because your father did not know how to write.'

Stephen went out into the road and gazed up and down it in dismay. No doubt his letter had not reached Albert.

—*There was a delay in sending it on from town to the mission station.*

—*There was a swollen river.*

—*There was a shortage of horses going north.*

Stephen felt in his jacket for his pocketbook, extracted it and counted out his money. How was he to hire a cart or even a horse to complete his journey to the mission on the Indwe River? And would Albert have a fresh horse at the mission that he could ride further, heading east towards the country where, after his father's disappearance, his mother had settled with her brother's people?

It was his own fault, for he had added a postscript: *If by any chance you are unable to meet me, I will make my own way to your mission.* It had been a courtesy, like his objections when

46

accepting teas—an attempt at acknowledging the debt, knowing that of course Albert would be there, never keeping score or expecting a return.

Stephen picked up his bag and walked along the street, gazing all about him as he went in case he saw a trap with Albert riding high, flourishing his whip and calling his halloos. He trudged on until he reached the outskirts of the town.

—*I will make my own way to your mission.*

Perhaps, this time, Albert had taken him at his word. After all, how could Albert know how small his stipend was? It was his own fault that he'd been too ashamed to tell him, demeaned by the difference made between them at the synod.

—*Native deacons will earn half.*

Even those who'd been to Canterbury.

As Albert had not yet arrived in the Cape when Stephen had attended his first synod, how could he have guessed the truth?

Stephen walked on in the hope that any passing vehicle would give him a lift. He had his doubts. What would the people think of a clergyman covered with dust, without conveyance, his bag slung on a rough stick over his shoulder?

Most would believe he was an imposter.

That is what they had believed of the dear old Bishop when, as Archdeacon, he had tramped the diocese begging a night's shelter in a stable or a hut. He was often turned from a door as a rogue. And when he had declared that Jesus was born in a stable and always walked with his disciples, the retort was that if Jesus had had access to a horse—as any respectable Englishman in the Colony did—he would have used it!

Stephen also knew what it was to be treated as an imposter. How he remembered the sliding glances in an English teashop when he sat down to a slice of cake with Albert, the hastily withdrawn stares of women, the unconcealed curiosity of children, the slight derision on the faces of the men.

—*Who does he think he is?*

It was only the elderly maiden ladies or clergy wives who hustled him into their drawing rooms, showering him with food until he felt like a pigeon in a park, stuffed with left-over crumbs from a Sunday cake.

Stephen walked until well into the afternoon, when a cart passed by. He called out and, some paces further down the road, it slowed and the driver stood up, turned and beckoned. Stephen raised his hand. He proffered a fare and was invited to climb up. He sat on a sack, face to face with a lean dog, its shoulders hitched, its ears flattened back against its head in the wind. It curled a lip each time he moved. He avoided its malevolent gaze and exchanged news with the driver.

It was nightfall when they reached a populous place, a mixture of huts and byres around a crooked church made of corrugated iron with a wooden cross on its gable. The driver of the cart pointed to it with his whip and, gingerly, Stephen alighted, the dog barking sharply as he pulled his bag down. It continued to bark as the cart trundled away, weaving back and forward across the tailboard, hackles up.

The Minister at the crooked church was a Nonconformist. He offered Stephen supper, welcomed him into his house but seemed ill at ease, allowing long silences to punctuate their conversation until Stephen mentioned Albert Newnham.

Ah, he knew the *Mfundisi* by sight. Always so neat. The man pointed to his eyes and laughed. '*Mehlomane*. Four eyes,' he said. 'A person from this district is helping him to learn Xhosa. It is not easy—he does not hear the language.'

All those lessons in Canterbury for nothing? And Albert saying ingenuously, his finger on a word in his exercise book, 'For a savage language it's very complicated, Stephen.'

'Is an Englishman the only one who can have advanced thoughts?'

'Sorry, old chap, I didn't mean that. I meant—well, for a language that's only recently written, it has so many rules.'

It was much more fun for Albert to watch Stephen grasp the rules of chess than to twist his tongue around words he had never heard spoken in a real conversation in his life. 'You out-manoeuvre everyone like a general with his troops,' he'd said admiringly.

'Well, my father is *isandla sokunene* of a great chief,' Stephen had replied.

'What is that?'

'A man of weight and authority. He sits at the chief's right hand—*sisandla sokunene*—and advises him.'

'Would you have been a great *sokunene*—or whatever you call it—if you had remained a heathen?'

'I shall be a greater *isandla sokunene* if I am a priest—so you had better stop fooling about when I bring you my Latin.'

IN THE MORNING when wreaths of smoke from early fires drifted between the houses and the boys were driving the goats to pasture, the minister asked Stephen to join him in his church for prayers. The room was furnished only with a table for an altar and a wooden stand for a Bible. The table had no cloth or candlesticks. The windows were without arches and the pews were a set of benches. The floor was polished dung. How much the same and yet how different from his own small mission church with its formal altar, its cross and its rose-coloured frontal made by the parish ladies in Canterbury. And yet, in this simple church, not kneeling but sitting, head bowed, listening to the murmured prayer offered for them both, Stephen transcended, fleetingly, the awe he had experienced in a great cathedral in a foreign land.

He was not an imposter here—a curiosity—but a fellow man.

CHAP. 4:50

W hen Stephen was twelve and Mzamo sixteen they were sent to the Native College in Grahamstown. Stephen was chosen for his diligence, Mzamo for his intellect but also, the Principal suspected, because Mzamo was a handful at Rutherford's mission.

Rutherford had written:

He questions everything. He constantly asks why the English churches are so hostile to each other. Is their God not the same? (The Dissenters have a mission nearby so their influence on the local people has been pernicious.) He even had the impertinence to challenge me for drawing water from the river on a Sunday! He is a leader and has a keen sense of his own nobility and he is alert to the fact that the English Church is the church of Her Majesty and therefore the most prestigious (my wife has been reading to our boys the history of England. Imagine—they are well-versed in the Wars of the Roses!). Should you curb him he will be a great asset to our civilising mission among the Gaikas. Undoubtedly, he will be influential in time.

So off they went, equipped with new Blucher boots, a pair of moleskin trousers, their jackets repaired and lengthened and two flannel shirts each, sewn by the mission girls from fabric donated by the Bishop's wife. They were joined by another three scholars from a distant station who had all chosen the name 'George' on their baptism, in honour of the Governor.

'My goodness, three young Georges!' Mrs Rutherford had exclaimed. 'Surely we could be more original than that!'

It was not a matter of originality but of respect.

Was it not the custom among English sons to take the name of their fathers? George Mandyoli Maqoma, grandson of the great Xhosa general, had already been in England for a year, along with Boy Henry Duke of Wellington Tshatshu. They were being educated by the Reverend Savage at Nuneaton.

'What lions they will be!' the Bishop had rejoiced.

Since then there had been a plethora of Georges, and the Governor, Sir George Grey, had pronounced before his departure for a posting in New Zealand that, despite the distance, he was still the father of them all. No matter how numerous his sons, those named George, it seemed, could claim his eternal interest—even if their letters to him went unanswered.

'What name will you choose?' Stephen had asked his brother when, after months of instruction by *Mfundisi* Rutherford, he was considered ready for baptism.

'I am Mzamo. You are Malusi.'

'Those are not the names of a Christian.'

'They are the names given by our father.'

'*Mfundisi* Rutherford says we cannot be considered Christians without a Christian name. I am Stephen now.'

'Yes. You are Stephen,' said Mzamo. 'Until you change your mind.'

'Why should I change my mind?'

'Do you know who Stephen was?'

'He was a martyr who was stoned to death,' said Stephen.

'Yes! And without complaining. What use is that? He should have raised his voice, taken up a stone and hurled it back. '

It was without any sense of irony that *Mfundisi* Rutherford chose to call Mzamo 'Saul', St Stephen's persecutor. It was a name Mzamo refused to acknowledge, despite its being written on his certificate of baptism and entered in the Mission Register.

'I am Mzamo Mzamane,' he insisted stubbornly. An indication of intransigence which did not go unnoticed.

THE NATIVE COLLEGE in Grahamstown was set on a hill among the grander houses and villas of the town. The dormitory windows looked out at the road running past the toll house. Beyond, the wagons climbed in steady procession along the pale sand track, the teams of oxen sending up plumes of dust in the dry weather. When it was wet the wheels often stuck in ruts and the students were summoned by the toll-keeper to help him lift them out. Mzamo and Vuyo Tontsi sometimes boasted that they would climb aboard one day and disappear into the interior to seek their fortunes.

Both of them bridled at the restrictions of the College, both had been mission-trained too late to have forgotten the freedoms of their homes. Even at their rural missions they had been allowed to hunt with sticks within the grounds. They had explored the pastures and the bush and helped milk the cows.

Here, the nearby veld was out of bounds, nor were students allowed home until they had finished their education. They were to speak English at all times. They were called by Christian names, baptised by the Principal, *Mfundisi* Turvey, and blessed by the Bishop. Each was supplied with a blue serge jacket to wear to church. Rice or porridge was served morning and evening. Midday dinner was potatoes from the College garden and meat every second day. There was soup on Thursdays and a pudding made of dough and raisins after church on Sundays. They did their lessons in the morning and were instructed in carpentry or printing for two hours after school.

On Saturdays, once they had done their laundry and cleaned the school and dormitories, *Mfundisi* Turvey coached his pupils in cricket, reliving his youthful triumph as a batsman at the Missionary College in Canterbury. A local curate, along with the cowhand, the carpentry master and his assistant, Eleazar Mbanda, made up the numbers on Turvey's team. With enthusiasm Turvey arranged matches with the local colonial schoolboys and their masters. He was a shrewd manager, determined to temper the hostility of his neighbours for running—on their very doorsteps and within the walls of the College for their sons—a mission institution for Africans. He also knew the value of games and the benefits of playing in a team. He rejoiced when his eleven won, knowing their success did not go unnoticed in the town. He was proud of their behaviour on the pitch, their respectful sportsmanship.

On Sundays the students trooped behind his broad, bearded figure to the first Bishop of Grahamstown's small stone Memorial Chapel in the cemetery and, on weekday afternoons, they worked together in the vegetable garden while he, shaded by a large straw hat, sat at the edge of the bean beds in a folding chair, one eye on his newspaper, the other on the students digging with their hoes.

The boys who had come from their own homes in Kaffraria, and not from a rural mission station as Stephen and Mzamo had, complained that planting, weeding and harvesting was women's work. No man tilled the land. Stephen did not complain. He was used to working in a garden. At *Mfundisi* Rutherford's mission he had been sent into the fields with the other boys, young as he had been. And, in time, he had been allowed to weed around the fruit trees in the orchard.

'Ah, Stephen,' Mrs Rutherford had once said, sadly inspecting the wasp-stung peaches, 'this is not like an English orchard. We will never harvest a decent crop.'

'I wish to see England.'

'It is very far away and much too cold for a native.'

'It is often cold here too.'

'But it's always wet in England. The damp gets into the chest and eats it away. Little children are often carried off.' Stephen had gazed at her, perplexed. 'Their guardian angels take them to God.'

Alarmed, he had questioned her, and Mrs Rutherford had reassured him that a guardian angel was uniquely his, associated with his baptism, his growth and his salvation: one who could be appealed to at any time, more accessible, it seemed, than God. Stephen wondered then if the child's body rose from the grave to be borne away in the secret hours of dark, nestled between huge feathered wings like those of the angels pictured in a print beside the altar in the church.

Mzamo held another view.

'You are confusing angels with ancestors,' he said. 'It is they, not angels, who watch over you from birth. Angels were never human so why should they care for you more than your grandfathers who are your family?'

'Ancestors do not have wings. They cannot fly. How can they reach God who is in Heaven?'

'The ancestors live under the earth or in great pools. They have homesteads and herds of fine cattle. There is no need to fly.'

'I don't believe in ancestors and nor should you,' Stephen had replied doggedly. 'We are not heathens.'

Besides, there was evidence of angels everywhere. They were in the mission church, they were in the illustrated Bible, they were sung of in hymns and when he was sent to school in Grahamstown, almost the first thing Stephen had noticed was the angel in the hall of the Principal's house, painted white from head to toe. But, mostly, angels were in the cemetery on the hill above the town, carved in marble or cast in bronze.

He had often been one of a party of students coerced, once a month, to weed the graves in the section set aside for

Anglicans. Along those sequestered rows he had made the acquaintance of every kind of angel: militant angels with drawn swords; weeping mother angels; baby angels with wings as small as a sparrow's. Many had lost their limbs, victims of vandals. There was one whose helmeted head perched on his foot, his glare unquenched.

All of them were English, like the pictures in the Bible. But it was not worth pointing that out to Mzamo. Nor to Vuyo Tontsi. They would only laugh.

But even if they laughed, neither wished to tarry among the angel-guarded gravestones in the cemetery. The *Mfundisi's* promise of one free afternoon a term to any boy who offered to weed there had failed to raise a single volunteer. No one dared, fearing to be sent alone. After that, it became compulsory for everyone.

The students would trail through the town under the supervision of the carpentry master, picks over their shoulders, spades and sacks wheeled in a barrow. The cemetery was, to most of them, a fearful place. Here the dead waited in rows, a great company, without the comfort of a byre full of cattle or a homestead busy with passers-by and the smell of cooking. The tall, gaunt cypresses along the perimeter were fearful too, dry and scaly, no haven for the birds. Once, Stephen had encountered a chameleon clinging to a frond: an emissary of the dead. He had turned from it in fear, hastily finding a fork to pry weeds from a nearby mound.

He had studied the fading letters on the stone, brushing the sand away. It was a soldier's grave, a relic of a distant war:

Killed by barbarous Gaika Kaffirs, 1839.

There was nothing barbarous about Julius Coventry Naka even though he was a 'Gaika'.

He was an object of awe.

Newly returned from four years in England, another of the

Bishop's 'lions', he had been educated in the hope of training him for Holy Orders. On his arrival, he was invited by *Mfundisi* Turvey to address the students at the Native College.

Polished and assured, with a white waistcoat and cutaway jacket, he stood before them in the refectory and told them of St Nicholas's Parish in Nuneaton, of the Reverend Dr Savage, the trains, the ships, the horse-drawn carriages. And of the death of George Maqoma, who had been one of his fellow African princes in Warwickshire.

'He was the grandson of our great General,' Julius had said. 'Confined as he is *esiqitini*.' On the prison island. 'My friend George would have been a Ngqika chief, a man to bring the word of God to all our people. But,' snapping his fingers, 'he was called in a wink to appear before his Creator.'

'We heard that it was while chasing vandals in the churchyard that he fell and struck his head,' *Mfundisi* Turvey remarked.

'That is what they like to say,' said Julius. 'It is better than admit his lungs have been the cause. England is not a healthy place.' He laughed. 'There are times when the smoke and soot made everybody's faces black and I did not feel so different myself!'

Mzamo looked sceptical. 'How is it the English do not suffer with their lungs?'

'They do,' replied Julius. 'The poor people suffer very much.'

'Are there poor Englishmen?' Vuyo was astounded.

'There are some so poor they are kept in what is called the workhouse.'

'What work do they do?'

'They break stones. '

There was a murmur of disbelief among the boys, a collective sigh, rippling across the row of upturned faces.

'No white man breaks stones,' returned Mzamo boldly.

'Oh yes they do,' said Julius. 'Mostly if they are Irish.'

'*Mfundisi* Turvey is Irish.' Mzamo turned to look at the Principal with his bland, broad face.

'Especially if they're Irish!' snorted *Mfundisi* Turvey. 'How right you are.'

There was a silence. Then Vuyo Tontsi said, 'Can you teach us to make guns, brother?'

He was cuffed by a master for impertinence.

JULIUS NAKA WAS kept on at the Native College as a teacher. He did not prove satisfactory.

The Dean was offended by his coming to Communion in the Cathedral instead of accompanying the students of the Native College to the first Bishop's Memorial Chapel in the cemetery.

'It is a subject of much triumph to the Dissenters,' he said to the Bishop, 'when these educated lads strut about the town and give them a chance to ridicule us for our folly. Did you notice what he wore to church? Black gloves which he waggled about for all to see in a most ostentatious manner.'

'My dear Dean,' replied the Bishop, 'you cannot imagine the trials and confusions a young man like Julius has been exposed to—cut off from old habits and associations.'

'My Lord.' The Dean was impatient. 'This young man with his fanciful name has been petted and spoiled. I heard him describing the dinners and croquet parties he had been to with the gentry of the land. It's preposterous. I don't know why Turvey allows it.'

'I believe it's high time you invited Mr Turvey and his students to the Cathedral for a service,' said the Bishop, enjoying the Dean's displeasure.

'What?' The Dean's voice rose. 'If you will forgive me, my Lord ... I cannot allow Turvey to preach in my Cathedral. He drops his haitches like a common workman. He has a brogue that no one understands. It would be a scandal.'

The Bishop regarded him quizzically.

'I believe,' continued the Dean, affronted, 'that he was educated in a Clergy Orphan School.'

'That may be,' said the Bishop quietly. 'But he is the best missionary in the diocese, make no mistake.'

MZAMO AND VUYO were entranced with Julius Naka. As they were among the older students at the College, they were housed not in the dormitory but in a small brick shed near the carpentry master's cottage. In the evenings after prayers, when none of the masters were about, they and the apprentices would invite Julius in to talk to them, eager to hear more.

Often, he would tell of his voyage, of Coventry and Nuneaton—quite unimaginable despite his eloquence, his grand gestures of height and scale and volume—and of the Missionary College in Canterbury, the 'Foreigners' Building' shared by the students from China, India, Burma and other countries of which none of them had heard.

'Were there many?'

'Not many—but we were all taught English together, to speak like gentlemen, to mind our manners and write letters to our sponsors.'

'Did you ever travel on a train?' asked Vuyo Tontsi.

'How does a train go?' Another, interrupting.

'Is it drawn by horses or oxen?' Yet another, recently arrived from an isolated mission station.

Supercilious though he was with the ignorant, Julius Naka was expansive. Mzamo, alert to every nuance of his speech, learned never to ask a question which might expose his ignorance. He listened intently. He watched. And he envied Julius Naka's fine hat, his slim-toed boots, the wing collar and the fob watch he wore tucked in his waistcoat pocket. It was a trinket Mzamo had asked to see—carelessly, as if it didn't matter one way or another. But Julius was eager to confide. 'Given to me by a lady,' he said, dangling it above Mzamo's casually proffered palm. 'There was a place called Fortune's Alley.' Julius slipped the watch into his pocket again, tipped back on his heels, breathed in deeply.

Mzamo caught his eye, inclined his head, grinned, seemingly complicit. He had no idea what Fortune's Alley was. But one day—when he was chosen to go to England—

58

he would know. In anticipation of that time, he gleaned from Julius Naka, in an easy camaraderie, the tricks and pitfalls of making his way in England, of finding fellows worth imitating: the signs of distinction, Julius said, were not difficult to recognise.

'They make a great fuss of rajahs and princes and the sons of other great men. The old ladies like it especially. They shower gifts on those with rank.'

Mzamo's father was *isandala sokunene*, a great chief's councillor. There would be no need to recall that he was a labourer breaking stones on the Governor's road.

It was also from Julius Naka that the students at the Native College learned most about the chiefs and headmen banished *esiqitini*, to the island just across the bay in Cape Town where once Nxele, the prophet, had been held and had drowned trying to swim to the mainland.

'It is a place the white people call Robben Island. Not long ago the students at the College in Cape Town sent a memorial to the Governor to ask for their release. There were many of us whose fathers were prisoners on that island, living in shame and poverty with only seals and wild fowl and lepers for company.'

'What is a memorial?' asked Vuyo Tontsi.

'It is a document we all must sign saying that we, as the sons of chiefs and councillors, demand the release of our fathers.'

'But what use was it to ask for their release?' said Vuyo. 'They are still there.'

'We must not stop asking,' said Julius. 'Our chief, Maqoma, is old. He will die soon. Now his grandson, George Maqoma, is dead too and they say George's brother, who was also in England, has disease in his lungs as well. What are our people to do? The white men are making fools of us. It suits them very well to have us die. And we must send another memorial too, asking for our farms.'

'What farms?'

59

'Before I went to England,' said Julius, 'when I was at the College in Cape Town, the Bishop there promised each and every one of us that we would be given land in recompense for what the government took from our fathers in the last war. I have a paper to prove it. You must get your paper too. A bishop cannot break a promise.'

It was not the Bishop of Cape Town who had broken his promise. It was the Governor, Sir George Grey. Letters had been written, title deeds prepared, the Governor flushed with his own largesse. But, when he left for New Zealand, the land had been left unsurveyed and the matter had been quietly postponed.

'I wonder how many natives in New Zealand will be promised land?' the Bishop had said acerbically to his wife.

'And how many will be baptised George!' she had replied.

The new Governor in the Cape was not concerned with the land claims of the sons of incarcerated chiefs: he would never have been foolish enough to have ventured the proposal in the first place. The Bishop of Cape Town could complain all he liked of the government's broken promises—it was not he who had gone back on his word. Besides, bishops should be kept at a prudent distance. They were always after funds.

WHEN JULIUS COVENTRY Naka left the Native College in Grahamstown for a distant mission—hustled off reluctantly by the Bishop who foresaw a disturbing influence at work—the students relapsed into their accustomed diffidence.

Except Mzamo.

He had had no scruple in asking *Mfundisi* Turvey to explain to him the way in which a memorial could be composed.

'To whom do you wish to write a memorial, sonny?' asked Turvey.

'To the Governor,' said Mzamo.

'Well, I'll be blessed!' Turvey hid a smile. 'And what, my good lad, do you have to say to the Governor?'

'That our chiefs must be released from the prison on Nxele's island. That place—*esiqitini*. They have been there too long. Their graves will be in the middle of the sea where their people cannot honour them.'

Turvey sighed and put his hand on Mzamo's shoulder. 'The Bishop in Cape Town has often made the same request,' he said. 'In vain.' He searched for the right words. 'The law and what is just is not always the same thing. Governors and bishops are obliged to obey the law.'

'Whose law is that?'

'The laws of England.'

'We are always told that the English are the most just people on the earth.'

'As we, the Irish, are also obliged to believe,' *Mfundisi* Turvey murmured to himself.

IT WAS SOME months after that that Mzamo was sent away from the College by the Bishop for insubordination: twenty years old, his education put aside, his examinations suspended.

It was a Saturday in summer and the heat was unrelenting, the air so still only the uppermost leaves of the trees twitched in the hot wind. Clouds thrust up, dissolved and disappeared. The students rose early. They trailed in reluctant relays to the washhouse. The stragglers hurried for roll-call, pulling on their boots. They had been told after prayers the night before that the Bishop had sent a notice instructing them to walk to Southwell for service at St James Church.

'How far is Southwell?' they wanted to know.

Mfundisi Turvey did not seem too eager to reply. At length he had said, 'We will set out tomorrow morning, which will give us all day and plenty of time. Accommodation has been arranged in the schoolroom for the night but we must take our cooking pots and blankets. There will be two services on Sunday. You will return on Monday.'

Vuyo Tontsi was the only one who knew of Southwell. 'It's many, many miles away!' he exclaimed once the principal had left. 'I do not know why we should have to go to Southwell for church! When *Mfundisi* Turvey goes there he takes a horse and is gone all day and often for the night.'

'The Bishop wants him to show off our singing,' said Mzamo.

'To a crowd of farmers? They will probably chase us from their church and we will go without dinner.'

'The Bishop is trying to raise money,' said Mzamo. 'Besides Julius Naka, there were another four students in England who came from the Native College in Cape Town. They are learning to be missionaries. Weren't you listening when the Bishop spoke last week?'

'Yes,' said Vuyo defensively. 'He spoke of Kona and Toyise —and I don't remember the others because they were Basothos and Baralongs.'

'Moroka and Morosi,' said Mzamo. 'The sons of very great chiefs. You should know that.'

'Well'—Vuyo was nettled—'what has it to do with us? They were at the school in Cape Town. They even lived in the Bishop's own house.'

'Not any more,' said Mzamo. 'Mr Gawe told me that the Bishop's wife didn't like "little savages" playing with her children. So the Bishop sent them to another place. Imagine a woman telling a Bishop what to do!'

There was a sudden silence and the younger boys stared at Mzamo in consternation: the Bishop in Cape Town had ears; he could hear words, know thoughts, snare sins from a distance just as clearly as God.

Mfundisi Turvey had once said so.

Mzamo was unconcerned. 'One of us will be chosen to go to England next time. The Bishop in Cape Town is looking for the favour of our Bishop here.'

'Why should he want a favour? He's the Archbishop,' said Vuyo.

'Of course the Bishop in Cape Town wouldn't care about us if he didn't need our Bishop to support him in making our colonial Church independent from England. He'll make sure one of us goes from Grahamstown to keep our Bishop on his side.'

'What are you talking about?' asked Vuyo.

'You will never be a man of influence, Tontsi, if you don't understand these things. Churchmen are no different from the men in the government or a chief looking for tribute from his neighbours.'

'The choice of who goes is God's,' intervened one of the other senior students.

'This has nothing to do with God,' said Mzamo. 'It has to do with votes and favours.'

'You are irreverent, my friend.'

'If God made the choice, he would choose you,' said Mzamo. 'God likes pious fellows.' Then he added, without a hint of self-congratulation, 'If our Bishop makes the choice —or, maybe, I should say the Governor—he will choose me. I am a senior councillor's oldest son.'

'But you will never make a priest,' muttered the other, retreating to the door. 'And a Missionary College—here or in Cape Town or in England—is there to train priests.'

THE FARMERS OF Southwell did not evict the Native College students from their church. They participated heartily in all the hymns. During the offertory the College choir sang alone, ranged in three rows in front of the pews. The plate was passed about and the weekly portion which had once been sent to England for the Lancashire Cotton Famine or, more recently, to the missions in India was set aside for the College's fund. Two pounds three and four pence.

—*The native students behaved very nicely*, wrote a parishioner to a friend. *Their clothes were a little shabby but neatly got up and they sang surprisingly well.*

63

—Afterwards the native students were treated to tea and buns. They seemed most grateful for the refreshment which was supplied by Mrs Long and the ladies of the Guild: the report in the Church Quarterly.

—Listening to them one would scarcely believe that they lately came from savage homes.

—Certainly, wrote the Rector, more enthusiastically and better informed, finer singing has not been heard in my small church before. Their soloist was splendid.

It was Mzamo who sang the solo.

His voice, despite his youth, was full and rich: a voice for hymns, for praise, for hallelujahs. As he sang, Stephen stood intent, his damp hands clenched against his sides, willing every note into life, alert to each expression on the watching faces of the congregation. There never was a voice like Mzamo's! But if it was a voice singing English hymns, it had a darker vibrancy, a note of lament. The congregation was suddenly alert, all attention on the tall, lean figure in his winged collar with his carefully parted hair.

The congregation almost clapped when he fell silent, forgetting they were in a sacred place. Turvey beamed, his face alight. He inclined his head towards Mzamo in acknowledgment. Mzamo stepped impassively back into line.

Stephen knew he could never match Mzamo's dignity. That presence, that reserve. Even around the tea table, he remained the noticeable figure among the crowding boys— taller, freer, moving with an ease, a grace. And, at that moment, there was no doubt in Stephen's mind that what Mzamo had said the night before was true: *He will choose me.* Who else could represent the Native College at a Missionary Institution in a foreign land? Who else could command such attention?

It was a long walk back to Grahamstown. Far longer—or so it seemed—than the journey out. Mfundisi Turvey had returned home on horseback, reaching town hours before they had even tackled the steepest pass. He had already settled in his study with a cup of tea and begun his *Quarterly Report* to the Society for the Propagation of the Gospel in London by the time they topped the crest:

> As we set out for St James, Southwell—a distance of 24 miles from Grahamstown—it was quite romantic to see the young people walking along the road with their bundles of clean clothes which they intended to put on for the Sunday service the following day. They reached Southwell at dusk and the night was spent in an adjacent school room. There were two services in St James on Sunday to which many of the local farmers came. I can report with pride that while the offertory was being taken my boys sang (with great effect) a chorus from the Messiah, 'Lift up ye heads, O ye gates'. I was most gratified that the sum of a little over 2 pounds was given to us for the College on this occasion as all diocesan offertories of late have been going to the relief of the Lancashire Cotton Famine or to the Indian Missions. I am pleased to have been able to accept this contribution to our ongoing work.

Worn out from two nights on the rough floorboards of the draughty school, the choir had set off from Southwell for town. They trudged up the passes, their backs to the mysterious stretch of blue that lay flat on the horizon and which, on the outward journey, Vuyo Tontsi had exultantly declared to be the sea. So few had ever seen the sea. Only Vuyo boasted that he had swum in it, dashing at the waves, fearless in the rush of foam.

The smaller boys soon lagged. Some removed their boots and examined blisters swelling on their heels. Most had soles too soft to walk on the stony ground for they were not allowed to go barefoot at school.

'My boots are done,' said Vuyo Tontsi to Mzamo. 'Where will we get leather to repair them?'

'The College must replace them,' said Mzamo. 'We

cannot do it for ourselves. I will speak to *Mfundisi* Turvey when we are back.' He turned and surveyed the following students. 'We should go to him together and protest. We should act as one. We will write a memorial and demand it.'

It was then that Mzamo went to the front of the column and, raising a sturdy stick he had broken from a bush, sang out a note, rallying the stragglers. Half-laughingly, half-mockingly Mzamo sang a phrase. '*Izihlangu zethu zonakele.*' Our boots are destroyed. 'The boots, the boots! Who will repair the boots? *Ngubani na oza kusilungiselela?*'

The refrain was taken up. 'The boots! The boots! Who will repair the boots?'

A phrase repeated until it became a march, a fighting song, Mzamo swinging at the head of the column chanting in Xhosa, the forbidden language. The phrase swelled among the older boys—the rhythmic ululations, the bass leader's summons breaking out—soon followed by the youngsters, filling their lungs with dust, marching on, singing up into the fading white of afternoon.

It was already dark when they arrived back at the edge of the town and stopped at the spring to drink and bathe their feet. Mzamo instructed them all to sling their boots around their necks and, instead of branching off as they were meant to do and taking the byways to the College from the eastern side of town, Mzamo led them straight down the hill in front of the Cathedral with its squat, square tower, at the head of the main street. He paused, the students gathering round him. Raising his stick, he cried as he faced the church, 'The boots! The boots! *Ngubani na oza kusilungiselela?*'

—*Ngubani na?*

—*Ngubani na?*

—*Ngubani na?*

Quite unexpectedly the Dean appeared in the porch, accompanied by a group of laymen, a deacon and a curate.

They stopped, stunned.

Mzamo hesitated. The students hung back. Then Mzamo

66

said quite clearly, coolly—even rhetorically—'Ngubani na oza kusilungiselela?'

He wheeled and raised his stick, pointing down the road, and started away again, followed by the straggling band.

Only when they were out of sight did they quicken their pace, cross the *sloot* and race up the other side, turning left at the mill and pulling to a serried halt at the College gate. Mzamo used his staff to rap at the front door. *Mfundisi* Turvey opened it and stared in surprise at the throng, each with his boots laced about his neck.

'*Mfundisi*,' Mzamo said, 'the journey was too long. Our boots are worn through.' He paused—not lowering his gaze. 'We will walk barefoot from now on until they are replaced.'

Calmly, without a hint of recrimination, *Mfundisi* Turvey said, 'Go to your dinner, lads.'

But it was while they were at table that the Dean arrived with the Chancellor and a number of gentlemen from the town. *Mfundisi* Turvey's voice could be heard in the vestibule, the voices of the delegation. The students sat alert. The door opened and Turvey came into the dining room and walked heavily to the seniors' table. He said quietly to Mzamo, 'Come with me.'

AND SO MZAMO left the College.

At the Bishop's insistence, he departed the next afternoon in a cart heading east, back towards Rutherford's mission, five days' travel across the hills, a letter from the Bishop included in a parcel of securely packaged books and documents. Mzamo had no pangs of conscience as he unpicked the string, examined the books and, on finding the letter, prised off the seal. He read:

Dear Rutherford,
The bearer, Mzamo Mzamane, has been excluded from the College for fomenting insurrection. To my sorrow, he was by far the best of Turvey's students. I had hoped to send him to Dr Bailey at the

Missionary Institution in Canterbury next year, not only because he will have political sway with his people in the future but because he is a young man of considerable intellectual gifts.

However, I have been compelled to insist on expelling him though I had a deal of trouble convincing Mr Turvey (who has that independence of mind common to the Irish of a certain class) and who told me that he 'liked his spirit'. Nor did he himself inform me of the incident—I had to hear it from the dean who, after an unsatisfactory interview with Turvey and the culprit, arrived at my door in triumph with a posse of gentlemen to remonstrate (yet again) on the folly of educating natives.

Most annoyingly (and I'm obliged to confess I agree), they implied that this turn of events had been influenced by the recent presence of one of the first youths sent to England, one Julius Naka, who spent some weeks teaching at the College before I realised it was prudent to pack him off elsewhere. The former Governor's selection of candidates favoured lineage above ability (I have warned often of the folly of political choices).

I suggest you keep young Mzamane at the mission so he does not make mischief among his own heathen people. He would be a competent teacher, secretary or interpreter. His English—both spoken and written—is excellent. As his original sponsor I hope you will feel it within your power to do what you can to prepare him for future employment. I will use my influence to find a suitable post for him but, for the moment, it would be wiser to separate him from his friends over whom he holds considerable sway. I do not want the expense of his education to be forfeited and it would be damaging to our wider educational plan to allow him to fall away.

Our travails are indeed burdensome! May the Lord deliver us from the darkness that surrounds us.

Your brother in Christ etc. etc.

Fomenting insurrection: these were words Mzamo had not heard. He would have to discover their meaning and consider them.

Perhaps even act on them.

He folded the letter and returned it to its envelope, carefully tying the string of the parcel and smoothing the wrapping. God was greater than a missionary, a bishop or a king. If He was just—as had been preached so often—God would prove that justice. If not—then there was no God. It was a possibility he would defer for now.

CHAP. 5:70

Stephen was desolate at Mzamo's going. His presence and protection, no matter how remote it may have seemed, no matter how condescending, was security. It also ensured Stephen's consequence with others.

On the sports field, playing against the white boys from the school next door, he remembered how the captain, Fred Hillier, had pointed at him and said to his teammates, 'Fellows, this is Mzamane's brother!'

They had appraised Stephen—dark, slight, even delicate —remarking sceptically, 'Is he as good?'

No, he knew he was not as good. He could never match the skill of Mzamo's 'wicked spin' or lob a ball from the boundary. Nor could he debate. Nor defy anybody's patronage and make it seem like charm.

It was only when he went, at last, to Canterbury that he became 'Stephen Mana' in his own right—where, for the first time, he was not the younger brother but 'the chosen', with *Mfundisi* Turvey's warm commendation of his humility and sportsmanship.

And there, among scholars from every corner of England and the world, he alone could have made comparisons and wonder how Mzamo might have triumphed in his place.

Perhaps he would have been like Joshua Morosi, the star in the missionary firmament or—more likely—the terror of the bowling line-up or the mighty-smiter in the First Eleven. Or perhaps he might have been disgraced like Nicodemus Ngubane, dismissed for importuning the Warden's housemaid.

Who could ever tell with Mzamo?

Yet, if Stephen did not quite match Mzamo's physical vigour, his agile mind and his propensity for challenging everything the missionaries said, his merit was not in doubt.

He was dependable.

The Bishop and *Mfundisi* Turvey concurred: *That is the virtue we should value most.*

MZAMO WOULD HAVE challenged that as well: *He is dependable* —oh yes. *Unoloyiko.* He is filled with dread.

Dread of the Devil. Dread of sin—the consequences of which catechist Mjodi had enumerated nightly when they were children in the mission boarding house.

—*You shall strive against the sins of the flesh until your hearts break within you. Only then will you be ready to lick the Word of God.*

But what if one had never heard the Word of God?

It was something that had troubled Stephen since he was a child and for which he found no answer. Salvation seemed random. A matter of luck. Of timing. Alighting like a fly on some and not on others.

His fears had germinated when he was ten. It had been a Sunday at Rutherford's mission and there had been a scuffle in the porch during service. A young man, barefoot, dressed in a grimy coat, was evicted by a catechumen seated at the door. Voices were raised. People turned to stare. *Mfundisi* Rutherford, delivering his sermon from the pulpit, paid no attention but droned on.

At last, the service over, *Mfundisi* Rutherford had given his blessing and gone into the vestry to unrobe while Mjodi led the congregation out. Under a tree in the yard stood the man. Mjodi approached him briskly, gesturing the curious away.

He was a young man, a poor man, a man who had sometimes worked a day here, a day there, when labourers were needed to dig a furrow or repair a track, who drifted off when the work was done to the limbo between the mission and the colonial farms, the edges of the towns and the drablands where nothing grew.

Stephen watched silently, small enough to be unnoticed, close enough to hear.

'You know you may not come into the church dressed like that. Also without your shoes,' Mjodi remonstrated. 'It is disrespectful.'

'Where can I borrow clothes? I must speak to the *Mfundisi*.'

'The *Mfundisi* has been taking service. *Udiniwe*.' He is weary. 'And it is Sunday. There is no work here.'

'I have not come for work. My wife ...'

'I know you do not have a wife.'

'She has sent me,' said the man, pleading now. 'The child is just a few days old. He is very sick.'

'There is nothing *Mfundisi* can do. He is not a doctor.'

'She says he must be baptised. She is very much afraid if he is not. She is weeping. She says if he is not baptised *Mtyoli*'—the Devil—'will take him.'

'What can she expect? She is not your wife. She is a sinner.'

'I must speak to the *Mfundisi*.'

Mjodi relented. 'Wait here,' he said, retreating to the church in search of the missionary.

Stephen, a grave small figure in the shadow of the porch, did not move away. It was hot. Still. A thunderstorm was brewing. The man, standing by the tree, was still as well.

Mfundisi Rutherford did not come. He went home to his dinner. He said to Mjodi, 'It is Sunday, the day of rest, and Mrs Rutherford has prepared the family meal. I will speak to the man presently.'

Presently.

That is what the man was told before Mjodi, too, went home to his dinner.

Stephen did not slip away. He could not go and leave alone this man whose hand clasped and unclasped the front of his coat, whose eyes never left the path to the rectory.

At last *Mfundisi* Rutherford had appeared. The man gathered his coat about him, went forward, eyes averted, head bowed, speaking softly, urgently. The *Mfundisi* listened, then walked briskly down the road with him towards the boundary fence as if edging him away. Stephen could not hear what they said. But after some time, when it was clear the *Mfundisi* talked a lot and the man listened, Stephen watched him hurry off, his pace quickening, hastening, disappearing at last among the bushes as the rain began to fall.

The next day *Mfundisi* Rutherford and Mjodi were not at the mission. They had ridden out early. It was said that they had gone in their compassion to baptise an infant who was ill. When Mjodi came back Stephen heard one of the catechists ask him, 'Whose infant?'

'*Ngudla-mhlaba.*' A drifter.

'But the mother is a woman seeking God.'

He shook his head. 'The child was long dead when we came there. *Walila kabukhali.* Such wailing!'

'Poor soul.'

'The father asked the *Mfundisi* to bury the child in our cemetery. The mother said that there, at least, the child would be safe.'

'What did *Mfundisi* say?'

'We cannot bury an unbaptised person in a Christian cemetery, Devil or no Devil.'

'The child has not sinned.'

'The will of God,' Mjodi said.

'No, *mfowethu*,' said the catechist. 'It was a matter of *Mfundisi* Rutherford not wishing to miss his Sunday dinner or wet his coat.' To which Mjodi had no answer.

73

STEPHEN HAD LEARNED to lick the Word of God. Not, as Mzamo believed, out of fear of sin or the Devil, but in search of certainty.

God would not abandon him.

And if *Mfundisi* Turvey at the Native College had encouraged such belief, he also knew that Stephen could not rely on God alone. 'God likes a chap with grit,' he'd said to Stephen in his third year. 'You're strong but you're small, lad. You're such a quiet chap you get pushed around.' Affronted, Stephen protested. 'Oh, I've seen it! Younger brother—all that. If you are to get on, you must know how to put up your fists if need be.'

And so *Mfundisi* Turvey had taught him to box.

'It's us fellows who have to roam the backstreets who need it,' he'd explained. 'And believe me, in our line of work, you will. I've fought a few bouts for God, Stephen. Sometimes I came off worse—but then I've stood up again and given them hell.'

Nor was it something he advertised to the parishioners of West Hill.

—Just like an Irishman to think of teaching savages to fight!

—Whatever will the Bishop say?

The hardy old Bishop had no objection. He had already marked out Stephen as the candidate for Canterbury in place of his brother. There would be no one to protect him.

So, twice a week, Turvey took him and some younger boys into the carpentry shop after tea and taught them to use their fists—to weave and dance and parry. 'You can run, lads, but it's better to turn and face him. That's the ticket, Stephen. Put some fire in those fists.'

Mfundisi Turvey had also taken Stephen and a number of the other students to catechise with him in the dingy outskirts of the town. 'When we go among the heathens,' he had said as they set out the first time, 'they will greet you with "*Ncazela*", give me tobacco. His Lordship does not want what he calls "Tobacco Christians" in our church but I've

74

found it's best to let the old men smoke their pipes for they always say, "Wait for us to light our pipes for then we hear you better."' Turvey had chuckled. 'It's a chance for me to light my pipe as well!' He had added more seriously, 'The first and most important lesson is—teach them to sing! There's nothing like hymns to stir the heart. Sing—and people will draw near.'

And so they went of an evening and catechised among the heathen, the displaced, the poor, going from street to street with a small group of boys to harmonise the choruses and swell the prayers. They chose moonlit nights, when the shards of the mimosa thorn gleamed white and the plovers called in the open lands beside the mill. At other times the dry wind gusted in from the hinterland bringing dust and the dread of drought. Sometimes they ventured to the clusters of huts gathered around a goat pen or a patch of garden. Sometimes they made their way to the poorest hovels where canteens had sprung up and the beer was laced with illicit brandy bartered from soldiers in the alleys behind taverns in the backstreets of the town. Here women loitered in the shadows, shrinking back when they saw the students picking their way along, led by *Mfundisi* Turvey.

'Ah, dear,' the *Mfundisi* might sigh, hurrying the students past but saying cheerily in Xhosa, 'I will be back, ladies, to have a small talk about what our Lord Jesus had to say to Mary Magdalene.'

'These are very bad women,' one of the boys had said to him, almost admonishingly.

'These poor souls have no pleasure in their lives. It is not for us to judge.'

'But you have told us it is the gravest sin for any of us to approach such a woman.'

'You are fortunate you do not have a brood of children to feed and no other means of earning money,' said *Mfundisi* Turvey peremptorily, shepherding them along.

'Why do you speak to them, *Mfundisi*?' a senior challenged him.

'How can they know the word of God if everyone shuns them?' he retorted fiercely. 'What will become of their children?'

'But ...'

'Enough.' *Mfundisi* Turvey had marched to the front of the column of scholars. 'Let us sing.'

The note was taken up immediately without further direction: *Mfundisi* Turvey always led them with the same hymn, striding down the hill towards the town:

> *Return, O wanderer, to thy home,*
> *Thy Father calls for thee;*
> *No longer now an exile roam*
> *In guilt and misery.*

Once Stephen had asked *Mfundisi* Turvey why he always chose it. He did not answer the question. He simply said, 'It is hard to be an exile, lad. But it's harder to return.'

IN HIS FINAL year, when his training as a teacher had already begun, it was announced that Stephen Mzamane had been chosen to go to the Missionary College in England—that mysterious, that weighty and majestic realm. Overwhelmed and suddenly afraid, Stephen had asked *Mfundisi* Turvey if he might go home and be reunited with his parents before he sailed. What if the wet and damp that Mrs Rutherford had talked of long ago invaded his chest, abandoning him to a foreign grave, truly gone from them forever, like George Maqoma?

'I wish very much to see my mother's face,' he told *Mfundisi* Turvey.

'There is no money to send you,' Turvey had said kindly, laying a regretful hand on his shoulder. 'I am truly sorry, lad. We have accounted for every penny we may spend and you must travel with the Bishop when he goes on furlough for you cannot go to England alone. There is not enough time before the *Briton* sails.'

But it was not a matter of money.

Regretfully—and on instructions from his Metropolitan —the Bishop had told Turvey to refuse, knowing only too well how critical it was to keep chosen students from the influence of home, despite the advantages of their education and the reassuring bulwark of their new religion.

'It is not necessary, Mr Turvey,' the Bishop's wife had declared when he had called one evening to plead Stephen's case with her husband. 'The native's home does not thrive on the same family affections and sensibility as ours. I never see the mothers cry when they are parted from their children.'

Turvey knew better.

Le nto indoyisile: this thing which is beyond endurance or the proof of tears. Turvey had witnessed it many times. Nor, Turvey might have added, could such mothers—in the bewilderment of parting—have grasped the distance of such a separation when they themselves had never ventured further than they could walk, knew nothing of the place from which white people came, had seen no settlement bigger than a trading station. Stephen's mother might have wept, *'Umke namangabangaba aselwandle'.* He is carried off by seabirds. Gone. Leaving nothing of himself behind.

How else could she imagine it—she, who had never spoken to a white man, only marched in fear before the scarlet-coated soldiers on their horses, long ago, when their people had been driven east from their ancestral lands? How could she imagine the *Briton* or even picture Stephen dressed like the trader's son, reading from a book and singing songs which she had never sung to him as a baby lying against her back as she hoed the fields?

She did not even know his name. To her he was Malusi.

On boarding the *Briton* in Algoa Bay, Stephen had been intrigued by the gentle rocking of the ship at anchor, the sea

77

stretching away to the horizon—so vast, so shining in the morning sun. The great pale dunes of the eastern shore were edged only by a low seam of surf. The water breathed against the hull, the masts stood bare against a windless sky.

But the tide caught them as they sailed from the bay. The wind swelled the unleashed sails, the keel rolled and the passengers hurried below decks.

Stephen lay seasick, a bucket at his side, berthed with the crowding crew, far from the Bishop and his party in the cabins and saloons. Praying did not seem to help. The motion did not stop for days—not until they rounded the Cape and sailed into calmer seas. He came on deck at last to gaze at the great flat-topped mountain in Table Bay, leaning his head on his arms every now and then, his eyes closed, willing away the motion of the boat which seemed to still possess him despite the sudden calm. A fear—that warning, that small dark dread, that isithinzi—lodged in his throat.

Should he escape the ship, run away, journey east, not to Grahamstown or the mission, but beyond the Kei River—to his father's homestead and his mother's house—before there was no way back?

The Bishop approached him at the rail, coming up silently behind him. Stephen shrank away, alarmed, as if the old man had read his thoughts. 'You've had a rough passage, Stephen,' the Bishop said, putting a hand on his shoulder. 'But you'll find your sea legs long before we reach England and start to enjoy the voyage and feel like your old cheerful self.'

'I do not very much like the sea,' Stephen said.

'I do not like the sea very much,' the Bishop corrected him, adding kindly, 'I have felt the swell myself and my chaplain has not left his bed.'

Stephen was silent, holding tightly to the rail. The Bishop seemed to revel in the scene. He pointed to other ships, guessed their destination or where they had come from. India, China. Australia. As they anchored close to shore he spoke with a sunny triumph of cargoes and trade. And of England.

To the starboard, the swell reared up from the jagged teeth of a breakwater, dark against a summer sea. Small figures moved back and forth in gangs, chanting, heaving, falling back then straining once again, hauling boulders.

Forgetting himself, Stephen pointed, saying, 'What are children doing there?'

'Children?'

Stephen pointed again.

'Those aren't children, Stephen,' the Bishop said. 'Some of them, alas, may even be grandfathers. They are Bushman prisoners. They are building the sea wall to protect the harbour.'

'Why are they in prison?'

'They have taken to hunting sheep and cattle instead of wild game. Farmers do not like that. Perhaps these are the fortunate few. Most are simply shot like animals.'

Stephen gazed. 'And yet, that is fearful punishment for men so small. It will surely break their bodies.'

'I fear,' said the Bishop, 'that that is what may have been intended.'

EVERY ENSUING SUNDAY the Bishop held a service on deck, attended by the passengers and crew. Once or twice he had chosen Stephen to read the lesson, coaching him beforehand in the correct pronunciation of the words. 'The manner of speaking is important to the English,' the Bishop had said. 'It is very strange, but you will find that how a man speaks, rather than what he says, seems to count! People will see you very differently if you talk like them. They may even overlook the colour of your skin.'

Through all the weeks at sea, they read together every day —slowly, deliberately, the Bishop re-pronouncing every word until, when Stephen spoke, he closed his eyes and listened with a smile. 'Splendid. Yes, we will get on very well in Canterbury.'

The sailors took a fancy to Stephen once he had overcome his seasickness and could stroll about on deck. He seemed to intrigue them. They would question him, cock an ear—without condescension, even fondly—anticipating something droll: *Yes, a nice cuppa tea would refresh me.* Artlessly obliging. *Thank you, sir.*

He also seemed to be a propitious sort of talisman, a charm against a storm or sudden calm. They taught him any number of sea shanties: 'The flag that braved a thousand years', 'Then do let me go, my darlin' gal', 'O Jenny Riley, O'.

'I don't know that it's suitable for Stephen to be fraternising with the sailors,' the Bishop's wife said to her husband as he sat in a deck chair, dozing. 'He's always laughing with them. I have never seen him laugh before. I fear he may be learning rough talk.'

The Bishop had opened one eye, squinted up at her and replied gruffly, 'Laughing is good, my dear. It keeps a lad from being lonely.'

'He has us and the other passengers. Perhaps I should do some extra Bible readings with him.'

'Leave him be. He's going to a world where he'll hear much rougher talk from the inmates of a workhouse.'

FROM THE TIME the ship docked and the vessels, wharves, warehouses, spires, towers, churches, carriages, carts and crowds appeared through a grey drizzle—more smoke than mist, more mist than rain—until the time he walked through Fyndon's Gate at Canterbury, Stephen had seemed frozen. He and his luggage were taken charge of. He was borne along on a tide of hurry and distraction, almost forgotten in the bustle. And although the Bishop and his party's words of encouragement and farewell had been warm and enthusiastic, he felt despatched like goods, parcelled off with relief. He had been unable to respond, to raise his eyes, to grip a hand.

—*Buck up, lad. Here we are.*

—Godspeed.

—I shall pray for you every day, dear Stephen.

—Be a credit to your College.

He had wished to cling to them. Call them back. Instead he watched them dissolve into the terrifying gouts of steam at a railway station. He barely looked up at the black-clad man who had come to fetch him. 'Blunsom,' the man said. 'Mr Blunsom, the porter at the College.'

In the vastness of the station, the hiss and clatter, Stephen followed the porter blindly to a train, dragging his luggage. He was all but hauled into a carriage—the maw of a beast—and crouched in his seat, almost flung to the floor by the first jolt as the train started away.

'Hold on,' said Blunsom.

A pause, another jolt which made him cry out, and then the train gathered itself. It left the station and Stephen barely dared glance out at the vast, sunless, ghostly vista. It seemed an eternity before they left the city, before the buildings thinned, straggling out into fields. At last they steamed into soft sunlight. Peering out of the window then, he was astonished by so much green.

Blunsom had seemed unsure of what to say beyond 'You'll become accustomed', which he repeated every now and then as if it were a well-worn litany for newcomers. At last he said, leaning forward and studying Stephen sitting small and pinched beside the window, 'Are you a prince or a chief?'

Stephen looked up startled, uncomprehending.

'Do you speak English?'

'Yes, sir.'

'Then tell me—are you a chief or a prince like them other foreigners?'

'Foreigners?'

'Them that lives in the Foreigners' Building.'

Stephen was mystified.

'Last fella I fetched from the ship was a Indian prince.

Surprised 'e left 'is elephant at 'ome—'e'd so much luggage. Real bother taking 'im back again.'

'Taking him back?'

'Didn't last.' Blunsom sniffed. Stephen was silent. Blunsom went on as if to himself. 'Like the Heskimo. Didn't last. Like the Zoola from Africa. And all them others.'

'What happened to them?'

'Didn't last. '

'Why not?'

'This and that.' He shook his head. 'Some was sent 'ome. Some died.' He scanned Stephen—so young and slight. 'You ever feel poorly and need a dose of anything you just come and speak to me. Mrs Blunsom keeps a cupboard full of remedies. Much better than the sawbones at the 'ospital. Specially good with digestive complaints.' He winked. 'Especially them that's not accustomed to our ... you know.' Again, Stephen stared at him, mystified. Blunsom leaned forward confidentially, his shaggy head close to Stephen's. 'A dose of castor oil fixes that.'

The twin towers of the great College gate—ancient and venerable and glistening in a sudden shower of rain—looked like the pictures of the Gates of Paradise in Mrs Rutherford's Bible.

Perhaps he'd died. It seemed to him as if he might have.

Except that Blunsom was not a guardian angel, not with his wild white hair and his hat pulled down to his bushy brows and resting, somehow, on the tips of his large, crumpled ears.

'Here's another Zoola,' Blunsom exclaimed cheerfully to a group of students standing in the forecourt. 'He's a likely lad, I tell you. Just you wait and see.'

—*Didn't last. Like I said.*

Stephen's luggage was abandoned in a porch and he was hustled through a door into a hall where he blinked away the gloom, his blood beating in tumult in his throat.

'Wait 'ere, lad,' said Blunsom. 'Dr Bailey's on 'is way.'

If he had not been Mzamo's brother he might have flung himself on the stone-flagged floor and howled.

IF MZAMO HAD been chosen to go to Canterbury instead of Stephen, it was unlikely that he'd have chosen Albert Newnham as a friend. He'd have thought him far too modest a companion. Debate was not Albert's forte and although he was a splendid cricketer he did not have the remotest idea about which coat or hat was the most desirable, which novel the most fashionable nor, indeed, much knowledge about the missionary lands to which he and his fellow students would be sent. Kaffraria in the Cape had not occurred to him. He was not quite sure, before Stephen came to the College, where it was. A brother and a range of uncles in the army in India seemed good enough for a posting to a hill state. 'I love rambling among mountains,' he had said to Stephen. 'I believe, the mountains in India are rather bigger than here.'

After their first meeting in the carpentry class, it had been enthusiasm on the cricket pitch that had clinched their friendship. Albert was a steady batsman and Stephen's bowling rarely missed the mark.

'Where did you learn to bowl like that?' the senior captain had exclaimed at Stephen's first trial.

'At school, sir,' Stephen had replied, as respectfully as if he had been standing before a master.

'We also learned to bowl at school,' put in Albert. 'But not like that!'

'I think, perhaps, at school, you did not have to hunt birds with sticks.'

Albert whistled admiringly. 'With sticks?'

'It's our custom to bring down birds with sticks,' said Stephen. 'At the mission where I grew up we were allowed to hunt. There was not much food so we went out on Saturdays after lessons. At my College in town our Principal said it was to our great advantage in cricket that we could throw a stick

83

so straight. The colonial boys hunted with guns. So, you see, our bowling was usually better.'

'You always won your matches?' said the captain, impressed.

'Mostly.'

And at the Missionary College in Canterbury with Stephen in the team they had mostly won their matches too. How astonished Mzamo would have been—except he would probably have taken most of the credit for Stephen's skill himself! Quite rightly, Stephen admitted. Anything but bringing down a partridge at the first throw was unacceptable to Mzamo. Stephen had practised stick-throwing himself for hours and hours behind the boarding house. It had made him almost—but not quite—equal to his brother.

Nor would Mzamo have persisted in calling any senior student 'sir'.

It took time for Stephen to break the habit, even when speaking to Albert.

So ingrained was it—with downcast eyes and tentative handshake, the hallmarks of diffidence and respect—that it seemed impossible to change.

'Come on, old chap,' Albert had cajoled him. 'I can accept Blunsom calling me "sir", but not my teammate.' Then he flushed a little and looked off, not meeting Stephen's eye. 'See here. I'll help you get a picture of the way we do things. But only if you want and no offence. It'll help a lot with the old ladies in the parish when they ask you in to tea.'

'Tea?'

'Oh, they will ask you, believe me. It's a feather in their bonnets to sponsor one of—how did I hear Mrs Bailey say it?'—intoning shrilly—'"the Sable Sons of Ham" and to have a claim in civilising him. It's all rot of course. I'll help you be a step ahead.'

So it was that Stephen learned to shake a hand—a male hand—with a firm grip and look the fellow in the eye, to smile—so disrepectful to grin at elders—and exchange

84

pleasantries instead of keeping silent. Albert often nudged him into laughter. 'I must show you the Warden's report in last year's Christmas letter,' he said. 'It was something about the "lugubrious glum native ..."' Perfect mimicry again. '"He is not at all an attractive person, being rather vacant-looking as a rule but this is soon corrected when his shyness is overcome—for ..." Wait for it ...' Albert folded his hands just like the Warden. '"The native's splendid teeth are made for smiling!" Isn't that just like the old fellow? I believe he's quite a connoisseur of horseflesh! He'd consider you a thoroughbred when you smile and show your teeth, Stephen. Only, you always look so *serious*, especially in church.'

'We were not allowed to smile in church.'

'God's not a spoilsport!' said Albert. 'He never said you couldn't laugh and sing and dance. Or, for that matter, enjoy a decent dinner.'

'He doesn't allow laughing and singing or dancing and feasting where I come from,' Stephen had said. 'That's for heathens.'

'What a jolly lot they must be!' exclaimed Albert gaily. 'I think I shall have a grand time trying to convert your heathens. If the fellows there are anything like you, old chap, it'll be a capital posting. We must work together.'

But the 'fellows' there were not like Stephen.

How could they be?

Nor was it a 'capital posting'.

Nor were they sent together. They served more than a hundred miles apart.

There were no heathens to sing and dance and feast near Albert's mission—they had been sent to live beyond the White Kei and Albert's parishioners were Mfengu, shifted in to fill the gap. They lived in daily fear of reprisals from the Ngqika and Gcaleka.

Lugubrious and glum would have been entirely apt.

AND STEPHEN'S MOOD was glum now, as he shifted his bag on his shoulder and trudged on towards Albert Newnham's mission through the weary, dusty day. The drought had lasted for so long, the country been so razed by war, that there were few homesteads where he could stop and ask for water. Even the shadows of the trees seemed to have died, withered as the grey grass with bark of bone. He kept his eyes on his boots, pressing on, hour after hour, rarely looking up.

Ngubani na oza kusilungiselela? Ngubani na? Who will repair them?

Who indeed?

What would he find at his mother's people's place? Would they have retreated east in search of pasture, drawing further and further away? And what of Albert? He had not answered Stephen's letter. What if he'd retreated too?

CHAP. 6:87

'The spade, hammer, plane and saw should take the place of playing chess with Lady Bountiful ...'

So had run the report in the Cape Colony's newspaper by the Chief Inspector of Education on the Church's policy of educating Africans in England. It was a rap over the Metropolitan's knuckles from a distinguished government official. And, by association, from the politicians. No more students to England to indulge themselves in seeking the patronage of country parishes, no more young black Englishmen. The climate had defeated them: two had died and four had been repatriated before they had graduated for fear that they too might contract consumption. On their return to the Colony there had been a further death, and only one had proved himself suitable for Holy Orders. The others had acquired a worldliness and independence over which the Dean in Grahamstown crowed to his Bishop, 'What did I tell you, my Lord!'

Furthermore, they had roused up their fellow countrymen to continue lobbying for the release of the chiefs still incarcerated on Robben Island. Even in SouthAfrica, too many who had been students at the Anglican native colleges in Cape Town and Grahamstown had had to be sent home ill or as 'unsuitable'. Since then many had returned to their people and reverted to heathenism while others had quit the Colony rather than suffer the indignity of colonial scorn:

—*Impertinent.*

—*Indulged.*

—*Absurd. Why, that fellow's wife wears finer dresses than my daughter!*

The experiment was an expensive failure. Unless Stephen Mzamane was the man to prove the critics wrong.

'He won't fail us,' Henry Turvey said to the Bishop.

'He's such a deferential fellow, though,' lamented the Bishop. 'Pity about his brother. I had real hopes for his development.'

'If you start a fire you cannot complain when it burns you,' said Turvey drily.

'He wasn't your choice?'

'Vocation makes a priest,' said Turvey.

The Bishop sighed. 'And all too rare amongst the best of us?'

'All too rare.'

STEPHEN DID NOT see the article but the Warden, Dr Bailey, was sent it by the Metropolitan in Cape Town. Bailey wrote a letter fierce with protest but it found no place in either the local or the colonial newspapers. By the time it reached the Cape the matter had been forgotten. Nor would his anger have been shared. The colonial argument had always been that the missionaries were wasting time and money in educating Africans in anything but trades. Book learning was a spur to sedition and discontent.

—*It makes them crafty.*

—*It encourages them to aspire beyond their proper station.*

—*It gets in the way of land reform.*

It was a hopeless situation. What was the point, Warden

Bailey wondered, in writing to the paper and informing its readers—against all expectation from the Colony—that Joshua Morosi had headed the class lists at the Missionary College, outperforming Englishmen with an English education? Had he not been chosen as the most able, pious, worthy student of his year? Where was the disparity between him and the English students?

But Joshua had died of typhus while on a holiday in Shropshire and all hopes of a triumphant Christian heir to a paramount Chief, ordained into the Church and returning to lead his people, were dashed. All that was left was a marble gravestone in a country churchyard and a stained-glass window of St Philip converting a eunuch.

Joshua had been four years older than Stephen and inspired a reverence for his seniority, lineage and cultivation that ensured Stephen's deep deference in his company. If, in speech and manner, Joshua had been an Englishman, his presence and bearing had been those of a chief. Stephen, the only fellow African that year, had held him in silent awe.

At the end of his first term, the Warden had called Stephen into his study and informed him that as no other invitation had been forthcoming for the Christmas holidays and as it was not desirable that he should stay alone in the Foreigners' Wing, an arrangement had been made with Joshua Morosi: Joshua had been persuaded to allow Stephen to accompany him—as a sort of attendant—when he visited the home of a former fellow student.

They had travelled by train, puffing through the countryside, Joshua absorbed in a newspaper while Stephen pressed his face to the window as the fleeting fields and flocks passed by. Stephen had carried the luggage and sat respectfully listening to the pronunciation of every word when Joshua had taken out his prayer book and read a passage aloud. There had been little further conversation although Stephen was aware of Joshua's shrewd—and not unkindly—appraisal. He felt curiously protected.

They had stayed in a large rectory, the guests of Joshua's former classmate's parents. Joshua's friend, Norbert Whitmarsh—sensitive to Stephen's youth and shyness—attempted to include him by telling jokes which Stephen did not understand and which Joshua was too solemn to approve. At table he ate in silence except for answering, now and then, the nudging enquiries of the Rector or Mrs Whitmarsh.

'Would you fancy another slice of beef, Mr Mana?'

'No thank you, ma'am.'

'Whereabouts in the Colony is your home?' the Rector had said, laying down his knife and fork and wiping his mouth with his napkin.

It was not a question Stephen could answer with any certainty. 'I am not sure, sir.' He glanced anxiously at Joshua. *Is that a foolish answer?* Joshua held his gaze. 'I was raised at a mission in Kaffraria, sir,' Stephen said to the Rector. Joshua nodded imperceptibly.

'But you have parents?'

'Yes, sir.'

The Rector glanced at Joshua then. 'I thought all the foreigners at the College were the sons of the nobility.'

Stephen looked in confusion from one to the other, not understanding.

There was a pause, then Joshua said, 'I believe it is sometimes wiser to choose ability above rank. And, after all, each diocese must have its chance. In the event they might send those with particular attributes.'

'Aah.' The Rector leaned back in his chair and took up his wine glass, examining Stephen more closely. 'I see.'

'Do not make the young man feel conspicuous, my dear,' said Mrs Whitmarsh. 'Mr Mewroozi, another slice of beef?'

Whenever they took an afternoon walk—Joshua and Norbert Whitmarsh deep in discussion on theological matters—Stephen trailed a respectful pace behind. In fine weather they had wandered in country lanes, taken tea in village tea shops, bowed and raised their hats to passing ladies whose astonishment at seeing them was barely concealed. When it was wet they had played chess and it was from observing that Stephen first learned the rules.

Then, immediately after New Year's Day, Joshua had suddenly fallen ill. He had lain for a week in an attic room in a tangle of sheets. Norbert Whitmarsh kept a hovering distance and Stephen—wide-eyed with dismay—sat in vigil near the door. The village ladies, both curious and concerned, brought gifts and comforts, and Mrs Whitmarsh wrung her hands and wished the responsibility for the young chief had not devolved on her. The doctor came and went.

On the tenth day, as evening fell, Joshua died.

Stephen, faithful to his post, had heard him calling out. He had crept towards the bed, standing at the foot. Joshua had gazed at him with some abstracted recognition. Then he had begun to speak in his own tongue. Softly. Almost fiercely. Stephen did not know Sesotho but the cadences, the phrasing, struck a deep chord of remembrance and he answered in Xhosa, tentatively at first and then more firmly. The words went back and forth, words learned long before either took up a slate and chalk or was baptised.

Joshua spoke his own Sesotho name—Tsekelo—over and over, urgently evoking an older theology than the one they served. Then the names of the great ones of his people, calling them up, mustering a lineage. A clan. A place.

As evening came outside the latticed window and the beech trees picked up the stirring of the evening wind, Joshua fell silent. He set his face to the wall and said no more.

When they buried him, the whole village turned out. Stephen stood guardian near the coffin. The prayers were all familiar, the psalms chanted by the choirboys. But for Stephen, apart from the melody of the English hymn echoing in the nave of a country parish church, he sensed a counter-note that reached back across the leagues of sea to where the mountains of the Basotho kingdom reared against a southern sky, distant, still and blue.

In time, a stone slab with Joshua's name, his age, his date of death, was erected by the Rector through subscriptions from the village and the Missionary College. But the hopes of the Governor and the Bishop in the Cape of installing a black Englishman among his people—secure in his loyalty to the Colonial Administration—were laid waste. The heir to a paramount chief rested with the rural poor in a churchyard in England, excised from tribal memory.

Once there was a man, Tsekelo …

Once there was a paramount's son.

JOSHUA HAD GONE and no students came from the Cape at the start of the year.

There would be no more playing chess with Lady Bountiful! No more Stephens to challenge the wealthy and indulgent parishioners from the community who contributed to their education.

For Stephen himself, chess had become his chief delight. He was coached in it by the Superintendent of Students. He had learned to play diffidently—in time, often trouncing his tutor, but always with a self-deprecation, making excuses gracefully for his opponent's blunders. Once he was proficient, he had been taken about to the genteel houses in Canterbury, a showpiece who played with skill and ease.

He had sat in stuffy drawing rooms, tea and cakes pressed upon him, daughters kept well away from approaching too closely, sons sent out on errands, only the ladies and gentlemen—beyond any possible harm—his chosen fellow players. Warden Bailey was delighted at his success: a sure indication, despite the protests, that the College had not been unwise in admitting the sons of the African elite.

Joshua had been the brightest hope of all.

But he had died.

Not long after Stephen's return to College for the start of

the Spring term, Albert had called him from his books and said, 'Do you know how to carve stone?'

'I only know how to carve wood.'

'Well, today it's stone. The master asked me to engrave Joshua's name on the wall of the memorial crypt. Can you help?'

It was the place where the compline was sometimes said, a narrow vault under the College Chapel, entered by a single door. Except for the glow from a stained-glass window, it was dark. The roof was corbelled and low, and the damp came through the walls, leaving a mossy stain around the edges of the floor. A statue of St Augustine stood near the altar, a gift dearly bought by the students of the College, sacrificing the sugar in their tea for a year.

Around the walls, carved into the pale stone, were the names of the alumni who had died and the diocese in which each had served: Barbados. Nova Scotia. Guiana. Labuan. Grahamstown. Adelaide. Bombay. Cairo. Sarawak.

> Lumley Lough Burnaby
> Dashwood Dinzey Betts
> Charles Beauchamp Williams
> Casper Allnutt Cookesley
> Alfred William Brereton
> Fayaz Hussein
> John Merwanjee
> Henry Smith

Row on row on row. So many in so short a time.

'Isn't it a beautiful little place?' Albert had said, putting the tool box on a pew and lighting a small oil lamp. He read out some of the inscriptions, chuckling. 'Poor fellow, fancy being burdened with Dinzey or Allnutt! Think of the nicknames!' He held up his lamp and gazed at the dates. 'It reminds me of roll-call at school. All together answering *adsum* to their names. I think it's a grand idea. I would like to be here too one day, along with the fellows I knew at College. It would be jolly company, especially if I'd been bitten by a snake or eaten by a headhunter and no one ever found my body.'

Stephen did not laugh.

To be confined. Here. In this sepulchral green gloom despite its grace and beauty. Without the sight of sky or hills. With the perpetual rain sluicing down the walls. Unembraced by the living going about their daily tasks nearby, giving the passing news about the harvest or the calving of the cows.

Albert chalked the name on the stone: *Joshua T Moroosi.* 'That's not the way to spell it,' Stephen said.

'Oh dear,' said Albert, perplexed. 'That's how they always wrote it here. That's how I was told to carve it.'

Stephen said no more. He worked in silence. The ring of the chisel, iron on iron.

Joshua Moroosi. Stephen Mana.

—Who are we?

The question remained unasked. And it remained unanswered by Tsekelo Morosi. He had gone.

BEWILDERED AT FIRST by the endless chapel services— Matins, Sext, Evensong, Compline, Communion twice a week, private prayers until the curfew at a quarter to eleven— Stephen often seemed to blunder from hour to hour, dragged by the tide of gowned scholars and the constant ringing of the bell.

The life outside the walls was different. Voices, song, the cries of workmen, the whinnying of horses, the trundle of wheels on cobbles. People jostled in the streets. There was colour in the surge of crowds. And women—so absent from the daily round at College. Children too. He and Albert often ran down the street to their compulsory lectures at the hospital just so that they could leap the gutters, swing down a side road, stop and gaze in a shop window or throw their

94

hats to each other in an impromptu game. Boys let loose—
until they pulled up breathless outside the Senior Superintendent's door, set their collars straight, rearranged their
jackets, wiped their sweating faces and tapped respectfully.

Lessons in practical medicine were a necessity for those
destined for foreign missions. Stephen and Albert would join
a group of medical interns and future missionaries as they
went from bed to bed with the Superintendent or another
consulting doctor, listening respectfully to explanations of
illness or injury, sometimes stopping to say a prayer with an
anxious patient. Stephen watched procedures gravely, never
recoiling. In the wards his calm concentration impressed the
senior doctor.

—*They send those with particular attributes.*

That is what Joshua had said. And Stephen began to sense
something of those attributes in himself when he followed
the doctor around the wards. If, often, he did not understand
the lectures—the quick delivery, the unfamiliar terms—he
did not back away from the patients who were dying or
burden them with religious homilies. He could sense the
threshold he had known himself—so long ago, so young—
drifting inexorably into death. They were supported by his
fearless presence, the warmth of his living hand.

It was only the post-mortems that he found deeply
distressing. To mutilate a corpse seemed an outrage to its
spirit. If some of his companions had appeared intrigued,
even eager to draw near, Stephen had resolutely turned his
back.

'These are paupers from the workhouse,' the doctor had
said briskly on the first occasion. 'If their lives have been
squandered, they make amends in contributing to the study
of anatomy.' Adding, for his particular audience, 'God rest
their souls.'

Stephen would not draw near. Only sorcerers violated the
bodies of the dead.

The workhouse had been the end of another of Stephen's

preconceptions of England. He might have fled at the sight of the abject children had not Albert been with him. 'It's the very least we can do for the little ragamuffins and it's part of the College drill to visit,' said Albert. 'I always choose a jolly Bible story to cheer them up. And I never talk about hell like some of the other fellows. I think that's most unkind.'

'Are there any jolly Bible stories?'

'Of course! What about David and Goliath? That'll give them something to think about. It might rouse them up against the beastly Beadle.'

Stephen had stood silently at Albert's side at the workhouse gate, surveying the dank fungus on a wall. He had gazed at the roomful of children cowed by hunger—running noses, throaty coughs, small hands red with cold. They gathered in a ragged group as Albert read.

'Are their parents dead?' Stephen asked.

'No,' Albert said. 'They're kept across the wall. Men this side, women, that. The adults are put to work and they may not see their children while they're here.'

'Even the mothers?'

'Even the mothers.'

'I did not know that there were slaves in England.'

'There aren't!' Then Albert hesitated. 'Are there?' As if the thought had suddenly struck him.

EVERY FORTNIGHT ALBERT and Stephen had made their visit to the workhouse, returning to College in time for evensong. But one evening they had been particularly delayed.

'Damn, we've missed our tea!'

'You don't like it anyway,' laughed Stephen, 'unless it has two spoonfuls of sugar.'

Rain was falling, a sky of sludge, a sly wind, and the cathedral bell struck the hour.

'Run,' panted Albert. 'The gate will be closed and we'll get it from Blunsom. Down here. Quick.' He skidded round a corner into a narrow passageway.

Fortune's Alley.

A route the students were forbidden to take. It was out of bounds. Stephen hesitated.

'Hurry!' Albert urged.

The odd light flickered dimly in the windows of tenements in the creeping dusk. They hurried past a tavern, crammed with workmen. Somewhere a fiddler played. Voices were raised roughly from a doorway. Nearby, where a stairway led up the side of a crumbling building, a small girl sat huddled. Albert raced past but Stephen stopped. 'What are you doing here in the rain?' he said. The child started up, gave a little shriek, began to scramble to her feet.

A door opened at the top of the stairs, a shrill voice calling, 'Effie?'

'A darkie, Ma.' The child began to back away, losing her footing. Stephen put out his hand to steady her. She clutched a bottle to her, shrinking away in fear.

There were hurrying footsteps, a dim tongue of light. A woman pushed past the child, pulled herself up short and gazed at Stephen.

'Ma'am.' Stephen raised his hat.

'Well, I never! Fancy a darkie calling on me.'

'Stephen! Come away at once!' hissed Albert, turning back.

'It's very cold, ma'am. I saw the child in the rain. I thought she might be lost,' Stephen said, a gust whipping his neck.

'Stephen!' Albert all but roared.

Stephen ignored him. 'Is she your child?'

'What's it to you?' said the woman. 'Are you coming up or not?'

'Stephen.' Albert pulled at his arm.

There were footsteps behind them. A small man, muffled to his eyes, had ducked out of the tavern. 'What's the rumpus, Dora?'

'Why'd you send me a darkie 'oo doesn't seem to know why 'e's 'ere, frightening our Effie?'

'I didn't send no darkie.' The man turned on Stephen. 'Wotcha doin', nigger?'

'Excuse me,' Albert intervened. 'There has been a mistake. I am so sorry. My friend was concerned about a child sitting in the rain.'

'It's her job to direct traffic,' said the man. 'Isn't it, Effie, my girl? Directing traffic. Upstairs.' He pointed skywards aggressively. 'Rain or no rain.' He turned on the child. 'Wotcha making such a fuss for? Where's the gin?' The child continued to sob. 'I'll give you somethin' to snivel about.' And he reached over and cuffed her roughly on the side of the head. She dropped the bottle and it smashed on the steps.

'Don't you hit my Effie,' stormed the woman. 'She hain't to blame. She was frightened, seein' as she never seen a darkie before. And now look what you done. I hain't paying for the gin.'

'You brute!' Albert exploded, interposing himself between the man and the woman. 'I shall call the police.'

'The police?' The man laughed, shouting over his shoulder. ''Ere lads. This fella's calling you out. Look sharp!'

A small crowd of drinkers pushed through the doorway of the tavern. Men and women, dodging the rain cascading from broken gutters.

'A darkie!' someone exclaimed. 'Oooh, ain't 'e an 'andsome fella?'

'You'll please excuse us,' Albert said firmly. 'It has been a mistake.'

'Wotcha doing 'ere then?' said the man.

'I assure you ...' Albert squared himself, white with resolution as much as with fright. 'I shall make a report.'

'Is that so?'

'You can sod off, duckie!' called a woman.

'We want the darkie!' A squawk somewhere in the mêlée of voices.

'He has absolutely no wish to stay,' said Albert, dragging at Stephen's arm.

'You insultin' our Dora, then?' Mimicking: ''E 'as habsolutely no wish to staaay.'

'Excuse me.' Albert shouldered his way out of the throng.

Stephen stepped up behind him. 'Be good enough to let us pass, please,' he said quietly.

'This darkie talks like a toff!'

'Them's Bible-boys,' cried one of the men. 'The only niggers in this place is Bible-boys. '

'Let us pass at once,' said Albert, his voice rising.

'Let 'em go,' shouted Dora, pushing at the man who had struck her child. 'Shame on you.'

'Shut up, Dora, or you'll find you're out of a lodging.' The man shoved Albert. 'Go find Jesus somewhere else!'

Albert stumbled, lost his hat, turned, his fists clenched. The man stepped forward, caught Albert full on the jaw with a blow that sent him sprawling backwards on the cobbles.

The blow was returned, side-on, by Stephen. The man reeled. The crowd crowed.

'Give us the darkie!' the woman shrieked again.

'You can 'ave 'im, darlin'.' A leer from a workman. 'Only don't be shy to tell us hall about 'is battle-haxe.' Screams of laughter. Stephen was half-lifted from behind, strong arms pinning him. 'Come and get 'im, girls.'

Stephen wrenched himself free, let fly a barrage of blows —aimed, timed as accurately as *Mfundisi* Turvey had taught him.

—*Put some fire in those fists, lad. That's the ticket.*

He wheeled, dragged Albert to his feet and bore him swiftly along the street.

Albert's hat lay abandoned in the gutter.

THE NEXT DAY, Albert was ordered to the Warden's study, summoned from the choir procession as it trooped back to the College from the Cathedral. He entered and, at a signal from the Warden, closed the door and approached the desk.

On it lay his hat.

'I believe this hat is yours.'

'It's mine, sir.'

'Ah. It was given in at the gate to Mr Blunsom by a woman,' the Warden said. 'For the "Bible-boy".' He was silent a moment. Then he resumed, enunciating, '"And the darkie."' He did not add that she had told Blunsom that 'the darkie and his friend' would always have her thanks and welcome to it.

'It was my fault, entirely,' Albert blurted before the Warden could continue.

'Unforgivable, Newnham. I should send you both down.'

'Both?' Albert's face blazed. 'Send me down, sir. But not Mr Mana. He had no idea—'

'Do you have the slightest notion, Newnham, of the nature of native people?'

'Sir, I must tell you—'

'I was speaking,' said the Warden.

'Sir.'

'I have been a Warden of this College for years. I have the confidence of dozens of missionaries in the field—especially in Africa—on the most intimate subjects.'

'Sir.' Albert turned his prayer book in his hand, the ruff of his choir robe dipping from the heat of his neck, the starched white edge thrown up in reflection against the underside of his chin.

'Immorality is the abiding folly of the native races. It is the first issue the missionary must tackle. It was reprehensible of you to throw temptation in Stephen Mana's way.'

'Mr Mana had no idea who the woman was, sir.'

'Indeed ...'

'We would have left immediately after we had spoken.'

'You spoke?'

'She spoke.'

'Who spoke?'

'Mr Mana stopped and spoke—'

'Ah, encouraged.'

'To the girl.'

'Indeed.' A glint which sent Albert's blood thundering in his ears. Despite his best intentions, fumbling for words, he could not meet the Warden's eye.

'The second folly, Newnham, which will not surprise you once you have been some time in a colony,' said the Warden, glancing shrewdly at the swelling on Albert's jaw, 'is the native's propensity to fight. Another barbarity which the missionary in the field will encounter. This propensity is especially evident after spirits have been drunk ...'

'It was the people from the tavern—' Albert interjected.

'The tavern?'

'Let me explain ...'

'I was speaking.' A silence. 'You remember well, in your first year, how a young student from Africa was sent down ...'

'Yes, sir.'

'Do you know the reason?'

'It was said he had flirted with the housemaid.'

'You are naïve, my dear fellow.' A pause. 'As I might have expected. You have no idea of the gravity of the issues with which we must contend. The slander and the intrigue fomented by our detractors, the difficulties of justifying our position regarding native students, the opposition from colonial governments and less forward-thinking clerics ...' He picked up a sheaf of papers and put them aside, out of the range of Albert's downcast gaze. He slipped a blank sheet of paper on top of them—a slight, Albert felt, sending the flush higher in his face. 'Students at a public house ...'

'But we never ...'

'Especially one of our native students,' the Warden continued, ignoring the interruption. 'It could bring the College down about our ears.'

Albert felt close to tears.

'You have put us in a very grave position, Newnham. It is fortunate you were not seen by someone of consequence in this town!'

'Sir.' Albert did not contradict him. He shifted his gaze to the cross on the wall behind the Warden's head.

'You will learn, Newnham, when you are finally in the field, that too deep a fraternisation with the natives is undesirable. For all our worthy intentions, we—as races—will never be the same.'

'That's not what the Gospels—' Albert began, almost severely.

But the Warden silenced him, one finger slightly raised. 'My boy ...'

—*My boy?* Albert almost retorted again: he was twenty-one years old and planning his marriage.

'Do not forget this conversation,' said the Warden, signalling dismissal. 'You will do so at your peril. And, believe me, you will have reason to recall it in times to come. Mission work is a soul-breaking, dangerous business.' He appraised Albert. 'Men's work, Newnham.'

Albert met the Warden's eye. 'You are not sending us down, sir?'

'No.'

—*Why not?*

'I should. You were out of bounds.' He stood. 'In Mana's case I have both reasons and constraints. In yours ...' the Warden hesitated. 'I may reconsider your posting.'

Albert held his gaze. The implication was clear: he and Stephen would be parted.

'I will not mention this incident to Dr Wills,' the Warden added briskly.

Albert was silent then. There was no escape: the Warden had deliberately offset Stephen against Unity. He should have revolted against such duplicity. Immediately. Risking all. Instead, he had stood bewildered, outmanoeuvred, a school-boy in a choir cassock.

'You may take your hat and go.' The Warden inclined his head.

Albert picked up the hat, turned and opened the door. As

he walked away through the cloister he put it on his head and pulled it straight, a small defiance. When he reached the courtyard, he crossed to the far side, went behind the buildings and, with a curse that would have had him 'sent down' irrevocably, flung the hat across the wall into the street beyond.

When he reached his room Stephen was there. He rose from the chair. 'What did he want?'

'He found out about last night.'

'How?'

Albert cast about. 'Blunsom told him that we came in late,' he mumbled unconvincingly. 'And the bruise on my jaw.' Albert put his coat down and fumbled for his handkerchief. 'He doesn't miss a trick, even in church. Even when he is supposed to be saying his prayers.'

Stephen stared at him, panic dawning. 'Is he sending us down?'

'No.'

'Why not?'

'I don't know.'

It was the first betrayal.

CHAP. 7:104

The winters in England had been very different from the one through which Stephen now trudged on the long road to Albert Newnham's mission. Here, there was a dry emptiness, an unending distance. There, the damp seeped in, the chill of tombs. Mrs Rutherford's words, spoken so long ago in a sunny orchard on the mission, had stayed with him:

—*The damp gets into the chest and eats it away.*

She had been right. Joshua Morosi, George Maqoma. Would he be next?

He had fought any suggestion of a cold and submitted to Mrs Blunsom's gruesome weekly dose of chlorodyne.

He remembered his first sight of snow in England, his astonishment at its whiteness, the blue of its shadows, the feel of it. It was so different from the film of bleak, hoary rime that had sometimes frozen the tops of the higher hills round the mission. This snow was the clouds come down to earth; this was the flying light foam he had watched for hours at sea in the wake of the ship. Abundant billows in drifts and on hillsides, weighing down the branches of trees.

Albert and he had sometimes walked out to the meadows

beyond the town, a brisk trot after midday dinner, and plunged knee deep, thrown snowballs, slid laughing into ditches. Others had no boyish delight in it. Manoah, a student from Antigua, took to his bed when he first saw it and refused to get up: it was a sinister magic, despite its sparkle.

But, as the darker days set in each winter, rain and wind reduced the snow to a grey and muddy sludge and it was necessary to read at a window or light a stub of candle, even at midday. A terrible damp pervaded the College, where only a small fire burned in the dining hall at evening. Services seemed ice-bound, and in assemblies the College tutors were always reminding the students of the privations they would have to endure in times to come.

—*You will remember our English weather with affection. Simply bracing!*

Albert had once muttered, after a particularly irksome homily during supper, 'We must all be mad. There's plenty of wood in the shed. Why on earth are we enduring this?'

'For the love of God,' said Stephen.

'Bosh! My father has a fire in his study every day and he's a clergyman who serves God very well,' adding, 'and no one would say he wasn't a frightfully good fellow.'

The privations took their toll. One student after another in the Foreigners' Building went down with fevers, coughs, bronchitis. Three were taken to the hospital. Three others repatriated hurriedly. Stephen kept his chilblains to himself. He acquired a pair of gloves so the beady-eyed Mrs Blunsom would not pounce on him.

Spring came. Summer.

No longer considered a novice, Stephen was asked to spend the holidays supervising the incoming foreign students who had nowhere else to go. In between duties, he volunteered to help the doctor at the hospital, watching each procedure, wishing he could practise them himself, holding the instruments with some reverence, imprinting their use, their shape, their size in his mind.

Summer drifted into autumn. The winds blew cold again and Albert had taken to accompanying Miss Unity Wills to her home after her lessons at Sunday school, offering his arm in sunshine, his umbrella in rain. He was sometimes invited for midday dinner. Feeling guilty, he brought back small treats purloined from the table for Stephen. 'Do you think it could be counted as dishonest?' Albert asked. 'Taking two cakes for myself rather than one and hiding the second in my pocket? I have told Miss Wills rather gruesome stories about the food at College so she'll make up little parcels for me to bring back. I have omitted to tell her they're for you. You won't let on?'

Stephen had sat munching a small jam tart. 'Certainly not!'

'I don't like to think of you having only bread and butter twice a day and a bit of slop in between.' Albert mimicked the nasal snuffle of the Supervisor of Students. '"Such strict regard to economy and frugality of habits will fit you, my dear brethren, for the future hardships you'll endure." Looking at him, I imagine he has plenty of cake and ale in his study. He gets rounder every year.'

As the chance to play sport diminished with the onset of rain, duties in the workhouse and the hospital increased. The city's poor were in the grip of every ill that winter brought. There were always ragged groups gathered in the graveyard round mounds of newly turned soil.

It was then that Stephen was recalled.

The Warden sent for him late one afternoon. 'Mr Mana,' he said, indicating that Stephen should sit and make himself comfortable. It was an ominous sign. 'I have had a letter from your Metropolitan in Cape Town. It is a distressing situation but, really, we see no alternative but to act on it.' He hesitated, folded his hands in his lap, looked down at his fingers. 'We will be sending you back to the Colony. Very sadly, you will miss your final examinations and graduation but that will not stand in the way of your being ordained as deacon once you are home. We have never felt comfortable

106

returning a student without support on the journey and I have recently heard that the Bishop of Bloemfontein is sailing for South Africa with a party of men he has recruited for his diocese. I must take this opportunity to repatriate you as another might not present itself for some time and it will save much expense if you are included in his party. Besides, your health is always a worry. We really cannot have you getting ill.'

And so it went. Kindly spoken, sadly regretted. Incontrovertible.

Stephen knew it had little to do with his health. It would be a directive from the politicians, not the Church. A practical expedient. The Warden's regret seemed real—but his hands, he said, were tied. 'Our sponsors here at the English parishes also believe it may be better to train more English recruits for the colonies rather than bringing colonials here at such proven risk to themselves. Nor—confidentially—is the present Governor in the Cape as forward-thinking as his predecessor. I fear there have been disappointments, deaths and—I regret—those who simply haven't been up to the mark.' The Warden caught himself, sensing he might have blundered. 'Not you. Mr Mana. Certainly not you.'

Stephen was not convinced.

'It is a very great blow to your Metropolitan. I fear it has affected him quite woefully. I feel his disappointment as keenly as if it were my own.'

Stephen could not speak. Every protest died. Whose vocation was it? His, the Bishop's or the Warden's? Or was it only the pecuniary concern of the treasurer of the Society for the Propagation of the Gospel and the sponsors from the parishes of Hereford?

And what of his graduation? That longed-for moment when the Archbishop of Canterbury would bless his scarlet and black hood, the mark of a scholar, the badge of his great achievement?

The Warden looked at him kindly. 'I am really very sorry, Mr Mana. You have been a worthy student.' He smiled again. 'And a great credit to our cricket team.'

Stephen left him, apologising as he backed, bowed, fumbled with the door, his palms slipping on the knob. He started down the long, echoing cloister, the patterns of the multicoloured floor tiles blurring. His steps hastened— faster, faster—until he was running where no one was allowed to run.

A service was being held in the Chapel. He did not climb the stairs and join the other students in the pews. He went instead to the crypt where the names of dead missionaries who had once studied at the College were carved around the walls. He sat, clenched, recovering his breath, willing his blood to subside, his racing heart. At last he looked about him.

There was Joshua's Morosi's name, more newly etched than some. Stephen gazed at it. What would the Warden have said to Joshua? The same as he had said to him?

No: all that dignity, that presence could not be ignored. And he knew, too, that had he been his brother Mzamo, he would have drawn himself up and challenged everything the Warden had said, word for word.

He did not weep—either in regret or anger or self-recrimination. He felt deeply weary.

He was tired of being grateful.

Albert found him in the crypt. He slipped into the pew beside him. 'I've been looking for you everywhere.'

'I am being sent away,' said Stephen.

Albert was aghast. 'No! Why?'

'They are afraid I'll get consumption. '

'Are you having trouble with your chest? My dear chap, why didn't you tell me?'

'There is nothing wrong with my chest,' said Stephen. 'I am just one more of their disappointments. '

'Impossible.'

'It seems we "foreigners" just "aren't up to the mark".'

'What about Joshua? He always came first.'

'Well, he wasn't up to the mark, was he? He died.'

'He can't be blamed for that.'

'Who pays?'

'What does that have to do with it?'

'Everything.'

Albert seemed bewildered. 'Surely ...'

'You haven't worked in a colony yet,' said Stephen. 'Whenever I get a copy of the *Quarterly Review* from our diocese it's always about money. Or rather—no money. God hardly gets a mention.'

Albert was at a loss. 'What are you going to do?'

'I will write to Reverend Turvey and ask him if I can teach at the Native College in Grahamstown. I have to get on with my Latin and Greek or I can't be a priest. He'll help. At least until you come. After that we can start our work together and prove them all wrong.'

'Of course,' Albert said hastily: if he repeated it often enough, perhaps he'd be able to convince himself.

Unity was quite another matter ...

—*How can you think of such a thing, Bertie? Taking me to live in a tent in the wilderness with Mr Mana? My family would be appalled!*

'Of course, old chap,' Albert said less confidently. 'Certainly! Yes ... Do you think there might be a master's post for me at the College too? That would be capital—until we— Miss Wills—my wife—becomes accustomed ... you know ...' Stephen said nothing. 'She's never been to a colony before. Even though her father was once in Barbados.' He clasped and unclasped his hands. 'Oh dear.' And he bowed his head, sidestepping any further entanglement. 'Let's pray on it.'

Stephen waited for Albert to begin but the words did not come. Albert prayed silently—if he prayed at all. And Stephen sat staring at the statue of St Augustine near the altar. He said sardonically, 'I wonder how much of him the sugar for our tea has paid for?'

'What?' Albert snapped his eyes open and followed Stephen's gaze. Then he grinned, relieved to be able to laugh. 'Perhaps, between us, we've bought his big toe.'

Stephen took up his hat and left the crypt abruptly, Albert trailing after him.

That night he wrote to *Mfundisi* Turvey.

—*Put some fire in those fists, lad.*

Was he a disappointment to him too?

No—*Mfundisi* Turvey was not the Warden, he was not the Metropolitan in Cape Town, he was not the treasurer of the Society for the Propagation of the Gospel or one of the bewhiskered old benefactors from the Diocese of Hereford. He was Stephen's own *Mfundisi*—pugnacious, blunt and genial—who had taken great pains to learn his language, and not only in the imperative.

No, he would not be a disappointment to his *Mfundisi*. Turvey would welcome him in. One of his strays. As once he had been himself.

Return, O wanderer, to thy home ... The words came back to him, the blend and weave of African voices in the warm-wind nights, the moon shining on the mimosa thorns, the vast black sky, stars so low they could be reached and plucked.

Home.

ON THE DAY before Stephen left the College to embark for the Cape, he had given Albert a gift. It was the photograph of himself. The one taken in Baldwin's Studio. He had sat at his table for a long time, deliberating. The portrait had been intended for his mother, to be presented when he went to find his people.

He took it from his drawer and looked at it. That transcendent moment of being himself—most truly, most precisely—the significance of which he had not shared. He had met her gaze with a gaze of his own. Unimpeded and equivalent. It was his most personal possession. It was the best he could be. The best he could give.

He put the photograph back in his drawer and closed it.

No. It was his mother's.

He searched his bookshelf and his drawers, knowing there was nothing else.

He took the photograph out again, leaving the drawer open and muddled. What, after all, could his mother know of Baldwin's Studio, of the hat and cane, the street that ran towards the great cathedral, the sound of bells? What could she know of the tea shop, the cloisters and the classrooms, Dr Bailey, the tutors, the drawing rooms of Canterbury and the chess sets of the Ladies Bountiful? No doubt she'd never seen a photograph before. It would be a bewilderment even as the face could have no resemblance to the child she had last seen walking away to forage for food so many years before.

He would find another gift for her.

One to delight her. One which would not confuse her or bring forth questions he could not hope to answer: *What is this place?* Pointing to the landscaped canvas which had been the backdrop to every photograph taken at Baldwin's. *What sort of house is this which has no door?* The curtain draped beside an urn and then the painting of the sea beyond.

Stephen took up the photograph and rushed across the courtyard to Albert's study before he could consider further. He held it out on the flat of his palm—almost shyly, his eyes averted. And Albert, unaware of his gravity—*it is all I have to give*—had looked at it, grinned, then playfully mimicked the serious pose so that Stephen was obliged to laugh, ignoring the sudden tightness of his throat, saying awkwardly, 'It's a portrait of your lost hat, which I often thought was mine!'

'You're lucky that it wasn't!' Albert was almost grim.

'Such a pity it was lost! But here it is again.'

'To haunt me.'

OVER TIME, IT was not just the hat that came to haunt Albert. It was the photograph: the gift that—so long afterwards—recalled his own omissions. At the time, he had admired it warmly, propping it on his desk among his books and papers, such a vivid reminder of his friend. Glancing at it while he worked, he had often smiled: a gift for which he had unwittingly loaned five shillings—as if he didn't know! Dear old Stephen!

On leaving Canterbury it went home in his trunk and was left there, unremembered, until the trunk was emptied in preparation for his departure to the Cape. It was a journey long postponed by Albert's failure in his finals to pass his Greek. If he regretted having spent too much time pursuing his new enthusiasm for football, he regretted more that Unity's father, Dr Wills, had offered to tutor him for the supplementary examination as a favour to Dr Bailey. It was an excruciating arrangement: undoubtedly designed to decide on Albert's suitability as a husband rather than expose his ineptitude as a scholar. When, at last, he had graduated in early 1873 with the few other first-round failures and escaped from Canterbury, there had been so much anticipation of his forthcoming wedding in the summer— how happily he imagined being swamped by her—that he'd bundled the trunk into the cellar at home. He had only retrieved it on the eve of embarkation for the Cape when he had hauled it up the stairs of his father's parsonage and tipped the contents on the floor of his old bedroom.

Unity—busily proprietary in everything—had surveyed the mounds of books and scooped up the photograph which lay on top of them.

'Ah,' said Albert fondly, looking over her shoulder, 'I must get a frame for that.'

'Wouldn't it seem a curiosity having this among the family pictures, Bertie? Especially *there*, where it seems people are not so very fond of natives.'

'He's my closest friend.'

Unity made a small movement of her mouth, a retort he grew to know too well. 'Frames are so dear,' she'd said, delicately.

'He wouldn't understand ...'

'Have you considered *everything* we need for the household, Bertie? We can only manage to buy *essentials* on a curate's stipend.'

He had taken the photo and put it aside, out of her reach. She had cocked her head, smiling dimples at him as her eyes darted from the picture to the books as if she had a mind to sweep them all away.

—*We should take nothing that is not of immediate use, Bertie. That's what the Bishop said.*

More privy to the Bishop, through her father, than he could ever be.

—*That's what the Bishop said.*

Damn him.

Forlornly, Albert had slipped the picture among the detritus of his boyhood, also to be left behind in England. Albert knew that if Stephen ever came to his mission he would notice that the photo was not among the things displayed on the bookshelf, and then Albert would be obliged to say—deceitful once more, though he could not admit to the word—'The carrier left one of our boxes behind in Kent. It was such a terrible pity as so many of my treasures from College were in it. When I'm on furlough I'll bring it back ...' Knowing, all the while, that it awaited the moment when his mother might decide to spring clean:—*Oh! Albert's in Africa! He will not miss this!*

It was yet another small betrayal he would carry with him always: the remembrance of Stephen's hand, holding the picture on his open palm so as not to leave a thumbprint, looking down. *This is all I have to give.*

THE LAST TIME Stephen and Albert had talked had been on the quay before Stephen embarked on the voyage home. The ship lay at anchor out in the river, surrounded by a flotilla of small craft bringing supplies and luggage. They had strolled among the piled boxes, the bales and sheep pens, the lumber on the dockside, lifting their voices above the creak of rope and halyard, leaving the other students gathered about the group of missionaries destined for the Cape.

For Stephen, it was good to be without the irksome company of Unity, always clasping Albert's elbow, and they went together, walking purposefully, glancing back now and then to ensure that Stephen was not being called to say his last farewells. 'When do you think you will join me?' Stephen said.

Albert looked ahead. 'I really don't know.' He drove his heel into the walkway, flicked at a piece of paper with his stick. 'Miss Wills wants to go about the country and say goodbye to relatives once we are married.' He grinned ruefully, not catching Stephen's eye. 'There seem to be an awful lot of them. Also,' swiping a little wildly with his stick, 'the wretched Bishop has advised we wait till the spring before we sail. I believe the winter seas are very rough down south.'

'So long!' exclaimed Stephen. He turned to Albert, walking backwards, facing him. 'There's no doubt you'll join me? *Mfundisi* Turvey is waiting for me and I know he'll have you at the College though I haven't heard about that yet. I suppose it's the mails ... I wrote reams about your cricket and about you being young and energetic, and I told him that you had done printing and bookbinding and carpentry and were good at all of them. Those are things he was starting at the College when I left. He was building a stone carpentry shop. He ...'

Albert stopped and waved his stick at him. 'You'll trip and break a leg, you ass, and then you won't be going anywhere!'

Dexterously, Stephen sidestepped a bale, still intent. 'They promised.'

'We must go back.' Albert was flustered. 'They're getting into the boat ...' He looked this way and that, all angles—his thin legs awry, his hair on end, his face suddenly anguished. 'Come on, let's hurry. I don't like goodbyes.'

114

Stephen caught up with him. 'You'll be married when I next see you. I had better find a wife quickly so you don't become too ponderous and bore me to tears.' He took Albert's arm. 'We'll shake up a cricket team and I'll teach you to bring down birds with a stick to improve your bowling.' He grinned to keep his rising alarm at bay. 'Oh dear! I hope Mrs Newnham will allow it?'

Albert half-pulled him along, panting. In the distance one of the curates was waving his arms frantically, calling them. 'Where shall I write?'

'To the Native College in Grahamstown. I should start there as soon as I have made a journey to find my people.'

'You have never mentioned where exactly they live ...?'

'I don't know myself.'

Albert looked confused. 'Don't know?'

'My people were chased away from our land,' said Stephen. 'But my brother Mzamo has since found where they're settled. He'll come with me. It's a place I have never seen.'

His parting from Albert and the other students was different from the time he had wandered from his homestead with Mzamo, meaning to return, never coming back. Stephen had stepped from the English quayside suddenly invigorated by the occasion, the ceremonious farewells, grandly waving the cross the Warden had given him, the gift of a newly inscribed prayer book in his pocket, his legs astride, balancing himself as best he could against the swaying of the boat.

'Godspeed, Stephen Mana.' The Warden raised his hand in benediction.

'Three cheers!' Albert's voice floated out across the water followed by the hurrahs of the other students, hats in the air.

'Sit down, for mercy's sake, Mr Mana!' A fellow missionary, parrying the spray blowing in as they reached the open water. 'You'll upset the boat and we'll all be drowned.'

A woman weeping.

'Hush, my dear, you will worry the children.'

'I hope the Bishop of Bloemfontein and the rest of his party will not detain us too long. His train has not yet arrived.'

'If he's another Puseyite, I shall push him overboard.' This from an elderly clergyman returning to the Cape from furlough.

His wife, bridling as all eyes fell on him, had whispered, 'This is not the time for disputes, Mr Henderson. We will be confined at sea for weeks.'

'Anglo-Catholics!' the old man snorted, and settled into his shoulders, glaring at Stephen and his cross.

Stephen paid no attention. He was gazing back at the quay, at the receding figure of Albert Newnham. He could no longer tell if he was waving—or even if he was still there among the black-clad figures.

The parting had been swift. Too swift to feel its loss. That would come in time when, painfully, the shouts of herdboys passing on a hillside recalled the kinship of young men.

An hour later, the Bishop boarded in some state, proceeding to his cabin as the ship weighed anchor. Stephen, no longer relegated to the crew's quarters as he had been on the voyage to England, was berthed with a pair of mission workers recruited from the counties. He was, the Warden had assured them, a real gentleman. He was no longer a curiosity, wide-eyed and bewildered. He had his cutaway coat and his stiff wing collars. He spoke like an Englishman. He was, he realised, far better educated than his companions. They had been working men, salvaged from farms. Stephen even felt a little lofty in their company.

Many of the clergy sailing to the Cape had been in service there before. They included Stephen in their Bible readings and their evening prayers. They did not invite him to their tables. The wives raised their voices slightly when they spoke to him, affecting affability. They were happy to ingratiate themselves as long as he didn't ask for anything, as the colonial passengers were quick to warn: *Keep your distance, my dear, or you will be educating a horde of children and sending comforts to his mother.*

The Bishop held Communion on the deck on Sunday mornings. Otherwise he remained in a suite of cabins with his chaplain and his curates and one young missionary destined for a brotherhood. The Bishop had greeted Stephen after the first Sunday Eucharist and enquired about his future posting in the mission field, asked what subjects he'd been taught and probed the form of service at the College. He had not shown particular curiosity in how an African had adapted to life in England and, it seemed, he disapproved. All he had said was, 'Ah! I heard the sad tale of Joshua Moroosi. But, after all, what can you expect of such experiments? Such a pity ...' He had seemed distracted, flicked his eyes over Stephen, appraising him and saying again, 'Such a great pity ...'

Stephen had sometimes seen him walking on the deck with the young man from the brotherhood who carried a prayer book or a notebook in which he sometimes wrote, the Bishop leaning in when it was breezy, a finger on the edge of the paper, holding it down for him. More often they proceeded in silence or stood side by side watching the sea, rapt and gestureless, leaning on the rail. When they walked, they seemed to move as one, step to step: pause, turn, continue, then disappear up the companionway, avoiding the saloon, a door closed discreetly behind them.

Stephen never knew if it were prescience or not but the image remained vivid in his mind: two men standing side by side and watching the sea—the surging bow wave or the spiral of iron-grey water unfolding at the stern. A deep companionship of silence.

ALBERT HAD WATCHED the sailors pulling at the oars and Stephen standing in the boat waving the cross in an arc above his head. He'd turned away before the others had dispersed, hurrying, eager to catch the train for Canterbury, both guilty and relieved. It was not Stephen's going he was glad of but being able to forget—for a time—the Warden's words: *I will have to reconsider your posting.* Nor would he have to make excuses to Stephen about Unity or to Unity about Stephen. His time would be undivided. The worry about having Stephen as a guest at the wedding breakfast had also lifted, the discomfort that it would have caused. Who to seat him with? An over-enthusiastic aunt who would swamp him with questions? A supercilious colonial cousin who might either ignore or lecture him? One of Unity's younger sisters, tongue-tied in the presence of any male past preparatory school?

'Bertie, what are we to *do* with Mr Mana?' Unity had said before Stephen was recalled to the Cape. 'My mother does not wish him to be uncomfortable and, after all, it is really just a family wedding. Don't you think it would be better if ...'

—*No, Unity. It is not Stephen who will be uncomfortable. It is your mother. It is you.*

But he had not said it then and now the problem had dissolved as Stephen had diminished into the sunlit sea, the looming ship obscuring the outline of the small boat carrying her passengers. He was relieved too—dared he admit it—to be free of Stephen's acuity even if it was a matter of his own uneasy conscience. Stephen always graciously accepted any excuse that Albert might offer, never judging him. But Albert was shrewd enough to guess that it was not incomprehension that kept Stephen silent. It was generosity. That—and the burden of being beholden.

Perhaps every bun had its price.

AS THEY SAILED further south Stephen sensed the slow withdrawal of his shipboard companions. A cautious ebb in conversation. The invitations to visit missions, parishes and schools which had been so abundant when they embarked had faded as potential obligation loomed. One could remember the charming Mr Mana as anecdote, as self-congratulation; one did not wish to have him suddenly appear among one's colonial friends at luncheon.

A change came on Stephen himself: a wariness, a matching caution with fellow clergymen who mentioned, less enthusiastically, the Missionary College and English cricket and fell silent at his approach when they had been conferring together. Had other students sent from the Foreigners' Building felt the same the nearer they got to their destination, suddenly adrift from their chaperones, the tact once shown to protégés now ebbing into condescension?

He had once heard a missionary visitor to the College laugh indulgently as he told anecdotes of the last voyage to his mission in East Africa, accompanying a home-bound student. 'Fancy! While he was at College he spent his pocket money on wax dolls for his mother! His mother, I ask you! Well—as might have been expected, their faces melted in the heat when the ship reached the Equator. You cannot imagine how upset he was! He wept! Besides the expense, it seemed to him an evil omen. He was simply plagued by superstition after that! Mr Meshach Lavender—yes,' with a droll chuckle, 'that really was his name ... Mr Lavender, bless him, was an object lesson. The more I know of the native'—he had avoided glancing at Stephen, sinking lower in his seat— 'especially the African, the more I believe it impossible to eradicate the savage inclination.'

'Old fool!' Albert had muttered under his breath, his face burning on Stephen's account. A reassuring pat on the arm, a chummy nudge of the shoulder: *A lot of bosh!* Albert's favourite riposte when he took offence.

Alone on deck, Stephen had looked at the precious photograph of the woman, kept between the pages of his prayer book.

—*They even sang before the Queen. The lady told me so herself.*

Had *she* also felt suddenly diminished once she and her choir companions had set sail for the Cape, their little flurry of fame quenched by the indifference—the disapproval—of their fellow travellers?

It was easy to be affable when no commitment was required.

—*Should you ever return to England, do come and stay. We'd be delighted.*

Knowing it would never be.

Stephen walked the decks at night when the closeness of his quarters woke him, sweating. Perhaps his face would also melt into anonymity like Meshach Lavender's dolls, a waxy sludge unrecognisable to anyone he knew.

Almost superstitiously afraid, he would stand where he could catch the breeze, aching for sleep, wishing he could strip off his heavy flannel nightshirt and stand bare limbed. He did not dare.

—*There's a naked savage in the stern!*

Instead, he kept watch, gazing at the turning stars, adrift between two worlds. As they voyaged south, the northern constellations slipped from view, the new arising as they crossed the Equator and wallowed in the torpid heat. Somewhere beyond his sight he sensed—almost palpably—the bulk of the African coast.

When at last the ship had anchored in Table Bay, he hurried to the gangplank with a sudden sense of consequence and elation, searching eagerly for faces as dark as his own among the waiting crowds, wanting to reach down and shout aloud, '*Sendigodukile!*'

Already, I am home.

But he was jostled aside by the Bishop's chaplain and the party of curates, making way for the Bishop to disembark—a pageant of blackclad priests delivering him ceremoniously to a reception line of waiting dignitaries. Stephen watched them mount an equipage of carriages, the Bishop waving a pale hand at the gaping crowd. Beside Stephen, unnoticed at the starboard rail, the young man from the brotherhood stood staring after the Bishop's carriage as it drew away. He turned, caught Stephen's eye. Then he hastily dipped his head and hurried off, his brown robe gathered round his thin, slight form. Stephen almost started after him, putting out a reassuring hand. He knew that look, that dawning desolation.

When, at last, he stepped onto the quay, he was pressed aside by workmen, intent on their business, hauling bales. He had raised his hat to a gentleman who had failed to see him. A beggar had petitioned a fellow clergyman but ignored him. He had bought a newspaper and the vendor had scrutinised his coins for longer than was necessary.

He stood bewildered. In a moment he had lost his poise.

IT WAS ONLY the Archbishop who seemed enthusiastic at his arrival. When Stephen called on him soon after he had disembarked, he talked with animation of the missions, the need to send returning clergy to the furthest outposts, the lack of men to go around, the mighty task ahead of them all, his confidence in Stephen's vocation, his delight at seeing him so grown, regret at his recall—at Joshua's sudden death. George Maqoma's. Were his lungs quite well? Alas, consumption was the enemy of all their dearest schemes. Had he heard that soon after returning to the Colony, another of the earlier students had died? One of the Zulus. After all those years of training! He must appreciate why it had been decided not to send any more African students to England. The climate did not suit them. Was Stephen sure, quite sure—perhaps he should consult a doctor—that his chest had not been weakened? Stephen did not have a chance to speak. He sat on the edge of the chair facing the Archbishop's laden desk, a shadow among the looming bookcases and dimly draped lamps.

Then the Archbishop said, 'In consultation with your Warden in Canterbury and most particularly with Canon Rutherford, who, I believe, was your earliest mentor, I have a special commission for you.' Stephen gazed at him. 'It will be a hard posting and I am sorry that you will be on your own, but Warden Bailey feels that of any student in your year, you will manage.'

A sudden dawning: did Albert know? Albert on the dock, evasive in a way he had not understood, hurrying him along, wanting him to go.

'I have no doubt the Bishop of Grahamstown will be delighted to see you and have you serve in his diocese. Indeed, it's a matter of pride that one of his Native College students has done so well.'

Stephen made no reply. He knew he had not misinterpreted Warden Bailey's words, no matter how obliquely delivered. 'Not up to the mark.' Evidently, the Archbishop was only flattering him, greatly relieved he looked so well.

'I had a letter,' said the Archbishop, drawing a paper towards him. He put on his spectacles and peered at it. 'Ha, yes.' He took them off again and laid them on the desk. 'Dr Bailey is not a man given to exaggeration. He said,' the Archbishop smiled benignly, 'you had great piety and faith. And that's what we value most, young man. A true vocation.'

'I have hopes of being appointed to the Native College,' Stephen said. 'Mr Turvey's letters have been very encouraging. Mr Turvey has said he will help me in my study of Greek and Latin. He wrote that I would be a useful teacher of the younger boys while I am in Orders. I have also recommended my fellow student to him, Mr Newnham. He will be coming out after he has graduated. We have been promised a posting together.' The Archbishop looked as if he was about to interrupt and Stephen hurried on. 'It was very disappointing to come home early, so long before my final examinations.' He paused, said bleakly, 'My lungs are certainly well ...'

'You will be ordained deacon soon enough but, besides the Classics, it requires at least two years of mission work—sometimes many more—before you can be priested. There will be time to study.' The Archbishop rose, came round the desk, put out his hand. Stephen shook it briefly, fumbled for his hat and bag and followed him to the door. As the Archbishop opened it, letting in a flood of sunshine, he paused, turned to Stephen. 'After all, as a deacon you are still a clergyman and missionary, and you are needed urgently among your own people. It will be testing to be alone, I know, but you will understand that we have so many places to fill. Where there is a native clergyman we must use him to advantage. There are so few of you.'

Stephen began to speak again, stopped. The light seemed too bright in the open doorway, the voices in the vineyards beyond the gardens echoed loudly in the vacant corners of the room. He was borne along in the wake of the Archbishop's receding footsteps. 'Where are you sending me?' he said at last.

'Trinity Mission. At a place called Nodyoba.'

Nodyoba? The word would not form.

'It is a hill parish. Very fine climate. A pleasant prospect, I believe. Mountains, forests. Lovely ...' The Archbishop took advantage of Stephen's stunned silence. 'The church, I fear, is rudimentary and the Director of Missions will only manage to visit once, perhaps twice, a year. But you will be a pioneer, a true pioneer as St Stephen was himself. I am sure you will prove yourself well named—a "man full of faith and of the Holy Spirit".' As an afterthought, he added, 'It is in a Fingo location.'

'I am not a Fingo.' Stephen was alarmed. 'I am Ngqika. The people will not be satisfied with that.'

'You are a soldier of Christ. It does not matter what nation you belong to.'

There was no point in contradicting him.

Stephen boarded the ship for Port Elizabeth the next day. He stood often on the deck, gulls scudding in the wake, watching a wilder sea than he had known on his passage to the Cape. For the first time since the days when he had watched for his mother on the road leading to *Mfundisi* Rutherford's mission, he was assailed with a hopelessness that he could not shake off.

He sat alone in the stern. Albert was very far away.

CHAP. 8:124

Mzamo met Stephen off Cobb's Coach in Grahamstown. A finer fellow Stephen could scarcely have imagined. If he had come home thinking he was bringing the learning and sophistication of a world that none like him had ever known, it seemed—outwardly—that his brother matched him.

He was waiting with a horse and trap. Tall, upright, his hat brushed, a cane under his arm, Mzamo did not greet Stephen in Xhosa but spoke in English.

If accented, it was as fluent and as easy as Stephen's own. He was affable, expansive, and passers-by paused to stare: two such well-dressed black fellows laughing together, speaking English and hoisting travelling bags covered with labels into the trap.

'Does my father know I have returned from England?' Stephen asked as they drove away.

Mzamo urged the horse abruptly. It surged forward, startled by the whip. He whistled, deftly drawing it back a little, allowing it to calm itself, and then he said, 'No one knows where our father is.'

'Why did you not write?' Stephen turned on him.

'What could I write?' Mzamo answered. 'He bought some cattle, he built some houses. The drought came so he went away again to work. He has not returned. Our mother waits for him as she waits for you. She keeps his house as if he is coming there today.'

'When did he go?'

'It is more than a year. He went to work on the government's roads again.'

'You should have told me,' Stephen interrupted, his voice rising.

'And what could you have done, Malusi?' said Mzamo. 'It is the same with many men. They go to work. They are paid with a gun. Some return. Some do not. There are temptations.'

'My father would never leave his cattle.'

'No,' said Mzamo. 'Nor would he leave behind his gun if he did not mean to return.'

'What do you mean?'

'It was not so long after I was *ikrwala*.' Newly initiated. 'I was still at our home. The drought was killing the cattle. The crops failed again. He said I must stay to look after our mother and the homestead. He was going to earn money and a second gun.'

'What gun?'

'Men on the roads or those making railways or going to dig diamonds are paid with a gun, Malusi. Surely you know that. But a second is not easily given if a man owns a first. He wished to have another. He knows it is prudent.'

'Why? Who is he to fight?'

'You have been away too long, Malusi. There are things you do not understand.'

'But our father ...' said Stephen. 'A man cannot simply disappear. Especially not a man of consequence. He is councillor to a chief.'

'When a man comes into the Colony, Malusi, he is just another kaffir. If he ventures far from his home, who is there to know him? He will use another name. One that white men understand.' He turned and looked at Stephen sardonically. 'Stephen, perhaps? Or even Saul? Maybe George.' He snorted. 'If he's unlucky he will be named by his employer. Maybe Jim-Houseboy as distinct from Jim-Horseboy. If he dies—who is he then? What name is put on his grave?' He shook the reins. 'If he has one at all.'

Stephen Mana. Joshua Moroosi. Stephen did not comment. Mzamo was not the only one who understood a diminished name. Except that, stubbornly, insistently—courageously— he had never answered to his baptismal 'Saul'.

He never would.

'Does my mother know that I am back?' said Stephen.

'I sent a message once I heard from *Mfundisi* Turvey that you had sailed. You will be expected.'

'Are you coming with me?'

'Yes,' said Mzamo. 'We will have to go on horseback.'

'I do not know how to ride.'

'You will have to learn. A horse is as necessary to you as a church.'

'I hope both will be supplied.'

'After the expense of your education, it would be a scandal if they were not,' said Mzamo.

Stephen did not reply. He did not wish to tell Mzamo of his disappointment in his posting. He sensed it might be a triumph for Mzamo.

—*What did you expect?*

'Perhaps we should visit *Mfundisi* Rutherford's mission on the way,' suggested Stephen.

'No need.'

'I wish to bring him the greetings of Warden Bailey. They are old friends.'

'Rutherford? He's here in Grahamstown. He's far too important for any old station now. He's just been appointed Director of Missions.' He turned and looked at Stephen, examining his hat and necktie, his jacket and his bag. 'He will be your superior again but, as you're a real gentleman now,

Malusi, he will show you off to everyone in town and pat himself on the back for rescuing you!' They swerved past a wagon drawn by a span of long-horned oxen. 'At least you came back. I think I would have stayed.'

'I doubt it. '

'The freedom would have suited me.'

'Freedom?'

'I heard that you took tea and played chess in all the finest houses in Canterbury. You wouldn't be invited to play chess here and you'd get tea in the kitchen if you were lucky.'

'Those are trifles,' said Stephen. 'I was no more free in England than you are here. Not when it counts.'

'I don't believe you.'

'A black man is a black man, Mzamo. He is either a curiosity or a nuisance, wherever he is.' Then he added, 'Except to Albert.'

'Who is Albert?'

'My friend at the College. He is coming out as soon as he has graduated and is married. He taught me Latin and Greek and I taught him Xhosa. It was a good arrangement. I can be ordained a deacon now, but I need the Classics to be a priest and he will be no use on a mission if he can't communicate.'

'Who's doing best?'

'Neither of us!' Stephen steered away from the subject. 'We preferred playing cricket.'

They turned down a side street, going slowly between the houses. Behind them the Cathedral seemed as small as a parish church to Stephen, the proportions of everything diminished. Only the sky was a remembered summer blue, the wind warm, an undertow of heat never felt in Canterbury. He breathed in the scent of smoke, of dung, of maize cobs roasting on a brazier.

'You will meet my wife,' said Mzamo. 'She is Vuyo Tontsi's sister.'

'You wrote that you had married but why did you tell me nothing of her?'

'What was there to say?' said Mzamo carelessly.

'I would have been pleased to hear about her character,' Stephen said. Then he added, trying to make it sound more in jest than in complaint, 'Since you didn't answer my letters I thought, Ah, he's gone back to the red blanket and has taken half a dozen wives. He has forgotten how to hold a pen.'

Mzamo did not smile. He said with some irritation, 'I'm a very busy man. I am helping *Mfundisi* Turvey to translate the prayer book into Xhosa. I am directing the choir at St Philip's. I am a reader and a catechist in our church. I have my work with the Magistrate. I have committees and organisations to attend to. And now I have a wife and rent to pay to Vuyo Tontsi, who is my landlord because only Mfengu have title to property in Grahamstown.'

It was no excuse but Stephen let it pass, feeling the old subservience rekindling.

Mzamo was the only member of the family who could have written. Could he not have imagined Stephen's anxious lingering in the dining hall after tea, waiting for the weekly letters to be handed out? How would he have felt if nothing ever came for him but the quarterly bulletins from the Native College with a note appended from *Mfundisi* Turvey? What if Mzamo—the heir—had not been told of their father's disappearance?

Clearly Mzamo had never conquered his resentment. Nor did he wish to dwell on Stephen's triumphs even though Stephen's monthly letters to *Mfundisi* Turvey never failed to send his regards, his prayers, his admiration in whatever news about Mzamo he had gleaned from the reports.

'Did *Mfundisi* Turvey show you my letters?' Stephen asked.

Mzamo looked nettled. He urged the horse to a lively trot down the rough road and Stephen was obliged to hold onto the seat as he was slung from side to side. They drove in silence for a while. As they reached a narrow bridge, Mzamo turned to Stephen with a grin. 'Did you bring me a wedding present? I would have liked a present.'

AT LAST THEY reached Fingo Village: children, noise, boys playing in the street. Chickens, ducks and pigs in the yards. An albino horse dragging a rope around. A dog foraging.

Across the slope, beyond a stretch of grass and bog where donkeys grazed, was St Philip's Mission Church.

'*Mfundisi* Turvey is in charge now,' said Mzamo. 'A younger priest has just been appointed Principal at the Native College so that the *Mfundisi* has more time for parish work. Besides, he cannot see too well. One eye is almost blind.' He laughed. 'That old horse of his—you remember? The one called Gladstone? It's blind in one eye too. When they ride down the street everyone gets out of the way. Going down the hill to town the horse pulls to one side. Coming up, it pulls to the other.' He gestured with his whip. 'We call them *Oononkala*, the crabs.' He slowed a little, pointing. 'St Philip's and the parsonage were completed while you were away. The *Mfundisi* is still building a school-room.'

A stretch of levelled earth piled with bricks stood beside a small, tall-gabled church. A sturdy cottage, newly whitewashed, had been built at the edge of the yard. A fenced and furrowed vegetable garden, still devoid of growth, was laid out against the north wall.

Mzamo urged the horse on, flicking its rear with the lash. He raised his hand in greeting as he passed people in the road—haughty, handsome, adroitly steering his trap over potholes and corrugations. He drew up beside a house. It was as simple in design as the houses around it but there was an air of something more substantial. There was a sundial in the garden. There was a stable for a horse, a lean-to for the trap.

And there, at the door, was Mzamo's wife.

'Her name is Nokhanyiso,' said Mzamo. 'She is known as Miss Moonlight by the English.'

Stephen stepped down from the trap, doffed his hat and took her hand.

NOKHANYISO WAS A big woman with a handsome, impassive face. She kept her eyes cast down and was silent beyond the customary greeting. She was dressed in a frock as tuckered and flounced as any belonging to Miss Unity Wills. Her boots were tightly buttoned at the ankles. Only when she served tea did she put her gloves aside. When she had poured it she went away to let them drink it on their own.

'Would you believe that her father is a traditional red chief,' remarked Mzamo when she had closed the door. 'But she is a Christian. Vuyo made sure of that.'

'Why? Is he in Holy Orders?'

'Vuyo?' Mzamo snorted. 'No! But he is heir to the chieftaincy and he is preening himself for succession. He knows the best way to get on in life. He wears a top hat and frock coat. He persuaded his father to send his sisters to school at a mission. They were baptised so they might marry influential men. He calls on the Magistrate each Friday and, among other political business, discusses you.'

'Me?'

'It is a very fine thing to know a man who is being educated in England. You have quite a reputation.'

'But he hasn't seen or heard from me for almost three years.'

'Why does that matter? A name is good enough. "My friend, Stephen Mzamane, at the Missionary College." The English here do it all the time. They know it is to their advantage to be acquainted with a lord or a judge or a general.'

'A proper English gentleman wouldn't mention it.' Stephen took up his teacup. He ignored Mzamo's evident surprise. 'Tell me about my mother,' he said.

THERE WAS NOTHING that Mzamo could tell him about their mother that was at all familiar. Now that her sons had become *amakhumsha*—the elite—she wore frocks and shoes. Since the departure of their father, Mzamo had bought them for her. And a table and a bed and an easy chair. Despite these favours he could not persuade her to leave the hoeing of her garden to a servant.

—*What servant? What wife am I who cannot hoe my own garden? What would my husband say if he returned and found me sitting idle in the house?*

Mzamo had not seen her in more than a year. It was too far and he was too busy to go home, too involved in local political affairs—the Magistrate's Court, the Croquet Club, St Philip's Choir, the Teachers Association. A litany he repeated time and again, ensuring that Stephen appreciated his influence and status.

'Last year I had a square house built for our mother,' said Mzamo. 'It is the thing to do these days and it is a fine place. The clergy consider a round hut an invitation to immorality.' He looked at Stephen and Stephen was unable to determine if the expression was sardonic or not. 'You must get all your converts to build square houses, brother, otherwise, they will never get to Heaven!'

'I have come to preach the word of God, not build square houses.'

'Well, you will preach in vain if you can't build and plough and harvest like the rest of them.'

'They never taught us that.'

'Of course they didn't. Why would you dirty your hands? You are an Englishman.'

'It seems you are one too.'

'Only as far as it suits me.'

'How far is that?' Stephen was wary, remembering too well his belief in his own sophistication before he left for England and the shock—even the terror—of his bewilderment when he arrived.

'It did not suit me not to be a Ngqika or a man.' Mzamo looked Stephen over, mused. 'It will not suit you either.'

'Circumcision is forbidden,' said Stephen. 'It is not the fact of it. It is the depravity in the circumcision schools.'

'Then you will always be a boy,' scoffed Mzamo. 'And besides, you know nothing of such things. You were never there.'

'I would be excommunicated.'

'Yes! That is a way the English have of dividing us from our kinsmen, to deny us manhood. Pretending to be God gives them power over everything.'

'Then why aren't you excommunicated?'

'I didn't tell them—and it didn't suit them to enquire too closely. I am married to a Christian so they leave it at that. If they were to follow it up and examine the congregation at St Philip's they'd have to chase half of us away!' He laughed. 'Can you imagine? We'd run off to the Wesleyans and that would be a worse calamity!'

'You are making light of it.'

'What else can I do? It's ridiculous. Even *Mfundisi* Turvey thinks so.'

'Has he said that?'

'Of course not!' said Mzamo. 'He isn't a fool! If he objected they'd pack him off and what help would that be? But he gets savage when someone from the town comes to preach damnation. He never threatens it himself. It's learning our language that makes him different from the rest. I am helping him translate the prayer book into Xhosa.'

Clearly, it was a source of great pride to Mzamo. He repeated it many times in the course of the evening. 'And I told him, "*Mfundisi*, you must learn to be a native if you wish to speak like a native." And he said, "You have the impudence of a white man to talk like that!" And then he laughed. He really meant the impudence of an Englishman. I would like to know those Irish. I think we would have a fellow feeling.'

'There were many in the workhouse in England,' said Stephen. 'They are made to break stones until they break themselves.'

'They could not break me!' said Mzamo.

IT WAS NOKHANYISO—the improbable Moonlight—who disturbed Stephen's homecoming most. Despite her lowered eyes, he felt himself under scrutiny, subject to a sly intelligence.

He did not like her. Yet he could not give a reason why.

She spoke to him in both English and Xhosa. She answered his questions. She smiled when he smiled, though she made no conversation of her own. Despite an apparent diffidence, she had energy, an impatience that seemed constrained by her tight-fitting dress, her button boots. In the morning he happened to glance through his window and saw her standing in the yard, opening and closing a small parasol, flicking at its ribbons almost roughly. It seemed she sensed a watcher, for she turned suddenly and glared back at the house, a quick tilt of the head before she walked swiftly to a shed in the yard, let herself in and closed the door behind her.

The accoutrements of colonial life—including a stylish wife—may have been as essential to Mzamo's status as they were to the gentlemen of West Hill. But to her? Watching her, Stephen was aware of a fleeting ferocity: met and conquered as soon as it had surfaced.

THAT EVENING VUYO Tontsi came to the house followed by a horde of curious relations. Everyone was dressed in their best to meet the black Englishman. Stephen, his clothes still travel-worn, could not match their finery.

'My dear fellow.' Vuyo grasped his hand then spread his arms in a gesture of welcome, pumped his hand again. Affable, urbane and decidedly stouter than when Stephen had last seen him, he was expansive, almost magisterial. Even Mzamo was mildly deferential: Tontsi was a man of business, of consequence, a landowner, a stalwart of the Church.

A collection of nieces or younger sisters stood with their backs to the living-room wall, glancing curiously at Stephen.

Their whispers were silenced by a swift admonition from Vuyo's wife in her lace-frilled dress and tasselled shawl. She came forward, touching Stephen's hand briefly with gloved fingers.

'We have you home at last,' said Vuyo Tontsi. 'I will introduce you to all the great men of the town. Personally— at your earliest convenience. They are all agog at your coming.'

Stephen smiled. To be an object of admiration to Vuyo Tontsi and Mzamo was something he could never have imagined. Once ordered about, cuffed when he had made himself too visible, ignored unless he needed their protection, he had always been *Inci*, the little one. Now he was their triumph.

He would be appropriated, once again, by them.

Nokhanyiso brought tea and cakes. Vuyo Tontsi settled himself in the largest chair, the girls slipped out to hover in the kitchen: the chatter of birds as they laughed, peeped, withdrew and exclaimed, all admiration.

'How long are you staying?' Vuyo said, sipping his tea. 'Long enough, I hope, to introduce you to the members of our Cricket Club. Perhaps you'll play with us next Saturday. Which reminds me—Mzamane,' turning to Mzamo, 'have you arranged a Stranger's Pass for your brother? You must see to it at once.'

'A Stranger's Pass?' said Stephen, mystified.

'Yes, it gives you leave to be here for seven days. You may not stay in town without it. As a black man, I mean. But now you are an Englishman, perhaps you will be exempt.' He chuckled at his own joke, looking around for appreciation.

'They will not exempt him,' remarked Mzamo. 'Half the town will think he is a troublemaker and be delighted to pack him off and the other half will stare at him long enough to boast about knowing him.'

'Ah, and the Street Keeper will be along asking questions,' said Vuyo Tontsi. 'It is the very plague to have him here! Just last week he was enquiring about my houses, saying I am only entitled to one. How is a man to raise rents without property?'

'What is a Street Keeper?' asked Stephen.

'While you have been eating roast beef in England,' said Vuyo Tontsi, 'all sorts of regulations have been brought in here. Who may own a house, who may not. Your brother, Mzamane, does not own this house. It is mine. Simply because I am a Fingo and he a Ngqika and Ngqika are supposedly savages and Fingoes are good loyal citizens. And so it goes.' Vuyo Tontsi held out his cup to be refilled. Stephen took it. 'Thank you, *mfondini*.' He settled himself again. 'This Street Keeper is usually some rogue the Superintendent has in his pocket. It's his task to inspect each property and make sure the right people live on it. No squatters are allowed and the yard must be neat. Suddenly one day, you find him on your doorstep with a notebook and a pencil, telling you that you will be evicted. *Tyhini!* When one has so many matters to attend to!' And he sighed theatrically. 'I send him off every time. He knows the Superintendent dare not prosecute me! He would be run out of town!'

'Then I must see *Mfundisi* Turvey as soon as possible,' said Stephen. 'Before I am sent away by this Street Keeper.'

'I'll slip him a shilling,' said Mzamo drily.

'The *Mfundisi* wrote some months ago,' Stephen hurried on. 'He said he would like to appoint me as a teacher at the College. Now I find I am being sent into the country but I am sure there is a mistake and he will make a plan for me to stay.'

'I told you he was gone from the College and there is a new Principal.' Mzamo was impatient. 'As Tontsi said, things are always changing here. *Mfundisi* is in charge of the mission in this village. He is missionary-in-charge at St Philip's and attending to the translations with me. If you wish to change your appointment, Rutherford is your man.'

135

'Do you think it was really he who arranged my posting?'

'Of course. Now that he is Director of Missions he may send you wherever he pleases. Besides, you're my brother—I doubt he'd ever have had you teaching in his school.'

'Why not? When *Mfundisi* Turvey wrote ...'

'You may remember Julius Coventry Naka.' Mzamo was sardonic. 'Now there was a man! He could match them in every argument they tried. Land. Positions. Memorials for the release of our chiefs. He could run circles round them. So what do they do? They send him off *ehlathini*—as far away as they could to bring him down to size.' He pitched his voice to a quavering falsetto, not unlike the Dean's. 'The native must be humble. He must know his place!'

Vuyo took out his handkerchief, wiped his eyes and mopped his face. 'Ah,' he sighed. 'We paid a heavy price for Mr Naka, didn't we?' Ruefully, he turned to Mzamo. 'Without Naka's influence, we would have been entertaining you tonight as our returning English hero, *mfondini*.'

Stephen was silent.

'But'—Vuyo Tontsi raised a finger—'I will tell you, Malusi,' prodding Stephen with an elbow, leaning over confidentially, 'they didn't keep Julius Naka long. Imagine— he is now the proprietor of a hotel near East London. My dear fellow, he is making a very tidy fortune and living in style. He is a man of tremendous influence. Tremendous.'

'I thought he was sent to England to become a priest,' said Stephen.

'Of course,' said Mzamo. 'That was the intention. Yes, indeed. But if you stand on a snake it will bite.'

'And his vocation?'

There was a silence. Then Vuyo clapped his hands. 'Sister?' he called. Nokhanyiso appeared in the doorway. 'Bring us some of your excellent cordial.'

She hesitated a moment, shot a glance at her husband, then turned away. Mzamo went to a bureau, opened it and extracted three slim glasses. He put them on a small table near the door. In the sudden silence, Stephen rose and carried the tea tray to the kitchen. One of the young girls took it from him, bobbing a curtsey. The others pressed in: small titters, shyer smiles. Almost as shyly, he smiled back at them. One put out her finger and touched his watch chain. He took it from his waistcoat pocket and dangled it for her to see. Mrs Tontsi sat in a corner, a piece of sewing held close to the lamp. She glanced at him sideways and down, too deferential to meet his eye.

As he turned away, he saw, through the open door, Nokhanyiso emerging from the small shed in the yard carrying a jug. When she brought it to the living room she set it down beside the glasses and withdrew. Crossing the room, Mzamo took up the jug, filling each glass almost to the rim. He handed one to Stephen, one to Vuyo Tontsi, and raised the third, saying, 'Welcome home, brother.' He took a sip, savoured it.

Vuyo Tontsi rose from his chair and joined in the toast. '*Akazizelanga ke*. He did not come for his purpose alone.'

'No,' echoed Mzamo. 'He also comes for ours.'

Stephen glanced from one to the other. Tentatively, he raised his glass as well, sipped his drink. He neither exclaimed nor protested, but as Mzamo and Vuyo Tontsi toasted each other in concurrence, he walked quietly to the window, setting his glass down on the table, spilling a little on its dark surface. He wiped the liquid away with his finger, smelled the sharp scent of spirits as he lifted his hand to draw aside the curtain and peer out of the window into the darkness.

Outside, he could hear far-off singing, interrupted by the wind. Listening, straining to catch the notes beyond the voices in the room, the gusts of laughter of Mzamo, the rambling of Vuyo, he knew it was a hymn.

Perhaps old *Mfundisi* Turvey was catechising in the huts and hovels on the outskirts of the town. If Stephen could not hear the words, he could say beneath his breath the verses he had sung on moonlit summer nights when he had marched with his school friends behind *Mfundisi* Turvey:

> Return, O wanderer, to thy home,
> Thy Father waits for thee ...

There was neither father, nor home. Not here. Yet again, he was adrift between two worlds.

CHAP. 9:139

t is hard to be an exile. But it is harder to return.'

Stephen had not understood those words when *Mfundisi* Turvey had said them to him on the eve of his departure for England. Nor did he understand what they might signify to *Mfundisi* Turvey himself. Walking down the hill towards the new mission church in Fingo Village, he felt at odds with everything around him.

When he first arrived in Canterbury and lay in his narrow bed at night listening to the relentless rain, he had imagined the crown of pines on the eastern hill, the clamour of voices, women singing, the view from the College's dormitory window of Mr Beck's toll house, the pasture by the stream where his cattle grazed. But, in time, even in his dreams, the tastes, the smells, the sounds—his own language—drifted away and were replaced.

And now, taking the eroded track down the hillside towards *Mfundisi's* small cottage near the new church, everything that had once astonished him when he first came to Grahamstown as a boy, its size and dignity, seemed shabby. The pines themselves, those sacred trees, had thinned and shrunk. When Stephen stood at the open doorway of Mfundisi Turvey's cottage and the priest looked up from his breakfast plate, his napkin tucked into his collar like a bib, a smear of egg congealed on it, even he—gruff, broad, bow-legged, one-eyed titan—was diminished. His beard was not as abundant, his eyes no longer quite as blue. This was not the magisterial Dr Bailey on his Warden's throne delivering his benediction before meals, his face as austere as the frozen image captured by the artist in the portrait of him that hung above his dais.

Yet nothing of Mfundisi Turvey's voice had shrunk, nor his roar of welcome. He knocked over his chair as he struggled up. 'Bless my soul! Stephen, lad! At last! Oh, look at you!' Calling out, 'Mrs Turvey, come and see who's here. Well, I'll be jiggered! What a fellow!'

He steered Stephen to a chair, slapped the cushion to rouse a flurry of dust. 'It's the building sand,' he said, gesturing towards the window. 'Nothing we can do to keep it out. Worse than a plague of locusts.'

Mrs Turvey appeared from the kitchen, unknotting her apron, her face glowing from the heat of the open range. 'Oh my goodness! Fancy that, indeed! I shall have to call you Mr Mzamane from now on. Dear Stephen, what a very fine gentleman you are. Welcome home.'

'Tea, my dear. Bring our guest some tea. Now, lad, sit here and begin.' Turvey gestured with his broad workman's hand. 'Begin!' He pulled another chair closer, sat, leaned his elbows on his knees, thrust his head forward, his chin on his knuckles, scanning Stephen shrewdly. 'If you weren't so black I would say you were pale and peaky,' he said. 'And rather thin. I trust your chest is all right.'

'I shall be forced to suffer from a chest infection soon,' exclaimed Stephen, laughing. 'Everyone expects it. I'll disappoint them all for being quite well.'

'But not much grown. No sunshine. No good greens or amasi. No running about or hunting with sticks. I am glad they sent you back when they did. I remember the damp all

140

too well. Oh, that chill! I determined, as a mere lad in the Ragged School, that I would run away to sea and jump ship in the tropics.'

'You were at a Ragged School?' Stephen's astonishment overruled politeness.

'No doubt you were sent along to one of them to shine up the little souls with Bible readings. Oh my! I remember them well, and the visiting curate.' He chortled. 'He was quite as pink as a petal and fat as a guinea pig! We wondered what he ate to keep himself so well oiled.'

Stephen did not know what to say: those shadow children in their ignorance and want; the running noses, the swollen joints; the tiny graves, row on row, behind the workhouse. He could not imagine that *Mfundisi* Turvey with his learning, his vigour, his incomparable Faith, had ever been an orphan in a Ragged School.

Mfundisi Turvey cocked his head, amused. 'We're both cast-off fledglings, you and I, Stephen. Brought in from the cold. We should be grateful to those well-meaning folk who did it for us but it has always had its price.' He was almost fierce. 'Remember, lad, no matter what they say or do to you, God makes no distinctions.'

Mrs Turvey brought in the tea and a slice of bread with a scraping of butter. 'I'm so sorry, Stephen dear, but I have no dainties to offer you. So many come to our door I can hardly keep up and I have not begun the baking for the day. Bless you, lad, if only I had known, I'd have been prepared. You could have done with a biscuit or a cake.'

'So could we all!' said her husband. 'Besides our own four boys, we seem to have a dozen more to feed. Always hungry, always eager for a slice. She never turns a soul away!'

'*Ndicel'isilayi.*' Stephen cupped his hands and held them up, childlike, remembering.

'There's great want here in the Village,' said Mrs Turvey. 'Ever since the diamond diggings began in Kimberley the price of food has become quite unmanageable everywhere.

The way the traders charge, you'd think we'd struck it rich in Grahamstown too!'

'Men and lads are flocking north,' said Turvey. 'We've a shortage of labour and the drought has made things worse. The price of fodder is exorbitant. Poor old Gladstone is making heavy weather of it.'

Stephen laughed. 'My brother told me you had a horse called Gladstone!'

'My nag is very well named! He pulls left or right just as it suits him.'

They drank their tea and *Mfundisi* Turvey told Stephen of the Native College and his schoolmates, the positions they had found on graduating: teachers, interpreters, clerks, shopkeepers. 'Oh yes, some have gone back to their people and taken up the red blanket again, but most have found some work although, I fear, there is a great resistance in this town against employing them. One worthy said he'd rather "go to the trunk" than sit on a jury with an educated black man from our College. I ask you.'

'My dear, do not bother Stephen with painful stories,' chided Mrs Turvey.

'Ah well, poor lad, he will find out for himself soon enough!' said her husband. 'My great regret'—he turned back to Stephen—'is that I would have liked you to work with me on the translation of the prayer book.'

'I am afraid Xhosa no longer seems to be my mother tongue.'

'You'd get it back in no time. Your brother Mzamo is a splendid linguist, sharp as a blade, but I fear his heart isn't in the work. Confidentially, he is far more interested in training our choir for competitions or singing with the Glee Club than in translating prayers. I can hardly blame him. He is an active young man and now he has a wife he must take her about, make a splash, show her off.' He pursed his lips. Stephen caught a swift glance from his wife. 'Come, lad,' rubbing his hands together. 'How remiss of me. Another cup of tea?'

Stephen smiled at Mrs Turvey, aware of the sudden silence. He steadied his cup, a small nervous gesture, saying awkwardly, '*Mfundisi*, I had hoped so much to work as a teacher at the College and to continue my studies with you. When you last wrote you seemed pleased ...' He trailed away.

'Indeed I was! Certainly I was and so was His Lordship— since when he has been instructed by the powers that be to appoint a younger man in my position. You will learn, alas, that even the Bishop is ruled by a very distinctive Almighty. And I don't mean God.' He almost growled. 'I have been replaced by a fine fellow. He's a good scholar and a worthy cricketer.' Stephen knew *Mfundisi* was curbing himself, saying less than he might. 'Ah, and you may have heard that your old friend Mr Rutherford has taken on the title of Director of Missions and is here in Grahamstown now. A splendid promotion! He's been made a canon.' He slapped his hands on his knees. 'As for me—the Bishop wishes me to oversee the mission here in Fingo Village. He also wants to hurry me along with the translation of the prayer book, unbothered by other duties, so I have been put out to pasture like an old horse.'

—*They have any number of good reasons to have me here rather than offending the gentry on West Hill.*

It was not something he would have confided to Stephen. He rubbed his head, its wispy dome. 'Your brother,' he said, 'is a great help to me but you, lad, would have been a splendid addition to the team. My word, if I close my eyes and listen, I would believe you were an Englishman.' He beamed and sat back in his chair and folded his hands across his stomach. 'As always,' he said more seriously, 'it's a matter of economy. You would think us missionaries a bunch of bankers and usurers the way we go on about money. What have we come to?' He pulled at his beard, sucked his teeth. 'We are fitting one man to a number of posts to save on stipends. The new Principal at the College told me that any vacancy at the College must be filled by a master who can also serve as assistant chaplain at the Grammar School, take a lesson or two and coach the white boys' cricket. "What about my fellows," I said, "and what's best for them?"'

Stephen did not embarrass *Mfundisi* Turvey by challenging him. Of course: he would never be appointed chaplain at a white boys' school. Or be asked to coach them cricket.

'The current argument from Mr Rutherford, who recommends each posting now—in fact, decides—is that you are urgently needed among your own people.'

'The students at the Native College *are* my own people.'

'So I said!' Turvey hurried on. 'However, others can fill the post at the College. New recruits coming from England who do not know the Kaffir language yet. More suitable, I'm told, for married men with wives—not like Mrs Turvey—who baulk at isolation. A "breaking-in", if you know what I mean, before they are sent off to a mission station.'

'But how am I to get on with my studies and be ordained if I have no one to tutor me or lend me books?'

'My argument exactly!' Turvey muttered to himself. Then, taking the official line, he said wearily, 'We are all obliged to follow directions. Even the Bishop. Perhaps it would be wise to call on him yourself. Speak up. Tell him what you think. He likes a man with spirit.'

'I will go to him as soon as I have returned from my father's home. My brother is taking me to greet my people first.'

'Of course you must. Undoubtedly.' Turvey rose from his chair. 'Indeed, your brother told me that he would be away for a week and I assumed he was off on business to Port Elizabeth with the Magistrate again. I'm glad I was wrong and that he's going with you. It's not a journey you should make alone. We are praying that your father will return. It is a sad circumstance but all too familiar, especially now that so many hurry to the diamond fields. The list of "missing" here among my congregation is as great as if we'd been to war.' He patted Stephen on the shoulder, shook his hand, holding it a moment between his two rough palms. 'Damn me—if you will excuse the expression—if I didn't tell Mr Rutherford that you'd be an inspiration to the juniors. Why, I even told the boys in chapel that though you were the smallest boy in the school you turned out to be a fine, ferocious little boxer.' He looked at Stephen, quizzical, one brow raised. 'Did you ever have a chance to prove it?'

'I did. Once.'

'Did you knock the fellow out?'

'Cold.'

'Hurrah! I knew you had the pluck!' He looked fiercely at Stephen. 'I hope it was an honourable cause?'

'It was,' said Stephen. 'One you yourself taught me to defend.'

IT WAS A hot morning when Mzamo and Stephen left Grahamstown, taking the road to the west, passing the copse of trees at the summit of the hill above the town, following the ridge from which the land fell away in layer on layer of bush-clad slopes and rocky crests. Mzamo kept Stephen on a leading rein for the first few miles as the horse fretted, sensing an inexperienced rider. Stephen gripped the pommel of the saddle, felt the chafe of the leather on his inner thighs, repressed any exclamations of alarm if his mount stumbled. He felt again his gaucheness in his brother's company, his fumbling as Mzamo led the way with grace and ease, settled back in his seat, expansive in his conversation, a faint amusement in his voice.

It was a long ride, Stephen's stiffness and discomfort easing only on the afternoon of the second day as the landscape opened up, flatter, drier, wider, scattered with the homesteads of the Ngqika as if, at last, they had entered into a different world from the primal vegetation of the Fish River Valley, the thickets of impenetrable bush, the rust-red earth. Here were cattle, here were women hoeing in their gardens, the drift of smoke, a river running slowly between sand-banks, the bleat of sheep. A yellow summer sky.

A ROUND HOUSE, Mzamo had said, is an 'invitation to immorality'.

Here, on the slope below the bridle path, was the homestead of his father. It comprised several round huts, the thatch shining silver in the midday sun. A stone cattle byre stood in the yard before them.

KwaMzamane. The place of Mzamane. Councillor to the Chief. Absent. Fate unknown.

The gate of the byre was broken as if cattle were not kept there any more.

It was a place Stephen had never known and which had been built slowly through the years of road-breaking to a semblance of dignity. His father's early destitution had not stripped him of hereditary rights.

And yet, his *umzi* stood forlorn.

At odds—and at a distance—stood a rectangular house with square windows, a wooden door and a porch. 'You see,' said Mzamo triumphantly. 'There is our mother's house.'

'It's very handsome,' Stephen said.

And yet, despite the clean-swept yard, it, too, seemed deserted, hunched against intrusion. But as they dismounted and tethered their horses to a tree, the door opened.

Their mother.

Swaying slightly, she waited in the shadow of the porch. She was dressed to receive her sons in a print frock, her head-scarf soberly tied. Her face was wearied by want, quite different from the youthful mother Stephen remembered in her clay-red cloak.

At last she came forward, gazed at Stephen—seemingly without expression—and then, in a grave gesture, she took his hand. Her fingers were limp in his grasp. He could hear her breath drawn deeply, haltingly. It trembled in her throat.

She led him into the house, Mzamo following.

Stephen took his gift from his coat pocket, wrapped in paper, tied with string. It was a prayer book with gold-leafed edge, watered silk binding and a leather spine.

Stephen said, 'It is a prayer book, Mama.'

Standing at his shoulder, Mzamo laughed.

In the sudden silence Stephen's mother touched his arm and steered him towards a chair at the wooden table. She gestured that Mzamo should be seated opposite. She brought dishes, plates. Then she stood beside them, watching them eat, gathering Stephen in with her eyes as every moment passed and placing before him the food of his childhood: *amasi*, cool from the gourd, *imifino*, fresh from the veld, young maize grains stripped and steaming from the cob. More and more until he had to push the dish away, defeated. How different from the boiled dough and raisins of a pudding at the Native College or the gruel and suet served on chilly English Mondays as a mortification after Sunday meat and potatoes.

This had been a homecoming. These were loving hands making reparation for the years of want.

'You are home,' she said at last. She turned to Mzamo. 'Perhaps, now, your father will return.'

Neither could find words of encouragement. Nor was there anything that Stephen could say to rouse her again from her silence. She stood between her sons, her face so grave, so weary, so scarred by sorrow that all they could do was share the silence with her.

At last Stephen took up the prayer book she had placed on the table and opened it.

'*Masithandaze.*' Let us pray. 'Our Father which art in Heaven ...'

The mother listened, not to the words, for they were meaningless, but as if searching for a voice, intent to catch—far off—some distant tone, some echo of a child long, long gone. Before this grave young man with a book in his hands and a face that had lost its laughter.

THE BISHOP WAS away. He had been called to Cape Town by the Metropolitan on unexpected business. His chaplain was fulfilling his appointments until his return. Any requests from missionaries were to be diverted to Canon Basil Rutherford, the Director of Missions.

Stephen's heart sank.

He almost turned away, retreating to *Mfundisi* Turvey's cottage. How often, as a boy, he'd felt protected by his presence, a cup of milk from Mrs Turvey and the ubiquitous *isilayi*—a slice of bread and jam for comfort. But, this time, he knew *Mfundisi* would have sent him back to Rutherford. What else could he have done? He was as much in thrall to regulations as anyone.

Basil Rutherford met him at the Diocesan Offices beside the Cathedral. His promotion had given him a new pomposity. His hair had receded on the crown but was curled at the temples and oiled in place above his abundant side whiskers. He wore a pair of pince-nez which magnified his eyes—and his resemblance to a large and lumbering owl. His voice was deeper, loftier, more imperative. He strangled his A's in the manner of Warden Bailey, speaking of 'Khenterbry', which he remembered fondly from his visits when he was down from Oxford. He interviewed Stephen in his study, placing a chair for him opposite his desk. Stephen faced him, hat on his knees, eyes averted: once again a schoolboy at the mission, detained to be admonished for his writing or to recite by heart a monologue from *The Merchant of Venice* or one of the Psalms.

'I bring you the greetings of Warden Bailey,' said Stephen.

This seemed to please Canon Rutherford. He smiled almost self-deprecatingly. 'Tell me about my good old friend,' he said. 'I recall his sermons with so much pleasure.'

Stephen glanced at him in disbelief: those mind-numbing hours in the Chapel with only the diversion of Albert's outrageous sketches of the 'Old Man' in his robes to prevent a row of students from falling frozen from their pews and chafe them back to life with shaking shoulders and smothered glee.

'He seldom spoke to me for he only teaches the seniors. But, of course, he took the services and gave the sermons, especially on Founders' and Rogation Days.' Stephen cast about. Had Warden Bailey ever said that Basil Rutherford had been his friend? 'He was very kind,' he said at last. 'He gave me a cross and a prayer book when I left.'

'Ah. Well.' Rutherford peaked his fingers together before him irritably: he had neither cross nor prayer book from Warden Bailey to compare. No doubt the gesture had been a small condescension reserved for the foreigners at the College. He adjusted his pince-nez, pursing his lips.

Stephen, recognising Rutherford's brief hesitation, hurried on, gaining in confidence and enthusiasm, telling him about the subjects he had taken, describing the new Foreigners' Building which Rutherford had never seen himself, the hospitality of sponsors, his love of chess, cricket— almost boasting: *I can coach it too.*

Rutherford glanced at the clock on the wall. Stephen trailed off.

'I suggest you write a piece for *The Mission Field*. It will be of great interest to the readership at large.' Rutherford took off his spectacles and polished them on a cuff. 'You should send it to me first. I wouldn't want it going out before casting my eye over it.'

—Here are your mistakes, boy. Write out each correction ten times. I won't have careless work.

Stephen examined his hands in his lap.

'Now, as to your posting.' Rutherford was brisk. 'You will proceed to Fort Beaufort by the first transport and report to Reverend Chauncey at the rectory at St John's. That is the English church in the town. He has been instructed to supply you with much of what you will need and ensure it is transported to your station. He will explain the situation and I think it would be unwise to take your information from anyone else.'

Stephen was alert. 'The situation?'

'The last incumbent was called away in haste.'

Stephen waited expectantly.

'It was not a suitable appointment,' Rutherford said. 'I am sure you will wish to prove to us—and, of course, to Warden Bailey, who has taken such pains on your behalf—that you know your duty and the commitment that you made in taking the Missionary College Vow.'

'A vow can never be broken,' said Stephen, almost in challenge. 'I will always honour the College Vow.'

'See that you do.'

Roused, Stephen continued, saying more assertively than he had ever dared before, 'I am very much concerned about my posting, sir. It has been a puzzle and a disappointment. I believed I was to teach at the Native College where *Mfundisi*—Mr Turvey—could help me with my studies. I am determined to be a priest, as His Lordship and Mr Turvey had hoped. It will be very difficult to progress without books or a tutor.'

'Yes, yes,' said Basil Rutherford, taken aback by his tone. 'I suspect very well why Mr Turvey would have wished you to work with him.' He almost glared at Stephen. 'The translation is taking an unconscionably long time.'

Stephen met his gaze: *I am not my brother, Mzamo.*

'I had hoped to be a teacher while in Holy Orders,' continued Stephen. 'It's something I must also master if I'm to be of use on a mission.' Rutherford surveyed him, an appraisal that took long enough for Stephen to avert his gaze and feel his confidence desert him. 'In Canterbury,' he said, speaking hurriedly, determined to continue, 'we were promised we'd be sent into the field in pairs. I taught an English student my language. He tutored me in his. He also coached me in Latin and Greek—subjects I must pass if I am to become a priest. My vocation ...'

His words petered out. Canon Rutherford considered him, unblinking. Those tufty ears, that lardy face, those widely spaced, blunt-edged teeth!

Stephen blundered on. 'We were told—Mr Albert Newnham

and I—that we would work together. That was our particular aim ...'

Rutherford stretched across his desk, pulled out a few sheets from the pile, took up his pince-nez and glanced through them. 'Ah?'

'Sir?'

Rutherford put the papers down, placed his spectacles on top of them and said, 'You will go where you are sent. Our circumstances here cannot be fully appreciated, even by our revered College in England. The difficulties, the extent of our diocese, the economies we are obliged to practise. Besides, we have to be assured of your abilities.'

'But I must advance.'

'It is we who will decide how you advance.'

—*There are those who do not come up to the mark.*

Stephen was silent.

'You should always remember where you came from, young man. How providence put you in my way the day I found you. Who has paid for your very education, the abundance of God's goodness? I trust that you are grateful.'

'I am grateful for God's goodness, sir.'

'Demonstrate it, then.'

Stephen rose.

'It is your duty to go out and prepare the way for others,' said Rutherford. 'You were chosen to serve your people.'

'I believed that I was called to serve all Christians people, without distinction.' Stephen's voice was low but, for the first time, he dared to meet the missionary's eye.'

'That is very laudable, young man'—Rutherford at his most condescending—'but not the most helpful attitude to have here, as I am sure you realise. You are not in England now.'

No, he was not in England now. And so, alone, sent to 'prepare the way' before his ordination, Stephen had gone—in exile—to Nodyoba.

CHAP. 10:152

On his arrival in Fort Beaufort, somewhat dishevelled from the dusty wagon journey from Grahamstown, Stephen called at the rectory of St John's Church in the main street. The Reverend Thurston Chauncey was the incumbent.

Chauncey himself opened the door. 'Yes?' he said distantly.

'Mr Chauncey?' Stephen bowed slightly. 'Good afternoon, sir. I come from Canon Rutherford in Grahamstown.'

'Ah.' Chauncey stepped out onto the porch. 'You are sent to load up the supplies he ordered! Go round.' He pointed to a pathway that skirted the corner of the house. Before Stephen could speak, Chauncey had turned away and closed the door.

The path was overgrown with grass. A few leached fruit trees were scattered randomly beside a fence. A small Cape cart stood under a lean-to. Having gone through the house, Chauncey was waiting in the backyard. He was a dry little man of uncertain age, rather stooped, a slight palsy in his face, a lazy eye. 'Here,' he said hastily, indicating two stacked crates against which leaned a hoe and fork and spade. 'These boxes have a few necessaries. Salt, tea, sugar, meal and seeds. There are also candles and a lamp. I bought no meat or butter for I was not exactly sure when the gentleman would arrive. You may tell him that he will be able to get milk and wood at the mission from the people living round about and I will send up fresh supplies as soon as he comes.'

'Allow me to ...'

'I have had no end of trouble,' Chauncey interrupted, 'wondering when someone would come to collect this stuff.' He waved at the crates. 'Or even if someone would be sent at all after the catechist was dismissed.' He glanced at Stephen. 'I believe we are to expect a missionary who has recently arrived from England. It will be very satisfactory to have an Englishman on the station at last. And someone in Holy Orders.'

How Albert would have revelled! Stephen was tempted to play along.

'Push the cart out into the yard, will you?' Chauncey said. Then he turned towards the crates, putting the garden tools aside with a clatter. 'I see I will have to get the boy to help you load.' He went into the house, called loudly, 'Figlan?'

An elderly man came out onto the porch, wiping his hands on his shirt. Barefoot, dressed in a large pair of trousers tied around his waist with a length of twine, he looked at Stephen with some wonder. Stephen put his hat and coat aside, keeping his eyes averted. He was close to laughter, remembering Albert's *What a hoot, old chap!* at anything absurd. He and the servant wheeled the Cape cart to the edge of the porch and tackled the boxes between them.

'*Bambihaash*, Figlan,' Chauncey said, a pidgin Xhosa, waving the old man away to fetch the horse. Then he remarked to Stephen. 'You must bring the horse and cart back tomorrow. I cannot be without them. When the missionary arrives he will have no difficulty in finding a good mount here in town. The military sells them off every now and then. He should not buy a native horse.'

153

Stephen could not prolong the deception. He said respectfully, 'Sir, I cannot allow you to continue in this misapprehension.'

Chauncey thrust his head forward, startled. 'I beg your pardon?'

'I apologise for not speaking up before but I had no chance.' Again, Stephen almost laughed: how would he describe the look on Chauncey's face to Albert? 'I am Stephen Mzamane,' he said. 'I have recently come from the Missionary College in Canterbury. I have been there two years and am in Holy Orders. I should be ordained deacon very soon. I am surprised that Mr Rutherford did not inform you of my name.'

Chauncey's ears flushed. 'Have you been making a fool of me?'

—Perhaps it is you who has made a fool of me. Instead, Stephen replied respectfully, 'That was not my intention, sir.'

'It's months now since I was led to believe I should expect an English clergyman to join the native catechist at the mission.' Chauncey cast about, annoyed and mortified. 'In any event, the missions are not my business.'

'I am the clergyman, sir,' said Stephen. 'Or, at least, I will be very shortly. It seems our superiors were obliged to change their minds about the incumbent. I regret very much that I was sent alone. I had been promised a posting with an English friend from Canterbury. Perhaps, as soon as he comes out from England it will be possible for him to join me. At present, I believe, there is a shortage of men.'

'So it seems.'

With tact, allowing Chauncey to recover himself, Stephen said, his smile conciliating, 'I would be grateful if you told me something of Trinity Mission.'

'I have no direct contact with the mission,' said Chauncey. 'I am Rector of the English Church for Europeans although, naturally'—the flush still mottled his neck—'I expect to be informed about all diocesan matters. I am greatly over-

154

extended with my own work. Sometimes I do not know which way to turn.'

'I understand.'

'The military are a constant source of bother. They do not have a chaplain of their own at present. And then there is the school ...' Flustered, unsure how to proceed, he said, 'Will you take some refreshment, Mr, Ah ...?'

'Mzamane.'

'Ah, yes. Quite.'

'I will gladly oblige on another occasion,' said Stephen. 'But I think I should make my way as I would like to arrive before dark. 'Again, he almost laughed at the relief on Chauncey's face. He said, 'Could you tell me how to get there?'

'Ah. Of course. Aah. The road. Yes.' Again, Chauncey seemed vexed. 'I shall send Figlan with you to ride as far as the turning. He will point the way.'

Stephen put out his hand and shook Chauncey's firmly. 'I will certainly bring back the horse and cart tomorrow if that would be convenient.'

'No, no,' Chauncey interrupted. 'I have three services here tomorrow and a confirmation class. I shall send Figlan to collect them.'

'I hope one day to meet your wardens and congregation. I should be grateful if I may join you for the Eucharist when duties allow.'

'Indeed, yes.' Chauncey pulled at his ear, said hastily, 'My congregation are mostly colonials, farmers and tradesmen, you understand ...' He trailed off. 'Ah, Figlan!' He hurried to the steps, relieved to see the old man appear, leading a horse. 'Yes, yes. Hurry now. The gentleman has a stiff drive.' Turning back to Stephen, he said, 'There is a steep hill ... if I remember correctly. Of course, I am very much occupied here in the town. Is it there—or am I thinking of the one on the way to Middledrift?' He took out his handkerchief and wiped his hands. 'The hill, yes. You will have to rest the horse halfway up. Do not allow him to be winded.'

'I suppose I will not be expected?'

'Unfortunately, no. It's some weeks since Rutherford sent instructions to store supplies ordered from the local merchant. He has sent no word since, no notice of your arrival. It was a courtesy to Rutherford, of course. Mission work is not my province. No, not at all. As I said.' He steered Stephen towards the cart. The old man stood unobtrusively at the horse's head. 'I believe there is a fellow living near the chapel up there who acts as a sort of verger,' said Chauncey. 'His name is Candle or some such.'

The servant made a small sound in his throat. Stephen glanced at him but he remained inscrutable. 'I believe he is a Christian,' continued Chauncey. 'It was he who told my servant here the truth about the catechist. Naturally, I reported it.'

'It would be useful to know what has happened.'

'People were not allowed to pray in the church unless they gave an offertory. Nor do we know what the fellow did with the money when he got it. He was also very willing,' he added, 'to accept meat from heathens when they slaughtered.'

It sounded like an admonition: *Mind you do not do the same.*

Somehow nettled when Stephen did not react, Chauncey exclaimed, 'A thoroughly bad lot! One of Mr Turvey's fine young men from the Native College in Grahamstown!'

'I am disappointed to hear it,' said Stephen. 'Perhaps there was a misunderstanding.'

'I doubt it.'

Stephen climbed onto the cart. Taking up the reins and tipping his hat, he set out—another of Mr Turvey's 'fine young men'—with the ragged servant perched on the crates in the back. As he reached the edge of the town Stephen slowed and turned to the old man, indicating the seat beside him. He said, '*Mawuhlale apha.* Do sit here.' Clambering across, the man shuffled in, containing himself respectfully, remaining silent. Stephen looked at him inquiringly. '*Nodyoba?*'

156

The hint of a smile. 'Ah! *Hlelinje!*' As I live! '*KwaNodyoba.*'

'You know it?'

'*Singabakhaya, thini!*' We—we are neighbours now.

Stephen shook his hand, the light touch of husky skin against his palm. He spoke in Xhosa, deferring to the old man's age. 'I am Mzamane, *Bawo.*'

'Dyoba,' said the old man in some triumph.

'And this man, Candle? What is his name?'

'Dyoba.'

Stephen laughed. 'I should have known.'

KwaNodyoba. A PLACE of mists, high up against a hillside facing north. A place that draws distinction from the vagaries of its weather, the vastness of its sky, its unpolluted air. In winter snow may fall. In summer the earth is burned bare by the sun, the ironstone thrusting through upland grass growing in a spare skin of earth. In milder weather there are flowering bulbs, a fragrance from the warmth of pasture, the movement of wind and hazy distances. It is a place where warriors have passed and where small men once roamed armed with bows and arrows. Their paintings shelter in the caves along the cliffs, abandoned now.

There was a church. There was a house. There was a schoolroom. All were made of sun-baked mud bricks.

—*Rudimentary*, the Bishop had said.

They were less than rudimentary. They were a tumble of earth and stone and thatch. The only sturdy thing in that deserted yard was a tree—thorn and thicket thrusting from an ancient trunk. It had been there long before a man had cleared the earth to build this humble little House of God.

Stephen surveyed the yard with dismay.

This, this forlorn unkempt wilderness, when he had hoped for the Native College with its high, whitewashed walls, the triangular tower on the slate roof with the bell calling the students to prayer, the tall stone buildings of the white boys' College across the road, the deep-porched bungalow belonging to the Head, the flower beds and vegetable gardens. The old oaks. The chickens, cows and beehives. All the bustle of the town with the wagons rumbling up the hill. The clamour of the juniors in their familiar galatea trousers and flannel shirts, the bouts of sparring with *Mfundisi* Turvey.

—*That's the ticket, lad. Right, right, left.* The cricket matches on Saturdays. Raisin pudding for Sunday lunch. He would even have been glad to go on graveyard duty again and dig the weeds from the iron-chained plots.

He stood before the lopsided little church alone, the horse restless in its traces. It seemed, in the hush of afternoon, that the place had always been deserted. He turned towards the parsonage. Small, neglected, it stood further up the slope beyond an abandoned vegetable garden, overrun with thorny bushes and clods of dry earth. A sapling had taken root in the brickwork of the chimney.

He picked his way up the path to the house. The keys that Rutherford had given him were awkward in the unused locks. He had to put his shoulder to the door to open it. Bat droppings were scattered on the floor. The calico ceiling had a stain across it where the rain had dripped through.

A living room with a fireplace, a table and a chair.

A bedroom with a mouldy mattress and a bolster on the narrow bed. A washstand. A rush mat. The walls had been painted blue.

It was only at dusk that a woman had come with a bowl of *amasi*. He had watched her for some minutes trudging up a pathway on the hillside. She had appeared over the lip of the beaten yard, her face anxious, scanning the clearing for him.

—*No, they did not expect him yet.*

—*There has never been a priest. Only a catechist, Thomas Dema. He is not here.*

—*Where has he gone?*

—*He was called away.*

The woman's answers were reluctant, her demeanour so

158

gravely respectful he had found no further way, beyond his gratitude for the proffered food, to make her talk. She had hurried off assuring him that her husband would call on him the next day. He had gone to his brother's—*ngaphaya*—she gestured to the north. *KwaKhama*. The chief's place. The *Mfundisi* must excuse him. He had not been expected yet. No one had told them. No, the *Mfundisi* in the town never came up to Nodyoba, even though there were many here at the church who would be glad to greet him.

'My husband. He is *igqobhoka*. A believer,' she said. 'We are church people.'

STEPHEN DID NOT go into the chapel until the next morning. He had not wanted to bring his dismay to a sacred place: God —he suspected—would be as disappointed in him as he was in God.

It was barely light when he made his way along the edge of the garden and down the path to the churchyard. No one saw him. No dog barked. The homesteads on the hill below were still in deep shadow, the eastern sky fading into the fleeting green of dawn. Etched against the rising light, the tree beside the church had an architecture of its own: spiny, small-leaved, armed. It was an ancient tree, multi-trunked, scaled with lichen.

Stephen opened the chapel door.

He closed it behind him.

And stood.

He did not know how long he stood. But the gloom, the dusty darkness, ebbed at last into a cobweb-grey. He looked about him.

The altar was small, a table on a raised step. Behind, the wall was bare. The pews were benches. Only a bent brass cross and the rough, peaked, home-made arches of the six slim lancet windows declared the building to be a church.

There was a thumbed, close-printed Bible on the rudimentary lectern. Stephen took it to the window and examined it, wiping grit from the cover. The pages smelled of woodsmoke. A smudge of candle wax had made a few transparent spots. Written on the flyleaf, the ink faded now to pale brown:

Trinity Mission, founded 1865.
Nodyoba.

Stephen set it down where he had found it, gazed up at the high-pitched ceiling, the cross-poled rafters that held the roof: some venerable tree felled beside the river far below. He went to a window and looked out. A wedge of hills, a pale sky, lightening now. He ran his palm across the pane. Red dust. On the sill the desiccated husk of a fly.

It was time to pray. To sink to his knees and hear God speak.

He knelt on the dung floor and bowed his head.

He waited.

Far outside he heard a disgruntled cow's complaint. Another. And another. A herdboy's whistle, cattle being jostled from the byre.

Inside the chapel there was silence. No deep-throated summons from the cathedral bell, vibrating in the leads of a thousand stained-glass windows, sending the rooks from their roost, a black-winged congregation, streaming out into an English sky. No robed priest, no complement of solemn male voices raised in response to his words. No candlelight, no incense—the scent of holiness—drifting in the nave.

Just the soft smell of dung and dust and earth.

Still, Stephen waited.

No prayer came.

He had not wept since he was nine. He did not weep now.

When Stephen returned to the house there was a youth loitering near the door, armed with a broom. He took up his post on the porch and swept around and around, moving each small pile of dust in the wake of the next.

'What is your name?' said Stephen.

The boy hesitated. 'They call me Sidenge. The foolish one.'

'What do you call yourself?'

No more than a whisper. 'Sidenge.'

At midmorning an old man had arrived. He was Dyoba, the churchwarden. He wore a jacket and breeches, a stock at his throat, a felt hat on his head. He carried a cane. Stephen had difficulty following the rapid idiom and allusion in his speech. It was so long since he'd had a conversation with someone who knew no English and had never been to school. He realised that when he replied he was translating in his mind from English into Xhosa. No wonder the old man looked askance, head cocked with interest and dismay. '*Khawutsho imvelaphi yakho?*' Tell the news of the place from which you came.

'I have come from England.'

Disbelief. 'There are black people in England?'

At noon, Thurston Chauncey's man, Figlan, had come to collect the cart and horse. Stephen gave him tea and a bowl of rice. It was all he had to offer. He felt desolate as the cart drove away, the old man's hand raised in friendly salute. He seemed to be the only link with another, more familiar world.

Then the people came in ones and twos, passing by, driving an ox and sleigh or on foot, greeting him, the stranger: quietly examined, shrewdly assessed, respectfully hailed. Something of a wonder to the youngsters, this *Umkhumshi*, this stylish towns-man.

What did they make of him?

He did not catch the rapid repartee. It was an idiom he would have to learn. But from then on he acquired another name. He was *Mfundisi Ngesi*: the Englishman.

Others came too. The elders, their curious wives bringing maize, beans, *imifino*. Seeds. A gourd of *amasi*, a beaker of milk. Too tactful to gape, too polite to enquire. If there were questions that they wished to ask—just as he'd once longed to interrogate Julius Naka—they deferred them.

First they would see how he preached in church: they all wished to know—Christians, heathens, whoever.

Over the weeks that passed, he welcomed them all, and they in turn recognised his dignity and presence, despite his youth.

—*Ngumntu olinene.* A man of substance. A man of truth.

But, though his language was fluent, it was not the language of Nodyoba. They caught his hesitation in choosing a word, the way he tilted his chin as if to find it, a gesture of his slim hand, the slight frown. He also spoke of prophets and other holy men they had not heard of before. He wished them to kneel when they prayed.

This, they would not do.

He did not insist, though he knelt himself. If they gossiped in the intervals he admonished them—with humour, but with purpose. Nor was he like Thomas Dema who had permitted no one to enter the chapel without being dressed like a *gqobokha* or without money for collection. Ngesi even allowed the heathens—*Amaqaba*—to sit on the benches in his church.

For now, he said, he simply wished to see them in the congregation. They could choose if they wished to stay and hear the Word of God. They could go if it did not please them.

At last, a regular congregation assembled each Sunday. Stephen was aware that their attendance might have been to examine, at closer quarters, the black man who came from England. He had no doubt the story of his appearance at Nodyoba had been discussed on footpaths and at beer drinks.

Ngesi. The Englishman.

The worshippers were mostly old women whose husbands had long since died, or gone off to the diamond fields to seek work and never come back, or had drifted to the ports, or to neighbouring farms. Nodyoba was a place of old women, a patriarch or two, girls, a scattering of youths, small children. The church was a haven for the needy. As he could not celebrate Communion or engage yet in any of the rituals which had been so treasured in his life at Canterbury, Stephen had had to turn to Bible readings and prayers, remembering the chilling length of Warden Bailey's sermons and confining his homilies to the interest and attention of the smaller children and the oldest man. He remembered Albert's words:

—*We must not bore the boots off our parishioners! We have to make them laugh. God must have a sense of humour—otherwise, why would He have made us all so absurd?*

And once, after a visiting missionary had spoiled their Sunday evening recreation hour by droning on about 'Jehovah's Sacred Text' and 'The Blessed Volume' as if 'Bible' wasn't adequate, he had said 'I shall be like the Chaplain we had at school. He was a capital fellow! He could play dance tunes on a fiddle. If he saw a boy dozing in the pews, he'd say, "Oi, you, What's-Your-Name? I know what you're thinking and it isn't suitable in Chapel!"'

Though schoolboy humour would not have suited Stephen's congregation at Nodyoba, they relished parables. The children's faces were the test of inattention: through them he learned the storyteller's art. His prayers were short, earnest and to the point. Supplications for rain, good harvests, healthy cattle, steady work. His sermons were often stirring. Sometimes delicate. Never long. But if the days were busy and people came to help him clean and dig and carry water, plaster walls and smear the floors with dung—a workman and a builder after all—the evenings were long and solitary. He often stood on the porch at dusk and gazed down the hillside at the clustering homesteads, the drift of evening smoke, and listened wistfully to the sounds of children's voices, the companionable bleat of goats. Sometimes there was distant singing, a heathen dance at a homestead far across the valley.

163

—Remember, lad, the best way to raise a congregation is to let them sing.

It was time to introduce all the hymns he knew. He sang to himself as he arranged and rearranged his few possessions in the living room, doing it over and over again. He had an *Illustrated London News* which he had brought all the way from Canterbury—an old edition, discarded from the library, with pictures of the Siege of Cawnpore, a portrait of Lord Russell and a rather tattered image of the Missionary College taken during the Easter service. He had inspected it often. Now, he cut out the page. He would make a frame. He would hang it on the wall, buy a pane of glass to protect it. He held it to the light, trying to identify the small background figures, the choir processing from the Chapel in their surplices, the crucifer carrying the tall, slim cross with its gilded arms, the arches of the ambulatory behind.

He could still remember the day he had arrived at College and walked along it to the Warden's study, step by step on the Minton tiles, overwhelmed with fear and wonder, alarmed by the multitude of black-gowned students.

Now, he had another sort of fear: he might always be alone.

Instinctively, he took up his prayer book, let it fall open at the place where he kept the picture of the woman: the faint warmth of light reflected on her cheek, the small ring within her ear, the curve of her brow beneath the fold of her headscarf. How often he had examined her, never presuming to touch her face with his finger, only wishing her distant gaze was more direct, meeting his, reassuring him, no longer intent on an infinity of her own imagining.

STEPHEN GAVE NOTICE that he would reopen the school. He gathered together a group of women to smear dung on the floor of the lean-to which ran the length of the north side of the chapel. They laboured all day and he worked beside them, learning the art. A pair of swallows had nested in a corner of the eave. A woman fetched a stick to break the nest but Stephen stopped her. The birds must come and go as they wished. He watched them in the quiet times when he stood alone, looking up into the entrance of the nest. They had travelled—in faith—half across the world to their instinctive nesting sites. How many times did they set out, never wearying? Or did they sometimes lose their way high above some unfamiliar sea?

At first, Stephen's school had no books. He brought his own and laid them on the table. The Bible, the prayer book, Virgil. He fingered them wryly. They would be of no use to the three small children who had appeared, chivvied forward by their grandmothers.

Soon there were five.

By the end of the fourth month he had fifteen pupils ranging from six to fourteen years old. The best he could do was read to them and teach them hymns. He had nothing with which they could write, no rudimentary primers from which they could learn to read. He sent a letter to Canon Rutherford requesting school-books, slates and chalk. It was another two months before they arrived. But they were sufficient if gathered up each day, the slates rubbed clean by older children, taking care not to drop them.

He found that what he could not teach, he could learn. From his pupils the words and sentences, the sayings and the phrases gathered. With elation, he unlocked the language of his childhood, liberated the sounds to which he had been born. His speech became unfaltering, the nuance creeping in through adding to or subtracting from a word to give a subtle shade of meaning.

This knowledge made the pathways to the homesteads easier, it procured gifts from gardens. And if he was called Ngesi, the Englishman, it did not matter. It was not a slight, simply a distinction. It brought, at last, the few men in the district to his door. He listened to them speak of crops and cattle. Through them the world was differently described.

In the evenings Stephen sometimes brought his kitchen chair to the church porch that was his schoolroom and from where he could see the sweep of the valley uninterrupted. It fell away steeply to the river below, where bush wove along its edges through a ravine and turned north, out of sight. He would sit in the dusty fragrance, the scent of the newly smeared floor conjuring a fleeting memory of the sound of cattle tramping through the mud and dung at the gate of his father's byre, the wheeling swifts in the sky above, the white twilight along the edges of the hills.

The wind.

Its breath was nothing like the chilly gusts which turned umbrellas inside out on the rainy streets of Canterbury or sleeted across the cricket pitch and drove the players in to shelter. It was the voice of distance and of space. Warm. Forceful. Streaming dust across the sky. It was an upland wind, the breath of drought, the harbinger of flood.

It was here, in the ebbing dusk, so high above the valley, so close below the southern stars, that he found, at last, that he was able to pray. 'Our Father which art in Heaven ...' For then, as if in answer from every nearby thicket—after the brief and sudden silence of nightfall—the mustering of crickets, a vibrating dark. He began again. '*Bawo wethu osezulwini ...*'

IT WAS MANY months before Stephen felt confident to write his first full report to Warden Bailey, a further request for books to Canon Rutherford. To Dr Bailey, he was businesslike, meticulous and circumspect. He mentioned to the Warden that the chapel was in need of furnishing: prayerbooks, an altar cloth, a pair of candlesticks. If his friends in England could spare any article they did not need, he would be—as always—deeply grateful. He applied to Rutherford directly: he wanted more equipment for his school, money to repair the ceiling in his house. He was in urgent need of books to assist him in his studies.

To *Mfundisi* Turvey, Stephen wrote his regular monthly letter recording his impressions. They became more plaintive: a letter a boy might have sent to his father from his boarding school, full of news but with a certain unintended wistfulness that a thoughtful parent would have sensed.

—*When would Mfundisi visit? He very much wished to see his face again.*

—*Did he plan to come to Nodyoba?*

He scratched that out.

—*Please, if he could. Sometime soon.*

He must not worry about Stephen's chest. The air was very good up on this hill. He had planted pumpkins. He had *amasi* and greens from his neighbours.

—*Did Mfundisi still have Gladstone, the horse?*

He wished he had a horse. It was impossible to reach his outstations on foot in less than a day.

—*Very fond greetings to Mrs Turvey and to their boys.*

—*Could Mrs Turvey send instructions for making bread?*

He had not had Communion for many weeks. He did not feel he could impose on the Rector of St John's without an invitation. Could *Mfundisi* spare some stamps? Did he have a copy of Curwen's tonic sol-fa?

—*I am going to start my ministry with hymns.*

It was many weeks after his letter to Dr Bailey that he finally wrote to Albert. How could he confess to him that he was no more than a native catechist in a mud-brick chapel infinitely smaller than the schoolroom in the workhouse in Canterbury and just as shabby?

My dear old fellow,

Here I am at a place called Nodyoba. It is in the hill country almost a hundred miles east of Grahamstown. The people are Fingoes. I don't believe they know I am a Ngqika. They view me as an Englishman! Do you think I am?

The Rector in the town near here certainly wishes I was! He is Rev. Thurston Chauncey, which lends itself to one of your nonsense names. He was appalled to find that the fellow sent from Canterbury was a native. If you had been with me we would have disgraced ourselves—I could hardly keep countenance! He thought I was a servant—but one of those 'spoiled trousers and boots' fellows everyone complains about here. 'A thoroughly bad lot', as he said!

My mission is rather humble. I will have to learn to build. I fear the Chapel will fall about my ears if I don't prop it up soon. It appears that my predecessor ran away. Mr Chauncey claims he stole the offertories. My neighbours plough and have flocks but they don't have money so I hardly think he'd have been able to squirrel away more than a few shillings. There must have been other reasons which I have yet to discover.

I have a small parsonage and a garden which will be bursting with pumpkins and potatoes any day now. Please don't tell me to be grateful. I need to find another reason to be glad viz. you joining me here as soon as you can.

Please let me know, my dear fellow, if you have graduated, if you are married and when you plan to set out from England. I shall make a special effort to come and greet you when you reach Grahamstown.

Ever your affectionate friend and with warmest good wishes to Miss Wills.

Stephen Mzamane.

He propped the letter against a candlestick, knowing very well that Albert would never join him but generous enough to pretend he might. It remained there for a month. After he had reckoned on the postage for his official correspondence, the supplies he needed from the merchants, Jacobus Ockert & Sons, and had counted out the money in the small locked box he kept beneath his mattress, he had no change for a stamp until his quarterly stipend had been paid.

By the time the letter found its way to England, Albert had already gone from College and it lay with other unclaimed mail—some years old—in Blunsom's desk drawer, buried under chits and bills, notices and blotting paper. The longer it lay there, the less important it became to redirect it. How, after all, could Blunsom chase up every student? Some might be at home, soon to return, but others had set forth for places he had never heard of. How was one to trace a place called Sarawak? By then the news would be old—so, surely, as he grumbled to Mrs Blunsom, it didn't really matter. Besides, he liked the stamps from foreign parts. He had steamed off a fine collection of them and stuck them in an album.

CHAP. 11:170

The winter wind was desolate as Stephen tramped along the road from Queenstown towards Albert Newnham's mission on the Indwe. It was the bleakest road he had ever travelled on. A landscape of stone and doleful scrub, as dry and forlorn as a graveyard. Weary, hungry and dispirited, he had to shield his head with his jacket so he could see the track and keep the sand from his eyes.

This was not the sort of place Albert would ever have chosen to be a missionary. Stephen could only imagine what Unity Newnham must have made of it. She would have been shrill with reproach. Poor Albert, harried by his own accommodating nature into premature middle age. Perhaps, after all, he should have run off to fight in India like his importunate brother, Percy.

Stephen trudged on, his bag suspended on a stick, shoulders straining: their father trudging to dig the government's roads so long ago, heading west towards the Colony, coming back, the proud possessor of a gun.

His father going west again.

Never coming back.

And what of Mzamo? Perhaps, when he had been making

his way to Albert's mission, when the fighting was shifting back and forth across the eastern edges of disputed land, he had chosen a different, safer route. If he'd been riding Stephen's horse he might have cut across the veld, avoiding military patrols. On foot, he could have used the pathways of intersecting dongas for concealment. If he'd walked he might have carried his boots—those fine boots, burnished black—laced around his neck. There was no one now from whom he could demand a replacement. He would have gone barefoot, marshalling his soles to dust and stone and thorn.

A warrior's feet.

Had Mzamo come to ensure the safety of the mission bell? Had he brought the money to repay his debt to Albert as he had promised Stephen he would? And, if he'd failed, would Stephen now be honour bound to pay it for him?

With what?

The sum of his own debts had long defeated him. More demeaning than the failure to pay was the mortification of having to admit to Albert the difference in their stipends— over a hundred pounds a year—without sounding like a mendicant, without shaming Albert into saying, as he would: *Don't worry, old fellow. I'm sure to end up in Queer Street sometime. Then I'll be looking to you!*

And what if Mzamo had been captured even before he'd reached the mission and Albert knew nothing of his good intentions?

There was no way of knowing.

Stephen felt for the letter in his pocket. Soon it would be even more soiled as it passed from hand to hand at his uncle's house.

—It is a letter, Mama.

With what dread he would read it to her.

But first, before it was shown to the family to whom it was addressed, Albert would see it and tell him what to do. What prayers he should remember, what words Christ himself might have offered to a grieving mother. Most importantly,

171

perhaps, Albert would convince him that God still cared.

But if He did—why this desolation?

When Stephen had been abandoned at the mission as a child, it was the livestock that had died, the cattle sacrificed, the fields stripped bare: an act of will, of choice, his father wielding the sacrificial knife, calling on *iminyanya* to arise.

But now it was not the cattle that had died. It was the head of the lineage.

And he, Mzamo's successor, would be unable to perform the rituals the family required. As a Christian he could not slaughter a sacrificial beast. He could not eat the meat in homage to his brother.

He was not even a man.

Besides his uncircumcised status, there might not even be a beast to slaughter. Stephen had heard that byres had been plundered by colonial troops. Herds had been driven away to be impounded in a military barracks. Houses had been burned, crops flattened. And yet, the defeated had delivered the last defiance. The bells at all the mission churches had been smashed. Except for Albert Newnham's.

For Stephen it was a triumph.

Or perhaps the triumph was Mzamo's.

ON HIS RETURN to Grahamstown in 1869, more than a year after his initiation, Mzamo Mzamane had quickly proved his worth as interpreter in the Magistrate's Court and a sidesman at St Philip's. After a period of probation, *Mfundisi* Turvey had persuaded the Bishop to licence Mzamo as a Reader and Lay Preacher in St Philip's Church. He had often conducted prayer meetings or given the homily when *Mfundisi* Turvey was up at the Native College or holding services at Highlands or Southwell or Sidbury. When he was absent and Mzamo took the service, the church was packed with every passer-by: Christian, pagan, even Dissenters. The curious, the sceptical, the gullible, the faithful. They came to marvel at Mzamo.

Mzamo understood the power of the pause, the sudden burst of laughter or of wrath, the smile of conciliation. He played them all as skilfully as he conducted the church choir. If he did not directly evoke ancestral shades, he called on the great ones of the past to encourage the oppressed. He had also been complicit with *Mfundisi* Turvey in objecting to offertories being sent abroad at the suggestion of the Dean.

'Last week's pickings from the Cathedral have gone to Calcutta!' Turvey might exclaim with a snort.

—Or Constantinople.

—Or Rangoon.

'God have mercy on us! As if we aren't destitute ourselves! What next?'

But it was as choirmaster that Mzamo achieved his greatest triumph.

Even the Precentor of the Cathedral, for all his erudition, could not match him. The Mothers' Union, the Young Men's Glee Club, the full congregation—Mzamo directed all the music, teaching the tonic sol-fa with a facility learned in *Mfundisi* Rutherford's mission church as a boy. By the time Stephen returned from his years at Canterbury, Mzamo had as much influence with the congregation and almost as much stature as *Mfundisi* himself. Stephen's arrival from England was an extra adornment to Mzamo's reputation as a man of influence in Grahamstown. Mzamo could speak loftily of 'my brother who is in Holy Orders' and mention Canterbury as if he were as familiar with it as Stephen. And, while Mzamo made his way in the Church, garnering admiration and status and—as employee of the Magistrate—earnings more handsome (and uncompromised) than all but the more canny brewers of illicit liquor in Fingo Village, Stephen laboured at Nodyoba. He was a workman, not a priest: God's apprentice, indentured to a Master whose voice had once proclaimed His presence in the mighty tongue of the Canterbury cathedral bell.

At Nodyoba, all he had was the length of metal pipe strung up in the thorny tree with an oxhide thong, and, before he had found another length of iron—a piece of rusted stake purloined from the cemetery in town—he had used a tin saucepan to strike the rod.

Only *Mfundisi* Turvey would have understood, forgiven what seemed sacrilegious, although Stephen sometimes wondered if he was making light of worship by allowing men and women into the church on Sundays without shoes, not insisting that they bring a coin for the offertory. He was not even sure, as the alms bag was passed from hand to hand and came back almost empty, that more had been added than had been taken from it.

From the start, the old men had watched him sceptically, appraising him, inching closer, backing off, conferring among themselves. The young men did not come to service at all in the beginning. They were off with their hunting and their fighting sticks into the hills on Sundays.

'It is a day the same as any other,' one had said haughtily when Stephen admonished him. '*Liphum'ilanga, litshon'ilanga.*' The sun comes up, the sun goes down. 'Why does this *Thixo* of yours not show that it is different? If it is a feast day, why do you not slaughter a goat in *Thixo*'s name?'

He did much in *Thixo*'s name, mostly alone. The daily offices, the evening prayers, his voice echoing in the silence of his little church until he fell silent himself.

On this hilltop, it was only the wind that spoke, gusting bleakly.

When the rains came, the fragile porch that shaded the veranda where he held his school collapsed, then the south wall of the church, the unfired bricks dissolving in rivulets of red. The crude arched windows splintered as they fell; the jagged stone foundation, a jaw without teeth, was all that remained.

Stephen stood among the ruins and kicked in a pane, cursing, angry, almost blasphemous. Old Dyoba was watching him. Dyoba had looked grave, uncertain. Then he started to laugh. It was unexpected, oddly affirming.

It was then that Dyoba had summoned the few young men and boys still living in the nearby homesteads to make new bricks. It was he who constructed the moulds and sent his daughters out to collect the grass to bind the mud. It was he who wrestled the frames of the arched windows into shape.

And so the young men came and Stephen worked beside them, throwing off his jacket, rolling up his sleeves. And when the day's work was done he brought his precious cricket ball from his trunk, his College cap, fashioned a spar from a broken window into a bat, cut wickets from the craggy tree and taught them the rudiments of the game, God's solemn house forgotten for a moment in the laughter of boys, Sidenge, the foolish one, grudgingly given his turn along with the rest.

Summer lingered. Stephen planted sorghum. He planted pumpkins. He planted maize.

Locusts came. The rain ceased. The garden withered in the autumn. The mealies in the lands grated their stalks together and the bergwind blew. It was a fretful voice, without the promise of harvest.

As autumn deepened into winter, Stephen shared his monthly sack of meal with his neighbours. He cooked no more than a handful of rice each day. He learned to gather imifino in the veld, like the women and girls. He had no sugar in his tea. Much of his stipend was used to feed the children at his school, each bringing a bowl for a spoonful of porridge at midmorning.

It was a Sunday when, in a distant homestead on the opposite hillside, a great gathering of heathen made a supplication for rain. Far across the empty riverbed Stephen could see a clay-clad concourse, hear the sound of singing, stamping, see the smoke rising from a sacrificial fire. He heard the frantic shrieking of a goat. The declamations— over and over—of *igqira lemvula*, the rain doctor, rising above the chant of the people.

Stephen took his service in the church, aware of the diminished congregation. With more irritation than forethought, he chose for his text:

When ye pray, use not vain repetitions as the heathen do; for they think they will be heard for their much speaking.

It was a mistake. The young men, eager for meat, eager for occasion, had already gone across the empty river. The old men had followed. Then the girls, the children, trailing behind.

Even the grandmothers.

Stephen stood on the porch of his church in his surplice, watching them. Dyoba, the warden, watched with him. 'These are our kinsmen,' Dyoba said, lighting his pipe with care, squinting up at Stephen, one eye closed against the fumes. 'They ask for rain in faith. The same as you.'

'Are you going to join them?'

'I am going to join them.'

Stephen turned back into the church, took off his surplice and hung it on a peg. He trudged up the slope to his house, took down the Latin Grammar from the shelf and looked a moment at the picture of the woman.

For once, she could offer no consolation.

When the rain came at last it would be said that the *igqira lemvula* was a man of power and skill. Stephen countered the notion with a text from the Old Testament next time the people were at service:

Our Father sendeth rain. For He maketh the sun to rise on the evil and on the good, and sendeth rain on the just and the unjust.

'If that is so,' said one of the young men, 'what is the advantage of obeying God?'

The advantage could be offered only by example.

IN TIME, ALMOST imperceptibly, when the summer rains finally fell and the river flowed once more, the mission lands began to revive. By the end of summer, the produce of the gardens was sometimes great enough to sell off pumpkins to Mr Ockert at his store. The cattle thrived. Most of the children at Nodyoba went to school. Vagrancy and drunkenness and conflict waned. When men returned from town, some stayed.

Stephen could write his quarterly report, confident enough to state: *March 1874. Progress seems satisfactory.*

The following winter was mild. Spring came early and it was time to plant again. Cattle calved. Stephen acquired some chickens and a handsome rooster—a gift instead of an offertory for the alms bag. The mtsintsi were budding and the crop of mealies had started to sprout in his garden when an unexpected letter had come from Mzamo, brought by Figlan on a visit to his people. Stephen opened it eagerly, starved of news from beyond the rim of hills. Two closely printed notices from St Philip's Mission Church were included. Delighted to see Mzamo's handwriting, Stephen read the letter first.

20th September 1874

Brother,
From the enclosed you will see that a Choir Festival is being held in Grahamstown in early December. There will be entries from all the native churches of every denomination in the region. There is even an entry from a choir in Port Elizabeth which I was fortunate to arrange when I accompanied the Magistrate there on business. The members of the choir are Nonconformists but very fine ladies and gentlemen. Some of their members toured in England a few years ago. Imagine! They sang before the Queen. I was invited to their Croquet Club. It is a game they learned abroad. I wonder if you are acquainted with it?

No doubt you have already been informed by Canon Rutherford of the date of your ordination (18th December—see also the enclosed notice). As the Choir Festival is to be held only a week before, I will arrange an extension for your Stranger's Pass so that you can come to town earlier. As you know, you cannot stay above seven days without it but if I can arrange it you will have a chance to hear my choir as well.

—*They sang in England a few years ago.*

They sang in England …

Stephen had taken his Latin Grammar from the shelf and let it fall open where the photograph was stowed: *Kaffir Woman.*

What if she were real?

It would be too coincidental to suppose. And yet, those who had been educated at the Governor's largesse, the small, select handful winnowed from the thousands, could not avoid the likelihood that sometime, somewhere, at the margins of the society that had nurtured them and then rejected them, they would meet. They spoke English to each other, took tea, sent their children to the native colleges in Cape Town or Grahamstown, formed societies, clubs and teams. Ministers, teachers, interpreters, clerks. Churchmen and women. *Abakhutshane.* The elite. They married each other, became god-parents to each other's children, kept clippings from the native newspapers about each other's doings. They were the unanticipated marvels of refinement, banded together, no longer the lonely specimens of freak shows shipped to Europe decades earlier: *The Savage Bosjemans. The Hottentot Venus.* Not quite so quaint, perhaps—but a triumph of the beneficence of God, of missionaries, of Empire. And of Exeter Hall.

And yet—if she were real she could not remain immaculate. If she were real she could not be expected to sustain that ineffable poise.

Stephen put the picture away and returned the book to the shelf.

He took up the second printed notice that Mzamo had sent with his letter. It was a circular for all parishes in the diocese. It announced the dates for forthcoming confirmations, mission visits, ordinations.

Stephen scanned it eagerly. His name would be there, in print, he and any recent graduates from England appointed to the diocese. They would be ordained together in the Cathedral. A great celebration. A triumph of the Missionary College in Canterbury. Albert's name would surely be there as well. Surely Albert would have already landed in the Cape and be waiting for a passage to Algoa Bay.

Yes, Albert's name was there. *A J Newnham.*

But Stephen's was not.

He turned the paper over in dismay.

Notice of Ordination, St Philip's Mission Church: *Mr Stephen Mzamane of Nodyoba and Mr Gideon Boom of Rabula.*

No organ, no high altar, and the Bishop in a hurry to attend the next and more important engagement. He could feel the slow blood beating in his ears. Why had Canon Rutherford not written and informed him? Had the letter gone astray?

If, at first, Stephen was reluctant to protest, blaming the post, the pressures and preoccupations that the Director of Missions must contend with, he was goaded to react when, a few weeks later, he received a letter from Albert, written over months, it seemed, and finally posted from the Cape.

> *We have a daughter! We have called her Clementine Augusta (for the month she was born). She is a bonny little creature and I am already her slave. We are obliged to stay on in the Cape until my wife is recovered and Clemmie is old enough to enjoy a voyage!*

The rest was news from an earlier time, written at intervals on different stationery, put aside unfinished, rediscovered and continued sporadically. It recalled the revels at graduation in 1873—*Finally!*—College news and then, hastily dated 'Later', describing the joys of the wedding day, the scenery on his wedding journey in England, the anxious wait for the summons to set out, the irksome duties he had had to undertake assisting Dr Wills, made especially tedious as he and Unity had been obliged to stay with her parents until they sailed. 'No larks here!'

A new page, crisper and more recently written and dated July 1874, elaborated on the voyage, the debilitating heat at the equator, Albert's astonishment at his first view of Table Mountain. He playfully quizzed Stephen about whether he had 'captured a wife'. Most importantly, Albert had been given notice that he would be ordained as deacon in the Grahamstown Cathedral.

> Hurrah! I am sure it means we will be ordained together. It looks like there will be a 'job-lot' of Canterbury men! The Bp's letter was very welcoming. He seems a jolly fellow and I am determined to like him. He has invited me to join the staff of the Native College. I shall have to practise my bowling as I have no doubt the boys are as crafty at throwing sticks as you once were! I am also directed to assist at the Grammar School and teach the colonials Latin.
>
> Now, Stephen—this is an admonishment! Why haven't you written for so long? I have been disappointed, searching the postbox every day and mooning about it as I used to moon about Dr Wills's gate before I was married (or so you said!). I have been very anxious. I do not even know where you are.

So, his letter from Nodyoba which had leaned neglected against his candlestick so long ago had not reached Albert. Stephen knew he was at fault, the delay precipitated both by shame and by a small, subconscious resentment that he had been abandoned to a wilderness while Albert would have finished the academic year, graduated with the coveted red and black hood and certificate of merit, and perhaps gone off in triumph with Unity Wills to be married. And now—the final achievement—Albert had been given the post at the Native College that *Mfundisi* Turvey had once reserved for Stephen and which, ever since, he knew had been temporarily filled by itinerant English clergymen on their way to other parishes. No colonial boy would have accepted him as chaplain, let alone their parents, no matter what *Mfundisi* Turvey said. But there was no doubt that they would welcome Albert: teacher, theological student, cricket coach, chaplain. And now a father.

What more would Albert win?

—*Please don't tell me to be grateful. I need to find another reason to be glad ...*

He sat down to write a letter to Canon Rutherford. It was polite but unequivocal. He did not complain. He simply stated the fact that he expected to be ordained with the few alumni of his College in the Grahamstown Cathedral and requested an explanation.

He sealed the letter and wrote the direction in a large, bold hand.

–*Your writing is careless, Stephen. It shows a want of discipline.*

Not careless, sir. Angry.

Too angry—though unconfessed—to reply to Albert's letter either. What was the point, he persuaded himself, of shaming Albert into admitting he'd always been aware that they'd be apart? Perhaps it no longer mattered to Albert: Canterbury was too far away, too detached from the reality of their lives.

As, in truth, it always had been.

A LETTER FROM *Mfundisi* Rutherford arrived at Nodyoba a fort-night later, again delivered by Thurston Chauncey's man, Figlan. It was a reminder of the date of Stephen's ordination and a lengthy admonition asking why he'd failed to confirm receipt of the previous notice or write to the Theological Tutor to thank him for the recommendation to proceed. Everything had been included in the postbag sent to Mr Chauncey weeks ago.

Why the delay?

—*If a notice was sent, it has not been received. And Mr Chauncey has declared he is neither a local letterbox nor the*

Postmaster General. In addition, whenever I call, Mr Chauncey is invariably 'away from home'!

Instead, he wrote a brief apology stating that, in future, Canon Rutherford should send any correspondence to the general merchants, Jacobus Ockert & Sons. He would collect it quarterly, when he borrowed a cart and went to buy meal and seed. More conveniently, one of his neighbours might be happy to bring it to him if they made the journey to town.

—Mr Ockert is never 'away from home'. He turns a tidy profit, is eager to pass on gossip and says he will find me a suitable horse.

When I can pay.

But, if there were daily vexations like the post, the scarceness of offertories, the lack of a horse or the damage done by invading locusts, they were incidental compared to the disappointment of the notice of Stephen's ordination that Mzamo had sent.

That was the real trial of Faith for Stephen.

And though his congregation collected money for the journey—tuppence from a schoolchild, three shillings from the crowd of youths with whom he played cricket and who had begun to shadow him wherever he went, sixpence from Sidenge's grandmother, eagerly proffered by Sidenge, a shy tickey from the girl who always sat demurely at the side of the second bench during prayers, wearing a quaint blue bonnet —he would be an outsider to the 'job lot' of Canterbury men of whom Albert had so gaily written.

When, at last, he set out for Grahamstown, he was given a send-off by the whole community. Old Dyoba had insisted on lending him a horse. So eminent a man, if he could not take the coach, must ride, not walk.

The children ran alongside him as he turned from the churchyard and trotted down the track, sitting as upright and as dignified as he could, quite unsure if he would be able to control the beast which, reluctant to leave home, seemed unwilling to proceed. It was some time before he could relax, sit back in the saddle and look about him, the nervous sweat drying in the warm wind, cloud-shadow drifting over him as he took the slope and headed south.

He wore his gardening clothes, his only suit packed in a bag. His smart hat seemed incongruous with his labourer's outfit but he did not want to crush it in his luggage. He knew he would have to sleep under a bush or in a donga and arrive in Grahamstown caked with dust for he would also have to stick to the sandy road rather than risking shortcuts and being lost in the thorny wilderness of the Koonap Valley.

In the evening he hobbled the horse in the lee of a krantz where grass had sprouted in the run-off from the rock face. He unpacked the parcel of food that Dyoba's wife had given him. She, with her tusk tooth tipping her upper lip, unlatching it as she smiled up at him, rheumy eyes glistening. He had grasped her hand, bowed and touched the brim of his hat. He found, too, tucked unnoticed into his saddlebag, four slices of steamed bread wrapped in a square of clean cloth. They were a touch congealed in the centre where the loaf had not cooked through, but so delicately sliced and arranged that he knew it was a gift from the girl who wore the small blue bonnet to church, who walked eyes cast down, who went unshod beneath the skirt of her calico frock, tiptoeing through the chapel before the service to polish the crooked cross.

When, late the next afternoon, Stephen was in sight of Grahamstown, he stopped in a grove of trees to change into his 'Canterbury' suit. Black jacket (courtesy of Albert), wing collar (Albert again), striped trousers and well-shone boots, handkerchief and watch chain.

He rode to Mzamo's house.

Mzamo was not there. Only his wife, Nokhanyiso.

'He is practising with the choir,' she said. 'The competition is tonight. You are to be a judge.'

'Me?'

'Yes. He was worried you would not be here in time.'

'It is not easy to simply leave my mission,' said Stephen.

'The children are without a teacher while I am away. There is no one to help.'

Nokhanyiso gave him a bucket to fill with water for the horse and showed him the stack of forage Mzamo kept in an empty stable. He attended to the horse while she made him tea in the kitchen. He came inside and went into the living room, where he was astonished at the sight of a large dresser full of ornaments which had not been there on his last visit.

'This is a fine bureau, sister,' Stephen commented when Nokhanyiso appeared with a tray and a plate of griddle cakes.

'Yes,' she said brusquely. 'They are all from England.' It was a word she weighed, almost with a sneer. 'Indeed, *kanti ke, yintoni nje ...*' They are just trinkets.

Rebuffed, Stephen watched her pour the tea and said no more.

'I heard my husband say that you are to choose the best among the glees this evening,' she said, not looking at him. 'The Bishop, *Mfundisi* Turvey, *Mfundisi* Rutherford and the Headmaster of the white boys' school are the chief judges of the rest.'

'And who is to compete?'

'Choirs from all the churches. They are even coming from Port Elizabeth. My husband has arranged it.' She surveyed Stephen's suit, said almost smugly, 'He is often in the city. He is travelling far and near with the Magistrate.'

Mzamo's importance was clear: Stephen should not presume to overshadow him.

But Stephen made no such presumption. He said, '*Kanti* —indeed—his reputation is known everywhere. If I am fortunate enough to get a copy of *Isigidimi*, his name is sometimes mentioned. I am proud to be his brother.'

Nokhanyiso seemed satisfied. She rose and left him to his tea, shying away and busying herself with her embroidery by the light of the window, avoiding conversation.

It was almost dusk when Mzamo arrived home, banging the front door behind him, pulling off his collar and scattering the studs, calling for tea and pounding Stephen's back in greeting. 'It's going to be a capital evening,' he said. 'I only hope the guests from Port Elizabeth arrive in time. I've sent a scout or two to watch for them.' He sat in a chair, wrestled with his boots, indicated that Stephen should pull them off, never drawing breath to ask about Stephen's journey, too full of details of the programme and arrangements for refreshments to be curious about anything else. He ordered water to wash, told Nokhanyiso to hurry with her toilette and, surveying Stephen's suit, declared it a touch shabby. He lent him a taller hat, a newer necktie and a silk handkerchief for his pocket. He scanned Stephen again, nodded and disappeared to attend to himself.

They drove to the church in the trap, suitably late, Stephen squeezed into the corner by the volume of Nokhanyiso's skirt and cape. They entered the porch, Mzamo leading his wife on his arm. Stephen followed a pace behind, greeting elders here and there—a hand outstretched, a respectful inclination of his head.

A whisper went about among the young people in the pews as Stephen walked behind Mzamo to the flower-decked chairs at the head of the aisle.

—Yinzwana! *A handsome man.*

—Linene. *A gentleman.*

—Not as *fine-looking as his brother, though.*

—He *is not so tall. Nor so imposing.*

—It *is because he is not proud.*

—Kanti, unesithunzi mpela. *And yet, he has real dignity.*

Women craned to see, examining his face, dipping their heads when he glanced their way.

—He *is small.*

—But *he is strong.*

—Unobulumko. *He seems prudent.*

—Perhaps.

The Bishop, Rutherford and the Headmaster of the colonial boys' College had preceded them. Three such immense figures conferring together before they took their seats: the Bishop, lean and ascetic as a holy man from the wilderness; Rutherford, stouter, tuftier about the ears and nostrils than before. The Headmaster strutted in a way that pronounced his high opinion of himself. The children might have tittered among themselves if his reputation had not marked him out as a soldier with a gun, possibly vengeful. He had often been seen wearing a spiked brass helmet when he commanded the scholars' cadet parade. He was the subject of stories to terrify small boys, both black and white, into compliance. It was said he kept a blunderbuss primed to scare away intruders from his school, especially Non-conformists.

'It will be a very long evening,' said Rutherford to the Bishop, settling himself on a chair that was far too small for his vast frame. But the Bishop did not hear him. He had turned to Stephen and was shaking him by the hand, inquiring after the mission—if Mr Chauncey had been there to hold Communion yet, if the number he expected at his services on Sunday was satisfactory.

Stephen answered candidly, avoiding a mention of Chauncey—that was something he would keep for *Mfundisi* Turvey and tea at his cottage. 'My Lord,' Stephen said at last, 'may I ask when Mr Newnham will arrive in the Colony? I have been anxious for news of him.'

'Newnham?' the Bishop said. 'Ah, yes.' Beaming kindly. 'I have not met him yet but look forward to it very much. I believe he is married to the daughter of a most eminent clergyman, Dr Wills. Alas, he has been delayed in Cape Town.' A meaningful glance. 'His young wife was quite recently confined.'

Stephen understood. They exchanged a smile. Then Stephen said, 'We had hoped very much to be posted together.'

'It was thought more prudent by the Warden in Canterbury and, I believe, by his father-in-law, Dr Wills, to appoint young Newnham to the Native College until such time as his wife has settled.' The Bishop leaned in confidingly. 'Being a married man has its constraints, my dear fellow. You are a bachelor still?'

'I am not married.'

'Ah!' A pause. The Bishop seemed unsure of whether to congratulate him or commiserate. He resumed. 'Dr Ross at the Grammar School has been in need of an assistant chaplain for some time and we were told that Newnham is a fine cricketer. That will be a very great advantage to the schoolboys. Of course, it also means he will be fortunate enough to have the guidance of the Theological Tutor once he has been ordained deacon. It will accelerate his being priested. There is such an urgent need for clergy at the larger missions now. I hope he will prove suitable. Dr Bailey says he is ... how did he put it?' The Bishop fingered his robe a moment. 'An eager young man but in need of guidance. I believe he is given to boyish pranks.'

So there it was.

Decided by the Warden long before Stephen had set sail. As Albert had clearly known. Albert's tact was circumstantial —always generous in intent—but evasive none the less.

Before he could speak further, screwing up his courage to mention his ordination, *Mfundisi* Turvey appeared at the back of the church and called, 'All stand!' Surpliced, he came slowly up the aisle, his great beard full across his chest, his black-robed choristers processing behind him and taking their places on the wide step before the altar.

Turvey bowed in greeting to the Bishop, the eminent guests and the congregation in turn. He caught Stephen's eye and inclined his head, a wide smile warming his street-fighter's face.

He greeted the gathering in English and in Xhosa, moving from one to the other without hesitation, gesturing with his hands as if drawing them to him. He invited the Bishop to lead an opening prayer. Then, consulting a sheet of paper, he announced that the evening would begin with the choir of St

Philip's Mission Church, conducted by Mr Mzamo Mzamane, 'whose musicality has been a great asset to our humble church and whose fame as a choirmaster has stretched as far, even, as Port Elizabeth.'

The congregation murmured agreement, whispered and nudged and then settled, the children hushed into stillness as *Mfundisi* Turvey took the spare seat beside Canon Rutherford, leaning forward a moment to stretch across and greet Stephen.

Mzamo pulled his jacket straight, half-braced himself before his choir, raised his hands for attention, lifted his head, his slim-featured profile vivid in the candlelight, and held a pause just long enough to fix the attention of every watcher.

The choir opened with a hymn, '*Thixo, ndamkelele kuwe*'.

Knowing each remembered word, Stephen was instantly back at Southwell with Mzamo standing to the fore, his deep bass voice filling the church.

So long ago. So long since they had walked the soles from their boots on the road to Grahamstown. So long since they had stopped and gazed—as one—at the distant sea, felt the wind coming up the *kloof*, Mzamo and Vuyo Tontsi leading the parade, punching at the air with their imaginary fighting sticks.

'Rather a noble figure of a man,' said the Bishop to the Headmaster as Mzamo bowed to applause.

'Yes,' said the Headmaster, adding as he scrutinised Mzamo, 'but an impudent fellow, I dare say.'

Stephen shifted.

That eternal caveat. *Yes, but ...*

An anthem followed the hymn, a well-known slow lament, the theme taken up by the congregation—a collective sigh, Mzamo spinning harmonies. Then a glee and then a military march, Mzamo's face damp with the effort, his eyes triumphant.

The Headmaster, who had been dozing, snapped to

attention for the last item and applauded loudly. Mzamo acknowledged his choir with a gesture, bowed to the guests. He ushered the singers from the stage, returned to the dignitaries. The Bishop grasped his hand, spoke some words of approbation. Then Mzamo took his seat next to Stephen.

The congregation stirred, murmured, settled once again. From the back of the church there proceeded a soft humming, a vibration taken up by two voices, four, eight, twelve, until the sound was made by twenty strong. The choir from Port Elizabeth filed in, robed in white and blue, each holding a lighted candle. The glow reached the arched ceiling, illuminating the groined corners; the shadow of the cross flickered out above the altar. Each member mounted the chancel steps and faced the audience as the first words of the hymn began to sound.

Stephen closed his eyes, remembering the Cathedral in Canterbury and the treble of a choirboy escaping to the rafters like a bird in flight. There were no trebles here, only the sonorous harmonies of a gathered mass of singers. And then—suddenly—one soprano whose soaring voice filled the church with growing grandeur.

SHE IS AT the back, given no prominence for her solo, her words taken up, repeated, harmonised, swelling but not overwhelming her transcendent note.

Stephen almost starts up.

That face. That serene intensity.

That face which reposes—distant and aloof—between the pages of his Latin Grammar.

Luminous. Sufficient.

She is a Chieftainess, a Princess-of-the-Sky. A Queen.

Kaffir Woman.

He can do no more than glance—for if he gazes longer she will transform from that immutable poise, that fixed ideal, into a substantial shape: full-hipped, strong-necked, sweat sheening her forehead.

Mzamo whispers loudly to Stephen, 'Her name is Elizabeth Madikane. She is the wife of the choirmaster. I have met them on many occasions at recitals and in church when I have been in Port Elizabeth with the Magistrate.'

He barely hears Mzamo telling him these things or Canon Rutherford saying to the Bishop, 'Members of this choir went to England some years ago. They even sang before the Queen.'

'Did you hear that?' Mzamo persists. 'England and the Queen.'

Stephen examines his hands, his fingers tightly inter-woven as if, had he looked, he would have been instantly exposed, found out. An object of derision. An adolescent obsession. Beside him, Mzamo has fixed his bold gaze on her face in triumph. Nor does he look away until all the songs have ended and the audience has applauded and the Bishop bowed in ovation.

Stephen only glances up when Mzamo, as their host, rises to thank the visitors for coming and shakes the lumbering choirmaster's hand.

The Reverend PJT Madikane. Her husband.

Stephen remains seated throughout the long evening of performances, making his brief remarks on the winning glees without the least idea of why he has selected them, eliciting an exasperated frown from Mzamo. When the rest have risen to file out, he lags behind in the church until *Mfundisi* Turvey comes in search of him. He follows him into the schoolroom, where refreshments are laid out on old doors for want of tables, the congregation queuing patiently.

Mzamo, holding a small plate of cake, is deep in laughter with Elizabeth Madikane. Glancing round at him, Mzamo beckons. An impatient summons. Stephen stands before her then, jostled round by the choir competitors, the congre-gation, the readers and catechists and churchwardens, thronged together in the stuffy schoolroom. Mzamo introduces him, goading him out of his diffidence, his awkward silence.

Clearly he has been mentioned before. 'Here's that brother I spoke about. Soon to be Reverend Mzamane.'

—*Wake up, Malusi. Don't stand there like an idiot.*

'How do you do?' Stephen bows.

'How do you do?'

Mzamo speaks for him, not allowing contradiction even when he makes some exaggerated claim. 'He, too, has dined in the mansion of a lord.'

—*A baronet, brother.* But Mzamo would not have known the difference.

A string of pearls shimmers at her throat. Her fingers drift lightly across them: *she has sung before the Queen.* Her hand hovers a moment at the small hoops in her ears. They are the very same rings as in the photograph.

The conversation crosses him, note for counter-note, enquiry and riposte. Her gaze—neither distant nor serene— is entirely directed at Mzamo.

Across the room, Nokhanyiso sits alone, her frock spread across two chairs, her head tilted to advantage in the candlelight.

No one has thought to bring her a cup of tea.

CHAP. 12:192

Elizabeth Madikane.

She now had a name.

All he had was the face in the photograph. Unseen by her or anyone known to her—*Kaffir Woman*.

And that voice.

She was not a songbird. Not a nightingale. Her note had soared, stooped, towered. There was a terrible beauty in that voice. And in that face.

Its confidence, its power, was what he wanted for himself. That it was some form of idolatry did not occur to him.

ELIZABETH WAS NOT the name she had been given at birth. Whatever that had been was not revealed. It was put away, like the fragments of the language she'd once known, withering from want of use. It was only her face which proclaimed another ancestry: the structure of her cheek, the slim straight poise of her nose, the undertone of deeper darkness to her skin.

A name, Elizabeth—randomly chosen at the Wesleyan Orphan Home—was entered by the city's Superintendent of

Natives in his 'Register' as he marshalled the itinerant dwellers of each locality into a rough census. How often he had thrown his hands up in despair at a name that was unfamiliar and the owner could not spell. 'God knows! What next!' Arbitrarily conferred, there were innumerable Witboois, Swartboois and Veldmans—also the names of oxen. These anonymous were further classified by tribe:

> *Kaffirs, Fingoes, Tambookies*
> *Zulus*
> *Mantatees*
> *Basotho*
> *Hottentots*
> *Bushmen*
> *Gallas and Other*

He had designated her as '*Other*'.

An orphan, a pubescent foundling, she was part of the flotsam of a port, with its stevedores and harbour workers, its chancers and stowaways, traders and hawkers; its beggars, drunks, gamblers, thieves. She was fortunate not to have been snatched for her unusual looks by one of the pimps who lurked on the quayside but spied, instead, by a matronly licensed hawker and delivered to the Wesleyan Orphan Home in Strangers' Location instead of to Gubb's Farm where the vagrants squatted.

Strangers' Location grew like a fungus on top of the wind-blasted hill above the harbour. It was the dwelling place of itinerant black labourers, consisting of a warren of temporary shacks and huts interspersed with rows of small brick houses owned by the more prosperous and settled, the law-abiding and the God-fearing—the clerks and shop assistants, teachers and interpreters, domestic workers, churchmen and employees of the Town Council. A stream ran down the limestone *kloof* where water was collected and washerwomen came from the town, great baskets of laundry on their heads.

There was a view of the bay and the far pale line of dunes to the north-east. In time, there were two or three mission chapels, a graveyard and a school.

Elizabeth was sent with the other orphans to the school where all the children from the area gathered, mixed together, every age, every language. They were taught in English by the senior missionary, Mr Edwards, and kept neat and busy under the patient supervision of Mrs Johanna Madikane, the wife of the Assistant Pastor at the mission church.

She learned to speak Xhosa at the orphanage, English in the school, Dutch in the house where she took up domestic service when she was sixteen. She was valued by her mistress: she was diligent, respectful, clean. But she was valued more by the Reverend Paulus Madikane after his wife, Johanna, had died of typhoid, acquired while catechising with her husband among the heathen at Gubb's Farm. Typhoid was endemic there. Smallpox. Pneumonia. Every affliction of the destitute—the foragers in alleys, the 'harbour-rats' who scrounged the filth discarded by the ships —was found at Gubb's Farm, leaking inexorably into Strangers' Location.

Paulus Madikane buried his wife on the limestone hillside as he had buried many other people when some new pestilence took hold each winter. The graveyard grew larger and the graves spread further among the hardy, sand-thriving brush that clung there, angled horizontal by the constant wind.

Widowed, childless, soured, Paulus Madikane resolved to take another wife as soon as decency allowed.

She would have to be a Christian. Educated. Thrifty. One young enough to bear him children, even at his age; one who would help him in his work and adorn his dignity as a minister. He looked about him, furtively at first, then as boldly and purposefully as suited both his status and his age. He was *isoka*: a person of substance. A man.

His choice was Elizabeth.

A girl of the parish orphanage, she was without the encumbrance of parents or of clan who might object to the almost thirty years between them, or turn out to be traditionalists and demand *lobola*, or impose a stream of her younger siblings to be boarded and fed, schooled and clothed, and cause the endless expense which ultimately crippled so many men of means. She was without friends, without money and without protection. She did not even have a past she cared to recall. It seemed prudent not to ask.

Mostly, she was beautiful and strong.

She would bear him sons.

She would care for him in his old age.

She could not refuse him.

Besides, sacred music was his great preoccupation and hers was the finest voice in his church choir. Even in her girlhood, her voice could rise with power and depth.

Elizabeth was eighteen when she became Mrs Paulus Madikane. Over time, she cultivated an air of authority and presence which had been stifled at the orphanage and unapprehended when she had been in domestic service. If her mistress had let her go reluctantly—'so quick and clean and respectful, so unlike most kaffir girls'—she would not have recognised her in the street in her matron's frock and cloak, with her direct and penetrating gaze, the firm rhythm of her step. Her mistress would have been aghast to know that it was the voice of her ever-silent minion that had electrified an English impresario, stranded at the port but always on the lookout for exotic African entertainments, into signing up Madikane's choir for a season in England, all expenses paid. He had recognised at once something primal and disturbing in that voice. He had written to his partner:

They may appear civilised and be upright Christians but, despite his scruples, I have persuaded the choirmaster (who is also a clergyman) that his choir should sing tribal songs, got up in skins and feathers and beads. His wife—a savage, stately beauty—will take the place by storm. He demurred at first but has made a compromise as long as they can display their range of sacred music too. We will overcome his scruples once he sees how much we can rake in with a bit of barbarism.

Even the colonial newspapers crowed their delight.

—*Imagine? England? For natives from this city! It only goes to show!*

When the choir returned a year later, abandoned by their impresario and sadly out of pocket, though glowing with the approbation of the Queen, there was a mild celebrity, soon overshadowed by opinion in the town that they had been 'thoroughly spoiled'.

—*Fancy! They have started a croquet club!*

—*They are preening in all sorts of schmatte, got, no doubt, from unscrupulous Jews.*

—*Did you see that fellow in his yellow corduroys and green jacket, thinking he looked like a toff when all he could be taken for was a cardsharp or a bookmaker?*

—*It only goes to show!*

MZAMO ALWAYS ACCOMPANIED old Haddon, the Resident Magistrate and Civil Commissioner of Grahamstown, when he visited Port Elizabeth. At any excuse—official or on business for the Freemasons—Haddon boarded Cobb's Coach for an excursion to 'The Bay'. Mzamo was always eager to go, riding on the back of the vehicle along with the other clerks or interpreters, merchants or tradesmen's assistants flush enough to pay the fare, or whose employers paid it for them.

The coach always stopped overnight at the toll-house inn at the drift on the Sundays River. Here Mzamo was usually obliged to gillie for Haddon, who took delight in fishing, telling Mzamo about the sport he'd once enjoyed in Scotland. Togged up in his tweeds and gaiters and armed with an ingenious rod that could be dismantled and stored in a canvas tube, Haddon stamped along the windy riverbank at dusk and dawn while Mzamo trailed sulkily behind, slapping sand from his well-pressed trousers. But it was a small price to pay for a week in town, and Mzamo was always a privileged guest at the parsonage of St Stephen's, where Daniel Goba, an acquaintance from the Native College days, was the catechist.

Goba took great satisfaction in showing Mzamo off in the neighbourhood. It gave him a welcome fillip of prestige, something to match the gravitas of Rev. Paulus Madikane, the Nonconformist minister with his famous choir and his large and burgeoning congregation. He could not meet Madikane at the corner shop or in the small park where the prosperous gathered without commenting about this or that in connection with an anticipated visit from Mr Mzamo Mzamane, interpreter to the Resident Magistrate and Civil Commissioner of Grahamstown.

—Mzamane's brother was educated in England, you know. He was there for a number of years.

—He is a man of great learning. Acquainted with the Archbishop of Canterbury, I believe.

—He is known all over the city of Canterbury as a very fine chess player.

—He travelled with the Bishop of Grahamstown and the Bishop of Bloemfontein. He is intimate with both of them.

Stephen would have been astonished at the embellishments which must have been relayed to Goba by Mzamo himself. Or perhaps he would have laughed—knowing it was gossip far too potent for Goba to neglect, especially in the jostle of the Strangers' Location where prestige was everything and failure to rise meant slinking back to the rural countryside or—worse—being hounded across the kloof to Gubb's Farm to squat with the heathen. Still, as Madikane hinted dourly when Goba started on the merits of Mzamane's brother, none of this was quite as illustrious as singing before the Queen, as his choir had done.

Undeterred, Daniel Goba had been delighted to introduce the handsome, urbane and charming Mr Mzamane to the members of the Croquet Club and felt some triumph in observing Madikane's sour look when his wife tipped her chin in gracious greeting and Mzamo Mzamane had lingered over her outstretched hand.

Mzamo himself had been shrewd enough to return then to Rev. Madikane, asking, with great deference, if he could be allowed to listen to his choir while he was in Port Elizabeth, even invite them to Grahamstown at some future date. 'We are deprived of excellent music,' he'd said. 'We would consider it a great honour if you would agree.'

Madikane had smiled a little condescendingly.

'It would not be the same as in England, of course,' Mzamo was hasty to add. 'But it is our duty in a colony, don't you think, to raise the standard of the music we sing and appreciate. Perhaps, sir, we could arrange a choir competition? There is nothing like a competition to rouse us up.'

The Reverend Madikane had been flattered enough to invite Mzamo to attend a service in his church at the first opportunity. Bowing courteously, Mzamo had returned to Daniel Goba, going from group to group to be introduced during tea.

He circled at a distance, a darkly handsome moth courting the candle flame.

SHE WAS TALL. Not as tall as Mzamo, but a height that was stately rather than graceful, increased by the high coiling of her headdress. Unlike the other ladies at the Croquet Club, she usually wore a cloth turban which hinted, by the way it was arranged, at her unusual descent. Her frocks, carefully repaired with invisible stitching, were acquired in England, a gift from a lady too enchanted by her exotic beauty to be denied the privilege of showering her with cast-off gowns and collars made of lace. A tuck, a snip, a stitch would make them as good as new. And then, of course, there were the pearls, so greatly enhanced in lying against the dusky lustre of her skin.

Mzamo watched her at every gathering, fingered the chain of his fob watch, approached her only in company with her husband. They discussed the choir's repertoire, his attention fixed on the choirmaster, not the singer.

'What about "The Lark"? It has a delightful melody.' Mzamo imagined her taking the solo.

'We would prefer sacred songs.'

'Handel? "Lift up your heads, O ye gates"? We have sung that on several occasions.'

'I do not know it. '

'Pity.'

He watched her in church, insisting to Daniel Goba that it was a courtesy to listen to their choir, even if they were Dissenters. After all, he would have to clear prospective invitations to Grahamstown with the Bishop. Participating in their service could not compromise him: it was the only way to judge.

Paulus Madikane was pleased by the attention, scarce as it had been since the choir returned from tour.

Elizabeth Madikane made no comment. She had a distance as unfathomable as her past.

Mzamo offered to conduct the choir one Sunday. He did it without parade or his usual introduction. The congregation, wary at first, was delighted by his modesty.

—*You would not think he was a worshipper in the English Church.*

—*And he knows our hymns! I did not think a member of the English Church would know our hymns!*

—*Uyahlonela uMadikane. Such a gentleman, so courteous to Madikane.*

But the churchwarden, more observant and less beguiled by a handsome young man, had said: *Yinkewu le.* He is a rascal.

AFTER HIS PERFORMANCE, Mzamo was invited to luncheon at Madikane's home. His manners were irreproachable, his enquiries circumspect, coaxing them to speak of England. He dared not admit ignorance of the towns or cities that Madikane mentioned. Only Canterbury and London were secure in his mind from the tales of Julius Naka and his brother. He knew, of course, of Manchester and Liverpool, where the offertories from the Native College had been so often sent at the time of the Great Cotton Famine in the 1860s and over which *Mfundisi* Turvey had fulminated to his students. His own conversation, cautious to begin with, swelled at last with stories of Stephen, his younger brother.

'Aah. Your brother is a fortunate man to have had that opportunity,' said Madikane, absently sipping soup, eyes bent on his plate.

'If you come to Grahamstown and perform at our church, I will ensure that my brother is present to greet you.' Stephen was not there to contradict him. He continued rashly, 'He was a particular friend of the chief, Joshua Morosi, who, I am told, was the finest student at the College. They used to go on holiday together. The greatest of companions. My brother was privy to all the talk of his kingdom and his future plans. It is a tragedy he died.'

'Indeed?' said Madikane, now more concerned with the mutton his wife was handing him than with a Joshua Morosi.

'He sang solos in Canterbury Cathedral,' continued Mzamo, unabashed. 'My brother, not Morosi. I am surprised you did not meet each other at some recital ...'

'And if your brother went to England,' said Elizabeth Madikane, a little archly, 'why not you?' It was a challenge.

'I was a troublemaker. My brother was obliging.' It was a disloyalty. He added in mitigation, 'He is a principled man.'

'And you are not?'

AND SO THE Reverend Paulus Madikane's choir came to Grahamstown. The arrangements and the concert's great success were a triumph for Mzamo, even if his own singers could not compare with Madikane's. The clergy were impressed. The Headmaster of the College was impressed. The Bishop was impressed.

'Cooperation between denominations is commendable.'

'Although,' commented Rutherford ruefully, 'we were shown up as rather parochial, by comparison.'

'Well, it will spur us on. Young Mzamane has done us great credit.'

'So much finery and talk of England is to be discouraged.'

'We can hardly expect the native to emulate us English and then criticise him when he does,' said the Bishop.

'It depends *whom* among the English he emulates,' Rutherford dared to retort.

Mzamo would not have cared what Rutherford or the Bishop said beyond what it was prudent to remember to his own advantage. He did his work competently, took every opportunity offered him and was impressive in his address in the Magistrate's Court, even if the more perceptive among the legal fraternity sensed a sardonic humour in his courtesies.

In his own community, after a day at work and once he had entered the thronged roadways of Fingo Village, Mzamo walked with as much dignity as he did in town but more freely, openly, shrugging off restraint, expansive in his greetings, with a frank and biting wit when he shared his news and observations with his friends.

He was a good mimic of Haddon. Of the judges. Of the junior clerks. Vuyo Tontsi and his cronies were always eager for a laugh and though they did not frequent the taverns, they often gathered in the houses of the leading townsmen where sherry and brandy were discreetly served in good glassware.

To avoid collusion in what was illegal, their wives would go catechising among the poorer folk, gathering afterwards in someone's house for tea until the men dispersed, with only the smell of tobacco as evidence of their recent presence.

Though brandy was forbidden to the black residents of Grahamstown, traditional beer was not. Many of the wives in Fingo Village—some of the most upright, the most pious, the most well connected, like Nokhanyiso—made it for private consumption. Should the Inspector or his minion, the Street Keeper, arrive unexpectedly at the door, the sight of a beaker or two of beer would be inconsequential. It was only if the addition of brandy was suspected that the beakers would be confiscated for private analysis—sampled eagerly by the Street Keeper himself—and a charge laid. But, as Nokhanyiso herself had pointed out, why should the wives who brewed the beer be blamed if a case was brought? What the men might do to adulterate the drink was not their business. Most were too shrewd to be caught.

Except when someone bore a grudge.

Then, a hint dropped to the Street Keeper—no names, no formal complaint—was far more effective and less risky than a personal accusation which might lead to reprisals or, at worst, a charge of witchcraft. The Inspector and the Street Keeper earned a capitation fee for an arrest. Why would they betray the source?

It was a fine way to dispose of jealous neighbours. It was also a powerful weapon of betrayal. Nokhanyiso knew it. Perhaps, one day, she'd use it.

IN THE DAYS between the choir recital and his ordination, Stephen avoided being in Mzamo's house when his brother was at work. He sensed that Nokhanyiso resented his presence. She was awkward, brusque. If someone called she would hurry them into the kitchen or the yard, out of hearing. Nor did her callers seem like friends. They were a motley assortment of women and girls. A little shifty.

To avoid them, Stephen took to accompanying Mzamo from the house in the morning to spend the day with *Mfundisi*

202

Turvey at St Philip's, taking a class for him, going through the translations of the prayer book, struck by the interpretation of theological concepts into Xhosa, noting them.

On the afternoon before his ordination he walked into town. He crossed the stone bridge in the dip, went up the hill and paused to examine the scaffolding at the west end of the old Cathedral. It was being rebuilt. He'd been told that a tall stone steeple would be erected, with a gold-faced clock and a weathervane.

Passing unnoticed between the busy labourers, he slipped into the church. The light was dim, a pale yellow through the simply stencilled windows, etching patterns on the floor. He sat in a pew listening to the ring of the workmen's hammers far outside, echoing faintly back from the rafters of the nave. The brass cross on the altar was plain, the embroidered frontal was a little shabby, the carved memorials on the walls were powdered with builder's dust.

He had sung in the choir stalls of the great Cathedral in Canterbury with its lofty spaces, its ancient carving, its jewelled windows. But he was not thought worthy of being ordained here.

He went back to St Philip's. *Mfundisi* Turvey was in the vestry, tinkering with the latch on the old cupboard where he kept the communion plate, muttering in irritation. 'What's the matter, lad?' he said, looking up, startled. 'Come, hold the door steady for me, that's the ticket.'

When he was done, *Mfundisi* Turvey put down his screwdriver, glanced at Stephen. 'Why so glum?'

'I wanted to be ordained in the Cathedral like the others.'

Turvey snorted. 'I was ordained deacon in a mud chapel on a mission in the middle of nowhere.'

'Did you mind?'

'I am a workman, Stephen, not an adornment. So are you.'

Turvey led Stephen into the chapel, hand on his shoulder. They prayed together then, Stephen kneeling at *Mfundisi* Turvey's side, as he'd done so often as a boy.

203

IT WAS DUSK when Stephen returned to Mzamo's house. Mzamo was not home and Nokhanyiso was in the kitchen, cooking. Stephen took off his jacket and waited in the living room, absently examining the pictures on the walls and the contents of the dresser: teacups, a porcelain lady in a crinoline, an inlaid button box, a cherub and a plumed fan.

Mzamo, coming in soon afterwards, affable in his greetings, voluble in his news of the day, said, 'Ah! I see you are admiring the ornaments. I get something each time I go to Port Elizabeth. I had advice on the purchase of every item.' Glancing from Stephen towards the kitchen door. 'Tea, my dear?'

He turned back to the dresser and opened the glass door. 'It's important to get advice from someone with discriminating taste. I can't boast of having knowledge of these things myself.' He fingered the pale plumes of the feathered fan. 'This,' opening it, displaying the ranged filigree of the ivory vanes, 'has delighted my wife's friends.'

But it did not seem to have delighted his wife.

When Nokhanyiso came in with the tea, she slyly used the edge of the tray to push the fan off the small side table on which Mzamo had left it. Stephen saw her put her foot on it. He heard a vane snap. Mzamo did not notice—he was talking again, holding forth about Port Elizabeth, about Goba and the Croquet Club, until Vuyo Tontsi arrived in a flurry of consequence and good humour.

Throughout the evening meal Stephen listened to his and Mzamo's views, their various cases, their anecdotes. Nokhanyiso was silent beside him, irrelevant, like himself, in the business of their brothers. At last Vuyo left and Stephen took a candle to his room, bidding them goodnight, closing the door with relief.

His mission had not been mentioned.

It was the night before his ordination, when what should have been a moment of shared and solemn celebration had been tarnished by gossip. The journey he had made so faithfully to this climactic point since he was nine—his pilgrimage, its anguish and its triumph—had been diminished. His vigil, reminiscent of the knights of old, prostrated before God, should have stretched peacefully until dawn in prayer and resolution, ending in a state of grace.

Instead he lay down on the bed, angry and alone.

CHAP. 13:206

The ordination. That most solemn moment. Stephen's destiny decided on the road from Southwell when Mzamo had slung his boots about his neck in anger and the mantle of preferment passed to his brother. Or perhaps that destiny had been decided far earlier, predetermined even before Basil Rutherford had found him as a child, his filthy scrap of sheepskin drawn around him like a shroud.

'God's doing, lad,' *Mfundisi* Turvey had once said. 'Believe it and accept it gladly.'

And he *had* accepted it, never doubting his vocation, bound irrevocably to his Missionary Vow. And yet, as Stephen knelt before the Bishop beside his fellow ordinand, the humbly moved and weeping Gideon Boom, he could not bring his mind to grasp the words the Bishop said.

His restless night, his sense of inadequacy, the disappointment of the unpretentious church—St Philip's—in which the ceremony was held when he had hoped to be ordained beside his friend with the pomp of the Cathedral, left him wretched with a lurking sense of failure. He had not pleased God—or his superiors.

—*Too many have missed the mark.*

He must have missed the mark. And, despite his resolution to dwell on nothing but this most sacred moment, his eyes were drawn, again and again, to the place where she had stood and sung, translated from her silence to the surge of anthems.

Transcendently real. Unattainable.

And if the tears started to his eyes as the Bishop laid a hand upon him, calling him to the service of God, it was not in being awed by the great solemnity of his commitment. It was with an unremitting sense of loss.

He stood alone, unembraced. Even by God.

And when—his Stranger's Pass expired—he took the road back to Nodyoba, he rode almost recklessly, impatient to escape the piety and self-congratulation of those who'd witnessed the moment of his ordination as if, in an instant, it had changed him into someone else.

Perhaps it had.

Perhaps there would always be a presence at his side, like his Missionary Vow, inescapable for life, waiting in perpetual judgement. The censor he could not delude. His manufactured self.

The Reverend Mr Stephen Mzamane, deacon of the Church of the Province, incumbent of Holy Trinity Mission, Nodyoba, in the Diocese of Grahamstown.

He did not look about him—newborn into sanctity—or gaze in wonder at Creation, at the vast sky, the thrusting clouds, the sweeps of shadow in the hollows of the Ecca Pass, the distant curve of the Amathole, sun-capped by the late afternoon light. He swatted at flies and cursed the horse when it stumbled. He wished he could remove his clergyman's collar, so often had he run his finger round the inner rim to wipe the sweat away.

How Mrs Rutherford and the other clergy wives in the congregation had gathered round and gazed at it, exclaiming at how splendid he looked. Mrs Rutherford had put on her spectacles and peered at him, called him 'Reverend', laughing fondly that he should no longer be 'my little Stephen'.

'Oh, he used to kneel by his bed! "God bless Stephen Mzamane and make Stephen Mzamane a good boy."'

—*How charming.*

—*How very apt.*

The conversation had swelled around him—the jovial chortle of *Mfundisi* Turvey, the Bishop's gracious haste, Canon Rutherford, particularly hearty: 'What a triumph, my lord! My first acolyte! Put in my path, I might add, quite fortuitously. A sacred moment, indeed! Well, well, who would have thought it? Such a scrap of a child we didn't think he'd last the night. Those tragic times have afforded unforeseen blessings. Consider the harvest we have gathered ... .'

Even Mzamo and Vuyo Tontsi had called him '*Mfundisi*', glowed a little with reflected glory.

AT NODYOBA IT was different. After his return, the people claimed him not for how they'd benefitted him, as those in Grahamstown seemed to do, but rejoicing in what he was. As Stephen rode up to the lip of the last hill, the horse, though weary from the long ride, whinnied an enquiry, head alert. There was an answering whinny. Back and forth, again and again. The horse broke into a trot, its nostrils dilating at the scent of familiar pasture, ears pricked for the sound of familiar hooves.

There were the people, coming from their gardens, the old women dropping their hoes, the wood gatherers hastily stacking their bundles, the children scattering from the shadow of the porch of the church.

Old Dyoba clapped his hands when he saw the collar, raised up his arms. How very fine. Such dignity. '*Unesithunzi qho! Ungumaneli wethu.*'

You are our missionary now.

IT WAS SOME weeks later that *Mfundisi* Turvey forwarded Stephen the funds to buy a horse of his own. Dyoba had collected the letter from Ockert's shop and waited inquisitively for Stephen to open it, head cocked, sensing something pleasing.

I have taken the liberty of enclosing a percentage of the offertories destined for the General Native Clergy Fund for you to buy a horse. You cannot possibly be expected to carry on your work without one. Only His Lordship is eccentric enough to tramp about the diocese on foot! Besides, as you are not yet a bishop, I cannot allow you to be the butt of jokes and a horse is one of the surest means of maintaining a becoming dignity ...

Stephen had laughed. Old Turvey was enjoying himself! He and Gladstone were little short of comic themselves—and they knew it—as they wrestled their way down the tracks in Fingo Village, Irish curses roaring out as Gladstone went one way and Turvey the other.

—*Bavela oononkala!* Here come the crabs.

Whoops of delight, children running to meet the cart and pelt alongside.

—*Mind out, sonny! Whoa there! Steady on!* Rounding a corner perilously close to tipping over.

—*Out of the way, fool!* To a wagon and oxen lumbering across his path.

There was no advice in *Mfundisi*'s letter on how to choose a horse, so Stephen went on foot to consult with Mr Ockert at his shop in town.

'How much money have you fingered from the collections, Reverend?' Ockert grinned. He knew all about the catechist, Thomas Dema. '*There* was a fancy fellow, if ever there was one!' he said. 'Never came to me for a horse. Had to ask the Colonel of the Regiment. Impudent rascal.'

Stephen humoured him. 'Which, sir? The Colonel or Mr Dema?'

'*Allemagtig!* Such a pair! One as *skelm* as the other with the brandy bottle. '

'As for the offertories,' Stephen looked grave, pretending to be serious and whispered, exaggerating wildly, 'I took three weeks' worth, which came to the mighty sum of twenty pounds.'

'Let me invest it for you!' said Ockert, leaning forward, sharing the joke, hooking his thumbs in his braces, spittle gleaming between the gap in his front teeth. He wiped his sleeve across his mouth. 'Or perhaps, next time there's a race meeting I'll take a chance and gamble on the Colonel's Arab.' He looked confidingly at Stephen.

'Seriously—are you ready for a deal? I have a grey I'd be willing to sell you. Got it up-country among the Tambookies but it's well broken in. Triples nicely. Very steady. Good teeth.'

SHE WAS A broad, handsome mare, rather spirited but sure-footed. Stephen wrote to *Mfundisi* Turvey in delight.

> I wish I could send you a picture of my horse. She carries me most reliably to all my outstations. She pays no attention to me if I sing and has never strayed when I have taken a service in a stranger's homestead. I am able to visit all my outstations within a day now. But I am in want of a saddle.

Until he could afford one, he rode like a Thembu, tripling rather than trotting, leaning back, seated on a pad of old blanket, without his hat.

Rutherford, at the urging of Henry Turvey—always tenacious on Stephen's behalf—sent an old fashioned, somewhat careworn saddle with the post-cart. After that, Stephen's seat was so upright and dignified, his hat so firmly pulled over his eyes, his toes so correctly angled that, even if he rode a 'native horse', it was not so dreadful, after all, for the Rev. Mr Thurston Chauncey to have him attend the Eucharist every now and then—just as long as he knew his place and came to the communion rail last, to prevent anyone shrinking from the chalice.

But if dignity and a handsome seat on his mount gave Stephen the appearance of manly assertion, he knew it was an illusion. His thoughts dwelt on his single state and the gnawing shame of being uncircumcised. Nor was circumcision an option—not unless it was performed in a hospital under the supervision of a surgeon. And where was he to go for such an operation? How was he to pay? Until then, he could never have a wife. And the ceremony could never be performed while he was at Nodyoba, earning so meagre a stipend.

We declare that a life of chastity for the unmarried is not only possible but commanded by God.

So had run an article in the *Church Chronicle* written by the new principal of the Native College. Stephen had smiled laconically. How did *he* know? That worthy man had fourteen children, had married a girl-bride and had himself been no more than twenty at the time.

'Are Englishmen not circumcised?' Mzamo had challenged him once, shortly after his arrival.

'Yes. Many of them are.'

'Then why should we be different?'

'It is not the fact—but the manner. The initiation school and its evils.'

'Do you think it evil?'

Stephen bridled. 'That is what we were both taught at the College.'

'You should sometimes question what you're taught, Malusi. And think of what has been omitted.'

'Omitted?'

'The things that are *not* taught rather than the things that are. We are told that our circumcision custom is wrong. *Qha!*' With the sweep of his hand. 'How are we expected to be men if we are not given a realistic alternative?'

It was a matter that Stephen could not ignore during his time at the mission. Nor was it a topic he could have raised on his own account with Dyoba or the men of his community. He knew it was something the Church expected him to forbid among the few Christian youngsters still living at their homes at Nodyoba. But how could he speak with conviction in telling them initiation was a sin? He would be a hypocrite if he insisted.

And what could he have said—what could he still say—when the old men chaffed him about a wife: *I am not a man?* Instead he would chaff back, '*Kanti, ziphi iinkomo zam?*'And where are my cattle?

They knew that it was always said in jest. It was a great bewilderment to all of them that *Mfundisi* disapproved of *ukulobola*. After all, a man would not be 'buying a bride', as the white missionaries believed, simply ensuring his wife's security and that of her children. The cattle were a pledge, not a payment. What man could forego the tribute of *ilobolo* cattle in choosing a wife?

Even a Christian.

Stephen could not explain the Church's strictures on either circumcision or *ilobolo* without perplexing and offending the older men—or arousing their scorn. Instead he had said briskly, '*Ndingumnyolo.*' I am the one who goes alone.

Knowing him, they did not believe him.

NOR DID LILY, the girl in the blue bonnet.

Seemingly deferential to his status when he first arrived—*isinono*, a learned one—she had kept her distance. But, since his ordination, she had tracked him with her eyes from the fields where she hoed, from the yard of her father's homestead as he rode past on his big grey horse, from the bench where she sat in the church when he stood at the altar in his surplice, his voice lifting at morning prayer: *Thixo ungumThixo wam, ndiyakukufuna kwakusasa.*

That bonnet, so endearingly comic atop the motley bedragglement of her outfits—all the ragtag of the mission-box—could not diminish the quiet candour and attention of her face during Sunday prayers.

If, in her piety, Stephen thought he recognised something of his own boyhood innocence—*God bless Stephen Mzamane and make Stephen Mzamane a good boy*—he was aware, too, that behind the shy demeanour, the scrupulous respect for age and station, there was also a wariness, a scepticism, an incipient anxiety which had held her back.

When he had formed a choir, many had flocked to join it, but she did not come forward like the other young women of her age. When they practised on Fridays, she had gone instead to her mother's garden and hoed among the mealies until dusk had fallen and the first star appeared. But once, coming undetected from the chapel when the people had dispersed, Stephen saw her standing among the maize stalks, her head tilted up, her eyes closed. She was singing the last hymn that the choir had rehearsed, quietly, almost in an undertone, intent in some devotion of her own. He stood still, his hat in his hand, waiting. When she had finished and bent again to her work, he said softly, 'Lily?'

She turned, startled, dropping the hoe.

'Why do you not come to the chapel and sing with the others?'

She was silent.

'*Sizakukwamkela phaya.*' We will welcome you there.

She had appeared at last, joining the women and the schoolchildren, the young men and the old. She had stood unobtrusively to the side.

Soon after his ordination, searching for another way to include her, Stephen asked Lily if she would help in dying the unbleached bolt of calico that *Mfundisi* Turvey had sent him to be made into cassocks for his choirboys. She had bobbed a curtsey and waited in the yard, not following as far as the door of his house, while he fetched the cloth. He took it down to the church, laid it out on the table in the vestry and read her the instructions sent by *Mfundisi* Turvey.

Bark was to be stripped from dark-trunked trees and boiled with the cloth in a cauldron until the colour was an even black. A pattern for a cassock was included. Stephen turned the paper round and round in his hands. 'I cannot make head or tail of this,' he laughed. 'Perhaps your mother can help me.'

Lily Majola looked at the pattern and declared,'I will do it.'

In the days that followed, Lily Majola searched for dark-barked trees near the river, working with an energy and strength at odds with her childlike frame. Stephen directed the boy Sidenge to help her but she sent him away: had she not been chopping wood and carrying it on her head all her life?

Dismissed by Lily, Sidenge helped Stephen dig a fire pit in the yard. They filled a large black three-legged cauldron with water and placed it over the flame. When Lily was ready to begin she motioned them away and fed the bark and the cloth into the pot. She stood for the rest of the afternoon stirring it with a forked branch, stripped of leaves.

From the lean-to behind the parsonage where he was repairing the benches for the schoolroom, Stephen heard her singing once again. She sang not only the hymns that the choir rehearsed but the songs and rhymes he had taught the schoolchildren and to whom she must have listened while going about her daily tasks. The notes were plaintive bird-calls drifting away with the woodsmoke. Her blue bonnet had been carefully put aside and tied to a fence post, her long skirts hitched up out of the way of the flame, her small bare feet deft in avoiding the coals.

At dusk, Stephen walked over to her. 'Come, Lily Majola,' he said, smiling, 'you have worked too long. I will help you lift the pot from the fire.' He fetched a cloth for each of them so they would not burn their hands as they heaved it aside. He brought a spade and buried the coals in sand. 'Thank you,' he said.

A tilt of the head, a small smile hovering.

'Give my best wishes and thanks to your mother for sparing you from her garden. I am very grateful to her.'

Lily lowered her gaze, turned abruptly away, took her bonnet from the fence and carried it home in her hand instead of perching it on her head. Stephen watched her go, knowing that—unwittingly—he had offended her.

His blunder exacerbated his sudden loneliness, drove it home. There was no one, he realised, who could grasp his isolation and confusion.

Not even Albert.

Knowing it, Stephen failed to write, reminding himself daily that he must not procrastinate and finding reasons to forget. How could he describe his life with any sense of intimacy or pretend any longer that he hoped Albert would be joining him? Albert would have been bewildered at Nodyoba, even frightened. All this space, this vastness, the lonely wind washing like a tide across the empty hillside until even the hard old tree began to thrash.

More conspicuously, he did not take down his Latin Grammar at night or his Greek reader, even though he had promised himself to study for at least two hours after his meal. What impact could either Greek or Latin possibly have on the activities of his daily ministry? He taught all day in his crowded classroom, tilled the garden, chopped wood, took service morning and evening, attended meetings and catechised at distant outstations, sometimes setting out just after midnight to reach Fuller's Hoek by dawn, coming home via Mazoka at dusk, hardly having time to say his obligatory private offices.

—*Forgive me, Father. I have sinned. I did not forget ...*

I was simply too tired to begin.

Nor did he have the time to write more than abbreviated reports to the Society for the Propagation of the Gospel that paid his stipend. How could he explain the meagre offertories brought to service—sometimes as little as one shilling and sixpence—when *Mfundisi* Turvey could collect a pound or two each Sunday? The Secretary would think him incompetent—but what could he know of locusts, drought, failed harvests and the scarcity of work in the nearby town? Such explanations would be seen as excuses.

He knew the candidate priests in Grahamstown were faring better, having tutorials twice a week with the Theological Tutor, borrowing books from the library at the English Grammar School. They had no congregations, no outstations. They did not have to grow their own food. Nor were they called out at night to a child burned by coals, a woman suffering from a difficult labour, a herder bitten by a snake when watching goats. He was not just the *mfundisi* but the doctor, especially when the traditional *inyanga* failed. The lessons he had learned in the Kent Hospital with men hardened from labour among the poor had served him well.

—*You have an aptitude, Mr Mana. Do not squander it.*

It was not his vocation that was slipping away. He was adapting it, as others had before him, to a life which was beyond the comprehension of the Secretary or the officials of the Society in the great, gloomy building in Gower Street in London, from which instructions came. But if the governors and benefactors and their philanthropic sponsors knew something of '*Ora et Labora*'—Pray and Work—and applauded it, what did the Secretary or the governors of the Society in England know of *ubulolo*?

It meant so much more than loneliness. So much more than isolation.

To be one with his community and, yet, to be apart.

—*Come to the feast, Mfundisi.*

—*The young girls are going to the* intonjane *dance.*

—*It is a wedding, Mfundisi.*

But a heathen one.

These were things that, as a Christian missionary, he was not allowed to do. If Albert had been in the post instead of him, he would not have been invited in the first place, would not have had to refuse, nor incurred the disappointment of his own people. Albert was, after all, an Englishman.

Nor could Albert have understood the very nature of

Stephen's isolation. Albert had a wife. He had a daughter. The chance of Stephen's achieving those for himself had become seemingly insurmountable. How could he expect any young woman at Nodyoba to grasp the complexity of his experience, share its ambiguities? Albert, on the other hand, had had the choice of countless girls in Canterbury—the bonneted troop that came to church, the daughters of precentors, tutors, rectors, even bishops. Nor was an initiation into manhood necessary, a rite of passage accompanied by secret ritual and obligation. All Albert had to do was to reach his majority.

Stephen procrastinated, started many letters but did not finish them. What could Albert know of him now, so far from Canterbury?

Or he of Albert?

ALBERT WAS TWENTY-four when he married Unity Wills. She was barely twenty. They made a charming couple and the local newspaper wrote three triumphant columns about the eminent Dr Wills's youngest daughter's muslin and lace. It devoted half a column to the future prospects of the worthy young man whose family—unfortunately—was unknown in the city. If Unity's mother thought her still a child and Albert no more than a boy, Unity was determined she would prove capable of being a wife, running a house, leaving for Africa and starting a school. 'I am my father's daughter,' she had boldly announced to a gathering of aunts before the wedding day.

'Indeed!' they'd replied indulgently.

Her mother knew better.

Unity, with her brightness and chatter, her busy housekeeping and her love of friends, would have been challenged with the economies of a rural parish in England, let alone a mission station in Kaffraria. A comfortable living in a town—in Canterbury—would have suited her best. But it was all too late. Unity's mother observed with alarm her daughter's way of insinuating her neat, small, busy person far too close to Albert Newnham when he visited. She seemed to dab at him, rather like a she-cat dabbing at a captured sparrow; she had him in thrall.

'My, she has come on!' A cousin gaping at Unity as she hustled Albert to the tea table, an intimate hand at his back.

An aunt alert in their direction. 'What is known of the young man's family?'

Unity's mother retorting, 'He is a clergyman's son.'

'Rector or perpetual curate?'

Somewhat frostily, 'Rector, of course.'

A nodding silence, heads cocked, Albert under scrutiny.

A sharp-eyed matron, 'High time you called the banns.'

Unity noticed nothing of her mother's alarm or the surveillance of the nosing aunts. How could they doubt her? She did not doubt herself. When, at last, they were married and had embarked on a lengthy wedding journey, visiting every relation that could be mustered to delay their departure, they sailed for South Africa. By that time, Unity was in a delicate enough condition for Albert to spend his time bringing her little comforts in the cabin. Everyone was most solicitous as she sat on deck with a shawl about her, stitching an infant's bonnet. But eight months hence—what would Albert do if they were posted in a wilderness three days' ride from town?

To his relief, there had been that letter from the Bishop of Grahamstown upon their arrival in Cape Town, announcing that Albert would be employed at the Native College and as Assistant Chaplain at the Grammar School, where his services were needed. An addendum: *Are you a cricketer, Newnham?* It had been a heaven-sent reprieve. Albert could break the news to Unity with unprecedented relief. 'Definitely in town, my love! Society.'

'Such as it might be!' she'd replied pertly and not as delightedly as he had hoped. 'I hear it's rather dull there. That's what the Governor's wife told me'—pleased to have been noticed by that lady and a little smug. 'I confided to her that I wished you had spoken seriously to Papa before we left England about a posting in Cape Town. He might have influenced the Archbishop. It's certainly pleasant enough, even if—as she says—a little provincial.'

'Cape Town is another diocese from Grahamstown altogether. And that's where we've been posted.'

'Well, aren't they both in the Colony?'

Indeed.

Albert swallowed his exasperation. He had given up explaining that the Colony was on a somewhat different scale from England. Two adjoining dioceses could have their sees more than a thousand miles apart. Instead, he smiled indulgently, kissed her forehead and said, 'Quite true, my love.'

His brother, Percy, had cautioned Albert in a private note: *Marriage emasculates the average Englishman! Poor old Bertie! Hopefully, you'll be saved by being called to fight off the Kaffir hordes.*

But in the event, they did not leave immediately for Grahamstown. To Unity's relief, the doctors advised against it until she had been confined. The Archbishop, if a little exasperated by the delay, directed Albert to assist at his own Native College at Zonnebloem and gain experience of teaching native lads.

There was a further delay after the birth of their daughter, Unity insisting that it was unsafe to make such a voyage with so young an infant. It was only five months later that she reluctantly agreed to embark on a ship for Algoa Bay.

IN ANOTHER WORLD, unimaginable to Albert, Stephen kept his own counsel, did his work and gave thanks when his congregation swelled. He was preparing catechumens for baptism, the baptised for confirmation, the young boys at his school to serve as altar boys in preparation for his ordination as a priest when he would be allowed, at last, to celebrate the Eucharist. He coached his choir, preparing it for the first confirmations that would be celebrated by the Bishop on his diocesan tour.

Sometimes, in the afternoons, the Christian women helped him in his garden, where he planted maize, pumpkins and beans with seeds given by his neighbours. He formed a Mothers' Guild whose duty it was to clean the church, and bought cotton print from Ockert's store so they could make pinafores for the girls at the school. He spent part of every day in his woodworking shed, teaching carpentry to the older boys and the young men who had not been tempted to the town or gone off to the diamond fields.

The children in Stephen's school always asked eagerly for Bible stories. He told them without the book, the words translated to an idiom they could understand. He was Goliath. He was David. He was Herod and the Avenging Angel. He was Moses, he was Jonathan. He was Daniel in the lion's den, his voice, in turns, secretive or grand, ringing or flute-like. He rejoiced in his own language, appropriating it from his pupils, moulding it back into the Word of God.

AMONG THOSE WHOM Stephen was preparing for baptism were a woman and a man who wished to be married and an old heathen who often sat alone at the back of the prayer meetings, gazing thoughtfully at Stephen and detaining him after service, asking questions Stephen was often unsure how to answer.

'Why is it a sin, Mfundisi, to eat the meat of a beast sacrificed at the death of a relative?'

'Why, Mfundisi, if I have a home, wives, cattle and many goats should I give it all away for some reward after I am dead?'

Two infants were also to be brought for baptism. And one young child. A girl. She was three years old.

She was Lily Majola's daughter.

IT WAS LILY'S mother who confided in him. 'Her father is Thomas Dema,' she said.

'The catechist who was here before me?'

'The same.'

'Why did Lily not tell me? I thought the child was yours.'

'How could she tell you, *Mfundisi*, when she is unmarried and has sinned, when the father of her daughter is supposed to be a man of God? And has run away, leaving her behind? Lily was almost a child herself when her own child was born.'

'How old is Lily?'

'It was at the time of the Great Hunger.'

Stephen looked away. She could be no more than nineteen.

'He was a man of learning, that Dema,' said Lily's mother. 'My daughter wished to learn. She went to learn from him. Sometimes she cleaned his house.'

'Is this why he was sent away?'

'He went himself. One night. *Wabaleka nje.*' She gestured his escape. 'He knew that Lily's father was very angry that he did not wish to *lobola* or give a cow in recompense. That Dema said he was a Christian, not a heathen who would buy a wife.' She paused, seeming shamed, and said softly, 'He said that she was just a servant. *Isicaka.*'

'Go on.'

'We wished you to believe the child was mine because we did not want you to think ill of her. She was raised to love Jesus, not to sin.' She scanned his face, hesitating again. 'That Dema was *umkhohlisi*. A deceiver. So how could my child —how could any of us—know when first you came that you were not *umkhohlisi* too?' She paused as if waiting for denial but Stephen did not protest. 'Majola said that if you knew the truth you would not baptise Lily's daughter. He said that you would chase Lily from the church. But I told him, No—this *Mfundisi* Ngesi will not stand with Dema. He is an upright man.' She searched for words. 'My heart was not easy asking you to baptise this child without telling you the truth.'

'You are right to seek the truth, mother.' Stephen took her hand briefly, reassuringly. 'Of course I will baptise her.'

'Lily is afraid you will despise her.'

'May I speak to her?'

Lily's mother was silent a moment, then she said boldly—setting watch herself, a mother first. '*Kanti uyindoda.*' Yet you, too, are a man.

STEPHEN DID NOT speak to Lily directly, sensing that actions would be more effective. He simply went about his school work, his choir rehearsals and his prayer meetings with his usual quiet humour and compassion. And, one Sunday, when all who had been prepared for baptism gathered at the front of the church accompanied by their witnesses and families, Lily stood with her parents, her younger brothers and sisters, her small daughter dressed in a newly starched pinafore and holding on to her grandmother's skirt.

When the time came to anoint her, Stephen gently led her to the table on which the vessel of holy water was placed. The child gazed round in some bewilderment, pulled away. Stephen smiled, snaring her gently, and beckoned Lily and her mother to come forward. Lily's mother lifted the child up to have the cross imprinted on her forehead, admonishing her for fretting. But when the blessing had been given and the name conferred, Stephen took her from her grandmother and put her into Lily's arms. He said, looking beyond her, raising his voice for all to hear. '*UYesu wathi kuye: "Ntombi yam, ukholo wakho lukuphilisile. Hamba ngoxolo."*' My daughter, your faith restores you. Go in peace.

Lily Majola stood a moment, the child's head laid against her shoulder, held close with a small protective hand.

Stephen turned away, humbled. Such tenderness had long been lost to him.

CHAP. 14:223

Albert arrived at last, delivered to Grahamstown by Cobb's Coach with far more flurry and a great deal more luggage than Stephen had been. They were met by the Reverend Canon Amos Beazer, a former Canterbury man and an acquaintance of Dr Wills. Albert's connection with that eminent churchman gave him a certain anticipated lustre and Mrs Beazer had taken a great deal of trouble in arranging a room in their large stone house for Mrs Unity Newnham, the great Dr Wills's daughter.

Expecting a dignified young cleric and his lady, they were taken aback by the youth and volubility of their guests and the constantly squalling infant. Despite his scholarly spectacles, his well-cut coat and sunny manners, Albert Newnham's hair stood up in the most comical way, giving the impression of a small boy who had just left the playground.

And *Unity?*

Well! Mrs Beazer kept her comments to the privacy of her bedchamber, nodding her nightcap at her husband. 'I came upon them on the landing.' She folded her hands, plucked at the cuffs of her nightdress. 'How should I put it?'

Raising a brow, Beazer peered at her over the top of his journal.

'*Laughing.*'

'No harm in that.'

'And—not to put too fine a point on it, my dear—*fondling!*'

IT WAS MANY weeks before Stephen heard of Albert's arrival in Grahamstown. By the time a letter was delivered by Dyoba with the monthly bag of flour from Ockert & Sons, Albert, Unity and their baby daughter had been ensconced at the Beazers' for some time.

Stephen could hardly hide his impatience as he exchanged courtesies with old Dyoba in hearing the news of the town before hurrying inside and closing his bedroom door, fumbling with the envelope and cutting his finger on the sharp edge of the seal.

16th February 1875

My dear Stephen,

We are here at last! Grahamstown is a very quaint place for a city. I had no idea it was so small. But it is a pretty spot and we have been most warmly welcomed by the Bishop. We are delighted with him and his family. He is nothing like an English bishop. I was told he walks all over the diocese in handmade shoes. I had a good laugh when I heard it. Imagine our Bishop at home not riding in a carriage!

We are billeted with Rev. Canon Amos and Mrs Beazer (Geezer between you and me) who are known to my father-in-law.

Here, in the margin, was a cartoon of a bow-legged pudding with a Good Shepherd hat on its head, steam billowing from its ears.

We will be guests until our accommodation has been made ready at the Native College or the Grammar School. My wife is holding out for a house on West Hill (where 'Society' lives) but it is a most unlikely development despite the influence of her vigilant papa.

My dear wife was sad to leave Cape Town where she had made many acquaintances and where I helped at the Zonnebloem College so she could rest until her confinement. We did not want to leave and make the voyage to Algoa Bay until she and our little Clementine were strong enough. I am glad to say she is already quite a favourite in Grahamstown and has been taken about by Mrs Beazer and Mrs Rutherford visiting the important people. We dined with the Headmaster of the boys' Grammar School—a most ferocious gentleman and (my wife says) 'not quite the thing' (confidentially). As this is not Canterbury she should not expect too much! Besides, the lads all seem to be farmers' or soldiers' sons and a somewhat refractory lot so they need a firm hand and I am sure the Headmaster wields the cane as skilfully as mine did.

Another drawing, ragamuffins clutching their behinds and scampering in all directions pursued by an uncanny likeness of Dr Gould at the Grammar School.

I have played cricket against the schoolboys already. They are full of high spirits and larks which reminds me of the fun we once had. Sometimes it is hard to be a serious man of the cloth!

I met your friend Mr Turvey. What a fine old fellow he is and full of blarney! The first thing he wanted to know was if I could box and recommended lessons if I couldn't.

Here another cartoon: a gnarled old gnome of a man with an enormous beard and boxing gloves landing a knockout blow to a stick figure—wholly Albert—with a crest of hair, spectacles flying.

Mr Turvey told me you were ordained deacon last December so you have beaten me to it!

Here a sketch of Stephen looking strangled by a clergyman's collar, ringed round by a choir of small, bellowing black boys, musical notes tumbling into the air around them.

Will you be able to come for my ordination in June? I very much look forward to seeing you. I believe there is to be a dinner for all old Canterbury students two days before. There will be quite a crowd as a number of them are teaching at the boys' school in the interim before they are ordained and sent off into the wilderness! The dinner will be followed by a conversatione in the City Hall with the rest of Grahamstown 'society'. I am sure you will have been notified about it already and it will be quite delightful to see you.

Stephen had not heard about it.

It was not mentioned in the note Canon Rutherford had sent with the set of chalks and other odds and ends by the same post. There was no reference to anything called a 'conversatione'. Stephen looked up the word in his dictionary but it was not there. Nor did he question Albert's spelling.

He folded Albert's letter and put it in a drawer. Of course someone would have sent an invitation. If not Canon Rutherford, then the Bishop. He had been, after all, their particular prize, their only native export to the Missionary College in Canterbury. He had once had a warm letter from Warden Bailey commending his willingness to serve at Nodyoba. He had not yet replied—how could he when he had been so unwilling and when the fear of failure and temptation outweighed commitment? He would wait and write about the ordination in the Cathedral, the reunion of the Canterbury students. He would be able to send the greetings of Canon Rutherford, the Dean, the Bishop. Albert Newnham.

He convinced himself that the invitation to the ordination, the dinner and the 'conversatione' in Grahamstown had been delayed. It would come with the next post.

He wrote back to Albert at once, the diffidence and distance he had felt abandoned in the warmth of Albert's familiar boyish humour

How could he have doubted Albert? How could he?

—Of course I shall be at your ordination. Flood or fire will not keep me away.

He dispatched the letter immediately with a boy, allowing him to take the horse. The youngster rode off, whooping with delight at the privilege. Stephen could hear his voice all the way down the valley.

In the weeks that followed Stephen awaited the posts with anxiety. In his private prayers he reverted to English and kneeled before the cross that Warden Bailey had given him. It seemed to be insurance against a looming disappointment.

The posts brought no invitation.

—Of course I shall be there. Nor flood nor fire will keep me away ...

The absence of a formal invitation worried him but he persuaded himself that Albert's letter was confirmation enough. Albert would have told Canon Rutherford that he had written. Rutherford would see no reason to write as well. Stephen vacillated between doubt and the enthusiasm of Albert's letter. His own eagerness overruled his scruples and, arranging for Dyoba to keep an eye on the mission, he set out, at last, on the appointed day.

Funds were short and Stephen had to forgo buying food along the way in favour of forage for his mare. He rode slowly to conserve her energy, threading the paths across a wild stretch of countryside, winding down into the valley of the Koonap River. At his back, the Amathole rose far away in a haze of blue, the abandoned homeland of the Ngqika, the fastness deep with forest.

Stephen crossed a ford, the water running high against the belly of his horse. It stopped, unsure of its footing. Stephen sat quietly, afraid of startling it. He allowed it to choose its way, warily watching a current coil into a pool among the rocks downstream. The water stretched out, dark and still, shaded by a deep bank. The limbs of trees, the detritus of some distant flood, rotted at its edges. It was a strangely oppressive place, silent and remote.

He recalled Mzamo telling him when he was a child that the 'People of the River' lived in a submerged world of their own with their herds and homesteads; the same who, years before, had brought the prophecies to Nongqawuse that the dead would arise, the herds come forth and all white men be driven into the sea. All would come to pass if only, in preparation, the living killed their cattle and destroyed their crops.

Without that prophecy he, Malusi Mzamane, would still be tending his father's herds on the western slopes of the Amathole, clad in a clay-red blanket, bearing his fighting sticks and, perhaps, a beaded love-token from a girl. Instead, the Reverend Stephen Mzamane was riding a horse to an ordination in Grahamstown with his vestments in his saddlebag, neatly wrapped in cloth.

He gazed at the pool, almost waiting for a figure to emerge—a man, a bull, a herd of mottled cows—feeling the tug of the current, watching its drag deep beneath the calmer surface, its final sluicing out between the rocks where it foamed brown and thick with leaf mould.

He urged the horse on, suddenly afraid. It almost slipped in the shallows at the further bank but he steadied it and it scrambled up the incline. He goaded it into a trot. He began to sing—softly at first, then shouting out a rousing hymn, the one that he and Albert used to sing so energetically, Albert conjuring up trumpets, drums and cymbals, waving his arms like a bandmaster and bursting into laughter at the grand cadenza.

Yes, Albert would be waiting, an insurance against doubt. And he, Stephen, ten thousand miles from Canterbury, armed with his language and his knowledge of his people, would astonish Albert with his stories, his experience, his insight. He—ready to show off—would take him to Mfundisi Turvey's for tea and tell the grand old man of their sporting triumphs and their friendship.

Singing loudly, trying to imagine every delightful encounter in Grahamstown, wishing them to life, he kept on moving fast, afraid to turn and gaze back at the river and its silent pool.

Stephen left the valley and joined the cart road leading across the flats. Even though he often had to walk his mare and his progress was slow, he allowed himself to revel in imagining the festivities of the Canterbury men, making jokes about the Superintendent of Students, swopping tales of the times they threw water out of the upper windows on old Blunsom's head, lamenting—with laughter—the weekly fare of bread and tea and jam pudding. Mrs Blunsom's home-made remedies, her insistence on 'sanitary movement', her 'blue pills' and Epsom salts.

—*Will Mr Mana do us the honour of telling us of his experiences in England?*

—*Gentlemen. Humbly. It was a wonderful time in my life. A privilege for which I would like to take the opportunity of thanking my Lord Bishop …*

The mare stopped, pulled at the reins to browse at a clump of grass beside the path.

—*Oh, and the esteemed former Principal of our Native Institution, the Reverend Mr Turvey, without whose guidance and support I would never have been chosen …*

Applause and approbation.

—*Mr Mana is the first African student from Grahamstown to study at Canterbury and we are delighted to reminisce with him …*

Kind words of encouragement. Nodyoba would suddenly become a station all his fellow clergy would know. They would write to parishes in England asking for support.

Stephen occupied himself with these diversions all through a cold and hungry night, sheltering in a roadside culvert where there was grass to graze his horse. At dawn, he wearily rode along the Koonap Valley, past the inn at the drift, where he begged a bowl of milk, and up the tedious hot hill to the bare crest where the bush gave way to farmland and goats appeared among the thorn bushes.

His anxieties returned.

He could feel his awkwardness, hear his hasty, self-abnegating apologies to Canon Rutherford for not being able to present an invitation. Flustered, he checked the address on Albert's letter, returned it to his pocket. He pulled his shoulders straight. He would be safe: Albert would be there.

To keep his doubts at bay, between Fort Brown and the outskirts of Grahamstown, he went through his entire repertoire of hymns. As he rode within sight of the familiar copse of trees that stood sentinel above the town, there came, as if from nowhere—unrecalled, in all the years he had been at Canterbury—the words of *Mfundisi* Turvey's recessional hymn that he and the students had sung marching back to the Native College after an evening of catechising: *Return, O wanderer, to thy home ...*

ALBERT WAS WAITING.

Almost as soon as Stephen had knocked at the front door of a large stone house on a shady avenue on West Hill, Albert had burst out with a roar of greeting. How his spectacles danced, how his hair stood on end and his stock came loose and his collar flew up and his face was flushed and damp with heat and laughter! He clapped Stephen on the back, clasped his hand and pumped it vigorously, talked so fast, so delightedly, Stephen hardly had time to remove his hat and coat and ask if there was a place to tether the horse.

'You have a horse? My, but you are an important fellow! Do you think they will give me a horse? To tell the truth—I have never admitted this to you before—but I can't ride. I am terrified of the things. They have such vicious teeth!'

And on it went while Albert summoned a groom from the stables and then led Stephen up a passage and into a hallway which opened onto a back garden. He said in a whisper, 'My host, with whom we have been billeted rather too long, is an old cove! You must excuse him. Perhaps we will have a chance to talk more intimately when we walk down to the meeting at Vestry.'

230

'A meeting?'

'Didn't you know? An urgent summons by the Arch-deacon!' He squeezed Stephen's arm. 'It's delightful to see you, old chap. Quite delightful. 'Then, pulling his coat straight, fumbling with his collar, Albert composed himself, sent a wry glance back at Stephen and opened the door onto the garden. Beyond, under a flowering tree, sat Unity with their host and his wife. A laden tea table stood between them. The old clergyman stood, came forward to shake Stephen's hand.

Stephen bowed formally.

Unity—forgetting she was not the hostess—rose from her chair. 'Mr Mana! It has been such a long time. And of course when you last saw me I was still Miss Wills. Don't you think Albert looks remarkably well?'

'How do you do, Mrs Newnham.'

'Oh, how silly of me!' She clasped her hands, jiggling her curls. 'How do you do!' Stephen bowed again. 'I was just tell-ing Mrs Beazer that the passage to Algoa Bay was simply frightful! The ship pitched so much we almost fell out of our beds. I was laid up at least a week.' She laughed, a tinkling little scale of self-mockery. 'Poor Bertie! He ran about all day attending to me and little Clemmie. Didn't you, Bertie?'

'Perhaps we should introduce our friend to Mrs Beazer, my dear.'

Their hostess remained in her seat, her eyes alert. Already, she was wondering what would become of the china cup their guest would use. Her husband, sensing her concern, said abruptly, 'I fear there is no time for tea. We must be at our meeting in half an hour. It is a stiff walk and I still have some notes to complete. It is a pity you arrived so late, Mr Mana.' A tone of admonition.

'I had no change of horses,' said Stephen respectfully. 'We walked for much of the way.'

A silence.

'Well, that settles it, then,' said Albert. 'I wonder if we two oughtn't to start for town at once.'

The irrepressible Unity broke in. 'We made splendid friends on the ship to the Cape, didn't we, Bertie?' She turned to Canon Beazer, smiling prettily. 'Don't you find people particularly kindly on long voyages, Mr Beazer?'

'We really must go, my dear,' said Albert, taking her hand and squeezing it rather fiercely.

They escaped and Albert jingled the coins in his pocket. 'A quick visit to the tea shop. I spied one only the other day and it's just down the street and around the corner from the church.'

Stephen put his hand on Albert's arm. 'Not today.'

'We have more than enough time.'

Stephen smiled. 'They wouldn't serve me.'

Albert seemed bewildered. 'Why not?'

THERE WERE NOT enough seats at the meeting. Albert, quick to notice Stephen's discomfort—for he held back at the door—gave up his chair and slipped onto a bench beside one of the young student masters from the school. Stephen bowed formally to those around him, shook Canon Rutherford's hand.

'Ah, Stephen, I did not expect to see you. You have come all the way from Holy Trinity. I trust there is someone in charge and you have not left your post unattended?'

'No, sir,' said Stephen, his voice low, aware of the eyes of the gathered clergymen. 'I made all the necessary arrangements. 'He clasped his hands before him, just as he had done at school, an instinctive deference. 'I came to celebrate the ordination of Mr Newnham. He especially wrote to me ...' He went to the end of the table, the starch of his collar damp against his skin. He could feel the sweat at his back, the heat of his thick serge trousers.

—*I did not expect to see you.*

He glanced at Albert, but Albert, it seemed, had not heard. He was scanning a photograph his neighbour was showing him, smiling, patting the man on the back. 'Charming, really charming. 'A conspiratorial grin.

The Archdeacon called for silence and the opening prayer.

Stephen did not hear his words. He reached for his handkerchief to wipe his face, aware of the fresh, strong smell of nervous sweat. He dared not move. He raised his gaze to the framed portrait of the Bishop, hanging on the panelled wall.

—*What lions they will be*, he had said when the African students embarked for England.

Would he say that now?

The Archdeacon consulted his papers, ran his finger along his agenda and then remarked quietly, 'My Lord Bishop sends his apologies.' He drew his chair closer to the table, seemed to cast about for words. It was unusual for so measured a man. He folded his hands. 'It is my painful duty,' he said, 'to report on the reason for His Lordship's absence and I would urge each one of you to keep what I have to say absolutely confidential, though I fear it is only a matter of time before the newspapers pick up the scent.'

'Slanderers,' said Rutherford under his breath. 'They are already on the trail.'

Everyone was suddenly alert.

'His absence impinges on us particularly,' resumed the Archdeacon, 'as it seems it may be necessary to postpone Sunday's ordinations until he returns. He is doing his best to be home by tomorrow but it may not be possible.'

A general hubbub around the table.

—*Surely not!*

—*My people have come from Cape Town for the occasion!*

—*Who will run my parish if it's delayed? There is no one but me.*

—*What could have called him away at such a time?*

'The Bishop has gone to Bloemfontein at the request of the Metropolitan to investigate a matter, the delicacy of which it is difficult for me to describe and greatly painful for me to contemplate.'

There was no sound in the vestry.

'My Lord Bishop of Bloemfontein ...'

Rutherford snorted and gazed disdainfully at the opposite wall. 'It has been reported on reliable evidence,' resumed the Archdeacon, 'that my Lord Bishop of Bloemfontein ...' He hesitated. 'Has been consorting with a young member of a missionary brotherhood under his control. They were found —how can I put it? A case of in *flagrante delicto*.'

Stephen looked across at Albert, bewildered. Albert fiddled with a pencil, ran his hand across his cockscomb of hair.

'Surely not!' exclaimed an elderly clergyman. 'An English bishop! It's a slander broadcast by unscrupulous persons ...'

'I wish it were,' said the Archdeacon. 'The case seems quite clear. His Lordship has already admitted guilt, packed his bags and is preparing to depart for England. His only plea has been that no action should be taken against the brother.'

'On the contrary!' exclaimed Rutherford. 'I trust that he has already been arrested. These brotherhoods, like their Popish counterparts, are rife with vice. It's a scandal.'

'Gentlemen ... ' The Archdeacon's calming voice. 'His Lordship of Bloemfontein has taken full responsibility. There is no more to be said. Fortunately, his departure for home will obviate our own bishop from acting further. Justice will be in the hands of the Church in England.'

'But what about his accomplice?'

'I don't know if "accomplice" is quite the word,' said the Archdeacon.

'It's a crime. Of course he's an accomplice.'

The Archdeacon tapped the table. 'You can all imagine what a sensation the local press and society at large will make of this and, unfortunately, how the prejudice of members of other denominations may rejoice at our disgrace.'

'It's the Puseyites I blame,' lamented one of the curates. 'My brother at Oxford warned me about it long ago. In his last letter he wrote—'

'No one is to blame,' said the Archdeacon evenly. 'And it is for God to judge. We should pray together now for the redemption of the Bishop of Bloemfontein and continue with our business.'

'I don't think we should consider him a bishop any more.'

'He has not been tried, formally charged or excommunicated,' said the Archdeacon. 'Until then, it is not for us to speculate.'

'I won't pray for a sodomite!' exclaimed the Headmaster of the colonial boys' College. 'And nor should any of us. It's the Devil's vice we are condoning.'

The Archdeacon silenced him with a glance. 'We are not condoning it. But nor should we be guilty of bigotry.'

The tide of words ebbed. Stephen scanned the faces of the men around the table, all absorbed in private thought, each unable, it seemed, to meet another's eye.

A sodomite?

A word he had only heard spoken in an undertone. Something perilous—to harrow up the soul? In awe, he cast his mind back to the youthful Bishop, the windswept afternoons when the deck was almost empty, doused in spray, and he and the young missionary brother paced the decks or stood together staring out at the sea—a confluence of gesture that seemed to need no words. He remembered their slow retreat up the companionway, the discreet closing of the door. He remembered most the Bishop's troubled, wary eyes.

—It is for God to judge.

He wondered if God was judging him as well, his thoughts of another man's wife.

Was loneliness—or love—so easy to condemn?

THE MEETING ENDED late. Albert and Stephen hurried away together. Agitated, Albert whispered, 'I must get back to Unity, old chap. I promised I would help her prepare for the conversazione. She's very anxious not to put in a poor appearance. It seems … ' He was blustering, tripping over his words as he often had when he was embarrassed. 'It seems, old chap, that the merchants' daughters are all very fashionable. She's especially keen to appear to advantage, as there may be dancing and it will be her last chance.' He glanced at Stephen. 'You once told me dancing is very much frowned on, so once I'm ordained she'll have to sit out with the Mrs Beazers!' He grinned wryly. 'Also playing cards.' He hurried on. 'Did you know, the former Bishop often played at cards? I heard Mrs Rutherford telling my wife as if it were a scandal. He sounds a good sort to me. I didn't mention that I had two unopened packs in my trunk!'

'That's not what you wanted to say,' said Stephen.

Albert ran his hand over his head—that familiar perplexity. 'No.'

'Well?'

'I feel wretched,' he said, turning to Stephen. 'I expected that you would be invited to stay with us. After all, the house is so big and I mentioned what a close friend you were. I showed them your letter—well, the bit about not being kept away.'

He did not mention that Mrs Beazer had been perfectly prepared to accommodate a young man from Canterbury until her husband quietly informed her that he was an African.

But Albert had no need to mention it to Stephen for Stephen was already a step ahead. One glance at Albert's hostess had been enough. She was a colonial. No black person would be staying in her home. What, after all, would become of the sheets? He said lightly, 'Oh, I didn't expect that. I had already written to my brother, Mzamo, to tell him I was coming. It was a chance to see him too.'

Whether Albert believed him or not was irrelevant. He grasped at the excuse with relief and said, 'Of course, how silly of me. How could I monopolise you? It will be a fine thing to see your brother.'

As they reached the gate of the house, Stephen asked, 'What is this "conversazione" we are going to after our dinner?'

236

'A rather grand way of describing a social gathering where the tone of the conversation is supposed to be dazzling! I am sure it never is but the punch is usually rather good. They get the town hall up like a drawing room and everybody sends a piece of furniture. I had to help the vicar carry down their best settee and a big brass pot of ferns this morning. When you see it you'll believe we are back in one of the smart houses in Canterbury.' He laughed. 'Well, almost.'

They entered the yard and Albert went to call for Stephen's horse. A sash flew up and Unity thrust out her head, covered in curling papers. 'Bertie? Where have you been?' She peered down, saw Stephen. 'Oh, my goodness! Mr Mana! Do send Bertie up! I knew he would be dawdling all around the town. He has picked up your bad habits and has no idea of time!' She fluttered her hand at Stephen, meaning no offence.

'We couldn't get away until everyone had had his say. Blame the Archdeacon,' replied Stephen, raising his hat.

'There you are! I always said it! Men are much worse gossips than women. But they won't admit it!'

Albert appeared with a groom leading Stephen's saddled horse.

'Bertie!' The light-hearted banter gave way to a tone of vexation. 'Do hurry in. We will be late. And you must change your collar before you go to your reception. You look worse than a schoolboy.'

Stephen mounted his horse.

'I'll see you at the dinner,' said Albert, starting indoors. 'I'll keep a seat beside me.' He cast a glance at the open upper window. 'Oh Lord, I shall be in hot water!' He fled inside.

Stephen trotted down the road. He pulled up at the corner, out of sight of the house, hesitating. Mzamo was not expecting him. Stephen knew what he would say when he saw him:

—So, Malusi, you arrive without warning. Second choice, I see?

—It was a sudden journey.

Mzamo would look at him with that shrewd scepticism, instantly grasping the situation. No doubt there'd be some satisfaction in catching him out.

But, at heart, Stephen knew that his real motive for avoiding Mzamo was the issue of the former Canterbury students' dinner. He had been a coward and a fool to think Mzamo would be ignorant of it. It was likely that even the bill of fare would be published in the newspaper along with the speeches and the list of guests.

Mzamo might dismiss it as if it did not matter. But it did.

—*It should have been me.*

Yes, Stephen knew that too.

CHAP. 15:239

Mzamo's house seemed deserted. Stephen dismounted from his horse, tethered it to the gatepost and tapped with his cane at the front door. He waited some minutes then walked around the side and into the backyard. Nokhanyiso was taking down washing from the line. Her hair was unkempt, she was barefooted, her frock was pulled up to her calves and bunched at her waist.

'*Molo Mlanyakazi.*'

She spun round, startled. '*Ewe.*' She put her hand to her hair, loosened her skirts.

'How are you?'

'*Akukhonto.*' There is nothing.

'Is my brother in?'

'He has gone to Port Elizabeth.'

'Why has he gone to Port Elizabeth?'

'He has gone with the Magistrate,' she said, eyes averted, clearly discomposed by her appearance.

'When will he be back?'

'How can I know? It is men's business.'

'And your people? I bring my greetings to your brother, Tontsi.'

'He is at his home,' she said. 'I can call him if you wish.'

'I have a difficulty,' said Stephen. 'I have nowhere to stay tonight or tomorrow, nor do I have a Stranger's Pass. I need to wash and change my clothes.' He did not mention that he had not eaten since he had left the house at Nodyoba. 'I have a dinner in town. I must be there at seven o'clock.'

'I will speak with my brother, Tontsi,' she said.

She led him into the house. She fetched a cloth and basin, drew a bucket of cold water from the pump and brought them to the room where he had stayed before.

She went to her own room. It seemed a very long time before she emerged dressed in a cape and wearing button boots. She had wrapped her head in a turban of grey silk. 'Ndiya kwaTontsi,' she said. I am going to Tontsi's place.

Stephen had no choice but to wait.

It was almost an hour before Vuyo Tontsi appeared. The same hearty Vuyo Stephen had seen the night before his ordination except that he had grown even stouter. Perhaps prosperous would have been more apt. Stephen shook his hand.

'My dear fellow,' said Vuyo. 'How good to see you. What brings you here? I had no news that you were expected.'

'I wasn't,' Stephen said. 'Something has come up that needed my immediate attention.'

'Oh, we are all so pleased with you!' His voice, as once it had boomed round the dormitory, filled the room with largesse and authority. 'Believe me—the Bishop, *Mfundisi* Turvey! Every boy at the College. You are famous among us all.' He turned to Nokhanyiso, almost scolding. 'Sister, get along with you. We will take a glass of cordial.'

'I have to be at a meeting in town in less than an hour. I will be late,' said Stephen.

'My good fellow, there is no harm in being a little late. Except for an Englishman.' Vuyo beamed at what he perceived to be a joke.

Nokhanyiso brought glasses and a jug and a small plate of biscuits. Politeness prevented Stephen from reaching for

240

them hungrily but Vuyo helped himself and sat in the largest easy chair. 'Tomorrow you will dine with us and be a guest in our house,' he said. He cast a glance at his sister. 'I think you will be more comfortable and less inconvenienced.'

'I am not inconvenienced. I am disappointed, though, that my brother is not here.'

'Did he not write?'

'No.'

'He was always very bad at writing. I told him many times. Especially when a fellow writes with such a skilled hand.'

'Why has he gone to Port Elizabeth?'

'He is indispensable to the Magistrate,' said Vuyo. 'He has made himself so. Our Magistrate is acting in Port Elizabeth while their man is on furlough.'

Ah, the lessons of the Native College: the lists and lists of useful words and phrases handed out each Friday to be learned on Saturdays after sport!

Furlough: leave of absence; home leave.

—The Principal is on furlough.

—A furlough is granted every five years.

—Without the benefit of furlough, how can a man withstand the climate of the Colony or the isolation from his own people?

'He is also in communication with Rev. Paulus Madikane, the choirmaster,' said Vuyo Tontsi. 'It seems he wishes to arrange another competition. He said he was particularly struck by Madikane's choir when it was here ...'

Stephen caught Nokhanyiso's quick, unguarded glance. She rose and left the room. Stephen was immediately aware of the slow, dull thud of the pulse in his throat: that fleeting instinct; that age-old intuition. He took up his glass, emptied it, needing to escape. But Vuyo Tontsi became even more loquacious as he continued to sip his drink. At last, Stephen sensed the moment he could leave without giving offence, said his goodbyes swiftly, courteously, and, abandoning the idea of saddling up his horse, all but ran down the hill towards the town.

241

THE DINNER FOR the former Canterbury students had been held in the hotel. It had almost ended by the time Stephen reached the lighted doorway. The vestibule was empty and he mounted the staircase guided by the sound of an elevated voice and the murmurs of laughter from an audience. A sudden, short burst of applause, a communal guffaw, a cheer subsiding into a respectful silence as the speaker continued.

Stephen hesitated outside a double panelled door, pushed gently until it opened a fraction. Through a crack he could see into the assembly room, the long draped tables, the plates and glasses, the dozen black-suited men lounging back or leaning forward eagerly.

Somewhere beyond his gaze was the speaker.

To creep in would be worse than arriving late for Divine Service. People did not turn around in their pews to stare: it would signal their own inattention. But here, every eye would fall on him. The speaker would pause reprovingly.

That irremediable national fault: failure to be punctual.

Stephen suddenly felt resentment rather than shame. What could these men know of the distance from Mzamo's house, the formalities in seeking shelter, the rudeness of hurry, the necessity of accepting food, inquiring into the health of every family member, deference for a senior, the instinct for when to go without offence?

The delicacy of respectful, patient silence.

If he entered the room now there would be a reaching for pocket watches, as if he had defied the starter at the line-up of a race. He stood, hand on the doorknob. A last round of applause, three cheers, a return to the hum of conversation, the chime of passing plates. He turned away and sat on a decorative chair in a corner of the hallway.

His hunger was acute but so was his exhaustion.

He was awoken, starting up, at the sound of scraping chairs, then a silence but for the drone of a protracted grace. A tide of voices as the doors were pushed back and men— Albert among them—hurried out and streamed downstairs, eager to get to the conversazione in the town hall. Halfway down the steps, Albert looked up and saw him. He turned and shouldered his way back through the throng.

'Where on earth were you? I waited outside for ages till I had to go in.'

'It's too difficult to explain.'

Albert looked at him quizzically: *Ah yes, Stephen, you have lost your watch again!* 'I bet you haven't had any dinner.'

'No.'

'Well, that's rotten,' said Albert, taking his arm and all but dragging him into the emptying room. 'Here,' waving his arm at a waiter, 'leave that cheese, will you? My friend hasn't had his dinner.'

The servant looked askance, started to object. 'The Reverend here was delayed,' said Albert firmly. He took up an empty plate, tipped it to the candlelight to ensure it was clean and claimed the cheese platter. He strode over to the top table and inspected the serving dishes. 'This really is a scrappy affair,' he said apologetically. 'But I dare say we can get up something half decent and there will be refreshments in the town hall.'

Stephen did not stop him. He was almost faint with hunger.

'There,' said Albert triumphantly. 'Looks a whole lot better than what we had at College—if not too artistically arranged!'

Stephen laughed. Bread, cheese, pickles, cold potato and a random slice of meat.

'Bad luck you missed the pudding,' Albert said. 'Not a piece of fruit pie left, not a dash of cream! Everyone gorged like schoolboys!'

Out came the pocket watch. 'Oh Lord, Stephen! Unity— Miss Wills'—he laughed—'I mean, my wife, will behead me if I am another minute late.' He clutched his throat theatrically and staggered.

'Go,' said Stephen. 'I will meet you there.'

'You will allow this gentleman to finish his dinner,' said Albert loftily to the waiter who was eyeing them as he cleared the plates. 'The Bishop would be most annoyed if he heard he had been inconvenienced.' He spun on his heel, winked at Stephen, suppressed a laugh and flew from the room. Stephen could hear him descending the stairs two at a time.

Aware that the waiter was watching him with undisguised suspicion, Stephen said an elaborate grace, even making the sign of the cross, and settled to his meal. He dared not hurry and lose face. He contemplated each small portion, wishing he could gather up the discarded serving dishes and forage for more.

At last he laid his knife and fork aside, bowed his head for another grace and, glancing up to ensure the waiter noticed, crossed himself again. Then he took up his hat, signalled that he was finished and left.

He maintained the dignity of the dining room all the way to the town hall.

There was bunting and a garland at the entrance, carts and carriages and traps drawn up in the square. Light shone brightly in the doorway and Stephen could hear the orchestra tuning up. He took his hat from his head and stepped into the vestibule.

He was stopped by a man in livery. 'Sorry, you may not go inside.'

'I am a clergyman,' replied Stephen politely. 'My colleagues are waiting for me.'

The man surveyed Stephen, hesitated, suddenly unsure of what to do.

Stephen said calmly, 'If you would just call Mr Albert Newnham, who is inside, he will vouch for me.'

He was almost jostled by a group of guests sweeping past. Among them was Canon Beazer, Albert's host. He was about to call out but Beazer hurried on, head averted—the swift reaction of a man not wishing to be caught avoiding him, Beazer's voice suddenly loud and hearty.

Stephen watched him disappear through the arch. The message was clear. He should have had the foresight— should have known—to keep away.

Mzamo would not have kept away. He would have walked in with a flourish, handed his hat and stick to an attendant and gone straight to the Archdeacon to greet him and announce his presence.

Stephen did the same.

Except that no attendant took his hat and the Archdeacon, though he greeted him graciously, clearly struggled to remember his surname, failing to make the necessary introductions to the few clergy gathered round him.

Stephen bowed slightly and backed away. He looked around for Albert. He was laughing with a group of young men, Unity twittering among them, flirtatious, pert.

'Stephen!' Albert caught sight of him, hurried over and took him by the arm, steering him towards the company. 'How was your dinner?'

'Splendid.'

'I'm sorry I couldn't stay with you. Unity ... my wife ... sometimes she is a little shy with newcomers, you know. I couldn't leave her.'

Stephen forgave him: it was the raw young curates standing around her who were shy. She dipped and bobbed merrily among them, teasing them in and out of their awkwardness.

'Ah, Mr Mana,' she said gaily, as they approached. 'Here you are at last! Albert said he was quite bothered when you didn't appear for dinner.' Coquettish. 'Where *have* you been?' She tapped him with her fan admonishingly, as if he had been a mischievous schoolboy playing truant.

Stephen could find no light riposte. He bowed quietly to the group, recognising none of them.

There was a moment's silence. Then Albert said, 'Stephen here is a splendid cricketer. I am hoping we can get up a

245

game while he's in town. He'll certainly put us on a winning streak. What do you say, Stephen?'

'I haven't had a game for so long, I fear I'd disappoint you all.'

'No cricket in your parish?' said one of the strangers.

'Sadly, no.' Stephen smiled. 'Perhaps one day.'

'We should have enough fellows about these parts to have an old boys' team from Canterbury,' Albert hurried on, goading them all into conversation.

'We'd be scratching for eleven,' said one of the young men sardonically. 'We'd have to ask Beazer to be opening bat!'

They all laughed: Beazer had long been the butt of old-boy jokes.

'Did you hear about the time,' Albert began, 'when Geezer was playing for the College ... What was the story now ...?'

'Bertie! Really!' Unity took him by the arm. 'I cannot stand here listening to this nonsense about cricket. You haven't even said good evening to Dr Gould yet, or the Dean, and I have it on good authority that if you want to shine in Grahamstown you should not offend the Dean.' She fitted her neat, gloved hand around his elbow, gave it a fierce little tug and led him away.

The awkwardness returned: a remark from one young man to another, a laugh from a third, the small group shifted imperceptibly and Stephen, taking his cue, stepped away. He stood near a large pot of ferns, his hands behind his back, unnoticed.

Where was *Mfundisi* Turvey?

He scanned the room but he was nowhere to be seen. Nor was Mrs Turvey among the elderly ladies seated on the sofas. He glanced across at Albert. He was listening to Dr Gould from the Grammar School. By the way he was standing, rubbing the front of his shoe surreptitiously across the back of his ankle, Stephen knew he was trying to escape.

But there was no escape.

There was the Dean and the Precentor and Canon Beazer,

Unity aglow among them all: Dr Wills's charming daughter, no matter what Mrs Beazer had confided to the wife of the Dean over tea.

Stephen stood watching the company, the ebb and flow, the gusts of laughter, the treble of the young women's voices, the fiddler tuning up. A clergyman, balancing a glass and a plate of dainties on his way to join a group, greeted Stephen in passing and Stephen stepped forward, saying, 'Excuse me, sir. Have you seen the Reverend Turvey here tonight?'

The man paused, guarding his glass from spilling, smiled briefly. 'Didn't come. They say he was called away to someone who was dying.'

Stephen took up his station by the pot of ferns again.

—*We are delighted to welcome Mr Stephen Mana, our student from Canterbury …*

—*Tell us of your impressions of England, Mr Mana.*

—*And Dr Bailey.*

—*And the Cathedral.*

—*We hear you are a splendid cricketer. What an asset you will be.*

An elderly lady caught his eye, beckoned him. 'There are guests waiting to be served,' she said a little huffily. 'Perhaps you could fetch a jug of punch and some glasses. Be sure to bring a ladle.' Turning to a friend, 'It's usually rather sour, dear! It always needs a good stir.' Back to Stephen. 'Thank you.'

He walked away, collected his hat and coat and went instead to Vuyo Tontsi's house.

'MY DEAR FELLOW,' said Vuyo as he opened the door, his collar unstudded, his shirt tails out, his braces hanging loose from his waist. 'You find me in a state quite improper to receive you.'

'*Hayi, mfowethu,*' said Stephen, replying in Xhosa. 'I find I am a bullock in the wrong byre. Or, perhaps, simply an ox.'

'There is no shame in being an ox—you Ngqika, *ningabantu basemNzwini,* the people of Rharhabe's ox.'

247

'I had forgotten. '

Vuyo burst out laughing. 'The big *Ndaba* in the town hall?'

Stephen shrugged. 'This is not England. I am back in the Colony.'

'And you were left to talk to the kindly spinsters—or the servants bringing in the food, never daring to take a seat.' He drew Stephen into the room towards a chair by the fireplace. 'Besides, there would have been no meat—and what is a gathering without meat?'

'Cake and punch, I believe. '

'Women's food!' scoffed Vuyo. 'A drink?'

'A cup of tea would be most welcome.'

'Tea?' Vuyo laughed again. 'When your brother and I meet to talk we take brandy, not tea.'

Stephen did not insist. He sat with the untouched brandy glass beside him and let Vuyo Tontsi talk: old stories, jokes, wounds, misunderstandings, wisdoms, fears; the life that had been suspended while he had been in England, that had been taken up and lived here in this small town at the edge of its vast frontier—its ambiguous desires, its promptings, its pretensions, its perennial disappointments.

'After you left,' Vuyo Tontsi said, 'when you went off in the coach to take the ship to England, there was a terrible storm here in Grahamstown. There was hail thick on the ground all over the vegetable gardens at the College. It ruined the crop. That night there was a gale. You remember the big tree at the end of the vegetable garden where we used to sit and study? It was struck by lightning. I remember that one of the other students said, "It's a sign!"' Vuyo paused and took up the bottle and refilled his own glass. '"No good will come of this. It is not God's will." And I said, "What is not God's will?" And he said, "Sending our people to England. It is a sign." I told him he was an old heathen. I asked why God should be angry and he said, "Perhaps it is the ancestors, *iminyanya*, who are angry."' Vuyo turned to Stephen, holding his glass in both hands. 'We were never to speak of ancestors, you remember?'

'I remember.'

Vuyo Tontsi took a sip of his drink, held the brandy in his mouth a moment, swallowed. 'But Mzamo did speak of them before he went away from the College. He said to me once, "My father believes in our ancestors. Why shouldn't I?"' He turned and looked at Stephen a moment, scanning his white stock, his buttoned jacket, his carefully groomed hair. 'Mzamo may be an elder in the church here now—oh, he is very high in Church circles, believe me—but I sometimes wonder.' He swirled the liquid around in his glass, examined it against the light. 'I don't suppose you know, but recently he has been helping *Mfundisi* Turvey and also *Mfundisi* Rutherford with the translation of the prayer book into Xhosa. He was chosen even though he is not in Holy Orders because his English is so good through his work with the Magistrate. People go to court especially to hear him speak. I think he annoys the Magistrate by being so much more entertaining than he is!' He glanced at Stephen ruefully. 'Also, there has been no better choirmaster until those English singers from Port Elizabeth won the competition. Now, I suppose, being Mzamo, he will have something to prove.'

'What?' Stephen reached for his glass.

'That whatever is English isn't always better.' Vuyo Tontsi turned to him. 'Now that you're back, you'll have something to prove yourself.'

'I only need to prove myself to God.'

'Nonsense, *mfondini!*' Vuyo drained his glass. 'You have a duty to your people too. That is why God chose you.' He stood unsteadily, leaned against the mantelpiece and poked at the fire with a stick. 'You have unimaginable power right now. You know the English. You *are* an Englishman yourself. You understand their deceit better than anyone. Nor would they have cause to distrust you as they might Mzamo—after all, you are a priest.'

Stephen glanced away: so was the Bishop of Bloemfontein.

'Of course,' Vuyo waved an arm, almost knocking over the bottle, 'Mzamo's work on the prayer book has helped his reputation as a *Kholwa*.' He lowered his voice—a conspirator. 'But being a believer does not stop him from being a Ngqika first. Unfortunately, *Mfundisi* Rutherford's Xhosa is becoming so fluent as a result of Mzamo's teaching that he can understand rather too much of what Mzamo says when he takes a meeting or writes for the native newspapers! First *Mfundisi* said he was guilty of heresy. Now he says it is sedition.' He refilled his glass. 'Let me see—what did Mzamo reply?' His words were becoming thick. '"We will wait for judgement, sir. It may be a long time coming. But it will not be called either heresy or sedition then."'

Stephen picked up his drink. The unfamiliar taste. The sting in his throat.

Vuyo continued. He had begun to repeat himself. 'You are less impetuous than Mzamo. Instead of blowing up a great wind as he does, you can, more discreetly, let us know which way it blows—*sova singasemoyeni*,' he repeated meditatively. 'No one among our people has such knowledge of *ubuNgesi* as you. It could be used to great advantage.'

Stephen returned the glass to the table beside him, sliding it towards the lighted candle. Treachery? Betrayal? Was there a difference? Some refinement in degree?

'Englishness is not that easy to understand,' he said.

'Why not?'

'I cannot tell any more.'

CHAP. 16:251

The Bishop of Grahamstown did not return the next day to conduct the ordination of his diocesan deacons and priests. He sent an urgent cable. His business in Bloemfontein—the uproar among the disgraced Bishop's clergy and parishioners—would detain him for a further week. The disgruntled ordinands would have to wait it out.

'I will have to let my friend Stephen know,' said Albert at breakfast. 'I fear he will not be able to stay away from his mission any longer. It's all very disappointing.'

'Should he have left it in the first place?' said Canon Beazer, buttering his bread and poking his knife at the marmalade. 'Sometimes, my dear Newnham, omission is the kindest way to deal with tricky issues.'

Albert looked at him, mystified.

'In other words,' continued Beazer, 'it would have been better to avoid any mention of the College dinner in the first place, given that it was to be held at an hotel.'

'But he's a Canterbury man.'

Beazer sucked gently at his teeth. 'Perhaps,' he said. 'But it's not a regular or popular notion out here to send Africans to English colleges.'

Albert's teaspoon was poised above his egg.

'Being in such a far-off place, Mr Mana would not have known,' continued Beazer, 'if someone hadn't been rash enough to tell him.'

'And when he *did* know?' retorted Albert, rather too warmly. 'After all, he can read and you cannot even have a tea party in this place without a report in the *Journal* or the *Penny Mail*!' Albert was flushed. Unity, sitting beside him, plucked at his sleeve.

'The posts are very erratic in the country districts. It's not always such an inconvenience as one might imagine,' said Beazer.

It was an old trick in the Colony, the handiest excuse of all: *Post must have gone astray. Again!*

'Besides, what was the point?' Beazer was condescending.

Forgetting himself, Albert dabbed his forehead with his table napkin. Unity was scarlet with shame.

'He didn't appear at the dinner,' continued Beazer, taking the advantage, 'which was the height of rudeness, given the rush and inconvenience of persuading the proprietor of Woods' to allow him to dine at all. And then he hung about the town hall looking like a mendicant and perspiring most unpleasantly. I was relieved to see he'd slipped away. But, I might add, without taking his leave of the Archdeacon, who was his host.'

'You will learn,' Mrs Beazer wagged her head at Albert from across the table, a good opportunity for some admonishment for this and other lapses by the giddy young people she'd been burdened with. 'It's best to let sleeping dogs lie.'

Albert swallowed a retort. His own shame in abandoning Stephen at the conversazione, in allowing Unity to divert him, in neglecting to appreciate his friend's discomfort, was acute. 'If you'll excuse me,' he said, rising hastily, tipping his chair, catching it before it fell, 'I need to speak to Mr Mana before I find he has left town.' He did not glance at Unity or at Mrs Beazer. He bowed stiffly to the Canon and escaped from the room.

THE NEWS OF Sunday's postponed ordination was brought to Stephen by Vuyo Tontsi. Startled awake, Stephen found that he had slept in the armchair in Vuyo's living room. He leapt to his feet, appalled. Vuyo Tontsi laughed indulgently and said in English, 'My dear fellow, we had a marvellous evening. It was a tonic to talk and hear your views, especially on England. I wish your brother Mzamo had been here, it would have done him the world of good.' He picked up Stephen's hat from the floor and continued in Xhosa. 'I think it is time to introduce you to some friends of mine. Teachers mostly. Some are employed by the Native College. Some are concerned with their own business in the town. Some aspire to be newspapermen—even editors. Most of us are Mfengu —but you will forgive us that. A few are Ngqika or Gcaleka. Others you will remember from the time we were at school together. We are thinking of forming an association.'

'I must first go and apologise to my friend, Mr Newnham, for failing to take my leave last night,' said Stephen.

'My feeling, after hearing your—shall we say, uninhibited —views last night, is that it may be his duty to apologise to you.'

'No, no!' objected Stephen. 'You don't know him. He would never let me down. It's I who must explain.' Knowing, as he said it, that he could not—without excuses, without humiliation. How could Albert possibly understand?

It was all so wearying.

Instead, he took his hat and went with Vuyo Tontsi to meet his friends.

As he walked beside him, the sun glaring in his eyes, he wished that he could fall into the oblivion of the night before. Or tear the place apart in rage and still the unfamiliar thundering in his head.

ALBERT SET OFF for *Mfundisi* Turvey's mission to inquire where

Stephen's brother's house was to be found. He felt bewildered, worn down by the constant litany from everyone he met.

—*You can never trust a native to do what is expected of him.*

—*You are both new to the Colony, my dear.*

—*You will soon learn. It will not take long! It never does!*

Was it true?

Henry Turvey was not at home. A man pottering in the stable, crooning at the one-eyed horse, said, half-explaining, half-gesturing, little common language between them, that Mfundisi Turvey had been out all night with a sick young woman. He was attending now to her grieving family.

'Can you tell me where Mr Mzamo Mzamane lives?'

The man brightened, pointing in the direction of the hill crowned with trees. 'All the people know Mzamane. Simply ask. *Buza nje!*'

Albert started up the road, picking his way across stones, ruts, here and there a small gulley where water had drained too fast. The people up and down the street stopped to stare at the tall, thin Englishman with spectacles and legs like a spider, lifting his hat to every woman he passed, bowing, inquiring the way to the home of Mr Mzamo Mzamane.

—KwaMzamane?

—*It is not far.*

—*It is round that curve.*

—*It is up that hill—ngaphaya—behind the chapel.*

—*Before the school, near the windmill, close to Tontsi's place.*

—*Does the Mfundisi know Tontsi?*

—No.

Astonishment. Everyone knows Tontsi.

Albert had trudged on.

It was very far indeed. He stared about him, confounded by the bewildering warren of tracks and pathways, the rows of small cottages interspersed with hovels draped in sacking or branches, crumbling walls, fallen thatch. He baulked a little at the sight of thin dogs, mangy donkeys, vacant-eyed

254

goats nosing litter in a gutter. Naked children played together in a water puddle. Young women, barefooted, bare-breasted, bore great bundles of wood on their heads as they passed up a hill. Albert stared, caught himself, reddened, wondered if he should approach and offer his assistance, thought better of it and turned his eyes away, almost crossed himself. Stared again.

A ragtag of curious boys followed him, imitating his walk, their shadows nudging at his heels.

STEPHEN AND VUYO Tontsi had not returned from the meeting when, at last, Albert knocked at Mzamo's door. It was answered by Nokhanyiso. He introduced himself, putting out his hand to shake her limp fingers. Nokhanyiso did not appear to have heard of him. She greeted him respectfully but did not invite him in.

He asked her name.

'Mrs Moonlight Mzamane.'

'Is the Reverend Stephen Mzamane here?'

'He has gone with my brother, Tontsi.'

'May I speak to your husband, perhaps—Mr Mzamo Mzamane?'

'He is in Port Elizabeth.'

Albert was taken aback. 'Port Elizabeth? When did he go there?'

'It is some weeks.'

'I hope very much to visit you soon, Mrs Mzamane,' said Albert, raising his hat again. 'I should be delighted to meet your husband and introduce you to Mrs Newnham.'

Nokhanyiso stood silently with her eyes cast down.

Albert smiled, flushing. Had she understood?

She dropped a bob-curtsey and stepped back within the open door. Albert turned away, holding his hat down on his head in the blast of a hot wind that flurried up the dust and covered his jacket with a fine white powder.

He only reached the Beazers' rectory as the gong sounded

255

for lunch. His boots were crusted, his hair stood on end. He had no opportunity to explain. Unity did it for him with a torrent of apology stilled only by Canon Beazer folding his hands for grace.

Eager to give his own account of his dishevelment, Albert had the chance, at last, to tell of his walk into Fingo Village, describing his astonishment at the contrasts, the activity, the bustling, cheerful noise, lamenting the high dusty wind that had accompanied him back down the hill. Attempting to lighten the expectant silence that followed, he said with a smile, 'Mrs Mzamane's name is Moonlight!'

'Fancy!' said Mrs Beazer sourly.

'Moonlight?' exclaimed Unity. 'What fun!'

Albert sat, red faced and vexed, feeling suddenly mean. He added sheepishly, 'Really, she was very charming.'

Confused, he ate his lunch in silence: Stephen had deceived him. His brother Mzamo had not expected him. It was the first time Stephen had told him an untruth.

Or was it?

ON RETURNING TO Mzamo's house, Stephen heard that he had missed seeing Albert. He was glad, for the smell of brandy seemed to hover in his nose, his clothes were crumpled, it was painful to move his head.

But the next day he was wracked with anxiety and shame.

Early in the morning he went down into the town on horseback and drew up before the front gate of the Reverend Canon Beazer's house. The windows were still shuttered, the front door was closed. A dog barked and rattled its chain from the yard at the back. It was as impregnable a house as the many he had known in Canterbury. There was a time for calling and there was a time when it was unbefitting. Hospitality had its conventions. If he had learned anything in England, he had learned that.

Disheartened, he rode away with a sense of parting. Nor did he stop to gaze at anything familiar: the Cathedral where

—that very day—the ordination should have taken place; the copse of trees on the eastern skyline; the low smoke sifting in around the houses of Fingo Village where people were already busy with their daily tasks.

It was the first time since he was nine years old that he had missed Sunday service.

Riding up and out of the hollow onto the ridge and the track leading to the hinterland, he soon left behind the bare hilltops and the disturbed dust-laden reaches of the town and wound down again into a valley dense with tangled growth and thorn. Except for the scar of road, here was a primitive landscape undisturbed by habitation, the plough or even grazing goats. A shrike called—a ringing summons from the shadowed bush.

As the heat intensified, Stephen slowed his horse and allowed it to pick its way at its own pace. He did not think, then, of the meeting he had had with Vuyo Tontsi's friends. He did not think of the tide of words addressed to him— Mzamo Mzamane's brother—by the gathering of admiring, if self-important, men. He thought instead of the brief conversation with Nokhanyiso as he had saddled his horse and prepared to leave.

'Do you wish to live in Port Elizabeth?' he had asked as she stood in the yard, trim this time in a printed cotton frock and boots.

She had replied, 'There are many fine shops.'

Stephen had laughed. 'You are already a fine lady.'

'There is a finer one where he has gone.'

Elizabeth Madikane.

What had she to do with Mzamo? What did she have to do with him?

Nothing.

But she was there, staunching his prayers, driving what had been numinous and sacred from his heart. And now, added to his old confusion were the sins of drunkenness and envy.

He that speaketh evil of his brother and judgeth his brother speaketh evil of the law and judgeth the law ...

He said the verse over and over again as he rode towards Nodyoba. He said it as he knelt on the earthen floor beside his bed in the barren little room on the night that he arrived back at the empty parsonage. He opened his Bible to consult the words, proclaiming them:

There is one lawgiver, who is able to save and to destroy; who art thou that judgest another?

SIX MONTHS LATER, when Stephen was in the schoolroom coaching his confirmation candidates, a letter was delivered by a messenger from Ockert's Store. It was marked 'Urgent'.

It was from Vuyo Tontsi with news of Mzamo's fall from grace.

It was a letter full of self-righteous rage.

Mzamo had betrayed his wife, Vuyo Tontsi's sister, Nokhanyiso. He had disgraced the family, the position of Vuyo Tontsi as heir to his chiefdom, the relations with the important white men in Grahamstown.

—*All natives will now be considered liars, adulterers and fornicators.*

This was bluster which Stephen understood: it was incumbent on Vuyo, as Nokhanyiso's brother and the senior member of her family, to be angry. He must insist on damages. Not even Mzamo would have blamed him. If the business were not likely to come to the ears of the Church, Vuyo might have been indulgent. After all—what's a man to do if he is away from home and family? Who can blame him for a dalliance?

But such an indiscretion! Someone who was known—a woman who had been to England! The wife of a minister! It was clear, wrote Vuyo Tontsi, that Mzamo had been seduced: *It is always women who bring trouble. Bayenza bunyoka. They have the nature of snakes.*

To add to the outrage, it was believed that the Street

258

Keeper—that devious rascal—had been tipped off that there was brandy in Mzamo's house. It took a hefty payment to keep him quiet, but there was always the chance that he would be bought off by a higher bidder and then he, Vuyo Tontsi, could be forced, in scandalous circumstances, to give up his additional property leased by his sister's husband. Whoever betrayed Mzamo and Nokhanyiso, adding insult to injury, was a jealous rogue.

Indeed, jealousy is the root of all evil. Underlined.

That it might have been Nokhanyiso herself did not occur to Vuyo Tontsi.

Be warned, Malusi—if news gets out it could stain your own reputation as a priest. We will keep hearing, all over again, 'how foolish it is to send natives to England'. Mzamo himself will be severely punished—he is, after all, a lay preacher at St Philip's. You must vouch for your brother, Malusi. If you are asked by Rutherford you must deny any knowledge of his relations with this woman (or of brandy in his house). In this way you can save us the disgrace. Your word is all we have. Ungumsindisi wethu. You are our saviour. It is the only way.

Stephen folded the letter. Perhaps he should have burned it or buried it in a hole and planted a tree over it—some ritual, signalling his distance.

Mzamo had always managed to profane what was sacred.

Angels, Education, Englishmen, God.

Now, Elizabeth Madikane.

He thrust the letter into his Latin Grammar, abandoned, pushing it deliberately in beside the picture of Elizabeth Madikane, an admonition to himself for his fantasies and folly.

But he could not convince himself that the letter wasn't there. Its arrival could not have been less opportune. Canon Rutherford was expected at the mission in just over a month. He had given notice that he would accompany the Bishop on

259

his annual tour of the diocese to conduct confirmations. A date had been given.

What if he inquired about Mzamo? What could Stephen say? Pretend ignorance? Dodge the truth?

If his enthusiasm in planning for the Bishop's visit was suddenly blighted by anxiety, he was obliged to thrust his fears aside. There were constant streams of people at his door. Everyone wished to be part of the celebration. If the confirmation candidates were few, the community was eager for a feast even if he, Ngesi—the Englishman—had forbidden the brewing of beer.

He called the people together: the congregation, the schoolchildren, the members of the choir, the old women who tended the church and the schoolroom. They all came to hear him.

They would light fires and cook food.

They would harvest the best produce from their gardens.

They would send some boys to Ockert & Sons to buy tea and coffee and sugar and fine white flour for bread.

They would slaughter a goat. Not sacrificially, of course—even if, in their hearts, they wished it to be so.

They would gather *imifino.*

They would sweep the yard.

Stephen would stay in Dyoba's house so the parsonage could be prepared for the Bishop and *Mfundisi* Rutherford.

Lily Majola and her mother, old Mrs Dyoba and all the women in the congregation turned out to wash, scrub, smear the floors and shine the windows in time for the great event. The men repaired the leak in the roof of the church, some boys were sent into the rafters to banish the bats. All the schoolchildren had their clothes washed in the river and dried on the bushes nearby. Night after night Stephen composed and recomposed a welcoming speech.

The church was decorated with vines and leaves. The best altar frontal, made by the ladies of Canterbury and kept in waiting for this most solemn occasion, was unwrapped at last and hung on the altar. Lily went out at dawn on the day and gathered arums and ferns from the vlei, bringing them triumphantly to the parsonage, her blue bonnet wet with dew, her cheek daubed with pollen.

Stephen almost put out his finger to wipe it away.

NODYOBA WOULD ASTONISH the Bishop. It would astonish Canon Rutherford. Warden Bailey would surely hear of the occasion in faraway Canterbury and rejoice. It was only in the early restless hours of the morning before Stephen had risen to say his prayers that Vuyo Tontsi's words recurred.

If you are asked by Rutherford you must deny it all. In this way you can save us the disgrace.

How?

Ungumsindisi wethu. You are our saviour.

What was he to say? How could he deny what he had read in Vuyo Tontsi's letter? Would his words betray Mzamo? Or was it Elizabeth Madikane he feared betraying? Or—perhaps —himself?

THE BISHOP CAME. But he did not stay.

There was no opportunity for Rutherford to mention Mzamo as he hustled the congregation into the church. The men and women and children squeezed along the pews, lined the side aisles, stood shoulder to shoulder in the porch.

But the singing of the schoolchildren was cut short.

The confirmation and first Holy Communion were rushed through.

The blessing was perfunctory.

The candidates, dressed in clothes that had been carefully sewn over weeks by firelight and candlelight and lamplight, could not be solemnly paraded. The Bishop's sermon for which Stephen had written so considered a reply was waived.

Had he even noticed the altar cloth? Had he seen the lilies? The shining cross?

'We must get on our way,' Canon Rutherford had said to

261

Stephen in an undertone as they processed into the church. 'His Lordship has a number of mission stations to visit and he is anxious to return to Grahamstown as soon as possible. Mr Chauncey was very urgent with us to get back to town. It seems unrest may be expected any hour. Indeed, Rev. Chauncey could not be persuaded to accompany us.'

Stephen bit back the retort: *Not God Himself could persuade Mr Chauncey!* He said, also in an undertone, 'It has been quiet in this neighbourhood.'

'There are rumours,' said Rutherford. Then, another tack, closer to the truth: 'As we passed through Fort Beaufort this morning we had word that the Civil Commissioner will be organising a reception for the Bishop. He is, as you know, a very senior man hereabouts. It would be rude to be late for so spontaneous a gesture.'

Outside, half a dozen iron pots were already simmering on the cooking fires. The bunting, made by the schoolchildren and which Stephen had strung along the veranda of his house, was flapping in the breeze, little flags of welcome cut from coloured papers. Boys, with shouts and whistles, kept away the neighbourhood dogs, alert to the smell of stewing meat. The old heathen engaged to watch the Bishop's horses stood before them lost in a dance of his own, punching the air with imaginary sticks, startling them with sudden laughter and the stamp of feet.

All through the service, Stephen sensed the growing perplexity of the congregation, waiting for him to speak the words they knew he had prepared, subsiding uneasily when he said no more than, 'Welcome my Lord, welcome to our own *Mfundisi* Rutherford,' and gestured to the choir to resume their seats after only one hymn was sung. He could not scan the faces nor catch the eye of Dyoba. Like him, Dyoba had prepared his welcome as an elder and a brother of the distant headman. Stephen could not even glance at the representatives from his outstations who had made their way in darkness to arrive at dawn.

He stood, shamed, the blood beating in his ears as each candidate knelt respectfully, humbly, as he himself should have knelt at his ordination, awed by the presence of God.

When her turn came, Lily Majola—both ardent and tranquil—raised her face to receive the blessing, eyes closed, a faint quiver at the corners of her lids, her tongue tipping the edge of her teeth, her small slim hands lifted, palms up, cupped in thanksgiving.

He turned away in the presence of such calm certainty.

As they left the church after the service, the Bishop drew Stephen aside, took his hand in both of his and said, 'My dear Mzamane, it grieves me to hurry as I must, knowing you have been to a great deal of trouble to welcome us, but there are confirmations at three of four stations in the next few days and I am very troubled by word I have received of considerable unrest as well as warnings of roaming bands of cattle thieves.' He glanced about. 'As this is a Fingo community you will be secure among your own people and well protected, I imagine.'

Stephen let it pass. It was not only Mzamo who thought him an Mfengu.

The Bishop patted Stephen's shoulder. 'Of course we will keep you daily in our prayers and appreciate deeply what you have done to prepare the candidates for confirmation. A splendid record. Truly splendid.' They reached the horses. The Bishop gazed about him again. 'Good work, Mzamane.' He mounted and looked down at Stephen, his face shadowed by the brim of his hat. Then he glanced at the congregation standing expectantly in the churchyard and raised his hand. 'God's richest blessings!' Addressing Basil Rutherford, 'Very good, my dear Rutherford. I must congratulate you.'

As they turned their horses towards the gate, Canon Rutherford held back a moment, leaning down to Stephen standing in the road. 'I shall write to you.' Those owl eyes, those tufty ears. From the height of the saddle Rutherford loomed as large as he had when Stephen was a very small boy.

'Sir.'

'I need information in a matter it would be completely inappropriate to discuss now.' He cast him a searching glance. 'No doubt you understand me.'

'Sir?'

Another searching glance.

Stephen watched them ride away, his back to his congregation. He felt their silence, their bewilderment. He felt, too, his own anger rising. A great heat. He turned to the people, raised his arms and cried in a ringing voice, '*Silambile!*' We are hungry. '*Masitye.*' Let us eat.

The old heathen who had cared for the horses stood gazing after the retreating cavalcade. He sidled up to a cooking pot where a woman stirred the meat, saying, 'Why do the English hurry away when there is food?' He gazed a moment at the pot, said with a hint of inquiry, 'And we *abantu* —the very people—do not hurry away when there is beer.'

'Be off,' said the woman. 'We are Christians here.'

THAT SUNDAY STEPHEN gave a sermon. The congregation had never heard him speak so forcefully before nor read the Scriptures with so much fire. The old women glanced at each other and adjusted their headscarves. The old men listened gravely.

Sometimes you were publicly exposed to insult, at other times you stood side by side with those so treated ... We are not of those who shrink back and are destroyed.

It was a sermon they remembered and that they spoke of long afterwards—long, long after, when unrest had broken into war, and war had come and gone.

By then, the homesteads had been burned, the country emptied, and white men had come to the valleys round about and planted groves of orange trees. There they were, row on darkening row, pushing back the bush and pasture, eating up the cattle byres, emptying the river.

CHAP. 17:265

Stephen dreaded the arrival of Canon Rutherford's letter. When it came a month later, brought with the familiar bag of meal from Ockert & Sons, it squatted against a pitcher on the kitchen table, a little stained from its journey but addressed in the unmistakable and well-remembered hand:

—Write out 50 times: I will not talk in class.

—Write out 100 times: I am a Christian boy—I will not play games on the Sabbath.

—A satisfactory improvement, Stephen. Good progress! But there is no need for flourishes on concluding signatures.

If he does not read the letter there will be no obligation to answer it.

It stood against the pitcher for three days. But on the fourth day he opened it, conscience stricken. He slit it reluctantly with his knife. It was long. Some of the words were unfamiliar. He laid it aside when he had read half and went for a walk. He inspected his vegetable garden. He stood at the side of Dyoba's cattle byre and watched the boys milking the cows. He paused when he saw Lily Majola in the lee of her mother's house, bending down to her daughter with a swift maternal gesture, the brim of her bonnet almost cupping her small upturned face. He entered the church to pray, dusted the altar instead, walked back to the house, closed the door and took up the letter again.

Mzamo was an adulterer, appeared to have fathered a child, his co-accused 'the wife of a minister of another denomination'.

Did that compound the sin?

Certainly, Canon Rutherford was always dismissive of Nonconformists: the fault could only lie with her. Even though Mzamo was not in Holy Orders, Rutherford wrote, he was a catechist, reader and lay preacher in St Philip's Church. His work on the translation of the prayer book had been commissioned by the Bishop. Thus, his case would be tried in a specially convened Diocesan Court. It was likely he would be excommunicated. If not permanently, then for a number of years—at least until the Bishop was assured of his repentance.

In the meantime, he would be asked to leave the diocese. His influence could not be tolerated.

I trust you had no knowledge of this matter? You are a deacon in the English Church. You are a servant of God and the State. I shall not doubt your integrity should you be called as a witness.

Stephen put the letter down on the table and stood at the window gazing down at the church and the fall of the valley below.

Cows rested underneath the craggy tree—the twitch of an ear, the irritable toss of a head, a drift of flies. Early afternoon, that time of day when loneliness is most acute, the heat still piercing, empty of bird calls except for the forlorn murmur of mourning doves.

Ndivel' emaXhoseni
Ndikhumbul' emaXhoseni.

He returned to the letter again. Rutherford had written: *I shall not doubt your integrity.*

As if he already did.

It was then that Stephen had sat at the kitchen table and written to Albert.

My dear Albert,
I trust that you will understand my writing to you on the following matter. I need your counsel. I am burdened with a grindstone.

He crossed it out. That was not how he spoke to Albert. They had always joked when the matter was confidential. A signal rarely misinterpreted. He wrote instead: *You may not be the cleverest fellow I know (ha-ha) but you are the kindest!*

Albert had always insisted that Stephen was sharper than he. *Advise me. What should I do?*

What if Albert mentioned it to Unity? He wrote, underlining it:

Carry it in your chest. Yiphathe ngembambo.

He screwed up the sheet of paper and searched for another.

My dear Albert,
This is strictly between you and me ...

He outlined the case, inserting some of Rutherford's words. He re-read his letter, reconsidered. What could he say that neither judged Mzamo nor betrayed Elizabeth Madikane? He knew the letter might take a week or more to reach Albert but he would not hazard a reply to Canon Rutherford until he had heard from him.

He wrote the direction clearly:

Rev. Mr Albert J Newnham
The Diocesan Native College
West Hill
Grahamstown.

But the days dragged by. Why did Albert not reply?

Albert wrote at last but his letter came too late. A summons had already arrived from Rutherford. Stephen was to give witness at a Diocesan Court in early June. Rutherford intimated that Stephen's protracted silence indicated hesitation, that his failure to reply to the original letter was viewed very seriously.

—Do <u>not</u> *make the excuse that the post did not arrive.*

Ah, they knew their own tricks all too well! But sometimes it was true. His letter to Albert, it transpired, had been redirected twice. *Dear old chap,* Albert wrote,

I feel perfectly wretched for keeping you waiting but, in truth, I received your letter only this morning. I have been sent rather unexpectedly to supervise an up-country mission, St Paul's on the Indwe River. The missionary was called away on the death of his father and, it seems, he will be gone for some time. There was no one else who could be spared to stand in. Considering our situation with a young daughter, my dear wife was perfectly horrified. I wanted to leave her in Grahamstown but she would not hear of it. I trust we will not be here more than a few weeks and will then return to the Native College.

It would be so much better to talk to your shining black face and give you some encouragement in person on the matter about which you have written! Brothers—dear as they are—can be very vexing! Their misdemeanours are best not mentioned. That's why I never told you about my elder brother, Percy. He was packed off with the Army to India before he caused any more of a rumpus. I shan't say what—just as I think it would be in your best interests to keep quiet as well. As you are not implicated in the 'crime' that your brother has committed, there is no need for you to comment. Family honour—Rev. Rutherford should know that!

For Albert it was so simple.

Perhaps it might have been for Stephen, too, if he'd been an Englishman.

A FEW DAYS later Stephen rode down to the town and sent a telegram to Rutherford.

Arriving Grahamstown Tuesday 13th June stop SM Mzamane.

He called on Rev. Thurston Chauncey to tell him of his summons, resolved to ask him to go to Nodyoba at least once in his absence to take a service.

Chauncey was at home, pottering on his back porch among his ferns. They seemed as neglected and seedy as he. Stephen stood a few moments unnoticed in the yard, watching Chauncey clipping at stray fronds, chuntering away to himself.

'Good Heavens, man,' Chauncey exclaimed, suddenly looking up, startled. 'Why did you not ring the doorbell?'

'I did,' said Stephen. 'But I fear you did not hear it.'

'Figlan? Where is Figlan?'

'I have not seen him,' said Stephen. 'I took the liberty of coming round in search of him. I hope I am not disturbing you?'

'It is always better to send notice,' said Chauncey. 'You are fortunate to have found me in. I am always very busy about the parish. In fact,' he took his watch from his waistcoat pocket, 'I have a meeting shortly.' Of course. Mr Chauncey always had a meeting.

'Mr Rutherford has called me to Grahamstown on business,' said Stephen briskly, unwilling to mollify him.

'Ah.' Chauncey wiped his secateurs on his coat tail, not looking at Stephen. 'He wrote to me some time ago. He said you had not answered an urgent letter. Not having had a reply, I expect he was wondering if you were still at your post. I said I had no idea, I had little contact with the mission.'

'Excuse me, sir,' said Stephen, interrupting him. 'I have invited you several times to come to the church and take service with us. I have been disappointed myself in having no answer.'

Chauncey did not reply but his exasperation was evident: *Another of Henry Turvey's fine young men. As impudent as that scoundrel, Thomas Dema.*

Coolly, Stephen faced it down.

Chauncey tugged at his side whiskers, almost disconcerted. He said, 'I hear your brother has disgraced himself.'

'I cannot comment,' said Stephen. 'I have not been fully informed.'

'Why are you called as witness then?'

Chauncey, it seemed, knew more than he.

'I assume to give an account of his character.'

'Nothing else?'

'I know nothing of my brother's concerns,' said Stephen. 'He knows nothing of mine. He has never been to Nodyoba and, as you know, I cannot leave my mission unless summoned by my superiors.' Stephen would not be intimidated. 'If you will excuse the liberty,' he said, with an asperity that did not go unnoticed by Chauncey, 'I would be very grateful if you would take a service at Holy Trinity while I am away. I have newly confirmed parishioners and it is very important that worship should be regular.'

—A demand? And from a mere deacon!

'I have a very large congregation of my own.' Chauncey was querulous. 'More to the point, the military have it on good authority that the kaffirs are agitating for a fight. The townsfolk have been warned to be vigilant.'

'My congregation is Mfengu.'

'Nonetheless.'

Stephen waited.

Chauncey fumbled with his scruples. 'I will see what I can do but I cannot promise. Indeed, I doubt the wisdom of it. The Colonel is very concerned. Very. Perhaps I can organise for him to send the military chaplain ... although I doubt it. He is not convinced of mission work.'

—Nor are you.

Stephen bowed and took his leave. He clipped the gate behind him briskly, put his hat on his head and mounted his horse, swinging her into the middle of the street.

'YOU ARE GOING away, *Mfundisi*?' Lily seemed dismayed.

'I am called to Grahamstown.'

Thomas Dema had also been called to Grahamstown. Or so he had said.

'Are you coming back?'

'Of course I am coming back,' said Stephen. 'And I would be grateful if you would care for my chickens while I am gone.'

She nodded, her eyes still on his face, her forehead puckered fleetingly.

Stephen left her crooning mournfully beside the fowl run. He went to call on Dyoba.

'It is said that the people up at Tini's are gathering arms,' said Dyoba.

'That is far away from here. Why should it be a cause for alarm? It is surely just a rumour.'

'No,' said Dyoba. 'It is not a rumour. Those AmaNgqika still left among us are always searching for a reason to quarrel with us Mfengu. They are jealous over land.'

'Perhaps they consider it theirs,' said Stephen.

Dyoba glanced at him shrewdly. 'You are Ngesi,' he said.

—*Until I am a Ngqika once again.*

But Stephen did not say it.

'There will never be agreement,' Dyoba continued. 'Never! Believe me, *Mfundisi*, the Ngqika and all the rest in Kaffirland will always be looking for a reason to fight with the Mfengu.'

THE SAME COULD have been said of the Diocesan Court that would try Mzamo Mzamane. It struck swiftly with its canons and its constitution. No mitigating factors. No circumstantial lenience. Mzamo would be condemned long before he appeared before the assessors. An example to all. A precedent must be established, no debate permitted.

Whatever was decided must be incontrovertible or the Dean and his meddlesome newspaper would use the case to goad his Bishop, the Principal of the Native College and the Reverend Mr Rutherford, Director of Missions, in their foolish notion of educating natives above their station, an endeavour doomed to failure: moral, political and spiritual. They should have heeded Dr Dale, the Superintendent of Education:

—*The spade, hammer, plane and saw should take the place of playing chess with Lady Bountiful* ...

The Dean was expansive in his letter to the *Grahamstown Journal*: the Governor had been mistaken, the Bishop was mistaken, the late Metropolitan had been especially mistaken. In short, if they'd been less arrogant and ambitious in their aims and remained faithful to Canterbury and the Church of England, such cases would be unknown. The Dean's fulminations—*this spectacle of insincerity and fraud* —delighted the people of the town. His outrage was so much more entertaining than the gloom of the drought, the failed crop, the price of wheat. Somehow, the tribulations of the accused were incidental. What could one expect anyway? The scandal had arisen at a Croquet Club! What, in Heaven's name, were natives doing playing croquet if not to get up to mischief?

THE WEARY ROAD to Grahamstown once again. This time Stephen did not forget his food or a bottle of cold tea. He packed a blanket and an overcoat into his saddlebag. Late in the afternoon he came across a wagon taking hides to market. He slowed to ride beside it. The silence of the driver was less oppressive to him than his own. He helped outspan the oxen near a drift in the Koonap River that evening and he shared a meal with the driver and his *voorloper*. Stephen was invited to sleep under the wagon.

He went ahead the next morning as the oxen toiled up the pass out of the lowlands. He stopped at the crest of the hill and looked back along the valley. That blue distance, the heat of drought, the sloughed bracts of aloes, bone-white among the ironstone. No sound. No bird call. Not even the stirring of the dry bergwind.

He plodded on.

It was almost evening when he reached Vuyo Tontsi's house.

'I have been expecting you,' said Tontsi. '*Mfundisi* Rutherford told me he had called for you. Why have you taken so long to come?'

'Where is my brother?'

'He is staying with *Mfundisi* Rutherford. The *Mfundisi* has insisted that he have no contact with witnesses and I am sure he will take the opportunity to trick him into a confession.'

'What is there to confess?'

'Mrs Madikane and her child have been cast out by her husband and the congregation. They say she has been taken in by heathens at a place called Gubb's Farm, which I know is full of drunkards and thieves. My sister has returned to our father's home. That is accusation enough.'

'I must see my brother. I do not know the facts.'

'Rutherford has forbidden it. He does not want any witness to be compromised.'

'I have nothing to say.'

'You had better say a great deal,' said Vuyo Tontsi. 'You had better speak of your brother's services to the Church, his faith and his good character.'

'I thought you were very angry with him. He has shamed your sister. You called him *umkrexezi*. An adulterer.'

'That's as may be,' said Vuyo Tontsi. 'A family matter. There are more important issues at stake here.'

'Your reputation?'

'Yours as well.'

Stephen laughed grimly. What was a reputation when there was no one to recognise or share it?

'This is not personal,' said Vuyo and Stephen did not catch his eye, knowing better. 'It's for the organisation we are trying to form. What notice will the government take if they think our members are disreputable?'

'Ah … '

'You are the only one whose word has real weight, *mfowethu*.'

'Except if I lie.'

'There are different ways of conveying a truth.'

Stephen let it pass. 'Who are the judges, and who is representing my brother?'

'He is representing himself. He wants no lawyer.'

Stephen would have guessed as much. Who could speak more fluently in his own defence than Mzamo?

'The judges are the Archdeacon, Canon Rutherford as the Director of Missions, the Chancellor and two clergymen, one of whom is Dr Gould, the Headmaster of the colonial boys' College.'

'Then he is condemned before he opens his mouth.'

'That is why you are here.'

Stephen took up his hat.

'Where are you going?' said Vuyo Tontsi.

'To *Mfundisi* Turvey.'

'No,' said Vuyo Tontsi. 'You will come with me and consult with the other men who are concerned in this matter.'

'No one is concerned in this matter except my brother.'

'You are mistaken.'

'I will not bear false witness.'

'But you will go to Mr Turvey, one of *them*, one who will condemn him?'

'*Mfundisi* Turvey is a man of God,' said Stephen. 'He knows it is not for him to judge.'

'*Kanti, mntanam*,' said Vuyo Tontsi. 'Even yet, he is an Englishman.'

And implicit in his glance, *Are you?*

Too suddenly shamed to argue, too weary to resist, Stephen did not go to *Mfundisi* Turvey's. Instead he went with Vuyo Tontsi as he'd done before.

AND SO THE Diocesan Court was convened. It gathered in the old Chapel at the Grammar School, long vacated for a newer, more elaborate building and left dark and echoing with its high lancet windows and groined oak ceiling, its worn pews appropriated by an audience of churchmen, officials and invited laymen.

Mzamo stood alone before the Archdeacon, Canon Rutherford, the Chancellor of the diocese, Dr Gould and another unfamiliar priest. The Dean—an unwelcome observer—was in attendance, too, with a number of cronies from his congregation. It was a chance to put the Bishop on trial as much as the magistrate's impudent interpreter.

The Chancellor of the diocese rose. 'The sins you have committed—adultery, perjury and false witness—are very serious offences against God and man. The offences are so grave,' he said, 'that you must do all in your power to undo the evil that you have done.'

Then the prosecutor came forward and stood before the accused. The room fell silent. Stephen sat at a distance, his hat on his knees, Vuyo Tontsi beside him, his fellow witness. The shadowed room was chill, well remembered by him as a chapel, furnished once with an altar and a large wooden cross. The three lancet windows on the east side had been stripped of their stained glass but the air of a church remained. The ghost of past injunctions once painted on the walls had been inexpertly washed over with lime:

> *Raised for our Justification,*
> *Delivered for our Offences*

The bench on which he sat was an old pew, scored with the rat-tooth gnawings and chippings of bored schoolboys. F *Hillier. Mullins maj. G Bowker.* PWC—1862.

Where were they now? Long gone to farms in some dry hinterland? Or to the diamond fields or some colonial regiment? Perhaps, to their graves. Who was there to resurrect them now?

'According to the Constitutions of the Canons of the

Church of England,' read the prosecutor, 'notice of the intention to adopt proceedings, known as The Articles of Presentment and containing a statement of the charge and a copy of the information on which it is founded, was served on the accused together with the names of the clergy chosen to be assessors. As the offices of catechist, subdeacon and reader are recognised as offices in the Church, the Bishop may revoke, withhold or renew the licence of such persons as serve in one or more of these capacities. The churchwardens are also officers of the Bishop from whom they derive their ecclesiastical authority. It is their duty to complain to the Bishop if notorious evildoers be admitted to Holy Communion through which the parishioners be thereby offended.' He paused, looked directly at Mzamo.

Mzamo stood upright, facing the Archdeacon and assessors, his back to the gathering. No light from the windows fell on him; only his stiff white collar gleamed, disembodied in the shadow.

'As the accused, Mr Saul Mzamo Mzamane, is a catechist and lay reader at St Philip's Church and has also been commissioned by the Bishop to assist with the translation of the Book of Common Prayer, it is appropriate that he should be tried by a Diocesan Court and not a civil court. However, as this is not a civil court, evidence cannot be given under oath. Therefore, a solemn declaration is substituted and it is incumbent on all who are witnesses at this Diocesan Court to remember that they are conducting themselves in the sight of God.'

The prosecutor came forward, nearer to Mzamo. 'Do you promise, as in the presence of Almighty God, that you will speak the truth unequivocally and uprightly, whether in the declaration you shall make or in the answers which you are about to give?'

Mzamo's response could not be heard. Nor did he dip his head in assent. A moment's silence and the prosecution proceeded.

'On the twentieth of January of this year, the Bishop received a memorial written to him by the Reverend Mr Paul Madikane of Port Elizabeth. The document was signed by four members of his congregation, all office-bearers in his church, attesting that in March 1875, while Reverend Madikane was away attending to the harvest at his family home in the Alexandria district of this Colony, the accused, Saul Mzamo Mzamane of Grahamstown, had connection with his wife, Elizabeth, at their residence, in consequence of which Mrs Elizabeth Madikane gave birth to a son in the first week in January.'

Stephen glanced across at Mzamo.

'The document claims that it is suspected that Mr Saul Mzamo Mzamane is the father. Reverend Madikane had been married many years to his first wife, and, on her demise he married his present wife in 1866. He has never fathered a child.'

Stephen examined his hat. What thoughts, at this moment of accusation, did Mzamo have? Scrutinised now by five grave priests?

What thoughts—fleetingly imagined by himself?

In the photograph he had brought from Canterbury, Elizabeth Madikane had remained poised, almost sanctified, even apart from the voice that had swelled with life and power in St Philip's Church, giving her substance and warmth. It was an outrage that they—voyeurs—should examine what concerned no one but Mzamo and Elizabeth Madikane.

He closed his eyes, forcibly detaching himself, catching the voices far outside the building: the running feet of schoolboys going by to lessons; the bucking of a cart passing along the rutted road; the whistle of the driver guiding his donkeys up the hill. But she was there still, Mzamo claiming her as he had always claimed whatever Stephen valued most. Witnesses were called. Three had come from Strangers' Location in Port Elizabeth, hostile to a court convened by what they called 'Roman Englishmen'.

The reputation of their own denomination was at stake. Old men, shabby in their waistcoats and jackets, they sat in a glum row, suspicious of the fully robed clergy occupying the judges' bench, bearded patriarchs from the Book of Job.

Reverend Madikane was not among them. He had been taken ill. He would not appear in court. It was demeaning to him to discuss relations with his wife. It was demeaning to be scrutinised as a man who could not father sons.

One by one his wardens gave their witness.

'It was noticed in Port Elizabeth at the Croquet Club that Mr Mzamane liked to speak to Mrs Madikane.'

'What is peculiar in that?' said the prosecutor.

'A man does not laugh with another man's wife.'

—*She is known for her beauty.*

—*She is known for her singing.*

—*She is known for her learning.*

The prosecutor was patient. Mzamane might be a rogue but even he deserved a chance. 'Are these not attributes of which any husband would be proud?'

'She is a stranger. It is not known—even by her—where she comes from.'

'Being a stranger should not condemn her.'

'She is believed to be one of those people who has knowledge of *ubuti*.'

'*Ubuti?*'

Mzamo interrupted briskly. 'Foreign sorcery.'

'Inadmissible.' The Archdeacon glanced at the prosecutor. 'This is a Diocesan Court. We are not discussing sorcery.' Confusion.

'But it is the truth.'

'Let us proceed, and kindly outline your case against the accused,' said the Archdeacon quietly.

'It is claimed,' continued the prosecutor, 'that the accused has had casual connection on divers occasions with Mrs Madikane. It has been claimed that he has been seen going to and leaving the home of Rev. Madikane at various

278

times of the day but particularly in the evening. The woman, Mrs Elizabeth Madikane, has continually insisted that the child is her husband's. It appears that her husband wished to believe it but that there is so striking a resemblance to the accused that he could not delude himself. Moreover, the wife of the accused ... .' The prosecutor consulted his brief, scrutinised it for a moment, resumed, 'The wife of the accused, Mrs Moonlight Mzamane—who is not available as a witness, having left the marital home in Grahamstown and apparently gone beyond the jurisdiction of the Colony—has refused to give witness. She simply stated to her brother, Mr Vuyo Tontsi, that a young woman knows when her husband is unfaithful for he no longer wishes connection with her.'

'That is hearsay,' said the Archdeacon.

The prosecutor hesitated, glanced round at him, resumed, 'It may be relevant to note that neither married couple has children. The birth of this boy, involving a spouse from each of the marriages concerned, seems to put the matter of paternity beyond doubt.'

Mzamo did not react.

'In what capacity were you a visitor to Reverend Madikane's home?' asked the prosecutor, turning to Mzamo.

'I came to consult with him about our choirs meeting to sing together.'

'Why should you go so far as Port Elizabeth for this purpose? There are many church choirs in Grahamstown.'

'I was there on my employer's business.'

'Did your employer know of your acquaintance with Reverend Madikane?'

Mzamo was haughty. 'I do not inquire about my employer's connections. Why should he concern himself with mine?'

The prosecutor looked at him sharply. Vuyo Tontsi smiled.

'I put it to you that the attraction of the Reverend Madikane's choir was due to the presence of Mrs Madikane,' said the prosecutor.

'Certainly,' said Mzamo. 'She is a soloist who has sung before Her Majesty the Queen. The choir is known as the foremost in the country.'

The Dean snorted. *In whose opinion?* He made a note in his pocketbook.

'Did you have connection with Mrs Madikane?' said the prosecutor.

'I was often a guest in her house.'

'Answer the question.'

'I have.'

Nettled, the prosecutor glanced at the Archdeacon. A slight inclination of his head, settling back into solemn meditation, his arms folded, each long hand slipped into the fold of the opposite sleeve.

'You visited the residence of Reverend Madikane when he was absent, took advantage of the situation and imposed yourself on his wife.'

'There was no imposition,' said Mzamo without irony.

'The child is yours?'

'It is not unknown for elderly men to father children. It is something they pray for and prayers, as we all know, are answered.' Again, Vuyo Tontsi smiled. Stephen wiped his hands surreptitiously on his trouser legs, looked up at one of the lancet windows framing a distant cloud. He traced its edges with his eyes. Would these questions never end?

'The Reverend Madikane has ordered his wife from their home. It does not sound as if he is overjoyed by fatherhood.'

'It is a question you must put to Reverend Madikane.'

But the Reverend Madikane was not there.

—*You may tell a calf by its spots*, he had said, meaning that the woman's affection for the infant was disproportionate to her affection for her husband.

'You have submitted a report on the times you were in Port Elizabeth on business with the Resident Magistrate and Civil Commissioner,' said the prosecutor. 'It has been corroborated by that gentleman.'

280

'Yes,' said Mzamo. 'He has signed the document.'

'From this document it appears that you were *not* in Port Elizabeth at the time that the child could have been conceived.'

'You have the dates.'

'Where were you in the month of March last year?'

'I was at work in Grahamstown and I also made a journey to see my mother at Hohita.'

'Hohita?'

'It is a place beyond Queenstown,' said Mzamo. 'It is a long journey on horseback to reach it.'

'How many days did it take?'

'Four.'

'Where did you stop along the way?'

'I stopped with people known to me. I have a wide circle of acquaintances.'

'Is there anyone who can corroborate this story?'

For the first time Mzamo hesitated. Then he said, 'My brother, Reverend Stephen Mzamane.'

'Where does he reside?'

'Nodyoba, in the district of Fort Beaufort. '

The prosecutor turned to the Archdeacon and assessors.

'The Reverend Mzamane is incumbent at that mission,' interposed Rutherford. 'He has been called to give witness and is present.'

Mzamo turned then, suddenly alert. He scanned the assembly. Then he looked pointedly at Rutherford. Rutherford was impassive, studying the ceiling. He almost smiled. No, he had not told Mzamo that his brother had been summoned.

In his seat Stephen drew his finger across the initials carved in the wood, over and over.

'There will be no difficulty now,' Vuyo said to him. 'There is no one from Nodyoba to contradict you.'

But there is God.

Ungumsindisi wethu. You are our saviour, Vuyo Tontsi had written. *It is the only way.*

CHAP. 18:282

Vuyo Tontsi was called to give an account of Mzamo Mzamane's character. The Resident Magistrate, Huntley Haddon, who employed the accused, had also been approached but had declined. He was a member of the Scottish Church. He had no desire to involve himself in the intricacies of the canons of English ecclesiastical law. He did not see the necessity of appearing before a Diocesan Court. It was not a civil court and it did not have the authority to subpoena him. He had written a testimonial instead. Mr Mzamane's private affairs were unknown to him. He could vouch for his work:

He was an excellent interpreter. He has a thorough grasp of the law. For a native, he is exceptionally intelligent.

Besides, Magistrate Haddon was extremely put out. He might be criticised for being dilatory in his supervision. It also might be discovered—at home and abroad—that his absences were unnecessarily prolonged by a day or two so he could enjoy some fishing in the bay. On the pretext of other business commitments he generally let Mzamane go off— uninterrogated—to wherever he seemed so keen to go. It was a satisfactory compromise. The Magistrate's own escape was a reprieve from domestic annoyance. He could sit up with a bottle of port until after midnight if he wished. He could take breakfast at any hour he pleased. He could smoke his pipe in the bedroom of the gentlemen's club without being harried. Mzamane's independence in Port Elizabeth had suited him admirably. Damn the fellow for abusing it!

He had already confided in the Bishop that it would be very inconvenient to lose Mzamane's services, especially considering the number of incompetents he had previously suffered as interpreters in his court. Mzamane was worth his weight in gold, even if he was a coxcomb. Haddon knew that the dear old Bishop—despite his air of patriarchal sanctity—was a shrewd man of the world: as a young curate he had served among labourers and dockers on the Tyne. He had run a sanctuary for fallen women. Nothing shocked him. But, on the other hand, Haddon understood his wish to avoid scandal. Besides, the Reverend Madikane's memorial had come via his own Church's superior so, no doubt, the whole sordid story had been laid before the Nonconformists in Port Elizabeth and Grahamstown already. If it had been ignored, it would have caused a greater commotion.

'I suppose I shall be forced to let him go,' Haddon had grumbled during his meeting with the Bishop.

'My dear Haddon, it must seem precipitate,' said the Bishop. 'I can imagine what a nuisance it would be to replace your interpreter. On the other hand,' the Bishop had sighed, 'there are enough tiresome divisions among the Churches already. If we prevaricate it will be seen as feeble. I would have preferred to counsel the young man alone but the memorial has been circulated. We will never keep the story quiet. It seems to me, confidentially, that a likely sanction will be excommunication for a minimum of three years with the option of readmission if sufficient repentance is evident.'

'I'd throw it out if it were a civil case,' retorted Haddon.

'A transfer? Just for a time? I am sure it can be arranged. Think of the fracas the Dean will stir up in his newspaper.'

Haddon snorted. Yes, he knew.

—*Imagine allowing an acknowledged adulterer to partake of the Lord's Supper or represent the truth in a Court of Law ...*

'Justice?' The Bishop shook his head. 'If I were obliged to excommunicate every adulterer in my diocese, I fear my congregation might be sadly depleted. It is really very unfortunate that this has all become so public. I simply have no choice.'

VUYO TONTSI WAS nervous. His witness depended on his success in harnessing himself from saying too much. But Vuyo Tontsi always said too much. He relished his command of English, made little jokes, invented aphorisms, always competing with Mzamo whose facility embraced not only the slang of soldiers in the tavern, but the grave pronouncements of the Magistrate and the rhetoric of the preacher. He was a natural mimic and orator. If he had been a heathen he would, no doubt, have been *imbongi*, a praise-singer of a paramount, the lyric voice of a king.

Vuyo Tontsi, hand on his heart, declared that he would tell the truth. 'What is your relationship to the accused?' the prosecutor began. 'I am his brother-in-law.'

'For how long have you known him?'

'I was educated at the Native College with him since we were boys.'

'Then, you are well qualified to give an account of his character.'

'He was always the most accomplished student in the College.' A pause—just long enough for Vuyo Tontsi to elaborate and stumble into compromise. He hastened to fill the silence. 'Indeed, I believe that he was expected to be sent to England to take Holy Orders. We all had high hopes for him.'

'And did he go?'

Tontsi hesitated. 'No.'

'Why not?'

'His younger brother went.'

'Why was his brother chosen?'

'Oh, he was a very pious boy.'

'And the accused was not?'

'He was also a scholar—the brother I am referring to—very learned.'

'But Mzamame was older and, as you said, the most accomplished student in the College.'

'Indeed. Very accomplished.'

'Then why was he not chosen?'

'I cannot say.'

'As you have referred to the subject yourself, I believe I may mention that I recall he was not chosen because he was expelled from the College for insubordination. It appears that he is a volatile and impulsive man.'

The Archdeacon raised a hand, frowned slightly. 'We are drifting from the point of the case.'

'Mr Mzamane is a reader and lay minister in the Church,' said Vuyo Tontsi stoutly, taking the advantage. 'People come from far and near to hear him preach. He is a first-class choirmaster. There is no one who is not aware of the respectable and generous character of Mr Mzamane.'

'Respectable to the extent that the Street Keeper was called to his home to inspect it on suspicion that he had brandy in the house and that he regularly—generously, perhaps—entertained others with the beverage?'

Vuyo Tontsi was startled. Had the Street Keeper blabbed? After the exorbitant amount that he had paid him? He adjusted his waistcoat surreptitiously. He had begun to sweat. He felt a drop at the corner of his temple. He dared not wipe it away. 'That is an invention,' he said.

'By whom?'

Tontsi caught himself before he mentioned the Street Keeper's name.

'By whom?' repeated the prosecutor.

'Jealous people.'

'Jealous of what?'

'Mzamane is a successful man. People are always searching for flaws in successful men.'

'Even though—as you said—he is renowned as a respectable and generous character by everyone?'

For once, Vuyo Tontsi was at a loss.

'Have you ever known Mzamane to be intoxicated?' continued the prosecutor.

'Never.'

'Have you and he ever taken brandy together?'

Vuyo Tontsi drew himself up, the picture of affronted dignity. Again the Archdeacon interrupted. 'The line of questioning is more appropriate to a civil court. This is an ecclesiastical tribunal. Mr Mzamane is not accused of drunkenness or the possession of spirituous liquor, and the witness is not on trial.'

The prosecutor shrugged, consulted his notes. The Dean was writing in his pocketbook, glancing triumphantly, every now and then, at the assessors.

—Hah! Not only an adulterer but a drunkard.

The prosecutor began again. 'Do you have any recollection of where the accused was in March last year?'

'I assume he was in Grahamstown. I cannot quite recall. No, if I remember correctly—if I remember—he went on a journey at some time around then.'

'Are you sure of this?'

'It was more than a year ago and I am a very busy man. I do not interfere with my neighbours.'

'He is your relative and, I believe, occupies a house owned by you. You must be aware of his movements.'

Vuyo Tontsi was silent.

'Did he take a journey?'

Again, Vuyo Tontsi hesitated. 'Yes.'

'He took a journey?'

'I believe so.' Vuyo Tontsi paused again. 'Yes.'

'For what purpose?'

'To see his mother.' He seemed uncertain. He said again, more firmly, 'Yes. His mother.'

'It is generally known that your sister, Mrs Moonlight Mzamane, believed her husband had connection with another woman and that he went to Port Elizabeth very often.'

'Women say these things. It is gossip.'

'Did she say that to you?'

'I do not recall exactly. I take no notice of gossip.'

'What did she say?'

'Hearsay,' interrupted one of the assessors.

Irritably, the prosecutor changed tack. 'What course of action did you take when you became aware of your brother-in-law's conduct?'

'That is a matter within our family and concerning only my sister and her relatives.'

'But it is now a matter which is being tried in a Diocesan Court.'

'That was not my decision or my wish.'

'Do you condone adultery?'

Before the assessors could interrupt again, Vuyo Tontsi declared, as if he were taking an oath, 'I am a man of God, a Christian believer. I do not condone anything that is opposed to the teaching of Christ.'

'Even perjury?'

AT THE RECESS, the assessors and the Archdeacon went to their luncheon in the Headmaster's house nearby. Vuyo Tontsi was in a hurry to report to his friends about the proceedings: they must interrogate the Street Keeper. Who had he told? What had he been paid? He must be reminded that his own security depended just as much on the community's leaders as theirs on him. Reminded that it was no secret that, whenever he confiscated liquor, he disposed of it himself. Often immoderately, he and the cronies whom he lured to spy. Indeed, this was not about Mzamane and some woman any more. That was past. An unfortunate incident. More unfortunate because Tontsi's sister, Nokhanyiso, had reacted with such indiscretion, gossiped so loudly, perhaps even reported her husband to the Street Keeper, when everyone knew that she, a licensed brewer of traditional beer, prepared the beverage that now doubly condemned him. More pertinently, it was the fragile structure of community and reputation that was at stake—their freehold rights, their credibility. Would they be raided too? And the Dean—that *nyoka*, stealthy as a night adder—feeding the press with letters of complaint about the evils of liquor in Fingo Village even if the wine merchant was known to make regular deliveries to the Deanery!

Vuyo Tontsi's indignation was directed at Mzamo for the consequences of his thoughtless folly, but his greater anxiety was for the repercussions to himself and his organisation. The scandal had obliged him to act the outraged brother at a time when he was busy with greater and more urgent concerns. Mzamo's dalliance with some woman would have been a trifle if he had chosen less fastidiously. A clergyman's wife—and a celebrity to boot! And Nokhanyiso—if she had had any sense—should have appreciated her possessions and her status more and behaved as a wife was expected to behave. With tolerance.

Ludlolokazi. It was her childlessness that made her the betrayer.

Stephen, meanwhile, remained where he had been seated until the room had emptied, Mzamo escorted away, even *Mfundisi* Turvey shepherded out in obligation to the Chancellor who was speaking to him gravely, his hand on his arm. Stephen slipped outside and stood alone in the shadow of the building. He gazed up at the tall grey stone walls. It was here, so many years ago, that the wagon bringing him and Mzamo for the first time from *Mfundisi* Rutherford's mission station to Grahamstown had stopped after the five-day journey from the east. They had gazed in wonder at the high windows, the recessed arches, the heavy creeper, never having seen a more imposing place. They had been blessed in the chapel, the very place where the Diocesan Court now sat. It seemed much smaller now, dim, a little weary, parochial in comparison with the vast and ancient edifice of Canterbury Cathedral, the grandeur of Fyndon's Gate at the entrance to the Missionary College, the high crumbling fastness of the old Abbey walls. But when he had first seen this place, stood before it in his shabby trousers and his polished Blucher boots, it had been just as overwhelming, and he had been afraid.

He was afraid again.

He scanned the swags of ivy. Yes, wagtails still nested in the dense fronds. See, there it goes, the bird of the ancestors, tipping its tail up and down.

'Never kill *mvemve*,' Mzamo had once said. 'For then you must bury it with a white bead and ask *abadala* not to harm your calves.'

'We are not to believe that any more,' Stephen had retorted.

He watched a wagtail dip beneath the leaves above the studded door, said quietly, despite himself, the old invocation.

—*Camagu, mandingafikelwa ngamashwa*: let misfortune pass me by.

'YOU ARE REVEREND Stephen Malusi Mzamane of Holy Trinity Mission, Nodyoba, in the district of Fort Beaufort?'

'I am.'

'You are the brother of the accused?'

'I am.'

'You are acquainted with the charge brought against your brother?'

Assent.

'Were you aware of your brother's conduct with Mrs Elizabeth Madikane?'

Stephen began cautiously, sensing Canon Rutherford's scrutiny. He inclined his head, blocking him away. 'I live in an out-of-the-way place. News does not easily reach me.'

The prosecutor waited for him to answer the question but Stephen remained silent.

'Are you acquainted with Mrs Elizabeth Madikane?' the prosecutor asked.

'I have seen her.'

'Seen her?'

'At a choir competition in this town in December 1874.'

'At no other time?'

Oh yes, in Baldwin's window. There—that face among the bonneted widows and the troops of small, frocked boys, the gentlemen in hats with well-brushed whiskers, the potted urns and the draped curtains and the distant painted sea.

Kaffir Woman. In all her grace and beauty.

Yes, I know those little rings in her ears, that small, that unobtrusive scar beside her eye, that curve of forehead. Ah yes, a hundred times she has been slipped from the Grammar on the top shelf in my bedroom and I have scanned her face. I have dreamed of her: the curve of her back, the articulation of her spine; her neck, poised as a Madonna's. Her eyes—that quiet gaze, a distance that is far beyond my reach, perhaps the reach of any man.

Who would know?

Perhaps, yes, perhaps my brother, Mzamo Mzamane, knows.

'Reverend Mzamane?'

'No,' said Stephen. 'At no other time.'

Rutherford was watching him. And from a seat to the side, among the other clergy, *Mfundisi* Turvey, his old head bowed, hand to an ear. If he was blind in one eye like his horse, he was hard of hearing too.

The prosecutor continued. 'Where were you in March last year?'

'I was at my mission station at Nodyoba.'

290

'You have said it is an out-of-the-way place.'

Stephen hesitated. 'Sir?'

'Your brother has asserted that he called on you en route to visit your mother in a district known as Hohita,' said the prosecutor. 'I have consulted a map. It appears that Nodyoba would be a very inconvenient detour for anyone making such a journey from Grahamstown.'

'There are many reasons why a person might make a detour,' said Stephen, aware that the pause before he said it had lasted too long.

'And what reason would you suppose the accused had?'

'I am his only brother, sir.'

'And so he came to your mission station to visit you?'

Stephen had blundered into the trap. Only a direct answer would do.

'Indeed,' the prosecutor continued smoothly, 'it was recorded this morning that he claimed to have spent the night with you on his way to Hohita. He came?'

Another pause.

Across from Stephen, seated to the side of the assessors' bench, was Mzamo.

His brother.

That brother whose presence had dominated his actions and motivations throughout childhood. That brother who had challenged his sense of self-worth—a worth which had only triumphed by default, not through self-assertion but by acquiescence, claiming reward which had rightly been his brother's.

Older. More accomplished. More courageous.

A man.

If he betrayed Mzamo, he betrayed himself. If he betrayed him now, he would be lost to him forever. If he betrayed him, Vuyo Tontsi would be proved a liar.

If he betrayed him, he betrayed Elizabeth Madikane.

He would shame his own people.

Umngcatshi. A traitor.

Stephen looked directly at the prosecutor. 'He came,' he said.

He saw *Mfundisi* Turvey sink a little into his shoulders, close his eyes. Yes—*Mfundisi* Turvey also knew that he had lied.

Stephen turned from the bench, dismissed from further questioning, outcast even to himself, as if he stood accused beside Mzamo.

Vuyo Tontsi did not catch his eye. At this moment, a little distance would be prudent.

The Chancellor, as judicial spokesman, rose to address the court. The Dean, pencil in hand, eager to embellish on his words. 'Amongst his own people, this man, Saul Mzamo Mzamane, seems to have thrown aside every quality which raised him to a higher level than theirs.' The Chancellor turned his gaze on Mzamo. 'Unless the educated native may be trusted among savages to be very different from a savage, it would be better if he had never taken off his red blanket.'

A warning and an admonition to every black man present.

'Nonetheless,' the Chancellor continued, pointedly addressing his remarks to the Dean and the small group of laymen from the Cathedral congregation clustered around him, 'when a native comes to school and becomes aware of the degraded condition of his nation, he is not content to return to his former life in a hut surrounded by the horrors of barbarism. He consequently makes his way to town where at first he tries to live a life worthy of his Christian calling. But everything is against him, and he sees around him Europeans, whom he has been taught to regard with great respect, sinning with a certain amount of ostentation. So you see, even if any charge brought against the native Christian has any truth in it, we have not far to look for the cause.'

The Dean put his pencil away. He would not be lectured by the tremulous old humbug: missionaries had the irritating habit of making excuses for their own naivety. This dandy in the dock was the very scoundrel who had caused such an unseemly imbroglio when he was a student at the Native College. New boots, indeed! Oh yes, at the time, the Dean had scorned the protestations of that rustic, Turvey. He, with his notions of the redeemable savage! He had told Turvey then, in no uncertain terms, how it would end. But not even he had envisaged a Diocesan Court and the pious Nonconformists frothing with indignation. He could not wait to file his copy with the *Journal*.

The proceedings droned on. The three witnesses from Port Elizabeth were recalled.

—*Yes, the accused had been seen in Port Elizabeth in March last year.*

—*It was the time when Reverend Mr Madikane was called away to his family home.*

—*The servant of Mrs Madikane had confided the truth of Mr Mzamane's visits to the churchwardens.*

'Why would she do that when her position in the household would be endangered?'

'She had been the servant to the Reverend's first wife.'

'Is that relevant?'

'We do not like strangers in our midst.'

'He was seen to leave the house.'

'By whom?'

'People.'

'He was seen in the street.'

'By whom?'

'People.'

'Which people?'

'Our people.'

'No, sir, we do not like strangers in our midst.'

All hearsay.

The afternoon was fading. A short recess was called. The assessors withdrew to consult. When they returned, the prosecutor called on the Reverend Basil Rutherford to give evidence.

'I do not have much to say,' said Rutherford. 'In February

293

this year I had occasion to attend the confirmation service at Reverend Stephen Mzamane's mission station, Holy Trinity, at Nodyoba. I mentioned his brother to him, being aware myself of the memorial sent from Port Elizabeth. Even though I told him nothing about it, he seemed discomposed by my mentioning his brother's name. What is pertinent is that I have it from Reverend Chauncey, the rector of St John's and his superior, that Mr Mzamane told him his brother had never been to his mission. Besides, although I have always regarded Reverend Mzamane as a native of steady character, he has been known to fail in giving notice of his intention to come to town, which is a breach of diocesan rules. His superior in Fort Beaufort, the Reverend Chauncey, has since written to me about Reverend Mzamane's attitude, which he has described as 'cocky'. I was disappointed to hear it but, regrettably, we, in the mission field, are accustomed to disappointment. With regard to the accused, Saul Mzamo Mzamane has been known to me since childhood. I would not have confidence in his truthfulness at any time.'

That evening, the sentence, reluctantly composed by the Bishop on the findings of the Court, was handed down.

> *Whereas Saul Mzamo Mzamane, catechist and lay preacher in our Diocese, has after due trial in our Diocesan Court been pronounced guilty of having committed adultery with Mrs Elizabeth Madikane in the month of March last year in the house of the Reverend Paul Madikane at Port Elizabeth, I, as Bishop of the Diocese, suspend him for 3 years, during which time he will not be allowed to partake of the Holy Sacrament. If, subsequently, signs of repentance are observed, readmission may be considered.*

Mzamo smiled sardonically. And if the whisper went around that humility at such a time would have served him better—*uyazidobelela*, he brings upon himself a heavy punishment—Mzamo remained unmoved. Unrepentant. His responsibility lay elsewhere, beyond the grasp of those who'd tried him. The only person with whom he wished to speak was his brother, Stephen.

He had a commission for him that no one else could carry through.

CHAP. 19:296

S tephen left the Court by a side door. He had gone out as the Archdeacon was saying a prayer for God's blessing on the proceedings and for the repentance and rehabilitation of the accused. He walked away without a prayer, hastening past the back wall of the old Native College, the ablutions and the dilapidated cottages in which some of the senior students had lodged: Julius Naka regaling Mzamo with tales of England; Julius Naka speaking of the Parliament in Westminster, the debates, the justice of a great judicial system.

Julius Naka with his black gloves and his high top hat.

Stephen neither glanced at the familiar buildings nor greeted a group of students standing by the printing-room door. He walked fast. Down into the dip and across the stone-walled bridge, up towards the Cathedral, its new spire almost built, corseted by scaffolding, the walls of the old brick church now stoutly clad in stone.

He did not stop to admire it.

He turned left, striding past the Town Hall where, not so long before, he had slunk away from the conversazione.

Down the dip, across the *sloot*, into the busy thoroughfares of Fingo Village.

—*Molo Mfundisi.*

—*Molweni Manene.*

Respectful greetings made and returned as he passed along the street.

What would they say if they knew that he, a priest, had lied despite a declaration before God which had been as binding as an oath?

He turned in at Vuyo Tontsi's gate. He had come to collect his bag. No one was there except the nursemaid and a child. He left a note: he was returning to his mission. He saddled his horse and rode away. Up the hill, past the grove of stone pines, out onto the wild ridge above the town, down into the valley of the Koonap, the sludge of water pooled between the sandbars beneath its stony banks.

Thou shalt not bear false witness …

'He has gone,' Vuyo Tontsi said when, late that evening, Mzamo arrived at his door. He showed Mzamo Stephen's note.

It is urgent that I return to the mission.

'He has gone because he is ashamed,' said Vuyo. 'What will be the outcome now? We will all be discredited.'

'I think, Tontsi, that the only reputation you fear for is your own,' retorted Mzamo. And he turned away, returning to his house.

The windows were closed. The curtains drawn. He went in and stood looking about the bedroom. When Nokhanyiso had left she had packed only her clothes. Not an ornament or trinket had been taken.

It was a challenge. A final word.

He wondered if—in regret—Nokhanyiso would come back to reclaim her possessions one day. He surveyed the dresser where the fripperies from Copeland's Store were displayed. The gilded teacup, the Toby jug, the small painted box he had wanted to give to Elizabeth Madikane but which she had refused, saying, 'Give it to your wife', an edge to her voice, a hint of disdain.

At first, on receiving these gifts, Nokhanyiso had been delighted, ingenuous, greedy. Then, in time, she had become careless, breaking things, forgetting to dust them, a child indulged with toys, eager for more, valuing none. She had also watched him, listening from the kitchen when men visited to drink, loud and loose tongued from the brew she served. And when he had remarked to her, 'I am going to my mother at Hohita. I will be gone two weeks,' she had replied, holding his gaze, almost mocking, 'I will come with you. I must pay respects to your mother.'

He had turned from her. 'I am riding. It is rough country. You will stay and keep the house. *Mfundisi* Turvey cannot do without your help at the Sunday school.'

'And what of your duties in the church?'

'It is the only time I will have leave this year. I have told *Mfundisi* Turvey. He is quite agreeable. He says it is a good thing to attend to one's mother. He said he did not know his. If he had, he would have stayed with her, right to the end of her days.'

He had gone, riding out—not as if he were going on a journey into the interior, laden with necessities for a long-neglected family, but in his best suit and overcoat and hat. When she had remarked on his get-up, he had been cutting. 'My mother will be proud to know I am a distinguished man.'

But he had left the embroidered velvet pincushion she had made for his mother on his chest of drawers. She had put it away, hiding it beneath the petticoats in her clothes chest. Some time after he had returned—distracted, irritable, out of pocket—she had said, 'Did my mother-in-law like the gift?'

'The gift ...' He had hesitated so slightly, so imperceptibly, she would have believed him had she not known better. 'Of course. She was delighted. If she could write I am sure she would have sent a note with me.'

Nokhanyiso—coiled to strike—had smiled. 'Thank you,' she had said with a quiet triumph.

No, she was not deceived. He knew he would have to

brazen it out. *Banobunyoka.* They, the women, have the venom of snakes.

But anger is also pain. Nokhanyiso's pain was simple but profound.

She had no child.

NOKHANYISO HAD LONG gone and Vuyo Tontsi knew that if Mzamo left as well he would be obliged to lodge more relatives in his second house or forfeit his right to it. A fortnight after the trial, Mzamo informed him that he was to be transferred to Matatiele. The Magistrate in that far-flung outpost had had no interpreter for months and was eager to accommodate Haddon's proposition of employing Mzamo— a favour which might be returned at some point with a transfer for himself to a more congenial spot.

Mzamo was appalled.

It was four hundred miles away.

'I'll get you back sometime soon,' said Haddon. 'Once the fuss has died down and those reverend gentlemen have found another sinner to persecute.' He smiled a little thinly. 'Matatiele is a small place so I presume your salary will be somewhat reduced. Be a good boy when you're there. Go to church and behave yourself.'

'I am excommunicated.'

'What about the Methodists? They'll do.' Haddon laughed, gave him a guinea.

Somehow Mzamo was a small boy again, accepting marbles and five shillings from the Bishop. He left his senior with the slightest bow, retreating, angry with himself and with the world.

MZAMO SOLD HIS trap and the older of his pair of horses. He packed a bag with clothes. He wrapped his father's gun in oilcloth. He took only what he could carry on horseback. His furniture was crammed into an outhouse in Tontsi's yard, its lodger hastily evicted.

The ornaments and glass-fronted cabinet were set up in Vuyo Tontsi's living room, his wife delighted to appropriate them until Nokhanyiso should return.

'She will not come back,' said Vuyo Tontsi. 'How can she return when it is clear she betrayed her husband to the Street Keeper? He will round up more than Mzamane, you may be sure!'

'Who would have paid him more than you?' his wife said.

'Who said I paid him?'

Her glance was wry: Do you think I do not know you, Vuyo Tontsi?

BEFORE HE LEFT Grahamstown, Mzamo called on *Mfundisi* Turvey to return the notebooks containing his translations for the prayer book they had been working on together.

'You were so close to completing it,' said Turvey. 'So close. Your name would have been on it—a signal moment for a black Christian. I doubt Rutherford or I will be allowed to cite you as our fellow translator now. And who will replace you?'

'Ask Vuyo Tontsi.'

Turvey caught the cynicism in Mzamo's voice. 'Can you imagine ...' he began wearily. 'Can you have *any* idea of the damage you have done? You have compromised not only the Church but Stephen, a Christian clergyman. You gave him an impossible choice.'

'Yes,' Mzamo retorted. 'I did. And he made it himself. For once. That day'—triumphantly—'that day, Malusi was my brother.'

Turvey did not challenge him. How could he?

He took the notebooks from Mzamo and laid them on the table, saying, 'He did not come to see me before he left. That is not like Stephen. Not at all.'

'He is a native,' said Mzamo.

'That should make no difference.'

300

STEPHEN WAS NOT at Nodyoba when Mzamo came. He was at Jingqi, his furthest outstation. Dyoba had gone with him, riding at his side. They were to conduct a prayer meeting and a service and to interview some catechumens and prepare them for baptism.

First, though, Mzamo had called on Rev. Thurston Chauncey at the rectory in town to ask directions to Holy Trinity Mission at Nodyoba.

Figlan had opened the door and stared at Mzamo standing on the porch, his horse hitched to the gatepost.

'Is *Mfundisi* in?'

Figlan nodded, appraising the tall figure, the waistcoat, the blue silk handkerchief tucked in the breast pocket. The gun wrapped in oilskin in the crook of his arm.

Unconcerned with Figlan's dithering—should he close the door, or stand back and allow him in?—Mzamo pushed past him and walked into the living room. Figlan hurried off to summon Chauncey.

Mzamo strolled around the room, examining the pictures hanging on chains from a rail, their frames a mildewed black: tableaux from the Bible, English churches. The armchairs smelled of vinegar and damp. He had turned as Reverend Chauncey entered, followed by Figlan.

'Ah!' Mzamo came forward, put out his hand as if he were the host and Chauncey the intruder. 'Mzamane, sir. Your man was good enough to admit me.'

Noticing the gun, Chauncey had ignored the hand, recoiled.

Amused, Mzamo tensed his grip, shifting the firearm slightly. Chauncey stepped back, collided with Figlan, collected himself, and said—his voice unusually high—'What is your business here?'

'I have come to ask directions to Reverend Mzamane's mission, sir. He is my brother.'

The man, Figlan, cocked his head, a smile forming. 'Ngesi,' he said.

'Ngesi?' Mzamo grimaced slightly. 'Is that what they call him?'

'*Mfundisi* Ngesi.'

'See here,' said Chauncey, suddenly asserting himself. 'I don't think a fellow should bring a firearm into another man's house.'

'I was not prepared to leave it unattended outside,' said Mzamo. 'At a time like this'—enjoying himself—'it is very unwise not to be vigilant. Someone might seize it and use it to our disadvantage.'

Chauncey seemed to build up steam at this remark but prudently allowed it to subside. Mzamo, he could see, would not be intimidated. Yet another of Turvey's 'fine young men'. It was a scandal! 'Figlan'—lowering the register of his voice, clutching at composure—'show him the road.'

'Thank you,' Mzamo bowed slightly, glanced about the room again, head inclined—an insurance broker assessing the contents—and walked to the door. Quite in command of himself, he replaced his hat at the threshold, tipped it politely, adjusted his gun and walked away down the path.

Chauncey watched him through the window, twitching the heavy lace curtain aside.

Figlan had followed their visitor, held the reins as he mounted his horse. He was gesturing up the road with great sweeps of the arm, his voice raised as if declaiming. He said something and the horseman laughed, throwing his head back. Figlan laughed too. He continued speaking more softly, as the other leaned down to catch his words. They continued with their banter until Chauncey rattled the sash—safe behind the glass—and roared, 'Figlan, you rascal, come in at once.'

The rider raised his hat to Figlan, laughed again and trotted off, the firearm now slung across his back.

MZAMO REINED IN at the top of the long slope that led to Nodyoba.

There, beyond, was the church with its faded roof and its crooked cross.

There, the gaunt old tree, branches stark as bones.

There, a flock of goats resting in the porch of the deserted schoolroom.

What a place to send a man educated in England at the foremost Missionary College!

And the houses? Not a 'four-corner' among them. Thatched huts, mud-walled, smoke drifting through the roofs. Here and there an aloe sprouting on the apex—an *intelezi*—the sign of a heathen homestead; insurance against lightning, proof of the presence of the shades. Besides the chapel—church would be too grand a term—Stephen's little house was the only building which seemed to proclaim a Christian presence. For once, Mzamo was relieved he had not been chosen to go to Canterbury. If he had, he would have refused the posting to Nodyoba and become an interpreter, a businessman or clerk like Julius Coventry Naka.

He rode up to the house, past the vegetable garden and the mealie field where a small boy was chasing away birds. He tethered his horse and took the path to the front porch. He knocked on the door.

No one answered.

Laying his gun and bag down on the porch, he walked round to the back. Chickens scattered at his approach. A girl was washing laundry in a tub. She wore a blue bonnet, folded away from her forehead, tied in a bow beneath her chin.

'*Molo.*' Mzamo raised his hat.

A startled appraisal, eyes swiftly averted. Flicking away water dripping from her delicate, small fingers, the young woman replied softly, '*Molo, Mhlekazi.*' She did not look up again as she answered Mzamo's questions in a low voice.

—No, Mfundisi *was not here.*

—No, *he would not be back today. He was* kwaJingqi. *He must spend a night at that place. It is too far to go in a day.*

'Is the headman here?'

'No. He is gone as well.'

Vexed, Mzamo looked around. How could he leave the gun with a stranger, let alone a girl?

'Are you the servant of *Mfundisi*?'

She shook her head, said, 'I am not a servant.'

'But you are doing the laundry.' He gestured at the tub. He glanced at her feet. They were bare, her skirts pegged up at her waist at the back. Her apron was wet.

'Yes,' she said.

Mzamo suppressed a smile. He could draw only one conclusion. Imagine Rutherford's face!

'*Ndingumkhuluwa wakhe*. I am his elder brother,' he said. 'I am on a long journey and I cannot wait for him to return.' He would have to conceal the weapon without her seeing. 'I will leave a letter. Perhaps,' he continued, 'you could offer me some tea and a moment to refresh myself in his house.'

The girl dried her hands on her apron, shook down her sleeves and walked sedately across the yard. She opened the back door, standing aside to let him pass. He entered a low-ceilinged lean-to attached to the building which seemed to serve as a kitchen. There was a fire in the range. The girl took up a kettle and went outside again to fill it at a water-drum. Mzamo mounted a step and went through a doorway into a living room.

A table, a stool and an easy chair.

Three pictures hung on the wall in handmade frames. Two from the *Illustrated London News*, one a photograph of choristers in front of a great stone building. He looked about him for a place to conceal the gun.

Out of reach. Out of sight.

He stepped through to the bedroom. It was painted blue. An iron bedstead was pushed against the wall. Above it hung a handsome wooden cross. There was a chest and a clothes rail wedged across a corner. A bookshelf was secured to the wall high up near the window. It was long enough to lay the gun on it, hidden by the books.

Mzamo went back to the kitchen, said to the girl, 'Would it be possible to prepare some food for me? Or pick some cobs from the garden that I could take on my journey? I would be very grateful.'

He returned to the bedroom, closed the door and pulled the books down from the shelf, tossing them on the bed. Then—alert to sounds in the kitchen—he slipped unnoticed through the front door, retrieved the gun and his bag from the front porch and ducked swiftly inside. He lifted the gun onto the shelf, pushed it back against the wall and hastened to replace the books. Before he had finished there was a tap at the bedroom door.

'A moment,' Mzamo called hastily. He went through to the living room. The girl stood there with a cup of tea, flustered. She bobbed a curtsey as he took it.

'Surely you have a loaf of bread?' he said, encouraging her to retreat.

She shook her head, did not move. He sat at the table, put the cup before him and took his notebook from his pocket, saying, 'I will leave a letter.'

She did not reply, simply stood before him. 'Can you read English?' A little peremptorily. Again she shook her head.

'Have you fetched the corn?'

She went away then. A moment later he saw her through the window hurrying down the path to the garden, her bare feet light and deft. Yes, she was quaintly comely—but goodness, she was raw!

The room was stuffy and hot. Mzamo took off his jacket and laid it on the armchair, tugged at his collar to loosen it, then sat at the table and opened his notebook, tore out a page and, as a precaution against the inquisitive, scoured his vocabulary for the most obscure words he could think of. He took a pencil from his breast pocket and wrote in English, in a closely spaced copperplate, difficult to decipher amongst the flourishes.

Malusi,

I am grieved to have missed you. I am en route to my post with the RM and CC of Matatiele. I have concealed the evidence of compensation granted to our father for service to the Government (and which I have inherited on account of his extended absence). Concerned (through the counsel of others) at the possibility of confiscation or theft in such a distant place, I would appreciate your vigilant custody until I return. It is lodged with your Euclid and Virgil. Under no circumstances allow it to fall into uncongenial hands.

Your brother,

Mzamo Mzamane.

Rather pleased with his turn of phrase, he laid the note on the table, weighted it with his empty teacup and went outside.

The girl had collected an armful of cobs.

'Thank you,' he said. He returned to the house and collected his jacket and bag. He opened the bag and stuffed three of the cobs inside. 'Pity,' he said, 'but I fear I cannot fit more.' Straightening up, he put on his hat and touched the brim, saying in Xhosa, 'Greet my brother and tell him how sorry I am that he was away. I have left a note on the table. Be very sure to give it to him. *Yindaba etyhulu.*' It is a matter of importance. 'Do not forget.'

LILY MAJOLA WATCHED Mzamo Mzamane ride away. She had seen Thomas Dema ride away once too, dressed the same, his hair with the same glint of pomade as the sun had caught it, his boots burnished, his winged collar starched stiff beneath his chin. But, unlike Thomas Dema, this stranger had *ubunzima.* Nobility. Just like *Mfundisi* Ngesi.

She stood a long time watching the empty road. Then she went into the house, treading softly, as if there was a presence, hardly breathing. She lifted the teacup from the table and took it away to wash. She came back and picked up the note. She turned it this way and that. She had never seen such writing!

She stood another long moment at the bedroom door. She opened it, letting it swing back. She caught the faint scent of Mzamo's pomade, glanced about as if he might have returned and caught her prying. Three books lay on the bed. Frowning, she stepped across and touched them, almost reverently.

What was the brother doing with *Mfundisi's* books?

She took them to replace on the shelf.

A loose leaf fell from one, a picture from another, striking the floor.

She picked it up and looked at it. She took it to the window.

She stood. Gazed.

Had she been able to read she would have picked out the gold-lettered title, *Baldwin's Studio, Canterbury*, in the bottom right-hand corner.

She had never seen a face like that.

Such a collar. Such beads about the neck. Such a pair of earrings. So bright and finely hooped.

She touched the collar of her own frock, the bedraggled bonnet, the small, unadorned lobes of her ears. Who was this woman?

She sensed that she could never ask.

CHAP. 20:308

We had a storming synod,' said Albert, flinging down his hat and coat and flopping into a chair. 'Simply storming!'

'And I had a perfectly delightful time at Bishopsbourne with all the clergy wives,' said Unity. 'What a relief to be back and to have a cup of tea decently served! Still,' lowering her voice, 'whatever have we come to? My mother's daily tea service is better than the Bishop's best.' She glanced towards the door. It was closed. 'Just imagine what Mama would think! Oh, and while we were all at table, Nursey came bursting in all agog to say that when she was in the garden with the children there was an ox running wild down the street.'

'I put it quite strongly,' Albert continued, 'quite as strongly as you might have done. Surprisingly, so did the old Geezer. We both told them that the colonies wouldn't get students from Canterbury if they didn't shake up the stipends they offered to make it more attractive to leave Home.'

'Fortunately Clementine was upstairs in the nursery and not in the garden with the other children. The Bishop's grandchildren, I might add, are a fearfully rough lot. Their accents are appalling! And Bertie, you must stop calling him Geezer. You might let it slip.'

'So, to cool us off, the Dean marched us down to inspect the Cathedral's new tower. It's almost finished but looking rather naked still without the tip of the steeple. The Bishop said the new doors were a gift from Canterbury. I'll swear they're the ones I worked on when I was at College. I must have a closer look. I remember carving my initials into the inner edge, just for fun.'

'Bertie, are you listening?'

'Yes, of course.'

'Did you hear what I said about the ox?'

'What ox?'

'Albert!' Unity threw her sewing at him.

'I hang on your every word, my love,' murmured Albert, rising and kissing the top of her head. 'Where's my Clemmie?'

'You're unbecomingly sentimental about that child.'

'I'm her Papa, aren't I?'

The return to Grahamstown for synod had come at just the right time, Albert knew. They had settled back into their familiar lodgings at the Native College which, furnished as they still were with their own more permanent possessions, had been an instant relief and comfort to Unity. He had feared keeping her another week at St Paul's amidst the thorn trees and dusty dongas. She had even rejoiced in the journey back to Grahamstown, pointing out the plants and trees and distant hills to little Clementine, ensconced on her lap and diverted with sugar lumps whenever she became fretful.

It was a relief to him too. Alone with Unity and their small child among a ragged population of 'Tobacco Christians', always whining for hoes or seed or tools if he wanted them to come to church at all, had been a trial of Faith and had tested his cheerfulness beyond limits. He knew he was often 'taken for a ride', possibly laughed at for his willingness to please and conciliate, ending up both angry and resentful at being fleeced. But a resentful wife was worse. Especially when she played the martyr, a role she had perfected in their time at St Paul's.

She 'worked herself to the bone' to keep the house in order. 'If you can call this a house' was her riposte whenever he thanked her for her efforts. But when he encouraged her to employ a nursemaid for Clementine to give her time for a little leisure, she would be affronted and tart. 'Really, Bertie! You know quite well that if I employed a nurse she would have to be English. And how could we afford one?' Reproachful: *Papa warned me.* 'Besides, how could I possibly have a native girl in the house? Clemmie would start gabbling that barbarous tongue and the *bouquet d'Afrique* about the place would be overpowering! I simply cannot have a servant who does not wash at least twice a week. Nor could I possibly take on any of those young girls who like to smear them-selves with fat. And they all do, you know, even if they are dressed up in skirts and petticoats. Mrs Rutherford told me she was obliged to hide her face cream as every maid she has ever had has always helped herself!' After which Unity would invariably start to cry.

'I fear the people are offended that you have resisted their help,' ventured Albert.

'How can they be offended?'

'It is the custom to clean and cook for the missionary and nurse the children. The work and the money are very much needed.'

'Well, they will end up being spoiled by you and become all too familiar. And then, what will they do for luxuries when we have gone?'

'What luxuries?'

'Face cream,' she wailed irrationally.

Albert had begun to laugh. It was all he could do.

IT WAS AT synod that Albert heard the details of Mzamo Mzamane's trial. And at synod that he heard, too, of the doubt cast on the character of Reverend Stephen Mzamane by the Director of Missions, Canon Basil Rutherford.

'Where is Mr Mzamane?' he had asked at the recess after the opening session, looking about for Stephen. Yes, Gideon Boom was there. So was the senior teacher of the Native College, a newly appointed Mfengu in Holy Orders, only weeks away from being ordained priest.

'Mzamane has excused himself,' said Basil Rutherford.

'Why? He is the most dedicated fellow. Besides, he has been writing the "Rules and Suggestions for Missions to the Heathen". He wrote to tell me they were ready to be presented at this session.'

'You have been marooned in a backwater, my dear Newnham. I fear you will be disappointed to hear that there are some doubts about Mr Mzamane's reliability. We are not sure he should have our confidence.'

'Impossible!' Albert could not help retorting. 'If any living person ever taught me what vocation is, it is Stephen Mzamane.'

'Ah '—the usual old canard—'you have not been in the Colony long enough, Newnham. You will be sadly disillusioned, like the rest of us.'

Roused, Albert interrupted, 'I am very sure I will not be —' at which moment the Archdeacon glided in and drew Rutherford away to more elevated company, leaving Albert brushing his palm vigorously across his head, making the cockscomb bristle.

He looked about for Reverend Turvey and was making his way hastily towards him when he was collared by the Dean, alert to his return from St Paul's and determined to recruit him for duty at the forthcoming Cathedral Bazaar.

Albert listened impatiently, saying, in an effort to escape, 'I am very anxious to find out if something has prevented Reverend Mzamane from being here.'

The Dean—unctuous old humbug—remarked complacently, 'I doubt we will see him here again.'

'Why not?'

The Dean eyed Albert's hair as if he were taking notes for one of his editorials—*the lamentable quality of the incumbents sent to local missions*—and said, 'He was called as witness at his brother's trial. A most notorious affair with the wife of the minister of another denomination, the unfortunate product of which is now over a year old.'

'Yes, yes, I know all that,' said Albert, almost rudely. 'But what has it to do with Stephen—with Reverend Mzamane?'

'He said under oath that the accused had visited him at his mission at the time when the presumed "event"—you will understand me—would have taken place in Port Elizabeth, thereby implying that the child could not be the son of the accused.'

'Well, of course he did! The accused is his brother.'

The Dean's look was withering.

—*Didn't I warn you, my Lord, that the fellows coming from Canterbury were not up to the standard of those from our great universities? Take Turvey!*

As Albert hurried away, the Reverend Mr Thurston Chauncey was holding forth to a group of colonial clergy about 'that libertine, Mzamaan'. Overhearing, Albert stopped to listen.

'The fellow appeared at my door,' said Chauncey. 'Marched in, almost knocking over my servant, made himself quite at home in my parlour and'—pausing for effect, snuffling triumphantly at the unexpected attention—'armed to the teeth with a great blunderbuss of a gun. I told him, in no uncertain terms, to leave.' Conjuring the picture of affronted authority. 'If I've said it once, I'll say it again—having a Native College in Grahamstown right next door to the school for the sons of our foremost citizens is a very dangerous precedent. How can these "trouser Christians" possibly know their station when they are allowed to perform Shakespeare and play cricket together? And then—to send them to England? Well! I will not say who is to blame but

312

they will reap their just rewards, let me tell you.'

'I was in England with Reverend Mzamane,' interjected Albert from beyond the circle, his face red, his small spectacles slipping on the sheen of his nose. 'He is the stoutest Christian I have ever known and the most loyal friend.'

Rev. Chauncey, bolstered by the group around him, eyed Albert condescendingly.

'And,' said Albert, aware of the hostile stares and scoring the only point that he knew would carry weight with the colonials, 'he is one of the finest cricketers I have ever played with, either in England or here. A sportsman and a gentleman.'

'Ah,' said Chauncey huffily. 'We were not talking of cricket but of morals.'

'And let anyone here question Mr Stephen Mzamane's morals and I will take the greatest pleasure in knocking him down,' said Albert.

ALBERT DID NOT mention Stephen's absence to Unity; he wanted no reproof, no hint of an 'I told you so'. Feeling lonely and disgruntled he went to his desk and wrote a letter to Stephen.

March 27th

Dear old chap,

You were not at synod and I missed you. What detained you? It would have done me a world of good to see you and hear your news. I do not like getting it second-hand from others and am concerned that I might have given you bad advice when last you wrote.

We have returned to Grahamstown from St Paul's. It was not a pleasant place and my wife is very much relieved to be back in town. I have been assured that Rev. Jackson, the missionary-in-charge, will be returning to his post again within the next few weeks but I must be at St Paul's to hand over to him and pack up the last of our belongings. I have decided to leave my family in

Grahamstown and get through the business as quickly as possible.

Please send news. I am anxious to know that nothing is amiss. It's high time we had a game of cricket. Any chance of bringing a team to the College for a friendly next season?
God bless, old man.
Your friend,
Albert Newnham.

Dear old chap ... Stephen smiled as he read the letter. He had always been addressed by Albert as '*dear old chap*', spoken with real affection. Looking at the letter, following the jumble of words, trying to make them out, Stephen laughed out loud, as if Albert was right there with him, delivering the same friendly punches as he had at College whenever Stephen scoffed at his carelessness.

How could he return the gesture—*dear old chap*—when he knew that he had perjured himself in court?

Not on account of protecting Mzamo but in anger at those who had trapped him, crowing at their own cleverness. If God was not confused about his motives for supporting his brother, Albert might be. How could it be otherwise? He was an Englishman. He would trust the words of other Englishmen.

'I say, Newnham,' Stephen amused himself by addressing the fireplace, more cynically than in humour, parodying the clergy in Grahamstown. 'Heard about that native deacon, what's-his-name? The one who was at Canterbury?'

'Expecting a native to be a reliable clergyman'—mimicking the Dean—'is as foolish as suggesting that a woman should take Orders.'

Mrs Beazer this time, wagging her head at the fire irons. 'I hear he had a dalliance with a Dissenting minister's wife!'

A suppressed exclamation made him turn. Lily Majola was standing in the kitchen doorway, her hand across her mouth, her eyes wide.

Stephen laughed.

So did she.

THE REVEREND JACKSON did not return to St Paul's Mission on the Indwe River. Albert waited him impatiently all through April and May, riding out along the road every afternoon, scanning the track for a rider or a cart.

None came.

Anxious for information, he wrote to Rutherford, knowing how frantic Unity would be. He went into Queenstown to send a telegram to Rutherford, almost an ultimatum. He bought supplies to tide him over. It was a journey that had taken him all day and that obliged him to sleep in the Cape cart that night. He had not camped out alone before. He remembered the words of his churchwarden before he had left the mission that morning. 'Take care of reptiles, *Mfundisi*. There are many out at night at this time of year. They are very dangerous.'

How jovial and careless he had been when he had told Stephen so long ago that if he was bitten by a snake or slain by a headhunter he must carve his name in the memorial crypt at the College so he could bawl *adsum* at heavenly roll-call along with his old comrades.

It was no joke now as he sat upright in the cart, a rabbit on its hind legs, starting at every sound, too alarmed to step down even to relieve himself. Besides the ubiquitous 'reptiles', the trader in town had given him stark advice. 'I'd get back to your station in daylight,' he'd said as he loaded up the sack of meal and the bag of seed that Albert had bought. 'There's been trouble up at Nonesi's.' Before Albert left, the trader had given him last week's newspaper too. He read it uneasily.

May 17th: The natives are agitating for a fight. There has been a significant increase in the number and quality of livestock stolen in outlying districts in recent weeks. Cattle rustling being the first sign of men on the move, it is prudent for those affected to make arrangements to take their livestock to more protected regions …

He thought with rising anxiety of Unity and Clementine in faraway Grahamstown. What would become of them if rustlers arrived and murdered him? No, he would not alarm them with the news of livestock thieves. He took out his notebook and decided to compose a letter to Stephen instead.

> *Write to me, old chap—is there any danger? They say that the Galekas and the Gaikas are spoiling for a fight with the Fingoes. I have always trusted to your sense. I know you would protect my interests, no matter what—as I would yours.*

As a diversion he drew a cartoon of himself huddled in a cart, submerged inside his parson's collar, his hair electrified with fright, as a python with a predatory grin wound its way up the wheel.

He laughed. It was a croak.

He prayed. But the chirping and then the sudden silence of the crickets seemed a sure sign of watchers in the dark, and as the days dragged by, Albert considered deserting the mission. Despondent and impatient in turns, he listened out for news from every wagon and wayfarer that went by.

It was not encouraging.

A letter came from Stephen. It had crossed with his.

> June 3rd
> Dear Albert,
> *Events have overtaken me. We, at Nodyoba, are experiencing shortages of every kind, especially money. The harvest has been poor, the roads are in a parlous state and the drought has made us all alarmed. Pasture for cattle is dwindling.*
>
> *My brother Mzamo, in Matatiele, has written asking for assistance. It appears his work with the Magistrate in that district was unsatisfactory. He was obliged to sell his horses and all his goods in order to sustain himself. He wrote to Mr Haddon*

in Grahamstown, his former employer, asking for a loan so he could return to the town and resume his duties. It appears Haddon consulted with the Bishop and Canon Rutherford, who were not prepared to help. That is when he wrote to me. I consulted the bank manager in Fort Beaufort but he was not inclined to give me a loan—even of five pounds—which is the amount Mzamo needs to secure a ticket at the nearest railway station, which is none the less five days' walk from where he resides at present.

Would it be straining the bonds of friendship too much to ask if you could secure a loan with the bank in your name but on my behalf, which I will ensure is repaid as soon as Mzamo and I are able to honour it? His circumstances are so wretched that he has even had to sell his coat. It seems he is greatly repentant for all that has happened and wishes to return home and make amends with the Diocesan Court and be reinstated with his congregation.

Stephen ended the letter with Mzamo's address, care of the Anglican Church in Matatiele, where, it appeared, the incumbent had been generous enough to allow him to use the address in his extremity but not able or willing to advance a loan.

Albert sighed. What was he to do?

To go, yet again, to Queenstown, to endure another night in the cart? His deft cartoon suddenly seemed foolish, misplaced. Could Stephen know—could he begin to comprehend—his terror?

Albert read the letter again. Stephen had not asked for money. He had asked Albert to secure a loan because he, a black man, could not.

That was fair.

Albert knew that his own annoyance at the inconvenience was unjustified.

—I know you would protect my interests, no matter what—as I would yours.

But going to Queenstown again was wholly out of the

question. Jackson must surely appear at any minute and then he would be off before the sun had set, reptiles or no reptiles. He would not risk losing one more day than necessary in getting to Grahamstown.

He rifled through his trunk, packed and ready to depart. He found his winter jacket. A favourite. One Stephen had often admired when Albert had spruced himself up for courting Miss Unity Wills, promising to bring Stephen cake on his return. Remembering—penance for self-indulgence—he parcelled the coat up in brown paper. He examined his personal cash box. It was almost empty. Six pounds fourpence and the sum needed by himself for his own journey to Grahamstown. There was also the envelope containing a gift that Papa Wills had sent some months ago to buy 'Little Clementine and my dearest Unity some trifles on the occasions of their birthdays'.

A handsome seven pounds.

He counted it twice. He would replace it with the money he would get on loan from the bank in Grahamstown before it was needed. Unity would never know. If he had to tutor boys after hours for a fee, he would. He could not let Stephen down.

And yet, the thought crossed his mind—despite himself: Stephen might have let him down. Some omission in what he'd told him of Mzamo's history?

Just a flicker of doubt.

STILL MR JACKSON did not come. Basil Rutherford wrote:

June 20th
My dear Newnham,
I know you are anxious to return to us in Grahamstown but unfortunately I have some rather troubling news. It seems that Mr Jackson will not be returning to St Paul's after all. An alarming account has reached us here about his erratic conduct while he was in Cape Town. Although he has come into a handsome legacy on the death of his father, it seems the poor man

has lost his reason and deserves every sympathy in his condition. He has been admitted to an institution for observation until he is able to proceed to England. Under the circumstances I know you will appreciate that we cannot leave St Paul's unattended and desire you to remain at your post until further notice. The Archdeacon will do his best to find a permanent replacement so you can return to Grahamstown but, as a graduate of a Missionary College, you will be aware that your first duty is to your vocation in the field, despite its having been bestowed sooner than expected.

I hope Mrs Newnham will not find the change too inconvenient and will proceed to St Paul's as soon as possible to join you.

Yours ever in Christ,
Basil Rutherford.

He was appalled.

How in God's name could he tell Unity? How could he possibly break the news that he would not be returning to Grahamstown? That she and Clementine must make the journey north again, this time into the piercing chill and drought of winter? Into a district threatened by rustlers, reptiles and rumours of war?

His rage at Mr Jackson now found vent in language learned from his brother, Percy. It had seemed that Unity might have lost her reason, had the sojourn at St Paul's not been temporary. She might jettison it now in this strange little house with its whimpering thatch, its thumps and creaks and sly south wind that made the windows squeal faintly. She would be like a bird caught behind a window-pane, frantic to escape.

—Did you hear that, Bertie? Bertie, did you hear that? Someone is whistling. I know that thieves whistle to each other, pretending to be birds. That's what Mrs Rutherford told me.

How, too, could he justify bringing her here if fighting broke out? What use would he be if he could not leave her and visit his outstations? He must write to the Bishop and ask dispensation.

The Bishop was sympathetic. Mrs Newnham was welcome to continue in their accommodation in Grahamstown but Newnham himself would be obliged to stay at his post.

> Believe me, I am doing my best to secure an incumbent. At times like this you can imagine how difficult it is. I will deliver you into the bosom of the family just as soon as I am able. In the meantime you will be in my prayers and my wife will do all in her power to support your young family. I know I can rely on you and your Missionary Vow to overcome alarm and be a true soldier of Christ.

Yes—he would be a true soldier of Christ. Not to please the Bishop. Not even to please God. But because he was a man of his word.

Yet when war broke out in early August it was Unity who orchestrated his return. And Dr Wills who engineered it. A cable to the Metropolitan sufficed. Within two months St Paul's was left to its bewildered catechists and vagrant souls.

'I will be back,' Albert said, earnestly if rashly, shaking the hands of a small gathering of mission people on the day he left.

He knew they did not believe him.

Arriving in Grahamstown thin and dishevelled, he had been greeted with tears, caresses and fluting lamentations by Unity. She hung on him, dragging at his hand until he wished he could shake her off for a moment, loosen his stock and breathe, bathe himself and have a hearty dinner. Then take her to his bed. She wept and smiled and talked as if he were a small child, appropriated his handkerchief and blew wet tears into it. He went in search of little Clementine who, returned from a walk with her nurse, flung herself at him without reproach.

But not even she could assuage his shame.

CHAP. 21:321

The guns were called in.

There was a meeting at Nodyoba. The headman was incensed. Had not they, loyalists of the Crown, devoted subjects of Her Majesty the Queen, always defended the frontier against the Ngqika and the Gcaleka? Had they ever defected as the Kat River Hottentots had once done? Had they not been true subjects of Empire and the Colony?

Their guns were earned.

It was Stephen who had the task of mediating when the official notice came. The irony of his being Ngqika did not escape him. A Ngqika giving the news to the Mfengu that they would be disarmed. That their precious guns would be confiscated. That they would not be able to defend themselves in case of attack from the east.

That their loyalty was in question.

Stephen had loaded the weapons into Dyoba's cart. Sending Dyoba on an errand, he had gone reluctantly into his house to collect the gun hidden behind his books. He had wiped it briskly with a cloth, taken it up in his hands, examining it.

The patina of the butt, the buffed brass, the leaden barrel.

This talisman of his father's labour, of independence. Of manhood.

No one knew he had it but Mzamo.

And if Lily Majola had seen it he knew she would sooner be martyred than betray him.

He slid it back behind the books. And took the guns to town.

'How many weapons, Reverend?' the Magistrate's clerk asked.

'Fifteen, sir. '

'You're sure that's the final tally?'

'Can one ever be sure, sir?'

'Well, should there be any mistake and we find that weapons have been concealed, you realise that you'll be held accountable?

'Yes, sir.'

SCHOOL CONTINUED EVERY morning, work in the gardens every afternoon, but the carpentry workshop was silent, the enthusiastic games of cricket suspended. Most of the young men had left the mission. Some, unwilling to fight, had gone west in fear, some in despondency. Others, with mixed Ngqika blood and vacillating allegiance, had joined the rebels, urging their kinsmen to follow them east to join Chief Sandile's forces.

All along the skyline the fires burned, dull red patches in the night. The curls and shards of charred thatch drifted into the church, the parsonage, the houses at Nodyoba. Colonial troops marched in, scouring the valleys and kloofs, the gorges and riverbeds. From the surrounding hills and across the river, heathen and Christian drove their cattle onto the mission lands. The women and old men straggled behind with their household goods. Listless sheep and goats wandered across the drought-ravaged pasture, leaving nothing behind. Soldiers came and appropriated any fodder that had been stored against the winter. Children cried in hunger.

Lily Majola tended a cooking pot on the church porch.

322

She boiled bones and maize into a dough—a grey sludge that fed those who did not care what they were served or those stumbling into death as they reached the mission yard.

Stephen wondered if he should fortify the church. He inspected his makeshift windows, their rudimentary frames, their cheap panes of glass, the crooked hasps. A child could break the catch, a man simply push the structure in.

News came that his fellow-deacon, the devout and humble Gideon Boom, had been attacked at his mission on the Kubusi River. It had been burned to the ground. Boom— an Mfengu among the Ngqika—had fled.

Stephen was a Ngqika among the Mfengu. Would he be next? A reprisal?

News came of other burning missions, of Mfengu killed, Gcaleka killed, Ngqika killed. Chief Sandile was fighting once again all across the ancestral lands from which he had once been banished. A headline in the Grahamstown Journal read: Native criminals at the zenith of their boldness. The sons of the chiefs—'ungrateful "trouser and boots" natives'—had been 'dragging the colonial troops all over the Amatolas'.

And the editorial:

The opinion is gaining ground that there must have been something radically wrong in the treatment of the native to have caused so many of them to revolt. Yet, it is to be noted that in no case has any tangible cause of complaint been alleged by the chiefs. They have not been oppressed. They have not been made tributary.

A rebuttal from the Bishop:

We may regret but we can hardly be surprised to have it reported from the frontier that many Christian kaffirs have joined the ranks of the rebellion. It would be unreasonable to expect that no Christian kaffir would remain attached to the cause of his tribe and kinsmen.

Stephen smiled wryly. No doubt the dear old Bishop would be vilified (yet again) for his 'Exeter Hall sentiments' in the next edition of the *Journal*.

Julius Coventry Naka, Boy Henry Duke of Wellington Tshatshu and Edmund Gonya Sandile had joined the rebels. Jonas Ntsiko had been publishing poetry of which—had it come their way—the colonial newspapers would have trumpeted, '*Sedition!*'

—*If I must fight,* Gonya Sandile had said, *then I will choose to fight for my father.*

Mhala, the interpreter, had refused to serve in trials which involved his kinsmen. He was accused of treason on trumped-up charges. He was found in possession of a gun and arrested. He had protested to the Magistrate: 'It is very strange that the Whites should make me an object of their suspicions and yet adopt my suggestions as to securing the peace.'

A remark which elicited a flurry of scorn: imagine an Imperial Commander adopting the suggestions of a rebel chief! *It just goes to show!*

Like Stephen, all were products of the native colleges in Cape Town or Grahamstown, the elite of Canterbury and Nuneaton. The very men groomed for Empire and the Church.

—*What lions they will be!* the Bishop had once said.

Lions indeed! They had turned on their ringmaster and bared their teeth.

What if he, Stephen, were confronted with a band of Ngqika coming to Nodyoba to fire the mission? What would he say if he were suddenly challenged by Duke Tshatshu or Julius Naka?

—*Let's have a cup of tea, dear boys, and remember the larks at Canterbury? Think of old Blunsom!*

Then all in unison and in imitation: *Didn't last! Like the Heskimo. Like the Zoola from Africa. All them others. Didn't last!*

More news—from *Mfundisi* Turvey this time—in a letter

which, Stephen sensed, fulfilled the old man's self-deprecating dictum: *I shall not tell you what to do, only offer my experience,* Turvey wrote simply. And sadly. More in hope, it seemed, than in conviction: *Stick to your post, Stephen. The Christian voice of moderation is needed at this time. Do not sacrifice Faith to anger.*

But there were other words, more convincing, more urgent, written by Christian Africans in *Isigidimi* and other publications. Men who served both God and nation, men declaiming on an empire so much greater than the secular one they were expected to serve. Stephen had read with stirring conviction:

> *Look to the rock from which you were cut*
> *And the quarry from which you were hewn.*

> *Ngani ukuba uhlale ngedyudyu,*
> *usoyika ingqumbo yomcinezeli?*

Why fear the oppressor who is bent on destruction?

> *Ke wena, ngowam: you are my nation*
> *I give you my teaching and protection.*

> *For this is our sovereign Lord who defends his people.*

THE DROUGHT WORSENED all through 1878. Mr Jacobus Ockert did not rejoice in asking Stephen seventy shillings for a bag of corn that a year previously would have cost him ten.

'Bad times, Pastor,' he confided in the trading-store Xhosa that was as rapid and proficient as his voice was loud and hearty. 'The troops have taken everything but I kept this bag behind for you in case you needed it. I'll give it to you for seventy shillings cost price, as a favour. See here,' pulling a newspaper from beneath the counter and spreading it out, smoothing the wrinkled pages with his hand and running his broad finger down the columns of the *Market Report* from Grahamstown. 'Robbery, I tell you, Pastor. Rogues making money out of everyone's hard times. Besides mealies and flour, there isn't a piece of meat to be had at the butcher's except for something that is more likely to be an old donkey or goat. The dominee in my church said that the Lord was very angry with us all.' He turned to the front page, thrust his finger at it:

> Starvation looms. If the rains fail again this year's harvest will be ruined. The gaols are full to bursting, not with rebels and other felons, but with starving women and children, many of the latter having no idea of the whereabouts of their parents. Pitiful scenes are reported from King William's Town and Stutterheim.

'You got hungry children up at your place?' Mr Ockert inquired.

'Some. I know there will be more when the fighting reaches us.'

'You got a gun?'

Stephen hesitated. 'The guns have just been called in.'

'Pity.' Mr Ockert glanced around. 'If I was a kaffir and had a gun, guess who I'd shoot!'

Stephen said, feigning offence, 'Mr Ockert, my people call me *Mfundisi* Ngesi—the Englishman.'

'Well, you look like a kaffir to me,' said Mr Ockert. 'And a very black one at that! Give me a good kaffir any day. He will never be clever enough to be as *skelm* as an Englishman.' Stephen laughed. Mr Ockert, everyone knew, was no lover of the English.

DUSK. LILY'S STEP. Swift. Urgent. This was not the familiar scamper, preceding some breathless errand, some question for *Mfundisi* Ngesi.

Fists at the closed door.

'Yini?' What is it?

326

'They have come back.'

'Who?'

'*Abafana bakithi.*' Our boys.

'What's wrong?'

'The people are beating them.'

The shouting came in gusts from down in the river valley. A concourse of people in the late light of afternoon. Women. Men. Boys. The baying of women whooped up to aggression. Even Ma Majola shouting and waving her fist. Children standing at a distance, both frightened and gleeful, pressing closer.

Two young men were being flayed. Stephen's churchwardens, his elder sidesmen, wielded sticks as if they were harrying a pack of marauding dogs. Already there was blood in the sand. Astounded at the savagery, Stephen ran forward. '*Yimani!* Stop!' he shouted, pushing the women aside, roughly shouldering his way through the crowd. In the confusion, he was aware of two or three boys fleeing, chased by angry villagers.

'*Yimani!*' he thundered again.

The men stopped but, shouting furious threats, they picked up stones and threw them. The fleeing figures, running in panic, disappeared into the bush at the edge of the river.

Stephen gazed down at a bleeding form. He looked around, appalled. '*Bangabantu bethu!* These are our people!' he shouted. 'Would you kill your own children?'

Dyoba stepped forward. 'They went to the Ngqika to fight for them. Now they have come back because it does not suit them to be amaNgqika any more. Now they wish to be amaMfengu again. How can they go unpunished? *Bangabancethezi.* 'They are traitors.'

'They are sons of our village even if they are sons of mixed blood. They are also Christians ...' Stephen's voice rose. 'As we are! *Umninawa wakho lo ebefile wabuya waphila, ebelahlekile wafunyanwa.* This thy brother was dead and is alive again; was lost and is found.'

Dyoba was sullen. 'They had gone over to the Ngqika, who are our enemies.'

'Am I your enemy?'

Dyoba lowered his eyes, blood on his shirt. Ma Majola, the wardens, the sidesmen, the choir—all were silent.

'Am I your enemy?' Gazing at each in turn.

None answered but the crowd turned away, returning quietly towards the churchyard. A few men hovered as if to help him, but he dismissed them.

When they had gone, Stephen bent to the inert body. It was Sidenge. A contusion on his temple leaked blood. Stephen felt for a pulse in the neck, in the wrist, put his head to the chest to listen.

The boy was dead.

Stephen gazed at him. Sidenge, the foolish one. The first youth he had ever seen at Nodyoba, sweeping the porch with a broom, silent and wary; a boy who had smiled little, spoken less, a hoverer at the edge of the cricket field, ignored by the others for his lack of skill. But he had been at every practice, following the crowd, wishing for acceptance. Motherless, cared for by an Mfengu grandmother, he had a Ngqika father long since absconded. Perhaps, in a search for identity, he had followed the others to the rebels.

And had been rejected.

Dusk had fallen. Tentative crickets gathered confidence as the darkness deepened. It was the only sound. The houses nearby were silent. Somewhere in the distance, though, at the margins of the settlement, a woman was keening. Sidenge's grandmother, released from the burden of his care, without the solace of his company. A doleful mourning. On and on and on.

Stephen bent to the boy and touched his face, drawing his hand across his eyes. He made the sign of the cross on his forehead.

Dear God, why this savagery and madness?

Lily came down the path. She stood at a distance,

watching him. Then—unselfconscious in its innocence, beginning in a murmur, rising clear and true, 'UThixo, Nkosi Yethu', a gentle benediction, her slim hands raised as if in blessing.

Stephen came and stood beside her. They sang into the darkness, side by side, a faint echo sending each note back to them: an unseen listener.

In the morning, the men came to dig the grave. Dyoba, old though he was, toiled with the younger men. It was an act of contrition, a penance, as they worked in silence, digging into the earth that had once served as the cricket pitch. The boy's grandmother was secluded in her house with the body. The women were with her, preparing the boy for Christian burial.

'Are you going to report this matter?' Dyoba asked at last when the grave was ready.

'I have reported it to God,' Stephen said.

AFTER THE FUNERAL service, Stephen went alone to his house. He took out his writing paper. He would write to Albert, and, in doing so, regain his equilibrium, his certainty.

September 19th

Dear old chap,

I have omitted to report a matter to the authorities. So this is a confession because I cannot be sure I have squared the pitch—is that the right term? A boy was killed here in the village because he was known to have defected to the rebels. He returned. Perhaps he had been rejected. He was half Mfengu, half Ngqika—and thus to be trusted by no one.

We are at war, so, possibly, this act was seen as legitimate by the perpetrators. Had he survived he would, quite possibly, have met the same fate at the hands of colonial troops. Whichever way, he was lost.

So, whether I had the right or not, I have, in silence, committed him to God.

As Turvey had said, all those years ago: 'It is hard to be an exile, lad, but harder to return.'

When he had sealed the letter, Stephen went to the door and looked across the vegetable garden towards the church. The candlelight was dim behind the window of Dyoba's house. A low wind stirred the craggy tree. The night was very dark. Clouds had swept in from the west but without the promise of rain. Even the crickets were silent.

Stephen went to his bookshelf. He stretched up and quietly removed the books, laying them on the floor. He took down his father's gun and wrapped it in a cleaning cloth. He fetched a knife with a stout blade from the lean-to kitchen. Letting himself out of the house, he hurried down the path and quietly opened the church door. He felt his way from pew to pew until he reached the chancel step. Working deftly, he loosened one of the boards of the altar frame. He cut his hand and bit back a curse. He eased the wooden plank up. It took him over an hour to work it loose. He laid the gun in the cavity between the base of the frame and the floor and pushed the board back in place. He had lost the nail in the dark. He would have to secure it in the morning when he could see.

On returning to the house he inspected the side of his palm. The cut was clean but deep. Blood was smeared on his jacket. He bound it with a handkerchief. Then he replaced the books on the shelf, arranging them carefully. He opened the Latin Grammar and sat on the bed.

Elizabeth Madikane.

The pearls lay against her neck, curved across her collarbone, gleaming softly against her chest. The shadow in the indentation at her throat, the delicate lobe of her ear. That mouth, defined by a darker rim to sorrow or to scorn. The slim nose, the slight, fine flare of her nostril. It was not a gentle face. It was the face that gazed from a distant time. As distant as Canterbury. As unknown as the young man in his coat and brushed black hat, his polished boots, his cane beneath his arm, whose image now lay forgotten in a box at the bottom of a cupboard in Albert Newnham's boyhood room in Kent. The eager young man who had stepped into Baldwin's Photographic Studio and asked, 'Who is the lady in the window?'

Kaffir Woman.

A delusion. As much as he was to himself.

CHAP. 22:332

The height of hostilities. Stephen had not seen a fellow clergyman for months. He did not think it wise to leave the mission. The fighting was near, the Ngqika had had victories. So had the Imperial and colonial troops and their Mfengu cohorts. Daily he fed the starving, the wounded. Ma Majola had a coterie of small children, abandoned or orphaned, who she was looking after in her home with Lily. Stephen was called on to baptise those too weak to live and commit them to God before they died.

News came sporadically from Grahamstown. *Mfundisi* Turvey sent him the church notices from St Philip's with a letter of encouragement. Once a copy of the July edition of the Diocesan *Church Chronicle* came, enclosed with the printed forms for his quarterly report to the Society for the Propagation of the Gospel. It was a publication he read over and over at night after he had said Divine Office.

In it was the announcement of the forthcoming ordination to the priesthood of two deacons who had been far junior to him but who had taught at the Native College and who had had the daily tutelage and advice of Canon Mullins and Dr Espin, the theological tutors of the diocese.

There was no bar to their progress. No refugees, no starving children. No lack of books.

Far away in Nodyoba, Stephen did not have much more than the Bible, the Book of Common Prayer and the hymnal to instruct him; also his grammar, his Virgil and a small collection of old schoolbooks, *The Pilgrim's Progress* and an anthology of English poetry. He read them in turn, rigorously, the source of all knowledge and consolation, but how could he possibly have answered the more esoteric questions which could be posed in an examination paper or reference the works of theologians he had never read? He did not know the Canon Law in detail. He had no book to learn it from. He had written to *Mfundisi* Turvey asking for instructions but, as the roads were closed, the post erratic, letters might lie for weeks at Ockert & Sons. Nor could Chauncey enlighten him, even if he had chosen to—he had gone to the sea to recover his health 'in this time of trial'. No one seemed to know when he would return.

There was one passage, however, in Dr Espin's report on the examinations taken by deacons in Holy Orders, which he read many times and with a dismay which he directed at himself:

The other two longer-serving deacons have not shown satisfactory progress.

It echoed Dr Bailey's indelible words:

—*Most do not come up to the mark.*

He had no doubt that the other who had failed to reach the standard required was faithful, earnest, anxious Gideon Boom, inadequately educated from the start, marooned as he was from instruction, labouring alone until he was burned out of his mission by the Ngqika. Stephen remembered how Boom had also been asked to contribute to the 'Rules for the Guidance of those Engaged in Mission Work', as Stephen had. Perhaps they had both been given the commission rather as a fond parent praises the efforts of a child in a task beyond its reach.

—Humour them, my Lord. You never know, something useful might emerge!

Stephen had returned to the *Chronicle* again and again. Nor, over time, did the hurt abate—or his frustration both at the injustice and the lack of opportunity to refute it. At Canterbury he had so often guided Albert in a meaning or an argument, solved a knotty question of faith or interpretation, equal to any in debate. It was not something he had boasted of, but this was in print! What of the spiritual demands of an unwavering Faith? Of commitment? Of unremitting toil, hardship? Loneliness?

Knowing the words by heart, Stephen put the *Chronicle* on the shelf next to the Latin Grammar, taking it down and examining, for a long moment, the portrait of Elizabeth Madikane between the pages.

She had not changed. But he had.

He transferred the picture to the *Chronicle*, slipping it against the page on which the Theological Tutor's words were reported.

IN THE WEEKS that followed, Stephen was too preoccupied to think of ordination. There were sick and wounded to attend to. He became a doctor once again, bandaging, cauterising, cooling delirium with river water brought by Lily Majola, balanced in a bucket on her head. She never flagged, making trip after trip up and down the long, steep hill.

She helped him in the makeshift hospital he had arranged in the schoolroom where the sick were laid on heaps of grass. She had an unobtrusive deftness as she moved among them, shadowing Stephen without intruding. There was a gentleness in every gesture, a hand stretched out to touch a chest or face, to cup the shoulder of a child. '*Masithandaze,*' she would say, as she bowed her head and closed her eyes tightly enough to have the lashes quiver faintly.

Stephen might catch himself watching her, a half-smile on his face, forgetting to concur, '*Masithandaze.*' Let us pray.

News came.

> *The rebels have smashed the bells. All over Kaffraria churches on the mission stations—whether Anglican or Catholic, Methodist or Nonconformist—have been wantonly vandalised.*

The message was clear. The voice of the Christian God, admonishing and wrathful—that voice that promised earthly woe for heavenly reward—must be repudiated. If the bells could be stilled, so, too, could the voice that warned of man's damnation.

Stephen recalled the words of an old red-blanket heathen he had attempted to catechise on a trip to his furthest outstation when he had first acquired his horse. 'We were happy in this land. We had plenty of cattle, good country. What are you going to do to make us happier than we are?'

What, indeed.

Kanti ke sizokubulala ulwimi lwentsimbi. Therefore, we will smash the bells.

We will destroy the iron tongue of God.

It was then that Mzamo appeared.

It was a night of high winds. There was thunder over the Amathole, and the smell of rain was heavy in the air long before it fell. That very morning the congregation had gathered to sing a hymn in supplication for the breaking of the drought:

> *Sawulima umhlaba,*
> *Sahlwayela imbewu,*
> *Bulelelani uThixo.*

If it stormed now, Stephen would be lionised as the bringer of rain. The lightning doctor from Middledrift could stay away! *Amaqaba* in their heathen homes would have to ponder the reasons for the sudden change. 'Prayers are answered,'

Stephen said in satisfaction when he bid good night to Dyoba on the porch of the church at dusk after they had said the Evening Office together.

Dyoba had scrutinised the sky, turning, head up, as if tasting the promise on the wind. 'Indeed, it has arrived at last, *Mfundisi*.'

Late that night, as Stephen sat with his papers held to the light of a single candle, he sensed a sudden stillness. He looked up and listened. Then, far off, unleashed at last, the drumming of the rain. It came surging down the valley on the wind. The thatch of Stephen's house lifted, a flurry of dust swept from the chimney. He stood, fastened the windows and tied a piece of string suspended on a cotton reel around the latch of the door to secure it.

Near midnight the wind abated and the rain fell more softly.

There was a tapping at the door. Faint. Very tentative. The cotton reel bounced against the latch. Tap, tap, tap. Startled from his task, Stephen stared at it, alarmed. It seemed to be something disembodied in the sudden stillness. He started up, went to the door, listened, said huskily, 'Yini?'

'It is your brother.'

Swiftly, Stephen fumbled with the string, pulling it impatiently so that it broke.

Mzamo stood on the dark porch, draped in his ochred cloak. Other-worldly. Unfamiliar. Dripping wet.

'Brother,' Stephen all but croaked.

Mzamo stepped swiftly into the room, pulling the door closed behind him. He glanced about as if gathering in all the information that the place could give: the table and wooden stool. The single armchair. The sheepskin rug laid before it on the floor. He walked to the fireplace and looked a moment at the photograph above it of the missionary College at Canterbury, the rows of choristers in their surplices ranged before it, the ivied walls, the Gothic windows, far off the pediments of Fyndon's Gate above the shingled angle of a roof. He raised his fighting stick and touched the glass.

Stephen almost cried out, thinking he would smash it.

Instead, Mzamo stood silently before it, his head half-cocked. 'They chose you instead of me,' he said.

LITTLE MORE THAN a month later, Mzamo had been ambushed by colonial soldiers. Far off from the fiercest fighting in the Amathole, he was caught armed with an old gun and riding a large grey mare. He had been two miles east of St Paul's Mission on the Indwe in the country of the abaThembu.

He had been alone. On a journey to pay a debt, to reimburse his brother's friend, Reverend Albert Newnham, the money that had enabled him to travel home from Matatiele to Grahamstown. Once there, Mzamo had sold some of the trinkets from Nokhanyiso's abandoned collection. Vuyo Tontsi had been persuaded by his wife to buy them. It was a resentful transaction with conditions implied —especially as Mzamo had left Grahamstown almost immediately without confiding his destination. His brother-in-law suspected that he might be off to join the Ngqika in the Amathole where, it was rumoured, Gonya Sandile and Julius Naka were prominent amongst the rebels. He could not have known—or guessed—that among Mzamo's supposedly rebellious intentions would be a determination to honour a debt to Albert Newnham on a distant mission station. Tontsi might have been forgiven for doubting the importance of so insignificant an amount.

But it was a matter of honour to Mzamo as a Christian and, more importantly, as a challenge to Rutherford's angry rebuff of his request for assistance. An anger which would have been inflamed had he heard Rutherford's irritable expostulation to Magistrate Haddon: 'He may walk four hundred miles for all I care. I will not lend him a penny for the fare. He has been, and—mark my words—will prove that he still is, a thoroughly bad lot!'

ALBERT WAS NOT at Indwe.

As Mzamo rode into the yard with his gun slung across his back, his spear and stick laid across the pommel, bedecked with the amulets of a warrior, there was not a soul to challenge or to greet him. He did not notice a man peering anxiously from behind the church wall, sinking down into the shadow of the stones and watching as he tethered the horse to the tall pyramid of poles on which the church bell hung.

The man watched as Mzamo strode towards the house and rapped at the front door. He watched as Mzamo walked along the porch, glancing through the windows, then going round to the back before returning to the yard. He watched as Mzamo came towards the church, tried the latch, entered and closed the door behind him.

Had the watcher dared to peer through one of the windows, he might have been astonished to see a figure kneeling at the altar rail, his clay-red cloak draped about his shoulders, his head bowed. Had he not taken the chance to hurry away towards a distant homestead where a horse could be found, he would have heard a voice raised in chant, intoning the Lord's Prayer:

Bawo wethu osezulwini
Maliphathwe ngobungcwele igama lakho ...

Instead, he took the horse without permission or explanation and rode to the nearest trading station, eager for the reward promised to anyone who discovered rebels in the district or had information about who was smashing church bells. He accompanied the trader to the military camp to deliver his report. When a troop of soldiers came to the mission to investigate, he was not believed, for the bell hung undisturbed, nothing in the church had been tampered with, and no sheep nor chicken, goat nor bushel of forage, had been taken.

338

Angrily he watched the soldiers leave.

It was only later that a farmer's son was awarded the prize: he had seen an armed warrior on a large grey horse crossing at a drift, heading east. Alerted once again, the military had overtaken the rider, ambushing him in a ravine. He had fired at his pursuers until he had exhausted his supply of ammunition. Even then he had resisted capture, but the numbers against him were overwhelming. Wounded in the shoulder and the thigh, he was manacled, his horse commandeered and his gun confiscated. He was taken to Queenstown and dispatched to Grahamstown with others suspected of sedition.

Mzamo called for Magistrate Haddon. He called for the Bishop. He called for *Mfundisi* Turvey. To no avail. His messages were not delivered. With sixty other rebels he was transported to the Cape and sentenced by a military court to four years' hard labour on the Breakwater at the entrance to the Bay.

He protested vehemently on his own behalf and that of his fellow prisoners. He was reminded, by the military tribunal that tried him, of his personal luck in not being incarcerated on the Island with a much stiffer sentence, as Gonya Sandile, Julius Naka and the other sons of senior chiefs had been. His dignity sadly compromised, his status ignored, it was no consolation to Mzamo to be given less time and to labour on the Breakwater—the preserve, in earlier times, of Bushmen sheep-rustlers—in company with commoners. He wrote a long and eloquent letter to the *Cape Times*.

Too eloquent.

It might have occasioned protest from those fellow travellers who thought the rebels had a cause. At the discretion of the editor, it was not published.

Nor did Mzamo know that back in Grahamstown, on the day he had embarked for the Cape with the other prisoners to the local gaol and issued with prison garb, a sergeant with a mud-spattered jacket stuffed into a string bag had been dispatched to the Native College.

Albert was not at the College when the sergeant called. A master explained to the sergeant that he had gone with Canon Rutherford and some of the Theology students to catechise the labourers at the railway camp and hold a service. They would be gone all day but Reverend Newnham's wife would surely be at home with their child.

Stomping back down the path between the building, the sergeant came to the Newnhams' lodgings and rapped sharply on the door. It was opened by the nursery-maid, Beulah, who showed the sergeant to the parlour where Mrs Newnham was taking tea with an unsmiling Mrs Rutherford.

Unity rose in alarm, knocking over her cup on the occasional table at her side. The soldier was a rough fellow but cleared his throat, nodded his head, said gruffly, 'Beggin' your pardon, ma'am, but I am on the hunt for information.'

'What information?' Unity exclaimed, attempting to compose herself while mopping the spilled tea. Mrs Rutherford, cool and unhelpful, sat looking at the soldier over the half-moons of her spectacles. 'I hope nothing is amiss?'

'Two weeks ago, ma'am, Kaffir rebels was brought in from the Queenstown district. One of them was wearing a jacket.' The sergeant opened the bag and pulled out the garment, now stiff with grime and sweat. 'Do you recognise it, ma'am?'

Unity recoiled, as if it were alive. The buttons she had sewn back countless times. The familiar nap and stitching on the sleeve. And now, the stench. 'Albert's jacket. Oh, mercy!' she fluttered. 'Is he all right? Pray God there has been no accident.'

'No accident, ma'am. Never fear. But are you sure this is your husband's? Can you positively identify it?'

Unity bridled. 'Show me the inside of the collar.'

Eyeing her, the Sergeant reversed the collar.

340

'My husband's initials!' fluttered Unity, pointing and swiftly withdrawing as if she might be stung. 'There. I embroidered them when he first got it.'

'AHN,' said the sergeant. 'Those are your husband's initials, are they not, Mrs Newnham?'

'Yes,' Unity whispered, mortified.

'And when did you first miss this jacket?'

'Bertie did not say that it was missing.' Unity looked from the sergeant to Mrs Rutherford. 'Oh dear! It was a favourite of his. I think he bought it at Barstow's in Canterbury. I am not sure now. They had handsome jackets. Mama recommended it to him as the very thing to own ... .'

Mrs Rutherford was looking at her impatiently. 'Never mind where it came from! The sergeant wants to know when you last saw the jacket, dear.'

'Bertie had it at the mission. At St Paul's. Perhaps it was stolen when he was there alone and he didn't want to alarm me.' She coloured, fluttering her hands again. 'Now I think of it, I am certain he was not wearing it when he came back from the mission. And he was very distracted indeed. Not at all himself! Oh goodness!' And the all-too-frequent tears sprang to her eyes.

'If you don't mind, ma'am, but there's something else,' said the sergeant. 'This envelope was found in one of the pockets. It's addressed to your husband. We was obliged to open it to see what it contained. Five pound. And a note what said "With compliments, SMM".'

'A note?'

'On a sheet of writing paper, ma'am. "SMM," in a very fancy script. Would you know who SMM is, ma'am?'

'Oh Lord!' wimpered Unity.

But before she could say anything more, Mrs Rutherford had intervened. 'I do not think we can help you any further, sergeant. These are questions that need to be put to Mr Newnham, who I am sure will afford you a very simple explanation. Mrs Newnham will retain the envelope and the money, if you please, and I will ask Mr Newnham to call on you when he returns.' She turned to Unity. 'Mrs Newnham, do compose yourself.'

'Awful sorry, ma'am but there's a couple more matters,' said the Sergeant, eyeing Unity suspiciously.

'Yes.'

'The prisoner had a gun. It's important to know if the gun was stolen.'

'A gun?' Unity wailed. 'We had no gun.'

'It's an old-fashioned weapon, ma'am, of a type commonly used by natives working on the government's roads or around the diamond mines in Kimberley. All these guns was supposed to have been handed in by law. It's a felony for a native to own one now. Very serious crime. Treason, ma'am.'

'Mrs Newnham has said there was no gun in their possession, sergeant.'

'He also rode a horse, ma'am. A grey mare. Uncommonly well kept.'

'Our mission horse was a chestnut,' ventured Unity quickly. 'We never had a grey horse. Ours was a very bad-tempered animal. Not at all the sort you find at Home. I always said to Bertie he should sell it but he wouldn't listen.'

'If that is all,' said Mrs Rutherford briskly to the sergeant, 'we must not detain you any longer. I shall tell Mr Newnham to call on you when he returns. I think it would be best if he dealt with this matter directly.'

Rebuffed, the sergeant crammed the jacket back in the bag, nodded a farewell and departed.

'Now, Mrs Newnham,' Mrs Rutherford said firmly once the front door had snapped closed behind him, 'the last thing we want the military authorities to think is that we are'—she nearly said 'silly women', changed tack—'not in command of the situation. We have endless trouble justifying the missions without arousing their disapprobation.' She rang the bell and the nursery-maid appeared.

'Beulah, make a fresh pot of tea if you will and find me a bottle of salts.' She turned back to Unity, patted her shoulder lightly. 'There, there, dear! No one is hurt and jackets and guns and anything else that the natives fancy are stolen every day in this colony. There is no need to take on.'

'I thought something had happened to Bertie. That fellow barging in here and asking questions. What was I to think? And that jacket! It was the best he owned.' At the remembrance of which she wept again, complaining about the barbarous Colony and the sergeant's dreadful aspect. Then, looking wildly around, she rose to her feet. 'I must call for Clemmie.'

'You will do no such thing!' Mrs Rutherford was sharp. 'Do you want the child to see her mother in a pet? Such a bad example! Sit down at once.'

Unity dropped into the chair, shot a glance at Mrs Rutherford. Suddenly triumphant. 'Stephen Mana had a grey horse. So there!'

'Don't be foolish,' said Mrs Rutherford. 'Stephen Mana lives at Fort Beaufort and there are dozens of grey horses in the colony.'

'And he wrote with a beautiful copperplate hand.'

'Which I taught him,' said Mrs Rutherford, taking up the envelope and looking at it sceptically.

'And those are his initials. I have heard Bertie calling him some unpronounceable name beginning with M.'

'Pure conjecture!'

'Well, whose is it then?' Unity was defiant.

'I am sure Mr Newnham will find out soon enough,' said Mrs Rutherford, rising. 'Meanwhile I suggest you go and lie down before your husband returns. And when he does, rouse yourself. Remember that you are a clergyman's wife. Set an example in your household! Beulah may be a simple colonial girl but she's sharp. And a Methodist! She might gossip!'

Mrs Rutherford took her leave a little peremptorily. In the hallway she waylaid Beulah bringing Clementine in from the

343

garden. 'I have told Mrs Newnham to rest. She is upset.' She looked at the girl meaningfully, drew her beyond the open front door into the garden. 'Make sure that the minute Mr Newnham comes home—and before he sees his wife—you direct him to go at once to the military jail. He should ask for the sergeant who has just visited.' She wagged her head slightly. 'It would be a shame if he—how shall I put it? —got the wrong end of the stick before he had had a chance to hear the matter clearly.'

Beulah suppressed a smile. 'Yes, ma'am,' she said. 'I shall be sure to watch for him from the nursery window.'

'Good girl,' said Mrs Rutherford, pulling on her gloves and turning to the gate. She caught sight of Clementine, red in the face and damp about the edges of her tightly frilled bonnet. 'Dear me, why is that child trussed up in so many clothes on such a hot day?'

'Mrs Newnham does not want her to get a chill when she plays outside.'

'She should be running about in a shift and without her shoes in this heat,' said Mrs Rutherford in exasperation. It was just as her husband had always said: *You will know the potential of a missionary through the first meeting with his wife.*

How often she had recorded his sentiments when, as his amanuensis, she had copied out his letters to the Society for the Propagation of the Gospel in London.

My dear Hawkins,

Reverend Albert Newnham (or Broderick or Tweedie or Little or Garde—take your choice) is a good fellow and a very devoted clergyman but I would say he was more suited to a parish in a town. It is not a lack of gumption but a domestic situation tailored to try any man. In choosing our incumbents, I would say it is best to interview prospective wives long before the gentlemen concerned are even considered. It would save us no end of trouble and expense.

In short—Send us bachelors! There are any number of hearty colonial farmers' daughters to make splendid missionary wives. Poor Newnham—clearly he had been doomed to vexation from the start!

LATE THAT AFTERNOON, as Albert rounded the corner from the toll house and headed home to the College, Beulah ran out into the street and, assuring him that his wife was resting and that Clementine was resting, passed on the message that he should hurry to the military jail.

'What's it about?' said Albert, somewhat alarmed.

'A sergeant came this morning, sir, but I did not hear what was said. Mrs Newnham was a little anxious,' adding hurriedly, 'but I do not think it very serious—at least, it did not seem to be, as Mrs Rutherford was here. It was she who said you should report to the jail.'

Albert turned back down the hill, crossed the stream, and strode up the long slope towards the prison with its squat round redoubt and enfiladed window slits.

Why on earth should the military need him?

A feeling of dread gripped him. Had the bells had been smashed at St Paul's? Was the mission burned down or the livestock stolen? Hd the storeroom been ransacked? When Rutherford heard, there would be yet another inferno of indignation that he had left his post. He had endured it once on his unexpected reappearance in Grahamstown and been told, in no uncertain terms, that he would be obliged to return to St Paul's as soon as transport was available and he had recovered his sense and his wits. Damn Rutherford! And, for the hundredth time, damn Reverend Jackson for going mad and leading him into this imbroglio!

At the door of the prison, Albert explained his errand to the guardsman and waited for the sergeant to be brought. He paced up and down under a pale-barked gum tree and fanned his face with his hat.

At last the sergeant emerged. 'Afternoon, sir.' He tipped his cap. 'Might this belong to you, sir?' He held out the jacket.

345

Albert blanched when he saw it. 'Yes, it's mine,' he said, then hesitating, 'Where did you get it?'

'Worn by a rebel. Captured near the Indwe River, sir.'

'Oh my word!' Albert exclaimed. 'How good of you to return it. I must have mislaid it.' He ran his hand across his hair. 'When I heard you had called I assumed something had happened at my mission.'

'There was an envelope in one of the pockets, sir, with your name written on it. And money inside. Your wife has it.'

'My wife?' Albert's face flushed red. What was he to say? 'Ah!—the money her parents sent. It came in a parcel I picked up from the post office in Queenstown.' He chuckled unconvincingly. 'It was to buy little Christmas gifts for her and our daughter, so of course I didn't mention it to her.'

'And the jacket, sir?'

'The jacket?' Albert wondered if the sergeant had noticed sweat starting to bead on his lip. He dared not wipe it away. 'As I said, I must have mislaid it. I probably left it at one of my outstations. Very careless of me ... .' He rubbed his hand across his hair again, grinned ruefully. 'My wife always makes a fuss when I do that!'

The sergeant snorted.

Salvaging his dignity, Albert said 'You say the jacket was worn by a rebel. Is he here in the jail? I should like to see him. As a clergyman, I think I have that right.'

'Gone already, sir,' said the sergeant, war-weary and sour. 'I'd as soon have shot the lot of them as keep 'em here.'

'What was his name?'

'You've not been here long, have you, sir?' The sergeant scanned Albert's face as he stood there in his dusty parson's togs and his anxious boyish face.

Albert shook his head.

'Can't tell one from another. A native has every name under the sun—clan, family, age group—all of 'em unpronounceable. You get a different answer every time you ask, depending on their mood and the time of day.'

Perhaps it was better not to enquire further.

'Do you want to take the coat, sir?'

'No.'

'Want to see the horse?'

'What horse?'

'The horse the kaffir was riding. Wouldn't have minded keeping it for myself, if I could. I'll bring her around, if you could give me another moment, sir.'

Albert waited again in the shade of the gum tree and polished his spectacles abstractedly. At last the sergeant reappeared with the horse. Albert gazed at it in sudden dismay.

—*You have a horse, Stephen? My, but you are an important fellow!*

'You don't get mounts as good as this every day, especially not among the natives,' said the sergeant. 'The fellow probably stole it from a farmer up Dordrecht way. You don't recognise it, Reverend?'

'No,' said Albert. 'No. Never seen it in my life.'

CHAP. 23:348

am grieved to hear about your brother,' the old man said.

'I do not understand you, *Mhlekazi*,' Stephen replied.

'News does not lie in the road, *Mfundisi. Iindaba azilali ndleleni*.'

'What news?'

'Your brother was captured some months ago. He is now in gaol with some men from Grahamstown. All grand gentlemen indeed. *Zizinoni*. Very learned. Christians like you.'

'I did not know.'

'*Yeh!' intlekele!*' Indeed it is a great misfortune.

Somehow it was fitting that Stephen should have heard the news of Mzamo's capture not from some official, immediately suspicious of Stephen's own commitment, nor an exultant Mr Thurston Chauncey revelling in the disgrace of yet another of Turvey's 'fine young men', but *kwaJingqi*, at the Great Place of the late Maqoma, the most formidable of the former Xhosa generals. The dignity of the old man who told him of the event, his sorrow, his concern—his pride, even, in Mzamo's courage and reputation—offered a new perspective. No, Mzamo was not a rebel intent on destruction. He was a soldier. And, most importantly, a man of his word. Stephen guessed, with a sense of triumph, that Mzamo had been captured on his journey to repay his debt to Albert and to ensure the safety of his bells. But the triumph was mixed with dismay. And guilt. If Mzamo had not given his word to Stephen that he would go to Albert's mission, he would have been safely among his own people, unexposed.

As they sat together in the silence that the news required, with the old man meditative at his side, Stephen gazed through the doorway up towards the hillsides and ravines where the forests rose, rank on rank. It was the site of Maqoma's most famous battle, his routing of the British. Stephen felt an unexpected pride when the old man—as if echoing his thoughts—quietly recited the praises of their chief. And even though Maqoma had long been dead, he was still the guiding spirit, the rallying point of the AmaNgqika. The man recited, too, the praises of Maqoma's mottled ox, Jingqi, from whom the clan took its name.

No one knew where the bones of the great ox lay. Perhaps, like its master, it had been commandeered, branded with a number, its *isibongo*—its praise name—forfeited: just another ox. As, once, its master had been scorned as just another drunken old kaffir, haunting the doorways of the taverns of Fort Beaufort, begging a little brandy from passing soldiers.

Who could ignore the meaning of despair? Of the rage that injustice generates, the flame that cannot be quenched by logic or curbed by reason, spawning hate?

IT WAS ON the long trek back to Nodyoba on foot from the outstation that Stephen argued himself into making the journey to Strangers' Location to find Elizabeth Madikane. Perhaps he would persuade her to come with him to Nodyoba, to bring her son, to wait with him until Mzamo was released.

He dared not scrutinise his own motives. But he could not doubt his brother's. On the night he had come to Nodyoba to retrieve the gun, Mzamo had said, 'Why do you think I have had to ask for money?'

It had been because he had sold everything to protect her. To sustain her. To do what was honourable and right, even if, in the eyes of the Church, she could never be his wife.

—*She will be my Great Wife. It is my right to choose the mother of my heir.*

—*Then you cannot call yourself a Christian.*

—*God may judge it differently.*

And, as he had departed, Mzamo had said, 'You will fetch my son and bring him here. You will teach him, Malusi, to be a man like you.'

TO LEAVE THE mission was never easy. To leave it during a war, virtually impossible. But to leave Elizabeth Madikane and Mzamo's son without support now that Mzamo had been arrested was something he could not do. She must have suffered greatly in the last few months, none knowing of her plight.

And yet he prevaricated.

How could he bring them to Nodyoba? Under what guise?

His brother's wife?

His brother's concubine?

And to have her living in his house with him?

It was a fantasy to which he dared not surrender and one that came at night to goad him to repentance and self-recrimination when he woke.

He consulted his pocketbook three times a day as if, in doing so, the paltry sums of money recorded might increase. The Native Clergy Fund had paid out nothing this last quarter due to the shortages of war and the inability of people to contribute. He knew, too, that appeals urged by the Bishop fell on unsympathetic ears in Grahamstown.

—*This conflict is the mischief encouraged by the missionaries. Have you heard who is leading the rebels at the Hoek? Edmund Sandile, if you please! Once a teacher at the Mission! Once their star pupil!*

350

The eminent Cyril Mhala's trial for treason had brought about an unreasonably vehement squabble, even among the churchmen.

—*I will write to Dr Bailey about him. Can you imagine how grieved he will be to hear of Stephen's deceit?*

—*Well, serves your Dr Bailey right! Those fellows in England have no idea what a hornets' nest they have stirred up educating natives and forcing them to be above themselves. Give me a red-blanket kaffir any day!*

There was no money for a fare to Port Elizabeth. Not even with the only excuse he could have used in confidence to *Mfundisi* Turvey:

'I wish to marry, *Mfundisi*. I can no longer live alone. There is a young woman who I would gladly take to be my wife but she would not accept a husband who is not a man.'

Mfundisi Turvey would not scoff at him. How often had he done battle with the chapter when one or other of his 'fine young men' had run off to become *umkhwetha*, returned to take his place in church, marry and prove himself a devoted churchman.

'And who is this young woman?' Turvey would twinkle at him.

'Ah, she is a fine lady with a face like a Madonna, a high-curved forehead with a gold ring in her ear. She has been to England. She has sung before the Queen. I will take her back there on a ship and we will lunch at last with the parishioners in Herefordshire or in Shropshire. We will visit Joshua's grave, bring flowers to lay in front of the tombstone. We will make a pilgrimage to Nuneaton, call on Dr Savage, pay our respects to George Maqoma in the graveyard, tell him news of his brother, Edward, and of how he died speaking in Xhosa, returning in spirit—as Joshua had done—to the language of his forefathers. We will go to Canterbury and call on Dr Bailey. I will introduce my wife. We will take tea and I will tell him that I saw her first in the window of Baldwin's Studio and paid five shillings for her portrait. My brother will be dead and I will marry Elizabeth and adopt her son, and he will inherit my brother's farm on the banks of the Buffalo River which was promised by Sir George Grey so long ago, when we were boys at College.'

No. That would not be their conversation.

Instead, Stephen would look at his hands, twist them thoughtfully, clear his throat, making his voice firm, say, 'Her name is Lily Majola. She teaches the young girls to sew. She sits with them under the tree by the church wall and they sing hymns while they work. These girls are poor. They have no food when they come to the lessons, and Lily and I must make do with a loaf to feed them and perhaps some *imifino* from the garden mixed with flour. It is poor fare for growing girls.'

'And have you asked Miss Majola's father?'

'How can I ask her father when I am not a man? Why would she accept someone who is uncircumcised? And even if she would, I could not allow it. I am, after all, a black man, *Mfundisi*. You would think I learned the truth of this in England. No—I learned it here, among my fellow clergy.'

Mfundisi Turvey would be concerned, even distressed. 'She is not a Christian then, my son?'

'Oh yes, *Mfundisi*, she is a very devoted Christian. Baptised. She sings in the choir. There is no one who prays more earnestly than she.'

BUT STEPHEN COULD not go to *Mfundisi* Turvey. He could not ask the old man to lend him money which Stephen knew he did not have. He could not impose on him, for Turvey might then be forced to lie to Canon Basil Rutherford or his dear old friend, the Bishop. Nor could Stephen go to the men of the village. How could he tell them his predicament? They would not understand his wish to have the operation performed in a hospital, conducted by a white man, or his reluctance to follow the traditional rites. He went to Mr Jacobus Ockert instead, asked squarely for a loan.

'Ag man, go to the bush,' said Mr Ockert. 'No one will know. It makes no difference who does the operation.'

'But it does,' said Stephen. 'I cannot expect to be initiated with other young men and avoid instruction from the *ikhankatha*.'

'Cross your fingers and wink at the Devil.'

'I am afraid the Devil is likely to wink at me,' said Stephen. 'I will go to the hospital in Port Elizabeth. May I propose a loan?'

Ockert bridled. 'How are you going to pay it back?'

'I will give you my saddle as security.'

'Your saddle?' Ockert glanced at him, frowning. 'Don't tell me something has happened to that fine horse I sold you.'

'Stolen by the rebels,' said Stephen, not looking at him.

'Stolen?' A faint inquiry in his tone. 'You might have fixed on a good price with them. They would've paid it.'

'Why pay when you can steal?'

'Now, I am pleased to say, you are sounding like a good kaffir! I used to think that if I scrubbed you long enough you'd come up white. Ngesi, like your name.'

'I am a Ngqika,' said Stephen. 'And my name is not Ngesi, it is Malusi. And you can take your pick about what it means. Ma—lu—si.' Then he repeated it, 'Malusi,' the lilt of inflection too subtle for Ockert to differentiate between the two. 'One,' said Stephen, 'means a circumciser. The other, a shepherd. Which is it to be?'

HERE, AT LAST, was Gubb's Location. It squatted either side of a slope at the top of a *kloof* leading down to the harbour and the bay. It was a warren of wood and dung, mud and wattle. Sewage was thick in the clumps of grass and bushes, there was a smell of decay. Dogs scavenged. Children scavenged. Those trees that were still standing grew sideways, bent by the prevailing wind. The limestone earth was white as bone, ribbing up between the dusty clumps of grey grass.

There were men with hostile stares: strangers were not welcome. Resources were too few to share.

Stephen approached, dressed as a common workman. An apprentice, perhaps, or a storekeeper's assistant. There was no sign of the clerical collar. If challenged, he would say he was from Ockert & Sons in Fort Beaufort.

Where was he to find Elizabeth Madikane?

He could not go to Daniel Goba at St Stephen's Church across the *kloof* in Strangers' Location. Goba was a fellow clergyman. He would be obliged to report Stephen's presence to his seniors. He would be shocked at his appearance. Artisan's clothes.

He looked for her face among the crowds of faces. Asked discreetly. He chose a foreigner, a man with skin much darker than his own. The man spoke no common language and swiftly sidled off. He asked a woman, an old matron with a cluster of filthy children round her feet, attempting to cook on an open fire.

How could he describe Elizabeth Madikane in a way which would make sense?

—*She is a grand lady. She has sung before the Queen.*

—*What would a grand lady be doing in Gubb's Location?*

It was unwise to speak to strangers. What could their motive be?

She shook her head, was sullen. One of the children started to howl.

He went, in the end, to the Malay at a corner shop just beyond the reaches of the hovels. He was a man of information. He always spoke to strangers, especially if there was a profit to be made. He was also the only person who, in the course of the week, might see most of the inhabitants, especially on a Friday when the stevedores and labourers had been paid and came to buy a sixpence's worth of tobacco, a shilling's worth of tea. He could sell them meat every now and then.

Yes, the Malay knew the sorceress. He had heard the tale. A woman may not betray her husband even if he is the most

354

sour-faced, mean-fisted infidel. It was said to be *ubuti*—the bewitchment used by runaway slaves—potent, dangerous to any man, like the unfortunate dandy who had been caught with her and was the father of her child. Where was he now?

He looked Stephen over. The shabby jacket, the workman's boots, the hat fitting the contour of his skull from sweat and rain. 'What business would you have with her?'

'If you can direct me to where I can find her, I would be very grateful.'

The shopkeeper leaned forward, arms on the counter, lowering his voice. 'You look like a kaffir but you do not talk like one. Where do you come from?'

'I would be obliged.' Stephen was patient.

'I have *ubuti* too, if that is what you are seeking. From the East. We can discuss a price.'

'It is her I wish to see.'

The shopkeeper thrust his beard closer. 'I may have information—for ...'

'A consideration.' Stephen finished the sentence for him.

Stephen reached into his pocket, found some coins, even though each tuppence was already accounted for and had its future purpose. The shopkeeper scowled, slid the coins across the counter into his hand, looked at them scornfully. 'She has gone.'

'Gone where?'

'That rascal of a lover stopped sending her money.' The man scanned the shop for listeners. 'Perhaps her sorcery did not have the power to move him any more. Perhaps he just grew tired of her. She was always here looking for her money.' He leaned in as a customer came through the door. 'Very proud—as if she wasn't a kaffir at all. I am surprised no one here put a knife in her back.' Again he looked around, lowered his voice. 'People were afraid of her. Those women who come from who knows where, those ones collected from far up Africa, those ones with *ubuti*, they have the hearts of hyenas. Savage, every one.'

'Where has she gone?'

'Cape Town.'

'How could she go to Cape Town if she had no money?'

'Officials,' he muttered. 'From the Council, from the military. They have been clearing this place of vagrants and squatters. The men have been taken to work on the railways, the women into service in the Cape.' He glanced around again. 'In the Cape these people are paid lower wages than my people, the Malays. So whoever takes them gets what they pay for. Rubbish. Useless rubbish.'

He waited for Stephen to react. Stephen was resolutely silent.

'There were men, officials, who rounded up the women living here alone. Some kaffirs, mostly others who won't say where they come from. The bad ones. The ones that cause all the trouble with the harbour workers. The ones that spread diseases among men. They took them away in a ship. Even their children. It is a ploy to clear out the "vermin" who live here at Gubb's.'

'When?'

'Go ask Madikane at Strangers' Location,' said the shopkeeper triumphantly. 'He is sure to know what happened to his wife. He is sure to have directed these slavers to her.'

'I do not know the way.'

'I cannot send the boy without tempting him,' said the shopkeeper. Reluctantly, Stephen found another coin. The man pocketed it and disappeared into the yard behind the shop. He shouted in pidgin Xhosa. A youth appeared, scrofulous and thin. Stephen could not hear what was said but saw the boy cuffed from the yard, an abject figure tripping over himself into the street. Stephen left the shop to follow him.

From the doorway, the merchant watched them.

When they were out of sight, Stephen stopped the boy, said in Xhosa, 'I do not wish to see the *Mfundisi* Madikane. I

356

wish you to show me where the lady lived, his wife, the woman they say had ubuti and was a sorceress.'

The boy was disconcerted, shuffled his feet, looked about as if he wished to escape. Stephen took out his purse, extracted a shilling. The boy glanced at it, hesitated again, saying nothing. Stephen urged him to take the coin. Gingerly, he reached for it. Then, by a slight inclination of his chin, he beckoned Stephen as he changed direction, heading down the hillside, across rough ground towards a shambles of shacks and huts.

In approaching the place where she had lived, Stephen could feel the surge of blood in his ears, as if the shopkeeper might have been mistaken and she would still be there.

Waiting for Mzamo.

Waiting for him, his brother's emissary.

Surely this woman walking up the path towards them was she: very much thinner than when he had seen her in Grahamstown, her splendid frock exchanged for a jalimani print skirt and a loose top of no distinction, her head wrapped in the folds of a dark cloth.

He went forward to meet her, almost stumbling. 'Mrs Madikane?'

The woman glanced at him, hurried by. Her face was not the face of Elizabeth Madikane. It was a careworn face, leached of youth.

The boy was hovering now, scanning the buildings, unsure. He chose a fork in the track, rutted by the passage of many feet. They came at last to a labyrinth of small paths winding between shacks, deep in the shadow of the hill. The boy pointed out a yard. Before Stephen could even thank him, he had turned and fled.

Tentatively, Stephen made his way towards it, stepping over mud slicks where slops had been thrown out on the sand.

He paused. It was not the meeting he had always imagined.

In his visions, she would be magnificent. She with her pearls at her throat and her distant gaze. He would approach, put out his hand. 'How do you do?' A slight bow, taking his hat from his head, he in his frock coat and his burnished boots, his high-collared shirt, his cane. The man who stood before the canvas backdrop of Baldwin's Studio, upright, dignified and proud.

He peered about, the blood beating in his ears. The place seemed deserted: a gloomy lean-to with a broken door, a rusty pail lying on its side.

Then he saw her.

Beyond, in the shade of a scrubby tree, seated on a stool with her back to him, her dress spread out about her, the glint of a ring in her ear, her headdress coiled up wide and high: Elizabeth Madikane.

The shadows of leaves shifted across the pale folds of her frock, its frills and ribbons, its rows of covered buttons. A wisp of smoke curled into the air above her.

He stood, transfixed. Transfixed as he'd once been as he'd stared at the photograph in Baldwin's Studio in Canterbury so long ago.

Kaffir Woman.

That haunting face, that ineffable grace.

Would she turn and look at him? Would she remember him?

Would she see him? Not just recognise him but truly see him?

His longing?

His shame.

Or would she glance away with the same indifference she'd displayed when she'd met him at the choir concert?

Seeing only Mzamo Mzamane.

Her lover.

He moved a little closer, stopped again, afraid to startle her. She seemed suddenly much smaller, frailer. And so still that a bird alighted close to her.

In deference to custom, not presuming to speak, Stephen softly cleared his throat.

She did not seem to hear him but the bird, in alarm, darted away, alerting her to his silent presence.

She froze a moment, turned.

He stood, poised.

She raised her face.

He recoiled.

An old woman, skin withered and yellow as a wasp-stung Kei apple, a long tobacco pipe in her hand, stared back at him.

A parody.

He almost cried out.

If the dress had once belonged to Elizabeth Madikane, he saw at a glance that the hem was heavy with dirt, the neckerchief stained with the slicks of tobacco juice that had splashed each time it was jetted from between her teeth.

As she did now, narrowly missing the mark.

Had his imaginings turned her into this crone? Had the *mbulu* monitor lizard of folktales, passing itself off as a bride in stolen finery, suddenly exposed itself in its deceit by its scaly tail?

He wanted to run, in fear, as the boy had run.

'*Ewe?*' She eyed him with suspicion, her polyp mouth trembling.

He almost said, 'Mrs Madikane?', then felt his innate good sense return. Forgetting his disguise, he lifted his battered hat instinctively—the gesture of an Englishman. 'I am seeking Elizabeth Madikane.'

'I do not know that name.'

'But you are living in her house.'

'I do not know that name.'

Stephen took his purse from his pocket—yet again—an anger kindling now.

The old woman snatched the money, slid it down inside her bodice, said again, almost with a leer, 'I do not know that name.'

Stephen turned abruptly away, tears of anger rising.

How had it come to this?

The woman who had sung before the English Queen, the woman who walked in grace and beauty, whose voice had moved the mighty to bestow their gifts. The woman who was the mother of his brother's only child. He had squandered money meant for her and her son on rogues and charlatans. And yes, this mockery was all his fault: he did not come soon enough to rescue her, take her to a life of decency and order as Mzamo had asked.

Yet again, Mzamo had outrivalled him: not as a victor, claiming the prize—he was unaware that Stephen had any notion of her—but in pursuing his purpose boldly. If Mzamo had deceived others, he had not deceived her. Nor had he deceived himself about his motives.

But Stephen had.

Despite his prayers, despite his resolutions, his procrastinations, he knew that he'd deceived himself. That somewhere, buried deep beneath his piety and resolution— even his Missionary Vow—an angry and unbridled man wished to shake off the shackles and erupt.

What appalling treachery had been directed at Elizabeth Madikane all her life by those who wished to claim her?

Now she had gone, taken her child—as she should—and prevailed.

Beyond the reach of all of them. Except, perhaps, Mzamo.

But only if she chose.

CHAP. 24:361

Stephen walked away from Gubb's Location, facing a stiff wind blowing off the sea. A wind that whipped his words away, drowned his voice—not raised in prayer as it had so often been when he had ridden out alone to take a service at an outstation or to comfort the dying, attend to the sick or rejoice in a birth. It was a judge's voice, unequivocal, without recrimination but with truth. He addressed himself—Malusi Mzamane—without love. And without compromise.

He kept on moving—down the hill, past the shacks, past the graves, past the few wind-blasted trees. Past the hospital. Past St Stephen's Church.

He had no use for either.

He could not pray. Nor could he, in conscience, use the money that Ockert, the trader, had lent him to pay for circumcision when he had always intended it for Elizabeth Madikane and her child. It would have exacerbated his deceit to both of them.

He wished he could walk away from himself, leaving the husk behind, becoming a child again—the child who had crept into the shadow of a bush, untainted by shame, regret or guilt, and lain down, surrendering, at last, to weariness.

But Basil Rutherford had interfered and 'saved' him. As he, Stephen, had intended to 'save' Elizabeth and her son—if he'd been as bold as Rutherford, less prevaricating, less afraid. Perhaps, now, in his indecision, his consciousness of his own motives, his fear of sin—the spectre that had only needed opportunity for him to lunge at it, heedless of its cost —he had condemned Elizabeth and her son to a vagrant life. In saving himself, had he abandoned her? And yet, in Stephen's custody, the child would have had to face the same disjuncture that he had known, would have been coached in a lie for which he must always express gratitude. Until the boy was so tired of gratitude that he would rise in rebellion— or despair—to end it.

It was that disjuncture which, so many years before, had made Stephen stop, gaze and bind himself to the image of Elizabeth Madikane in the window of Baldwin's Studio in Canterbury on that cold winter afternoon.

Kaffir Woman: Kaffir Man.

Five shillings for an illusion.

STEPHEN MZAMANE RETREATED in confusion from Port Elizabeth, darting through the traffic, dodging wagons, carts, horsemen, mules, plunging his way through crowds as if he were in flight, too preoccupied to be aware of his surroundings. When the train reached Grahamstown, he had alighted and hurried down the platform, passing the first-class carriages.

Mrs Beazer saw him.

Craning stoutly through the carriage window, she had no doubt about the dark distinction of his face but was astonished by his shabby secular dress. Tapping vigorously, nosing out a potential peccadillo to be shared around the tea table, she called peremptorily, 'Mr Mana! Mr Mana?'

He paused, turned, looked directly back at her.

—*There will be no more playing chess with Lady Bountiful.*

He touched the brim of his hat—the gesture was brief, curt—and strode on.

IT WAS NOT only Mrs Beazer who discovered Stephen's absence from Nodyoba. On his route through Grahamstown after yet another sojourn at the sea, Reverend Thurston Chauncey was urged by Canon Basil Rutherford to take some duplicates which the Theological Tutor had set aside from among the books in the College library for Stephen Mzamane, whose neglected instruction had begun to weigh upon the Tutor's mind.

Chauncey had no intention of taking the books up to Holy Trinity himself or summoning Mzamane down to intrude on him. He sent Figlan.

Figlan collared a boy lurking about on a street corner and asked him to carry the box of books in exchange for a sixpence purloined from Chauncey's absent-minded pockets. The boy marched ahead, Figlan following, supporting himself on a stout staff.

At Nodyoba, Figlan found that the *Mfundisi* was away but he had a merry time of it with old Dyoba who, in the absence of his missionary, had appropriated some beer from heathen neighbours. He had also slaughtered a goat, the purpose of which—unadmitted—was to propitiate any of the ancestral shades who might be wrathful at the death of the boy, Sidenge. The lad who had carried the books so reluctantly got scraps of goat and feasted as he had not done in months.

Figlan sat on his haunches in Dyoba's yard as Dyoba's wife passed around the pots and beakers of beer. It was not an occasion he would report to Reverend Chauncey on his return to town, but he was less than cautious when describing the delivery of the books. When Chauncey asked him why he had taken so long—indeed, stayed away the night—Figlan inadvertently betrayed Stephen.

'No, the *Mfundisi* was not at Holy Trinity.'

'Where was he?'

Hesitating: 'He had gone on a journey. There are many sick people at this time to be visited. There is no food. He is a merciful man.'

'Who did he leave in charge of the mission?'

'There is Dyoba. A very good churchman.'

'Who is Dyoba?'

'The man who you call Candle. '

Chauncey looked sceptical then and Figlan became garrulous in praise of Dyoba, avoiding questions. Chauncey cut him short.

'Why did you not come back at once? You know you were needed here.'

'No, *Mfundisi*, I was not going to come in the night when there are rebels everywhere and men with guns.'

'Then why was Deacon Mzamaan not afraid of going about when there are rebels?'

'Perhaps he has no quarrel with them.'

Aha. Of course. Why would he? Hadn't half of Turvey's 'fine young men' joined the rebels? Perhaps, indeed—as one might suspect—Mzamaan might be a turncoat in their midst. A wolf in sheep's clothing.

It only goes to show!

'What did you do with the books?'

'I gave them to the woman at his house. '

'The woman?'

'It is a young girl.'

Chauncey checked himself. There was a girl who was implicated in the disgrace of Thomas Dema. More than implicated, if the rumours he had heard were true.

Yes, indeed.

It only goes to show.

'RUTHERFORD,' SAID AMOS Beazer. 'Why do you let these black fellows get up to such mischief at our missions? Can't you supervise them properly?'

Rutherford bristled. He objected to Beazer—a man with a common colonial wife and unrefined connections. Nor did he like criticism from the clergy with parishes in town—they with their congregations of mild old ladies! They with their

364

churchwardens drawn from the ranks of portentous tradesmen trying to insinuate themselves into the gentleman class of West Hill by abandoning their Nonconformist origins! Such colleagues could have no idea of his responsibilities to the missions, his far-flung obligations or the vexations caused by the demon drink among his Xhosa catechists. 'What are you driving at?' he said almost belligerently.

'My wife went to Port Elizabeth to visit relations,' said Beazer. 'At Grahamstown station she saw that fellow Mana get off the train. Not dressed like a clergyman, mind.'

'All natives look the same to white women,' retorted Rutherford. 'She must have been mistaken.'

'She called him. She said he tipped his hat and hurried off.'

'Any native would tip his hat if an English lady called out to him, mistaken or not.'

'No,' said Beazer, exasperated. 'We had him in our home when that fellow Newnham was staying with us and she cannot possibly forget him.' Casting about now as Rutherford snorted disparagingly, he added, 'Thinking back, we did not like him.'

'I will look into it,' said Rutherford, rising. Really, the sooner he went on furlough and escaped the irritating minutiae of this diocese, the better. He was quite harried by the endless scandals that assailed him and by ongoing rumours of the wretched Mzamanes. Thank God there were only two of them!

He raised the matter with Henry Turvey. 'Beazer's wife saw Stephen Mzamane at the station. Not dressed as a clergyman. Have you any idea what it means?'

If *Mfundisi* Turvey did have an idea what it meant, he did not express it. If Stephen had chosen, after all, to go for circumcision at a hospital, he would have gone to Port Elizabeth. And if he had, it was a private matter, not one he would dream of divulging to as strict a conservative as Rutherford.

'If he was going to make a journey I am sure he would have told me,' said Turvey.

'Perhaps your confidence is misplaced.'

'I doubt it.'

'Mrs Beazer was very clear.'

'And Mrs Beazer is the greatest busybody in the parish,' said Turvey sharply. 'She is always delighted to discover anything to throw at our fellows and discredit them. Ignore it.'

But Basil Rutherford did not ignore it. He wrote to Thurston Chauncey and asked if Rev. Mzamane had received the books from the Theological Tutor. Chauncey wrote back, eager to pass on the news that when his man, Figlan (a most reliable fellow), delivered the books, Mzamaan was not there. It was said that he had gone to visit the sick at a distance. A most unlikely event considering the state of hostilities in that part of the Colony. But, perhaps, as his brother was a convicted rebel, it might be possible that he had nothing to fear from roving bands. Moreover (underlined) Figlan found that there was a girl ensconced at the parsonage!

AND SO THE news seeped out. A matter of discussion in Vestry. A note to the Theological Tutor. Discussion at the College between the deacon masters.

—*Is it wise to place so much confidence in students of the Native College?*

—*Perhaps they are not ready for such responsibility.*

—*They are the first, after all, to have been captured from among raw, red kaffirs.*

—*No wonder they fall away.*

—*Look at that Saul Mzamane fellow. They said he was the best student at the College. Believe me, lust and drink are in the blood of every one of them.*

'I have never heard such a load of blarney,' thundered Henry Turvey, startling the grave priests gathered at Vestry. 'Never! Not one of you—not one—has any concept of the

366

journey a man like Reverend Mzamane has made to arrive at this point in his life! He is, in my opinion and in the opinion of his congregation and parishioners, a most worthy and energetic clergyman. Who of you ever witnessed the starvation here in 1858, who of you ever watched the mothers give up their children to us so they would not die, or witnessed their anguish? Who of you has learned the native tongue with the same facility with which Mr Mzamane and his brother speak yours? Schooled in Shakespeare no less, schooled in Holy Writ, and taking it to their hearts, I might add, with much more humility than I have ever observed among any of you. Lust and drink be damned! If the natives have learned to drink it is because the Englishmen of this colony have taught them how and encouraged them to buy it. If they can be accused of lust, one only has to go to New Street to observe the soldiers prowling in search of pleasure. If you insist that male converts may not be circumcised and be seen—perpetually—by their countrymen as children, it is because it suits you.' He was gathering himself. 'Which of you here, gentlemen, is not circumcised, may I ask?'

A shocked silence.

'We are in a sacred place, Mr Turvey,' said the Archdeacon.

'Indeed we are! And may it bear witness to what I have said!' Turvey stumped from the room, stood a moment alone before the chancel, head bowed, and turned on his heel.

WORD CAME TO Unity from Mrs Beazer, eager to deliver advice to a young woman who needed to be brought down a peg or two, despite being the daughter of the famous Dr Wills.

—'Our friend, Mr Mana', indeed!

Unity listened with alarm but, determined to defend Albert, would not concede to 'the foolishness' in fraternising with the 'kaffir clergy', despite her own long-held misgivings. If only Bertie had listened! If he had, Mrs Beazer would not be here, gloating over her!

'His brother is sentenced for sedition,' said Mrs Beazer.

'They say he has stirred up the other prisoners to rebellion.' Mrs Beazer was eyeing Unity's puckered face with some satisfaction. 'I always say and so does Mr Beazer—blood is thicker than water!'

For once, Unity had no reply.

'What can one expect when one raises natives above their station?' Aware that Unity's irritation was becoming anger, but not yet ready to desist from lecturing her, Mrs Beazer continued, 'I would advise you to encourage Mr Newnham to be a little more circumspect in his generosity and take counsel from those who have been here longer.'

'He does take counsel from Mr Turvey,' said Unity, feeling flustered. 'Mr Turvey taught Mr Mana and his brother at College.'

'Mr Turvey is an Irishman,' said Mrs Beazer. 'The Irish have always encouraged rebellion.'

'Mr Turvey is a dear man,' Unity snapped, aware, as she said it, of her own fulminations about the Irish, echoing her father at his loftiest. She added, more in defiance of herself than Mrs Beazer, 'Bertie quite depends on him.'

'It would be wiser to depend on Canon Rutherford. He is the Director of Missions.'

'I do not quite like his ears!' retorted Unity irrelevantly.

Unity had further cause to curse Rutherford, in a tirade that would have shocked the lofty Dr Wills, when the news came that Albert would have to return to St Paul's in January as no one had been found to replace him.

'We must pity poor Mr Jackson,' said Canon Rutherford, looming at her when he came to speak to her, enraging her beyond discretion.

'And what if my husband should go mad as well?'

'My dear young lady.' Rutherford was stern. 'It is your duty to support your husband. You are married to a missionary. Like all Englishwomen you are expected to have courage and resilience. It is what we are known for. I am sure your distinguished father would agree.'

'Papa,' retorted Unity, 'tried everything to discourage me.'
'Very wisely,' muttered Rutherford and took his leave.

RUTHERFORD HAD WRITTEN to Stephen, addressing him formally:

Dear Mr Mzamane,

It is with great regret that I have heard that you left Holy Trinity Mission some weeks ago without giving notice of your departure and that you were seen at Grahamstown station by a reliable member of this parish. Furthermore, it appeared that you did not wish to acknowledge your presence and were not appropriately dressed for your position.

I need to have an immediate explanation. It was also brought to my notice that the servant employed by Rev. Mr Thurston Chauncey was sent to deliver books to you at your mission and that you were absent. The explanation for that absence, relayed by your churchwarden, was entirely unsatisfactory.

Chauncey also brought to my attention that there was a young person at your house who took charge of the books and, by her demeanour, it has been concluded that her status could occasion the severest censure.

If it were not imperative that you stay at your post at this time I would summon you to Grahamstown to give a full account of yourself to the Bishop.

It is my painful decision to suspend you from writing any further exams in respect of your theological studies until the Bishop and I have satisfied ourselves with regard to your suitability to be licensed as a priest of the Church of the Province. This is a very grave matter to which you should give heartfelt consideration. It has been a most disappointing outcome considering the time, expense and commitment afforded you by the clergy of this Diocese and particularly painful to me who was responsible for saving you from heathen darkness.

Stephen could not even write to Mfundisi Turvey and explain, nor claim that his journey to Port Elizabeth in September had been for circumcision in a hospital. Though he knew he could have counted on *Mfundisi* Turvey's support, he had no intention of compromising him in the opinion of his fellow clergy—or of lying to him. For Mr Ockert, it had been simply a matter of a loan with interest and the security of the saddle. The merits of the case would be the least of Ockert's concerns.

But the money would have to be returned to Ockert. And, if Mzamo had failed to pay the five-pound debt to Albert, Stephen would have to reimburse Albert himself. Who should come first—Albert or Mr Ockert? And how on earth could he make up the difference unless his stipend was paid on time, and that time was still a long way off.

That Mrs Beazer had seen him was of no account.

That Chauncey had demeaned him did not matter.

Even if *Mfundisi* Turvey and Albert began to doubt him, he would not turn or falter. He would continue to serve God, despite them all. And yet, there was the letter from Canon Rutherford in which he had passed sentence on his vocation and his life.

Dear Mr Mzamane

The chill of his address. Not *My dear brother in Christ* ...

It is my painful decision to suspend you ... until the Bishop and I have satisfied ourselves with regard to your suitability to be licensed as a priest of the Church of the Province.

They would never satisfy themselves. How could they? He had lost their trust.

It was far more damning than having been tried—prosecution and defence—by an ecclesiastical court.

On his return to the mission from Port Elizabeth, Stephen had been informed, by the isolated old grandmother of Sidenge, that Dyoba had killed a goat and feasted. And that the people had gathered for a propitiatory beer drink in his absence.

Stephen did not question Dyoba about the goat. He did

370

not question Lily. He merely said to her, 'You all had a pleasant feast when I was gone.'

She cast down her eyes. How was it that *Mfundisi* knew things that none had spoken of? *Mfundisi* never needed to be told. He simply knew.

'We were hungry,' she said.

'Of course. We all are hungry.'

That great hunger. That deprivation of body and spirit. That longing. That weary wait. There was no way to describe it—either to her or to himself.

Well after dark, he had stood alone looking down from the porch at the valley and the far, dark ridge of hills. The wind swept in cold and strong, laden with mist. It was dense as the sea wind he had known when he had watched the night from the deck of the ship bringing him back from England eight years ago, wishing he could pull off his heavy flannel nightshirt and stand naked in the brace and thrust of a breeze.

Perhaps it was time to escape those constraints again—time, perhaps, to embrace traditional circumcision and, in doing so, gain the true acceptance of his community and, perhaps, of Lily Majola. Her familiar presence had become a touchstone of simple contentment. It was an echo of a lost time: his father's cattle byre, the cool smell of *amasi* in the calabash, the churn of dung at the gate of the byre, the warmth of the sun against his back when he leaned into the mud wall of their house, the drift of smoke from his mother's cooking fire in the time before there was no more food to fill it. Long before Canterbury. Long before Elizabeth Madikane, the woman who had sung before the English Queen.

But he could not.

He had made a vow.

—*Is it your deliberate intention to devote yourself with all the powers of mind and body which God in His goodness has given you to His service … ?*

—*It is my solemn intention.*

The relentless ambivalence of his situation had ensured the impossibility of clear choices. And when he had walked away from Gubb's Farm and passed the hospital with the remainder of Ockert's money still in his pocket, he had sacrificed the possibility of that communal world and the means of achieving it.

Ten pounds to liberate him. As once it had been five shillings to ensnare him, when he had begged money from Albert Newnham to buy a photograph in Baldwin's Studio in Canterbury—a moment of impetuosity in another lifetime which had led, inexorably, to this final reckoning. Then, he had been Stephen Mana. But he was also Malusi Mzamane, son of Chief Sandile's councillor, scion of the amaNgqika.

Who was he now?

Perhaps he was just *Mfundisi* Ngesi, a man without belonging.

NODYOBA. MAROONED ON its hillside.

As the months passed, Stephen withdrew into the limbo of his fractured world. In the evenings when he made his supper, he sat at table in opposition to himself, Rev. Mr Stephen Mzamane this side, saying his grace, Malusi kaMzamane that side: rebellious, reluctant, reclusive.

One evening he took down the pictures of the *Illustrated London News*, the photograph of the choristers of Canterbury. He stacked them on the floor. The next day, on returning from an outstation, he found Lily Majola putting them back, a duster in her hand. 'You took them down to clean them,' she said. 'I have done it for you.' She gazed a moment, then added gravely. 'I think they are beautiful.' Moved by their mystery.

As once he had been.

CHAP. 25:373

Hour upon hour Stephen walked, with the letter in his pocket announcing the death of Mzamo Mzamane on the Breakwater in Cape Town.

An accident.

An accident, the kind that happened with regularity to those who flouted prison discipline. A troublemaker trying to escape.

Did Elizabeth Madikane know? And if she did, how did it touch her?

The night before he left for Albert's mission, Stephen had taken the photograph from the *Chronicle* and examined it a very long time. There was no need to destroy the picture, or make a ritual of distancing himself. He slipped it into his prayer book in homage to Mzamo. It was simply there, immutable, witness to another era in his life, Mzamo's life. One that had passed, one that they had left behind.

Everything, sayeth the Lord, passes from us, even the bitter cup, even the joyous song. There is nothing we may keep and nothing we may cast away.

Stephen trudged up the hill to the summit of the ridge which divided the settler land from the kingdom of the

AmaThembu. It fell away, stretching westwards in the afternoon haze towards another and yet another range of hills. He walked on down the zigzag path among the bare rocks of the eastern slope. *Eyekhaba:* it is the season of aloes, armoured, red-cloaked, marshalling along the hillsides among the ironstone, dust drifting up into the sky as if those clay-clad battalions were on the march. He stood and gazed into the unknown hinterland.

The road to Indwe turned north into another range of hills.

It was long after nightfall when he reached the river and could see St Paul's mission church. He was exhausted. Hungry. Relieved.

ALBERT NEWNHAM KEPT his ear to the door. It was as if he could hear, minutely, the shadows of the trees brushing its surface. Just a door between him and the great dark wilderness outside and, too distant to be sure, the hollow tap of fighting sticks jostling each other, even though he knew it was just the wind in the upper branches of the thorn trees.

Though the war was over, the rebels arrested and sent to break stones for the harbour wall in the Cape or to the island where once the Xhosa chiefs had been incarcerated, little had changed. He had been told that gangs still roved the country and there was a sullenness about the people at the mission, conversations between his men he could not follow but which were silenced at his approach.

At night he closed the shutters and locked the doors. He never sat on the veranda in the evening smoking his pipe and looking at the stars as he had when he first came to St Paul's. Now, on each journey to an outstation, he was aware of every shadow, every flick of his horse's ears.

He often listened at the door, as he had the year before, armed with an old carbine that he had no idea how to load and fire. But, that night, as he stood alert, all he could hear was the sound of Unity sobbing in the bedroom.

Again.

Though she had repeatedly resolved to be a courageous, resilient Englishwoman, she had buckled very quickly after her return to St Paul's, despite her determination to support 'dearest, dearest Bertie, marooned there among the barbarous heathen hordes'. He knew she was overwhelmed with irrational fears. If she had rallied bravely at their first posting to St Paul's before the war, knowing it would end when Jackson appeared at last, the spectre of that unhappy missionary now seemed to haunt her. Seemingly at the brink of disintegration herself, she constantly used the drama of Reverend Jackson's descent into madness as a foil to her own despair.

'Unity, I will *not* discuss Mr Jackson any more!' Albert had exploded at last. 'Perhaps it was his wife who drove him to insanity.'

But it was not the Reverend Mr Jackson who had preoccupied Unity of late. It was something much more urgent, a conversation she simply dared not broach with Albert.

A letter that had come with a messenger while Albert had been at an outstation. A letter she had opened even though it was not addressed to her.

It was from Stephen Mzamane, announcing that he was coming to the mission to 'consult'. He did not divulge about what. The more Unity read the letter, the more alarmed she became, the victim of an imagination teetering at the edge of hysteria.

After all, it was Stephen's brother who had been arrested near their mission, armed, red-cloaked, a Christian turned savage, and when he had been brought to the gaol in Grahamstown, Albert could offer no satisfactory explanation for the jacket the prisoner had worn. A jacket that belonged to Albert. When she had pressed him, he had made a feeble excuse about leaving it in Queenstown, and then became quite unlike himself when she pounced on the fact that money in an envelope addressed to him had been found in the pocket.

Belligerent.

Bertie belligerent? She concluded that he was too proud to admit that he had been wrong about the natives—and about Stephen in particular.

Since then she had rifled through his correspondence and found the letter in which Stephen had confessed to not reporting the death of a boy to the police.

Concealing a murder!

—*I have reported the matter to God.*

As if that exonerated him!

And now he had written again, announcing his arrival, playing on Bertie's sympathy, wanting his counsel, eager to 'consult'.

And not saying why.

Unity had hidden Stephen's letter, convincing herself that it was the right thing to do. Albert was too trusting, too good-hearted to be cautious. Now—as the visit became imminent—she must find a way to entice Albert to take her into town. If Stephen Mana appeared he would find them gone.

He would go away. He would never come back.

Never.

But the longer she kept the news from Albert and tried to inveigle him to town, the more her fear turned to panic. The longer she left it, the greater would be her difficulty in explaining herself if Stephen arrived. And she knew Albert: the minute he saw Stephen, he would scamper to do whatever the wretched fellow wanted. Although the war might be over, Unity had it on good authority that the anger among the Gaikas and even the Fingoes towards white men was so great it bubbled underground and found expression in virulent attacks through the native press. All the more seditious because no one could read the wretched language! Mrs Rutherford had written that a former student of the

Native College and of Canterbury had been publishing poetry calling the Queen a 'voracious she-rabbit'!

It was all too horrifying.

If one of their polite, friendly and humble students could do that, why not Stephen Mana?

In short, if Albert came under Stephen's influence again —as he had in Canterbury—the chances of persuading him to return to England to a cultivated parish with civilised parishioners would be dashed.

She would not take the risk.

She lay awake at night trying to justify herself, woke in the morning and began again, pleading to go to Queenstown.

If Albert had no idea of the real cause of Unity's sudden distress, he was unable to leave the mission unattended. He knew quite well that her aim, using every excuse—from Mr Jackson's madness to Clemmie's boils—was to force him to take her away. If there was some other reason for wishing to escape, she would not say. She seemed to clutch at any notion, even trying to coax him about a sale of fancy goods at one of the dealers in town that she had heard about, weeping when he laughed.

He began to suspect that she was trying to orchestrate a return to England. On that he was determined to stand firm. He would not—could not—break his Missionary Vow. It was something she simply did not seem to understand. Nor could he do anything until a permanent replacement for St Paul's was found and they could return to the relative tranquillity of Grahamstown. The Bishop was well aware of his anguish. He had counselled him to have faith that all was being done to help. Albert knew that it was Rutherford who was recalcitrant.

—*I will not be dictated to by foolish wives! It's high time the clergy bucked up and took a stand.*

And now, on this windswept night, Albert listened, snatching sounds and magnifying them in his mind, almost as irrational as she.

377

What was it he had heard?

Nothing. Absolutely nothing.

He turned from the door and went to the kitchen to pour some water into a tumbler for Unity. He could feel the lameness in his arms, the unease. He glanced apprehensively at the window.

Was this night any different from any of the others during the late disturbances? Nights when he had sat and listened, his fork poised halfway to his mouth or the words on the page of his book read without sense?

He did not think so. It was all imagination.

No one had come then. No one was coming now. No one ever came. Not even his mission supervisor or his colleagues from the nearest town. He had asked the mission people why their bells had been left alone. No one knew except the old verger who said, 'It is because you are a good man.' Albert closed the kitchen door behind him, cocked his head to listen again and took the water to the bedroom. He said to Unity, 'Go to bed, dear. I have some work to do and letters to write.'

'I thought I heard something,' she whispered. 'Did you?'

'I think the horse whinnied, that's all. It's a windy night and he's restless.'

Albert quietly pulled the bedroom door behind him, leaving it ajar. He put another log on the fire in the living room and turned up the lamp. He read until he could no longer hear Unity moving about in bed. He opened his Xhosa notes, sadly neglected now. It was all too complicated to grasp.

He worked for an hour, drooping over the page. A log fell in the grate and startled him. He sat alert. The wind fingered the curtains but he did not rise to draw them or go outside to cotter the shutters. Instead, he tiptoed to the cupboard and poured a small tot of sherry into a glass, eyeing the bottle carefully. Perhaps he should add a drop of communion wine to make up the difference? Before he was tempted, he swallowed the sherry, blew out the lamp and went through to the bedroom, pulling off his shirt and trousers and leaving them draped on the chair before feeling for his nightshirt among the pillows on his side of the bed. He crept in beside Unity. She was asleep, her hand tucked under her cheek, the curling papers twisted into her hair like small white moths clustered in the gloom. Clementine, in a small bed in the corner, stirred once, turned and subsided.

It was after midnight when there was a tap at the outer door.

Instantly awake, Unity started up, shook Albert.

He pushed her hand away, listened, taut.

'You are not to answer that ...' Unity whispered.

'It may be one of our people.'

'They would have rung the bell.'

Albert reached for the candlestick.

'Don't you dare answer or I will go away and never come back,' Unity hissed.

He felt for the box of matches on the table but she almost snatched them from him. 'Don't, Albert, in God's name!' and her voice cracked then, emitting a small wail.

He crept from the bedroom without the candle and stood in the darkness of the living room.

Outside the window, darker yet, outlined against the indigo of midnight sky, was the shadow of a man. Albert caught the refraction of an eye, a face pressed briefly against the glass.

Concealed behind the front door, his ear to the wood, Albert called hoarsely, 'Who is there?'

'It is Stephen.'

Albert glanced back over his shoulder to where Unity stood, a fire iron in her fist.

'Didn't you get my letter?' The voice was indistinct, muffled by the sound of the wind in the eaves and the slight rattle of the door.

Albert did not catch the words but strained to catch the

379

tone, some recognition. He hesitated, panting. He could smell his own breath against the wood. 'Are you alone?'

'Yes.'

—*How can I be sure?* Albert did not say it but he hesitated, feeling the sweat on his soles. Then he said, 'Wait while I get a light.'

He went back to the bedroom, his footprints leaving clammy marks on the wood. Unity followed, clutching at him. 'Who is it?'

'Stephen.'

Wildly. 'Others may be with him!'

Albert shook her off without replying and, in the dark, fumbled for the matches and knocked over the candlestick. The candle rolled under the bed. Cursing, he took the matches to the living room and searched for another candle. 'I must go to him,' he said, lighting it.

Unity overtook him and tried to bar the way. He thrust her aside but she struggled with him still. The candle fell on the floor and went out.

'Don't open it!' she sobbed.

'Lock it after me!'

'Don't!'

'Lock it after me!' he said again, hurrying to pick up the candle and light it with a fresh match. His palms were wet with sweat. He wiped them, hesitated a moment, glanced back at her. Then, fumbling with the lock, he turned the key and eased the door ajar.

It creaked.

No one was there.

Lock it after me.

Stephen had heard the words through the door, had snatched his hand from the latch as if suddenly burned, had turned on his heel and run.

Betrayed.

—*Lock it after me.*

How firmly he had grasped the handle, eager to enter: cold, hungry, heart-weary and acutely relieved to have reached the end of his journey. Now he ran, plunging out of the yard and through a gap in the hedge of thorns that ran past the stable, not changing pace even when he heard Albert calling.

'Stephen!'

—*Lock it after me.*

'Stephen!' Now more distant. 'Stephen.'

Silence.

ALBERT, IN THE yard, was overwhelmed by a wretchedness he had never known before, his nightshirt whipped about his naked legs, the candle flame guttering across his anguished face.

'Stephen! Come back!' The voice rose higher, echoing against the stable wall. He could hear the bell rope twitching against the wooden poles of the belfry, the faint gonging every now and then when a gust caught the clapper, a soft, discordant counter-note to his rising sobs.

The candle flame went out. Albert stumbled back to the house and Unity unlocked the door, letting him in, almost crushing him as she slammed it again and turned the key. She was sobbing, drawing long, gasping breaths. 'You were right not to let him in! You were right!'

She fled to the bedroom, crouched on the bed, pulling a pillow into her arms. She rocked it, renewing her lament, waking Clementine.

Albert did not take the grasping hand. He could not comfort her.

Nor was there anything that she could do to comfort him. There was nothing she could ever do again.

CHAP. 26:382

Hohita.

A great plain scattered with numerous homesteads, cattle byres.

This was the land Stephen never knew, where his mother had come at the outbreak of the war to the safety of her brother's home, harried from the house that Mzamo had built for her, the byre emptied by the military, the gardens stripped. Here, among the amaThembu, pastoralists could come and go, seeking the best grazing. The herds ranged unhampered in wide pastures, the gardens were untrampled by men.

Here, there were no four-cornered houses.

There was no church.

As he walked, Stephen was aware of every footstep, counting them as he had all through the long night of his flight from Albert's mission, keeping at bay the sound of Albert's voice calling in the darkness, more a howl than a cry —'Stephen! Stephen! Come back!'

Come back. Come back ...

He paused only at noon the next day, suspended from himself, way beyond exhaustion, when he saw a group of youths sauntering along with their fighting sticks. He asked about the location of his uncle's homestead. An uncle he had never met, as distant from him in culture and experience as it was possible to be. A traditionalist, a sometime warrior, a man who had the skills of an *inyanga*—a herbalist who knew the secrets of the valleys and ravines, the plants and trees, the bark and roots, the lore of stars. A world from which Stephen had been lost since the cattle ceased lowing at his father's homestead, just as his mother's songs were lost, the ones she had sung when she had hoed her field with him bound firmly to her back. The ones he had tried to recall at night, lying in his bed at Canterbury, but which had melted into nothingness beneath the gonging of the cathedral bell, the harmonies of choirs, the anthems in a nave so sweeping in its grandeur that now, standing here before the undulating pasture, the broken backs of mealie stalks in winter gardens, it seemed impossible that both were part of one life, one experience, one imagination.

He stood in the pathway leading at last to his uncle's house, a little overgrown with dry thatching grass, small footprints in the sand as if a child had flitted past unseen, bird eyes watching from a thicket.

His uncle was an old man, dressed in a cloak, the red clay worn to a powdery patina along the folds. He smoked a slim traditional pipe decorated with copper wire. His face, angled deep by former want, had something of the calm assurance that called to mind Mzamo's dignity and presence.

He looked at Stephen enquiringly, believing him to be a stranger. '*Malume!*' Stephen said in greeting.

'Who calls me *Malume?*'

'The son of your sister.'

'*UMayile?*' The one who lives alone.

'It is she.'

The greetings were quiet, no voice raised. He followed his uncle to a hut—*intanga*—standing apart at the edge of the yard. A place set aside for strangers, widows, old women.

Chickens rustled in the shelter of the woodpile, a thin dog got up and sniffed the air, lay down again, with a small guttural growl, at a word from the old man. Stephen waited as he went inside the dark doorway. A soft word exchanged, an exclamation.

His mother emerged.

She was dressed as a heathen. The print frock had gone, the apron, the high collar. Her head was swathed in a black *iqhiya*, low across her eyes as worn by a widow. Her feet were bare, circled by amulets of root. Glancing at his face and its dawning bewilderment, she stood with her eyes bent to the ground as if suddenly ashamed.

'Mama?'

'*Mfan'am.*'

The clay of her cloak brushed his jacket, leaving its mark, the wrinkled cheek imprinted his with a sharp-smelling unguent of animal fat. A small beaded gourd strung about her neck sheltered in the hollow of her throat.

He stood back, said softly. '*Ndikubonile.*' I have seen you.

It was not the moment for Stephen to speak of Mzamo. He knew he should allow his mother, in her confusion, to calm herself and honour the age-old duty to feed him, to maintain the dignity, the courtesy of motherhood. She moved away to gather up what she could find—peering into earthen pots and enamel dishes, murmuring to herself, glancing back at him every now and then.

This son. This beloved.

Stephen's uncle drew him away to his own house, leaving the mother to her task.

'She is old,' he said. '*Wenza ngokuthi-phithi.*' She is confused. 'It has been so ever since she left her home. She believes her ancestors are angry that she let her children go to *gqobhoka* and forget their forefathers. She is bitter that your father gave you away.' He brought a chair out into the winter sun, indicated that Stephen should take it, sat on an upturned crate and filled his pipe.

'I am here with sorrowful news,' said Stephen at last.

'Yes,' said the old man. 'As I thought.'

'*Usitheliswe kukufa uMzamo.*' Death has hidden Mzamo.

The old man sat a long moment, his pipe unlit. '*Ndibethwa lusizi ngenxa yakho.*' I am indeed struck by your loss. He rose. 'We must empty the milk sacs to inform the shades. They must know that a man has died.'

At this gesture, as the milk gurgled from the full sacs onto the sand at the entrance to the byre, Stephen's mother, watching from a distance, understood the reason for his visit.

Stephen went to her then, unfolded the letter that had taken so many weeks to arrive, that he had carried with such dread. He read it to her, translating as he went. He left out the mention of Mzamo's son. There was no need to burden her with the knowledge of a child who would never now be part of his father's lineage. It was enough to know that the head of the Mzamane family was dead and that Stephen had come to inform them and—as they would expect—to carry out the rituals for the dead as the heir himself.

He who had no father. He who had no son. He who could not even call himself a man.

As he read, his mother turned her back and began to keen. Softly at first, then louder, a lamentation—isililo—to inform the shades. The sound brought the people of the homestead to the yard, the neighbours from their houses. The daughters, the sons of Stephen's uncle. Their wives, the nieces and the nephews. The grandchildren. They gathered round the still, small figure of Stephen's mother, silent now, lost too long to sorrow to shed tears. She sat, head bowed. In her lap she held the prayer book Stephen had given her on his return from Canterbury.

On seeing it, so long ago, Mzamo had laughed. Stephen could hear the echo still.

'WHERE IS HIS grave?' the uncle asked.

'I do not know. The writer of the letter does not know.

There has been no official notice of my brother's death. He was a prisoner. He was sentenced for sedition in the war that has already ended.'

'So you cannot bring the spirit home?'

'It is my belief,' said Stephen quietly, 'that his spirit is in God's keeping, his home with the Heavenly Father. Remember, he was a Christian.'

In respect for Stephen's station—*Mfundisi*—the old man did not contradict him, but his mother said suddenly, her voice trembling, looking directly at him for the first time, 'Why did you not save him?'

'I had no power to do it.'

'He said you are an Englishman. You have the power to do anything.'

'No, Mama, I am not an Englishman. I am a Ngqika.'

She was silent again for a long moment. Then she said, contradicting him, 'Your brother, who is dead, said you were an Englishman.'

'*Njani?*' In what way?

'He said that land was promised him by the government when he was a boy. He said it was pledged to those the missionary captured from among our children. The ones they sent away to become great men. He had a paper. He showed it to me. He said he would give it to you because you are an Englishman and they will not break their promise to an Englishman. He said he will build a fine *umzi* there for me. Like the house at your father's homestead. He will buy cattle. He will bring back the herd of his father's people. Those cows that were your father's pride.' She put her hand to her eyes then and bowed her head, turning it away. 'You will do this for him.'

Stephen waited quietly as she sat down on the floor, murmuring and rocking in her grief. Eventually, awkwardly, he said, 'Mama, I will never be an Englishman. They would treat me no differently from my brother.'

'Then why is it they took you and sent you on the sea, if

386

not to steal you away and change you into an Englishman?'

'Ndaguqulwa lilizwi likaThixo. I was converted to the word of God,' said Stephen. 'That is why they chose me. That was the only change.'

'Then,' her voice rose a note, 'if you are a Ngqika, you will honour the ancestors at idini.'

The old man cleared his throat, taking charge. 'I will go with you to buy an ox. My sister's son was an important man.'

'I do not have the money,' said Stephen. 'I did not anticipate that I would have to buy an ox.'

'Did you not mean to make a sacrifice?' The old man hid his dismay. 'His spirit will not rest without it. There are many here to mourn him. You should buy an ox.'

Stephen laid out all the money he had taken from the offertory box. He did not even reserve something for a train ticket back from Queenstown. Even then, his uncle counted it and shook his head.

They were obliged to buy a goat.

Nothing could have been less appropriate to lead Mzamo to his ancestral home. This idini would witness no venerable ox bellowing the news of the coming of the spirit of a warrior to take his place among the lineage shades. Only the shrieks of a goat, a beast without dignity.

THAT EVENING, STEPHEN went out into the pasture below his uncle's homestead. It was cold. Already there was frost on the leeward side of the opposite slope. The breath of the cattle in the byre rose like the smoke of cooking fires above the silhouette of the aloe hedge. He could hear the dull click of horns knocking against each other as they turned their heads.

Cattle.

Something else that he had never owned.

—He will buy cattle. He will bring back the herd of his father's people. Mzamo's promise to his mother.

Stephen's promise to Mzamo that he would care for his son.

Sir George Grey's promise to the 'young chiefs' of both the native colleges that he would grant them farms, sign the deeds of sale, securing them in perpetuity in recompense for the loss of their ancestral lands.

Izithembiso.

Pledges. Meaning nothing.

THE CEREMONIES TOOK three days. Stephen's anxiety at his absence from Nodyoba, his turmoil at all that had happened, at the choices he would have to make, the compromises, the words he would have to speak, could not be relayed to his uncle or his mother or any of the family at Hohita. If he was welcomed, he knew he was apart, watched with some bewilderment, followed at a distance by the children, his language imitated, sometimes with laughter. The business of the moment, the preparation for *idini*, was solemn, protracted; every ritual had to be performed with dignity, despite the sacrificial animal being a mere goat, only fit for inconsequential men and boys. And Stephen was expected to slaughter it himself, in a way that ensured that the animal cried out long and loudly, announcing to the *abaphantsi* that it was being butchered so they might eat and be satisfied.

Such a ceremony was always conducted by a man. But Stephen was *ingolosi*. Uncircumcised. A boy. Not mentioning the fact to his uncle was a grave omission. Perhaps, if the people knew, it would negate the *idini* and offend the shades. Perhaps it was the same as daring to celebrate Communion without having been confirmed, taking the name of God in vain.

STEPHEN PERFORMED THE ritual for his mother. She, who shambled through her hours, gazed sometimes into the air as if she saw passers-by, visions, *izinyanya zamafu*, shadows of the past, those of her own childhood here in the home of her father's lineage.

The neighbours came, the headman. The people from

across the hills. How could a single goat feed them all? And he, the *Mfundisi* Mzamane, a person of such substance—they could see by his bearing—where was the beast to honour his brother? The cow or ox?

No explanation was given.

Stephen's uncle directed him, standing at his side and speaking softly.

Stephen recoiled from the moment of slaughter, the frantic cries of the goat as it escaped from his grasp, its recapture, its struggle as it was wrestled back to him by boys bewildered at his ineptitude.

Why is this man not doing his work? Why does he shrink from killing the goat? The louder it cries, the more it will summon the shades: here is sacrifice; here is meat.

Stephen gripped the goat between his knees, pulled up its head and slit its throat. The blood, spurting over his hands, was caught in a basket by his uncle's son and carried to the back of his mother's hut.

Stephen did not know which words to say. His uncle, stepping in, recited.

'Camagu, makubehele! Mayekukhangele iminyanya yokuwenu neyamatshawe.' Let it be propitious! Let the departed of your people and chiefs look upon you.

Boys brought wood to prepare a fire at the spot where the animal had died. As he stood beside his uncle, stricken, Stephen prayed, his heart pounding, the sweat drenching his shirt despite the cold. Standing in the smoke, the logs sending sparks into the air, cinders dropping on his coat, he did not feel like the venerable *umcamagushi*, the lineage propitiator. He was Stephen at the martyr's stake, stoned on the orders of Saul. Condemned for his omissions.

—He should have taken up the stone and hurled it back.

On the fifth day Stephen left Hohita.

He carried a loaf that his mother had made for him from maize that she had ground on her grindstone, a ritual preparation which she performed in murmuring meditation. When it was cooked she had wrapped it in fresh mealie leaves. She had kept aside part of her own small portion of meat from the goat for his journey. That, too, was wrapped in leaves.

Stephen put them carefully in his bag.

His mother stood calmly beside his uncle as he said goodbye: a sacrifice had been made, the ancestors been appeased, her elder son had been honoured, even if only with a goat. Now it just remained for Malusi, her younger, to find Mzamo's grave and draw his spirit to the home that he had promised her. In his place, Stephen would claim it for him and, as his heir, would build the umzi out of respect for his brother's promise to her. He would secure cattle like those that had once been her husband's pride.

Stephen could hear her parting ululation as he climbed the hill.

Stephen walked the track leading onwards, upwards. He kept his eyes on the ground in front of him, lifting them every now and then to gauge if the ridge of hills to the west was becoming nearer. It seemed to move away into a blue distance, evading his approach.

Towards noon he saw a cart, donkeys transporting wood, bowling along, a merry youth singing as he stood unsteadily to wield a whip. Stephen raised a hand. He was given a perch aloft the logs.

Later, when he had left the cart at its destination and turned into the road to continue on his way, a horseman, leading another horse on a rein, greeted him in passing and Stephen, unabashed, asked if he could ride with him. The man hesitated a moment. Horse thieves abounded. Stephen introduced himself, pulled aside the fastening of his coat to show his deacon's collar. The horseman was a Christian.

A *Kholwa*. He would take Stephen as far as the mission—*kwinkonzo yaseRoma*—where the Catholic brothers had a school for the children of *abaTwa*, remnants of Bushmen clans driven from the mountains.

'The fathers there will be sure to greet you.'

It was a long ride but they came at last to a tall clay-brick building with a large crucifix in the yard and formal gardens edging a gravel sweep. Three great palms stood on the rise behind, a Calvary guarding the site. Strangely cast in this wilderness, the building reminded Stephen of the pictures of the Holy Land that he'd been shown at Canterbury by a visiting missionary.

He was courteously greeted by the brothers, given an armchair to rest in, a bucket of washing water and a meal of bread and cheese, which he ate at a refectory table with the silent monks whose glances, if wordless, embraced him as if he were one of their own. A seat was arranged for him in their cart which was going to Queenstown for supplies.

Despite his scruples and a fierce sense of shame, he was obliged to beg a train fare and in doing so could feel the sudden reluctance of the Superior to believe in him, as if, in asking, he had overturned the trust in their welcome.

'I will not be able to pay it back,' he said without excuse. 'But I would be very grateful. More grateful than you can imagine.'

Not having extended his explanation, his need seemed to satisfy the Superior more than if he had given him a story about his brother. He had learned himself that explanations about dead relatives—so commonly offered—were rarely believed. Even if it were true, it was better to be silent than excite exasperation. He did not wish to be known as *imbulu*, the monitor lizard, postponing debts and incurring more and more until he was an outcast, trusted by none.

If he had believed he could pay it back, it would have been yet another sum to add to the list in his pocketbook, now far beyond any possibility of honouring. How could he ever have contemplated going to the hospital in Port Elizabeth? Or getting married? What use was it to become a man?

In Queenstown, Stephen stood on the station platform. How different from the time he had looked about expectantly for Albert, imagined in his trap, shouting greeting.

—*Hullo, old chap! Over here!* Flourishing his hat.

391

It was not much more than a week since he had alighted from the train, looked round eagerly for his friend, anxious to seek his counsel, to pray with him, to sit in comfort in his company among familiar things—Albert's books, his funny drawings, a pot of tea, a cricket bat and ball flung on the sofa, a jacket hitched across a chair. Stephen's portrait in a frame on his desk.

He turned his back on the entrance and strode down the station platform, bought a ticket, and waited, hunched against a sly wind. No train was expected for at least three hours. He paced the platform on his own, counting his footsteps again—anything to keep at bay the turmoil of his thoughts. He took his prayer book from his bag, read, put it aside. He forced himself not to look at the photograph tucked between the pages. Half an hour before the train was due, a sudden throng appeared. Travellers of every kind, going south to find work, to make a journey home, men, women, youths off to try their luck in East London or King William's Town. A small group of colonists waited in the stationmaster's office, warming their hands at his fireplace, surrounded by children, toys, baskets of food, even a dog on a leash, chattering, excited. Their destination a matter of anticipation quite different from his own.

When the train arrived Stephen boarded swiftly, finding a seat in the carriage furnished with benches, set aside for 'Natives'. As the engine pulled away and slowly gathered speed, he leaned back and closed his eyes. He did not want to speak to the other passengers crowded on the benches. It would be a great release to sleep, even if he was jolted against the hard back of the bench with every shudder and surge. He lingered between dreaming and waking, assailed by strange images, longing for real sleep to assuage the great anxiety closing in on him, to block it out, never to wake to it again: *isimema*—the howling of dogs in the heart.

On and on through the winter landscape, the slow change from mimosa to a thicker, darker vegetation; on and on, the cold siphoning in when a door was opened, when a passenger alighted, the swaying making him feel almost as if he was at sea again. He closed his eyes: here was the ship, the tilting deck, the churning wave in its wake, the seabirds winging in a slipstream behind them; the Bishop and the young missionary standing on the deck, moving as one, conjoined step to step.

What had happened to them? Where were they now? Exiled to a life of scorn and shame. What great regrets there were in love. What great regrets in sin.

And he had sinned more greatly than he could ever have imagined.

That is what they would declare in a Diocesan Court when they came to know about his journey and the rituals he'd performed. A Christian clergyman conducting a heathen sacrifice, slaughtering a beast! Men had 'fallen away' for less.

He would be excommunicated. Disgraced. Cast out from the Church, shunned by his brethren, by Canterbury, perhaps even by *Mfundisi* Turvey.

And by Albert.

In taking part in that ritual, he had abandoned his Missionary Vow. No matter what the motivation, no matter what consideration for his mother, the turmoil of her mind, no matter what her loss and sorrow. That solemn oath was binding above all else.

Was it God who would judge him? Or was it men?

No—it was not he who had rejected his Missionary Vow. It was those who had demanded it and then rejected him.

One by one by one.

He left the train at Stutterheim and made his way to Eleazar Mbanda's house.

Mbanda looked at him shrewdly. He was concerned. 'You will stay awhile, brother,' he said. 'Yours has been a journey that has eaten up your strength.'

'I cannot stop,' said Stephen. 'I am already missed at Holy Trinity. I cannot even stay an hour.'

'It is most unwise.'

393

'It is my duty' was all that Stephen said and, knowing he could do no more, Mbanda went to catch and saddle up the horse that Stephen had left in his care and which had been borrowed from old Dyoba, the church warden at the mission. 'My wife will give you tea,' he said.

Stephen drank the tea scalding hot, barely able to answer the polite urgings of Eleazar's wife to stay so she could cook him a meal. She looked at him with pity. He was so different from the man who had called ten days before. It was as if he had been on a journey of years. She shook her head surreptitiously at Mbanda when he called Stephen to his horse and said once more, 'Really, mfundisi, you should rest. What use will you be to your people when you are so weary? What good will you do?'

HE STOPS AT a drift. He dismounts and leads the horse to drink. He stands on the bank a long while looking at the water, watching the suck of the current, the drowning leaves. It does not fill him with fear as the pool had done on the Koonap all those years before when, on his first visit to Grahamstown, he had recalled the People of the River, felt the shadow of doubt that had passed over him, and sung loudly as he rode away in haste, fearing something fleeting that he could not grasp.

He takes a portion of the bread from his bag, the sacrificial meat. He looks at them a moment then drops the meat into the water. '*Camagu! Mandingafikelwa ngamashwa.*'

May sorrow pass me by.

He breaks a piece of bread and it bobs, floats free, sinks slowly, turning in an eddy, drifting down.

Camagu.

A gesture of respect: the people of the river are propitiated, fed with food which is their due.

IT IS NIGHT when Stephen reaches Nodyoba. The old tree is creaking outside the church, for the wind is coming in from the southwest, bringing rain. A rain to cleanse and quieten the dust of drought. Already the houses are slumbering. Not even a dog heralds his return.

He unsaddles the horse and allows it to go free into the veld.

The sky is clouding over.

He fumbles for the doorknob, enters the lean-to kitchen. The familiar smell of woodsmoke and ash. He finds a candle and matches. Protecting the small flame with his palm, he goes up the step into the living room, closing the door behind him.

He sets the candle on the table, takes off his coat and hat, stands quite still, gazing intently at the furniture, the prints from the *Illustrated London News* hanging on the wall where Lily Majola has replaced them. He goes to the fireplace, leans down. The logs have been carefully laid, the tinders in a pattern, little shards of sneezewood below the logs to coax the sparks to flame.

Lily will have made it. Those small, neat, willing hands.

He straightens, looks at the picture above the fireplace. The ivied close at the Missionary College, the choristers, the chapter, the tutors, Dr Bailey. There—he and Albert side by side in their cassocks and their stiff white collars, the crucifer holding aloft the gold cross adorned with the *Agnus Dei*. Fyndon's Gate behind, the mullioned windows of the Great Hall. The paving and the flower beds.

He lifts the picture down, gazes at it one more time and lays it on the table.

Weary though he is, he fetches his paper, pen and ink, the candle dropping wax onto the unpolished wood as he briefly writes.

THE PEOPLE FLOCK to church early the next morning, glad to hear the summons of the lead pipe clanging from the craggy tree, even if the rain is falling, even if they are a little shamed for having feasted in his absence once again, ready to confess, repent, lend their labour to dig the garden or paint the porch as penance.

Dyoba, sitting on the front bench, scans Stephen's face for signs of disapproval—has someone told him of the slaughter of another goat? But there is no sign, no echo in the Mfundisi's face of censure, though Dyoba is startled by its weariness, sees the sweat glint in the hollow groove of the Mfundisi's cheek, even though the air inside the church is damp and chill. And when, at last, he speaks, his voice is not raised in praise, stirring in its declamations, glorifying God. It is low and steady and deep. He reads from the Gospels.

Let no debt remain outstanding, except the continuing debt to love one another, for he who loves his fellow man has fulfilled the law.

He looks down at the congregation—the old men and women, the children, Ma Dyoba, Ma Majola with Lily's little daughter asleep in her lap.

For none of us lives to himself alone and none of us dies to himself alone. If we live we live to the Lord, and if we die, we die to the Lord. So whether we live or die we belong to the Lord.

He turns to the altar and kneels. He needs to steady himself and raises his hand to the altar's edge, his fingers damp on the laundered lace of the frontal. 'Masithandaze.' Let us pray.

'Bawo wethu osezulwini. Our Father which art in Heaven ...'

He kneels for many moments in silence when the prayer is said. The congregation wait, a small stirring of perplexity. He stands, pushing himself up on the edge of the altar, turns to bless the congregation. He sings then a low note for the choir to take up. The singers wait, trying to sense the hymn that he has chosen.

It is a hymn they know though it is rarely sung. He leads them, his voice rich, firm, echoing around the whitewashed walls, resonating in the dark-stained rafters. Outside, the rain drifts away, all the pasture is alive, swifts hawking, swooping, wheeling out and away into the rising light.

396

He stands before the choir. They know the harmonies, they know the tone of the lament:

> Return, O wanderer, to thy home,
> Thy Father waits for thee ...

Lily Majola sings it with her palms raised, her eyes closed.

When he has blessed the congregation, Stephen turns and blesses the choir. He lays a hand briefly on Lily's bowed head, his palm cupped above the faded blue of her bonnet, lingering a moment longer, as if to impart through his fingers a warmth and benediction which he cannot speak.

The rain begins again quite suddenly, a stray squall driving in. The swifts disperse, the grass bends flat. The people hasten to their houses and Stephen stays alone in the church, hanging his surplice from a nail, lingering, his hand against its folds. He goes to the altar, closes the Bible, sets the frontal straight.

He kneels alone then, hearing the rain, smelling the promise of its coming. As he leaves the church, treading very softly down the aisle, he notices that one of the old lancet windows broken in the great rains when he first came to Nodyoba has been propped against the wall. He stoops to it, examines the inexpert joinery where he had tried and failed to recreate an arch.

The relic of another time.

He touches the contours with a meditative finger, rubs softly at an unbroken pane of glass, feels the rough joints. He had found no way to make them truly fit.

IT IS LILY Majola who finds him.

She stands at the threshold of that blue-painted room, poised within the angle of the half-open door. She sees only his shadow thrown up against the wall, as if it is his spirit hovering there among the shifting shadows of the tree outside, keeping vigil with the body of the man hanging from the rafter.

Not a prisoner on a gibbet, but Stephen Mzamane, the man who spoke at last, who raised his voice to witness the God he served.

To whom he'd gone now. Not with his words. But in his silence.

CHAP. 27:399

Henry Turvey opened the telegram. It was from Thurston Chauncey. It was the first time in his many years, in his long career of struggle and triumph, trial and laughter, that Turvey had wept openly.

Long and unashamedly.

Stephen Mzamane has taken his own life.

Who was this God who had allowed it? This God who had been constructed from punctilious rules and canons, laws and censures, that sour Archbishop in the sky with the heretics and heathens and all the damned of the earth under his heel?

Not his God. Not his staff and his rock.

Not the God he had revealed to Stephen so many years ago when, as a boy, delivered by cart from Rutherford's mission with his brother Mzamo, he had taught him not to be afraid of spectres, damnation, sin.

Not to be frightened to live, frightened to die, but to rejoice in youth and fight with his heart and his mind—and his fists—for what was right.

That was the God he had often seen reflected in the boy's face when he had prayed, the God he had even seen in

Stephen's fists when he put them up in challenge. The God who understood his diffidence but who knew, too, that there was fire and deliberation that could learn to outface fear.

'He has a flame within,' Turvey had once said to his wife. He would not believe it had been quenched.

Stephen Mzamane has taken his own life.

No, Chauncey. *We* have taken his life.

And the canons of the Cathedral. And the prejudices of the congregation on West Hill. And the soldiers who captured his brother and the court that sentenced him. And the expectations which were given him and then denied.

By all of us.

By our complacency, our omissions: that currency of cowards.

In hastening to find Basil Rutherford, Turvey barged into the Cathedral where matins were being said by a group of clergy. He paused, breathless, angry beyond weeping. His voice carried even to the vestry from which the startled Archdeacon emerged.

'The Reverend Stephen Mzamane is dead.'

Rutherford and the other clergy hastened after him as he stalked to the vestry, pushing the door aside. He turned to face the gathering. 'What have we to say?'

A silence, hesitation, as the clergy glanced at one another, waiting for Rutherford or the Archdeacon to speak. Then, in a murmur, muttered scraps of rumour, gossip, hearsay:

—*What about perjuring himself at his brother's trial?*

—*What about his going to Port Elizabeth without permission?*

'Chauncey said there was a woman living in his house,' said one of the curates.

Turvey turned to the speaker. 'It is an outrage to deny a man the possibility of a family, as we do every time we forbid a custom which is ingrained in the native mind and heart as the only rite to manhood.'

'That's as may be,' broke in Rutherford, taking charge.

'His faults are irrelevant at this point. Because of the nature of his passing, he cannot be buried in consecrated ground.'

'To omit to give him a proper Christian burial would be a sin so grave, so gross and so unjust that I would hand in my licence if it happened,' said Turvey, rounding on him.

'It is one of the rules.'

'Damnation to the rules!' thundered Turvey. 'Such a death —of a man in great distress, who has gone without counsel, or friend, or support from his brother clergy—cannot be considered a wilful sin. It is *our* sin, *our* omission for not supporting him. We took him up and then abandoned him. Our great mission to the heathen! Our great crusade for civilization!'

'Canon law states ... ' interrupted Rutherford.

'And God states, *Judge not, that ye be not judged.*'

'If the cause of death can be recorded as "taken his life when of unsound mind",' said the Archdeacon calmly, 'one can consider other options.'

'Unsound mind indeed!' snorted Turvey. 'If there are unsound minds, Stephen Mzamane's was not among them.' He turned on his heel, paused at the door. 'I will leave for Holy Trinity today and take the service myself, both there and at St John's in the town. A full requiem.'

'That sounds Popish, Turvey.'

'Well it might! I am an Irishman after all.'

WHEN THE CLERGY had dispersed, Rutherford took his pen and opened the diocesan records of incumbents of the missions. He scanned the pages for the name, *Mzamane, SM, Deacon. Holy Trinity Mission, Nodyoba.* He scored the entry through with his pen, wrote, *'Took his own life when of unsound mind.'* And the date. The entry would be expunged from the next edition. As though Stephen Mzamane had never been.

He sat a long while staring at the page, angry and remorseful, then closed the book, left the vestry and went back into the church. He sat down heavily in a pew. He knelt and tried to pray. The words were mechanical. He stopped, struggled up from his knees, rubbed them and sat again. He remembered his triumph all those years ago when the Metropolitan had praised him on Stephen's departure for England for his part in 'capturing and raising yet another flower for the garden of God'.

But perhaps Turvey was right. Perhaps the Church—perhaps he himself—had failed to nurture Stephen wisely. They had treated him as an exotic for display, grooming him and all the others they had 'lifted up from heathen darkness' without thought for the future. Look what had happened to so many of them: Naka, Maqoma, Mhala, Tshatshu, even Morosi, heir to a paramount. And now Stephen Mzamane, who was to have been the triumph of the College in Grahamstown, transcending the achievements of the scholars from the College in the Cape.

As he sat there in the quiet church, Basil Rutherford recalled the slight rustle in the bush just aside from the place where he had stood to relieve himself, faint as a bird moving in the undergrowth, the twitch of a leaf, the sigh of wind revealing a darker form among the shadows. Small boy, so close to death in his ragged sheepskin, legs drawn up, as if he had curled again into the safety of the womb.

What if he had left him to die? What if he had turned away —unseen—and mounted his horse, denying the presence, convincing himself he had not seen the small life fluttering, a moth in twilight? Would it have been a sin, an omission to ignore him? Would it have been more compassionate to have turned away?

Would it have been Christian?

Rutherford examined—unsparingly—what that word really meant.

THEY SHOULD HAVE buried him near the craggy tree beside his little church, which tilted at the edge of its hillside with its handcrafted windows, seeming as precarious as a small boat driving into the wind on a swelling sea. Perhaps he should have been among his people, high above the great sweep of valley and the far homesteads of both heathens and believers, the *Gqobhoka*, both Mfengu and Ngqika, whose children had learned in his school, whose daughters had sung in his choir, whose babies he had baptised and whose grandfathers he had buried, whose sick and starving he had fed and whose wounded he had tended in time of war.

The women brought offerings of food, the men stood gravely in murmuring concourse beneath the tree. A girl, comely in a blue bonnet, a small child trotting in her wake, brought lilies from the river. She laid the pure white spathes of the arums along the sill of every window in the aisle, a cross of them upon the altar. Turvey watched her, saw the grace of her gestures and the small bewildered sorrow of her face.

It was a suffering from which he turned in shame.

On his arrival at the mission he had sat many hours in Stephen's house, meditative, looking over the small collection of objects laid out so neatly on the table in the living room. As a boy at the Native College, Stephen had cared for his possessions as if each were a treasure. He had arrived with one change of clothes, one pair of boots and a small bundle of linen. They were always neatly stowed. Even the marbles the Bishop had given him—a reward for good work —were lined up against the back of his locker, counted nightly, never scuffed by being played with in the sand. Turvey wiped the moisture from his bad eye, put on his spectacles and drew the stool to the table.

There was a pocketbook, opened flat with columns of figures, and a small pile of books, some with the stamp of the Native College library inside them—the seconds passed along so recently by Rutherford. There was a Bible, a prayer book and a hymnal; a wooden cross of polished English oak, the standard gift of the Warden of the Missionary College to his graduates. There was a framed photograph of the students at Canterbury. An envelope addressed to Albert

Newnham and another with his own name written on it in Stephen's meticulous hand, *Reverend Mr Henry Turvey*, were propped against the books.

Turvey opened it. Inside was a much-folded piece of paper, the document signed so long ago by the Metropolitan, granting deed of ownership of fifty acres, a part-lot in a farm in the district of King William's Town, in favour of Saul Mzamo Mzamane.

There was also a letter.

7th July 1880

Dear Mfundisi Turvey,
These are my effects. I have no others.

The enclosed document was given to me by my brother, Mzamo Mzamane, for safekeeping. The promised acres should be transferred to my mother who resides at the home of her brother Hali at Hohita, Thembuland.

Please return the books to the library at the Native College. The Bible, Prayer Book and Hymnal should be for the use of my successor at Holy Trinity. My debts are recorded in the notebook. They may be settled if the stipend still owed me for this quarter is used for that purpose. The money enclosed with my letter to you was a loan from Mr J Ockert, trader of Fort Beaufort, and must be returned to him. Please add two pounds from my stipend in full payment of what I owe him and retrieve my saddle which may be given to my churchwarden, Dyoba. I trust my stipend will cover the balance of any incidental monies owed. However, please retain five pounds for Mr Albert Newnham and forward it with the letter you will find addressed to him.

In the unlikely event that there is any money in reserve it should be added to the offertories from my church. In distributing these, I would be grateful if a pound could be sent to the Catholic Mission in the district of Glen Grey with my thanks. If you can see to these matters for me I will leave no debt behind and will be deeply grateful to you for the trouble.

The wooden cross is to be given to Miss Lily Majola of Nodyoba.

The picture of the Missionary College is for you.

You have been a father to me.

But there is another to Whom I now return.

Your loving son,

Stephen Malusi Mzamane.

On his return to Grahamstown, *Mfundisi* Turvey said to his wife, showing her the photograph, 'Perhaps I should send this to his mother.'

'No, Henry.' Very quietly. 'That is not their world.'

—*Umke namangabangaba aselwandle.*

He is carried off by seabirds. Leaving nothing of himself behind.

AFTER THE CONGREGATION at Nodyoba had prayed beside the coffin placed before the altar in their church, and the choir had sung its long lament, without conductor, but as if each of them was still aware of the gestures which had so skilfully beckoned up their notes and harmonies, Stephen's coffin was loaded onto Dyoba's cart, pulled by Dyoba's horse.

The cart and horse, decked with greenery and directed by Turvey and Dyoba, slowly processed down the hill to the church in Fort Beaufort. A throng, almost a thousand strong, gathered and crowded into the English Church.

Robed and grave, Turvey took the service in both English and Xhosa. If no sermon had been preached in Xhosa in that church before, familiar English hymns had surely not been sung with so much fire.

After the requiem, a group of men—Dyoba and Figlan among them—carried the coffin on their shoulders to the cart waiting in the street. Heading the procession, Turvey led the crowd to the graveyard, the choir following behind. It was an echo of the moonlit processions that he had once led back to the College from the huts and small brick houses that had sprung up around St Philip's Church on the eastern hill of Grahamstown. The young treble voices of the past were transfigured into the surging sound of a thousand men and women.

He is laid in the Anglican section of the cemetery, in consecrated ground, flouting all the laws and canons, in company with pioneering priests and missionaries. Men of stature: Henchman, Steabler, Martin, Rowe. Here and there a rogue or two. It might have amused Stephen—or disconcerted him—that, not long afterwards, the Reverend Thurston Chauncey was laid in his plot a few yards to the south. It is a grave less visited than that on which stands the stone dedicated to

> Reverend Stephen Malusi Mzamane.
> Called to his rest, 8th July 1880.
> 'Return, O wanderer, to thy home.'

And if this place was where his body lay—to prove a point, to honour him in death, in the only way left, a concession to their omissions throughout his life—Henry Turvey knew, and Stephen's people knew, it was not the place where he could be found, there among the sad gums and the scrofulous grass, the haunt of stray cattle, the retreat of donkeys, released too seldom from the burden of hauling wood. His place is on the hillside above the river at Nodyoba, where the wind blows in from the south-west, where the little church is kept in order: here where the choirboys' cassocks are laundered, hung on pegs against the whitewashed wall of the dim vestry; where the altar frontal from Canterbury—made by the ladies of the Mission Society, oh so many years ago— is still hardly frayed even though the sunlight that lances through the crooked window in the morning has bleached the lilies on the left-hand border; where the Bible on the lectern still bears his name, written in the hand he learned at Mrs Rutherford's knee.

—Not too many flourishes, Stephen.

And where Lily Majola says her prayers before the wooden cross of polished English oak—the same prayers that she was taught by him. He is here where the swallows nest under the eaves, coming every year from across continents, belonging in neither one nor the other, dyadic souls in search of home.

IT WAS MANY years before Albert Newnham returned to England.

Unity prevailed at last: Clemmie's education must be English. How could she be schooled by the failed detritus of the English universities who slunk into the colonies where none could expose their shortcomings?

—Like me? Albert might have quipped.

But he did not react. He seldom reacted. He had taken his merriment and put it away. He seldom wrote letters; no more funny sketches. He had simply been, in his subsequent years in Grahamstown, a solid teacher, a diligent mentor to the boarders of the Native College, a handy bat or bowler on the cricket field. A player without fire. He had sometimes indulged in cards at the Gentlemen's Club. Once or twice he had taken brandy, briefly convivial again.

—Poor old Newnham. He'll be going Home soon enough and looking for a living in Tunbridge Wells or Taunton, if his wife finally gets her way!

It only goes to show.

When at last they went, it was neither to Tunbridge Wells nor Taunton, but a small parish in an undistinguished neighbourhood, neither too lofty nor too low.

'If Papa had been alive he'd have got you a more convenient living, let me tell you!' said Unity, secretly blaming him for his lack of lustre in the Church.

But there was nothing she could tell him. And there was nothing that he wished to hear.

He had been a failure. As a teacher. As a priest. As a friend.

Like so many others who had retreated back to England in defeat, he had not fulfilled his Missionary Vow.

But Stephen had.

Oh, indeed he had, no matter what the dignitaries of the Colonial Church might have said, or the gossips of West Hill have claimed to know.

Albert had been given Stephen's letter by Henry Turvey himself. It had not been posted, for Turvey sensed the need to be companion to a grief that the perplexed young priest would not feel able to share. It had to wait some months until Albert and his family finally returned to the Native College and Henry Turvey could choose his moment. He invited Albert to accompany him to take a service in the church at Southwell, needing a companion to drive the buggy now that his eyes were failing him. It was there, seated in a pew, when the congregation had gone, that Henry Turvey handed Albert the envelope that Stephen had left for him.

He opened it.

Inside was a small sheet of paper. And a photograph. It was a stiff *carte de visite* inscribed in gold with the name of Baldwin's Studio in Canterbury and an inscription: *Kaffir Woman*.

Albert gazed at it in puzzlement. He unfolded the letter.

Dear Albert,

Once, when we were at College, I asked five shillings of you. I did not tell you why. It was to buy this photograph. I could not pay you back, so I leave it to you now in recompense. It is companion to the picture of me that I gave to you on leaving England.

She is called Elizabeth as I am Stephen. But those are not our real names—valued as they once were for their promise, right as they were for their time and place. The story no longer matters, but it somehow serves as witness to a dream that you so generously shared. I leave its remnants in your trust, assured of your respect, your love and your remembrance.

We must not grieve, old fellow: 'Wounds from a friend can be trusted.' (Pr. 27: 6). I believe I always understood.
Your most loving friend,
Malusi Mzamane.

Albert sat beside Turvey in a pew, the light lapping on the whitewashed walls, the sound of farmland far outside, together in a thoughtful silence until the old man fell asleep —allowing Albert's tears.

IN THE YEARS after their return, Albert rarely accompanied Unity on visits to her family in Canterbury, claiming that he could not leave the parish until he had a curate to assist him. But, on the arrival of an energetic youngster fresh from College, Unity insisted that Albert support her in the essential if vexing need to console her mother in her widowhood, even though Papa had been dead for years. It was during this visit that Albert had made, at last, a small, private pilgrimage to the Missionary College, escaping from the confines of the family home, leaving Unity at the garden gate where once he had loitered so ardently.

The crypt chapel had not changed much since Albert and Stephen were students. Some new names were chiselled into the wall at the back where chairs had been stacked. He had to peer behind them to see the inscriptions. A piano stood against a corner. Climbing gingerly onto it, Albert saw older names, the diocese, the date of death carved above each. He scrambled down again and walked slowly round the walls.

Rangoon, Bombay, Labuan, Sarawak
Grahamstown

Old Beazer's name was there now. And Turvey's. And a frail fellow who had once been at the Native College but who had been suffering from consumption. He had been sent to drier and drier outposts: there was no cure.

409

Albert touched the inscriptions briefly. A greeting, faces suddenly vivid.

> *Grahamstown*
> *Edward Kona*
> *Cyril Mhala*

> *Basotholand*
> *Joshua Morosi*

Albert had carved the young chief's name himself, arguing with Stephen about the spelling, trying to cajole him from sullenness with a joke. But Stephen had been suddenly aloof, distant, turned inward on a world that Albert did not understand.

And one which, despite his long years of labour, had defeated him: its ambiguities, its mysteries, its sorrows.

STEPHEN'S NAME IS in the crypt now.

Low down near to the foundation of the north wall, an awkward spot. But it is clearly carved, correctly spelled.

Albert had carved it there himself, coming to the College with his collection of chisels, remembered by none, politely received, his whim indulged even though the practice of carving names had fallen away over the years. The burly porter had unlocked the door, letting in the light.

'Ever heard of Blunsom?' Albert asked.

No, the porter had never heard of Blunsom.

'Rattling great cove!' said Albert. 'But a fine old fellow, none the less.'

Ah.

The porter had left Albert to his task. Albert sat a long moment in a pew looking at the statue of St Augustine near the altar, bought with the money that the students had saved by giving up the sugar in their tea. Such a small, such a trivial privation in the light of all that followed.

He was deft at carving, a craft refined over years when he could slip away to his workshop and leave Unity to her garden and her gossip, her village visiting and her callers, to Clemmie and her children. He could take as long as he liked.

Grahamstown
Stephen Malusi Mzamane, sailed December 1871

When he was finished he sat back on his haunches and smiled.

—*Remember, Stephen, to put my name here if I am bitten by a snake or eaten by a headhunter. It would be rather jolly to be in company with everyone. A sort of roll-call, answering* adsum, *just like at school.*

Albert chuckled.

—*Get your hat, boy. It's time for tea!*

Clattering through Fyndon's Gate, turning down the high street, running now, leaping the gutter, nudging each other playfully, punching shoulders, scattering the pigeons which fly up in alarm into the high white sky of an English afternoon.

—*Two Welsh cakes and a penny bun.*

—*No, Albert, the tea shop closes at five. The bell will go before we're done and we'll be late.*

Ah yes, the bell!

AUTHOR'S NOTE

A *Sin of Omission* is a novel crafted from years of research into the history of the Anglican Church in the Eastern Cape between 1860 and 1885.

Much of the information comes from the records of the United Society for the Propagation of the Gospel in Oxford, the Diocesan Records of the Diocese of Grahamstown, the correspondence and letter books of the clergy working at that time, and other historical sources, both primary and secondary, in the collections of the Cory Library for Humanities Research, Rhodes University, Grahamstown, and elsewhere.

The inspiration for the protagonist, Rev. Stephen Malusi Mzamane, was the Rev. Stephen Mtutuko Mnyakama (d. 1885), a deacon of the Anglican Church at Holy Trinity Mission, Nondyola, Fort Beaufort. The life of Rev. Mnyakama moved me profoundly and had sufficient material existed for a biography and had biography been my métier, I would have preferred to honour the life of this young man with a meticulous history. As this was not possible because of large gaps in the record and, as I am a novelist, I created a character whose story, albeit informed—however transiently —by the life of Rev. Mnyakama, is none the less fictitious.

My interest in the subject was probably animated by the fact that my own great-great-grandfather founded the mission at Nondyola, where Rev. Stephen Mnyakama served, and so I feel a particular bond to the story and to the historiography of the Church's ministry among the people of the Eastern Cape. That said, I have juxtaposed some minor historical episodes in a way that is not historically correct but which serves to highlight a theme or idea I felt important to explore or which was particularly characteristic of the time.

Marguerite Poland
Durban, November 2020

ACKNOWLEDGEMENTS

Sins of omission are committed by everyone and I fear I will be guilty of a great number. Due to the fact that this novel took some years to complete, having suffered from prolonged interruptions, I apologise if any acts of kindness, interest or consideration may, inadvertently, have been overlooked. I am privileged in the number of people who have shared their friendship, knowledge, wisdom, laughter and love, especially those whose enthusiasm has brought my books to a wider audience outside South Africa. I thank, too, all who responded, when A Sin of Omission was first published, with such generosity and insight and whose opinions and scholarship I have long admired as well as the distinguished guests who agreed to launch my book on a number of memorable occasions.

Some have been actively involved in the progress of this work in providing information and untangling woolly thoughts and notions—in particular, Professor Francis Wilson, whose friendship has, as always, been an inspiration. He has shared a wealth of knowledge and been a firm and guiding hand. My gratitude is due to Professors Chris de Wet, Mbongeni Malaba and Dr Brian Willan for their friendship and encouragement. I acknowledge, too, my debt to the pioneering work of Professors Janet Hodgson, Jeff Opland, Jeff Peires and, in particular, Andre Odendaal. I greatly value and am honoured by the interest in and appreciation of my work by the Most Reverend Dr Thabo Makgoba, Archbishop of Cape Town and Metropolitan of the Anglican Church of Southern Africa, and by the eminent writer, Dr Sindiwe Magona to whom I owe particular gratitude for ensuring that the Xhosa text was correct.

A wonderful addition to the story was the offer by my friend, Dr Carol Baker Hofmeyr, former Director of the Keiskamma Art Project, to create four large narrative tapestries illustrating events in the book. Known internationally for their craftmanship, the talented embroiderers of the Project, led by Cebo Mvubu, took the story to their hearts. They produced four exquisite wall hangings, the sale of which was an important benefit to a community faced with pressing economic hardship.

Thanks and appreciation are due to Dr Cornelius Thomas and the staff of the Cory Library for Humanities Research, Rhodes University and particularly to my friend and former senior librarian, Elizabeth de Wet, whose enthusiasm for research matched mine but which far outshone it in expertise. To Elizabeth and Chris de Wet I owe the 'beacon day' when we went together in search of Stephen's mission: a profoundly moving event, as was the occasion of attending a service at Holy Trinity Church, Nondyola, with a congregation whose forebears had been parishioners of Rev. Stephen Mtutuko Mnyakama and my great-great grandfather, Canon Charles Taberer.

If the journeys to Holy Trinity Mission, Fort Beaufort, defined Stephen's South African experience, a visit to the former St Augustine's Missionary College (now King's School) in Canterbury, provided insight into his English sojourn. Through a number of coincidences, my husband Martin Oosthuizen and I visited the crypt chapel where